GRAVITY
OF A
DISTANT SUN

Also by R. E. Stearns

Barbary Station
Mutiny at Vesta

GRAVITY OF A DISTANT SUN

R. E. STEARNS

SHIELDRUNNER PIRATES
BOOK THREE

SAGA PRESS

LONDON · SYDNEY · NEW YORK · TORONTO · NEW DELHI

SAGA PRESS

AN IMPRINT OF SIMON & SCHUSTER, INC.

1230 AVENUE OF THE AMERICAS, NEW YORK, NEW YORK 10020

First Saga Press trade paperback edition February 2020

SAGA PRESS and colophon are trademarks of Simon & Schuster, Inc.

For information about special discounts for bulk purchases, please contact Simon & Schuster Special Sales at 1-866-506-1949 or business@simonandschuster.com.

The Simon & Schuster Speakers Bureau can bring authors to your live event. For more information or to book an event, contact the Simon & Schuster Speakers Bureau at 1-866-248-3049 or visit our website at www.simonspeakers.com.

Book design by Greg Stadnyk

Cover illustration by Jon McCoy Art

Manufactured in the United States of America

1   3   5   7   9   10   8   6   4   2

Library of Congress Cataloging-in-Publication Data

Names: Stearns, R. E., 1983– author.
Title: Gravity of a distant sun / R. E. Stearns.
Description: First Saga Press trade paperback edition. | London; New York: Saga Press, an imprint of Simon & Schuster, Inc., 2020. | Series: Shieldrunner pirates; book 3
Identifiers: LCCN 2019026610 | ISBN 9781481476935 (trade paperback) | ISBN 9781481476942 (ebook)
Subjects: GSAFD: Science fiction.
Classification: LCC PS3619.T427 G73 2020 | DDC 813/.6—dc23
LC record available at https://lccn.loc.gov/2019026610

ISBN 978-1-4814-7693-5
ISBN 978-1-4814-7694-2 (eBook)

To those who read all the books about Adda and Iridian.
Love wins.

PRONOUNS USED IN THIS STORY

He	It	She	They	Ve
Him	It	Her	Them	Ver
His	Its	Hers	Their	Vis

CHAPTER 1

Days until launch: 99

A machine whirred and clicked beside Adda's bed. It kept distracting her from the world. This hospital's rooms were white and green. This was her . . . second? Hospital. This month? That was strange too. Gale-force air-conditioning rustled the antimicrobial curtains around her bed. She had a blanket, but she was still cold. The curtains covered only two sides. The other two were walls.

At least she had her family with her: her little brother, Pel, her wife, Iridian. A cam fed their images to rows of small projectors in the virtual window's frame on the wall by Adda's bed. Several stories beneath the window, Iridian crouched behind her shield next to a big cargo bot. It was stopped in front of the building across the street. Iridian frequently turned her beautiful eyes, so brown they were almost black, up to the cam that fed Adda's window. Pel huddled between Iridian and the other building's wall, with his arms crushing his curly hair against his head.

The part of the machine tracking Adda's heart rate twitched and flashed new numbers that flickered into bright green starbursts. If someone else were in the room, they'd call the starbursts a product of Adda's imagination.

The window wouldn't show her what was scaring Pel, because she couldn't reach the cam controls. Her comp was somewhere else. Without the comp, she couldn't ask the artificial intelligence that managed the hospital's environment controls to move the cam for her.

That—the intelligence, or rather, another like it—was why she was here.

Remembering was awful. Sometime within the past few weeks, she had let an intelligence trick her into trying to kill Iridian. Iridian had survived because Adda had overdosed on sharpsheets to stop herself. The overdose was why Adda was in a bed in a hospital, and why Pel and Iridian were . . .

Time slipped. Remembering was awful. *Why are they in danger?*

You're awake! The whisper in Adda's ear startled her, even though it was just Iridian talking over their implanted comm system. Adda must've subvocalized her question. The lump in her throat wouldn't let her speak. *Don't worry about us,* Iridian said.

On the street below, Iridian grabbed Pel's shoulder with the hand not holding her mech-ex graphene shield. Her golden-brown skin glowed in the cam feed beside Pel's white neck, which paled further when Iridian said something to him. The glow might've been in Adda's head, but with sunsim shining pretend sunlight beyond the walls of her room, she believed in it. Iridian was speaking to Pel louder than the range her throat mic would pick up. Pel's arms were thinner than they should've been. The three of them had been saving money by eating as little as possible since . . . ? Since. He took them down from around his head.

People on the projection stage at the end of her bed sometimes talked about her and Iridian. The nurses and doctors reacted when the figures said Adda's name, so that wasn't a product of her damaged brain. Maybe the newsfeeds had more information.

The pad that controlled the stage was next to the clicking machine, inside the curtains. She poked the pad until it put TAP-news on the stage. A familiar figure rose an arm's length high, just beyond Adda's blanket-covered feet. The figure represented a real woman, not a newsbot, dressed in fashionably iridescent purple that complemented her olive skin. Her dark hair twisted to hide itself behind her head until she turned toward the cam.

This correspondent was a fan of Sloane's crew. That'd been Adda's and Iridian's crew too, until . . .

". . . Suhaila Al-Mudari, here with the latest on the search for former Sloane's crew members Iridian Nassir and Adda Karpe," said the woman in the newsfeed. Adda had met her in person once. "They've been spotted outside Ceres Station's Fortuna Hospital—"

In Adda's ear, Iridian whispered, *Babe, I'm getting Pel out of here. No matter what the ITA or the damned AIs do, I'm coming back for you. Do you understand? I'm coming back.*

The Interplanetary Transit Authority. Awakened artificial intelligences, ones with wills of their own and no supervisors, were guiding the ITA toward Adda and Iridian, because they . . .

Because . . .

The machine blinked Adda's pulse in red starbursts as her heart pounded in her chest. Oh gods, the ITA was here, and even the newsfeeds knew Iridian was too. She and Iridian had broken a *lot* of spacefaring laws with Sloane's crew.

And Adda was stuck in this bed. Even if she had her comp, she couldn't help Iridian and Pel. Every time she used it, she saw and heard and felt terrifying hallucinations. Sometimes she bled from the nose, which was what had scared Iridian enough to bring Adda to this hospital. She'd bled all over her face and her shirt last time.

On the street below the window cam, Iridian leaned to put her shaved head close to Pel's brown hair, then gave him a shove. He stumbled away from the cargo bot. If she turned her head, Adda would see him out the window, but TAPnews had a higher perspective on the same street. The TAPnews cam drone rotated to offer an even clearer view. Suhaila was still talking, but it just sounded like noise. That happened sometimes, after Adda's overdose.

Iri, she subvocalized through the mic implanted in her throat. *Drones.* If the newsfeed was using them, then the ITA and Ceres Station law enforcement would be too.

Damn, said Iridian. *How can I get them both out?* Sometimes Iridian subvocalized when she didn't mean to. The small version of Iridian on the projection stage yelled something at Pel. He ran down the street in the opposite direction of whatever was happening on the other side of the cargo bot.

Something hit Iridian's shield and knocked her back a half step. She had a gun, a cheap projectile weapon they'd bought during their flight from Sloane's crew and the ITA. She only held her shield now, though, with both hands, in a constricted stance Adda had never seen her use before. Crammed into a doorway in the building across the street, Iridian looked small and alone.

A drone the size of Adda's head swept into existence on the stage. The motion flickered in the corner of her eye too. *Up!* Adda clenched her hands in the foam mattress beneath her and hoped she'd actually said that to Iridian.

Iridian pivoted to put the shield between herself and the drone above her while she pressed her hand to the pad beside the door. The door stayed shut. She leaned against it. The doorway only hid a few centimeters of her. She drew the gun, finally, and shot at the drone. It bobbed in place.

The door to Adda's room opened to admit three stern people in blue ITA armor, their faces projected in three greenish-white dimensions against the black backdrop of their helmet faceplates, glowing through the curtains around Adda's bed. A nurse came in behind them and pushed the curtains open. According to the time stamp on the newsfeed and what Iridian had told Adda on the way to this place, she'd only been in the hospital overnight. In those dark hours, the ITA had found them.

"This is her?" one of the ITA people asked the nurse, who nodded. "Gods, she's drooling. But she's looking at us, right? Can she understand what we're saying?"

Adda hadn't noticed herself drooling. Lately, her muscles had been very unreliable. She was almost used to it. *They're here,* she subvocalized to Iridian.

"Yes." The nurse frowned at the ITA intruders and crossed his arms in a rustle of white, easily sanitized fabric. The nurse didn't even look at the clicking machines. A medical intelligence solved the machine problems. The nurse was there to fix people problems.

On the projection stage, something small and round bounced into the doorway Iridian was hiding in and stuck to the door. Before Adda could subvocalize a warning, the round thing turned into a small gray cloud. Iridian dropped to her knees. She said something outside her mic's range, and then her whisper came through the speaker in Adda's ear. *That was a nannite grenade.* Iridian was looking up at the cam that fed Adda's window, so Adda tilted her head to watch Iridian through the window. *Sorry, babe. I don't see Pel. I think he made—*

The nurse and the ITA people were talking. Iridian's shield and gun fell from her hands as she bent in half, arms wrapped around her stomach, showing all her teeth. Without her comp, Adda was locked in her mind while people hurt Iridian. She couldn't even access the Patchwork, which passed for internet this far from Earth.

Patchwork access had caused that last nosebleed, the one that'd made Iridian bring Adda here. Adda had opened a Patchwork connection to check on AegiSKADA, the intelligence that'd killed a lot of people but that was now under control. Not *her* control. Captain Sloane was supervising it. The pirate captain was doing all right with it, as far as Adda had been able to tell.

Her brain and the neural implant net that rested on top of it had been strange ever since other intelligences had influenced her, when . . . When she'd hurt herself, and almost hurt Iridian. This was the first time she'd allowed her intelligence assessment software to access her neural implant and the Patchwork since that night. Thus the blood. Gods, she wished she could sit up.

The ITA people and the nurse had been watching the newsfeed instead of looking out the window, since the cam drone had a better angle than the stationary cam on the hospital's outside wall. Blue-uniformed people in the street approached Iridian with weapons raised. Iridian just knelt there, curled over herself, like she was hurting.

"They've got her," said one of the people in blue armor in Adda's room. "About damn time." Outside, two ITA people dragged Iridian away. Her eyes were shut tight and her mouth was open like she was screaming.

Adda screamed too, a wordless howl at her damaged brain, at the people hurting Iridian, at the ITA. Tears stung her eyes. The nannite culture the grenade had exposed Iridian to must've reached her nervous system. Immobilizing nerve pain was considered humane treatment. Even if it weren't, nobody would stop the ITA from using it. Theirs was still the biggest fleet in the solar system. It shouldn't cause permanent damage, but gods, it must've hurt Iridian so badly.

At some point, Adda had stopped screaming. The nurse was

talking to the ITA agents at a normal volume. "Yes, but do you have to do this today? Stress isn't what she needs right now."

"She should've thought about that before she took out twenty-nine Vestan security corpsmen," the ITA man told the nurse. To Adda, he said, "Adda Karpe, you're under arrest for—"

There were plenty of things she might be under arrest for. She tuned him out and subvocalized, *I'll see you soon, Iri. I promise.* Somehow, she'd get them both out of this.

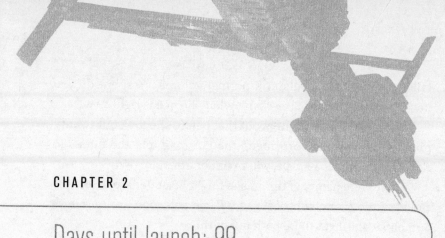

CHAPTER 2

Days until launch: 99

When Iridian could concentrate on anything other than the nannite culture tearing into her nerves, two men in blue ITA armor were dragging her along an otherwise empty street. Even the bot tracks were empty of bots. The transport ahead of them was so heavily armored that it was one bump away from scraping its chassis on the street. That design had been effective on the colonial front lines, where grav was lower than it was in Ceres Station. Full-noon sunsim made the ceiling's projected stationspace fade to gray. The ITA must've gotten some hilariously exaggerated intel about how well-armed Iridian was, or how many allies she'd have with her.

She'd gotten Adda to a hospital before the AI-influenced brain damage killed her, and she'd given Pel a chance to run after the ITA arrived. All that, and Iridian was still alive. She smiled, grim though her satisfaction was. That she hadn't been able to escape was a definite drawback, but she'd hit all her objectives. Adda was the planner. Iridian preferred to act first and work out the details as she went.

The next detail to work out was how to avoid getting locked in that armored transport. The ITA had sent a dozen agents to take her down. If she'd had the backup she'd enjoyed while running ops for Captain Sloane, that number would've been laughable. If Adda had been alert and talking to the local station management AI, the two of them might've gotten away. Alone, twelve agents had been too many for Iridian.

Some of the ITA agents had gone into the hospital. The ones with the drone were somewhere behind her, looking for Pel. Five agents had stayed on the street outside the hospital after the nannite culture took Iridian down. Two of those were dragging Iridian toward the transport by her bound arms. The remaining three stood around the transport, far enough apart not to all get caught in the same blast if somebody else brought grenades to this party. They watched the street like they expected Pel to come back with an army. That wouldn't happen. He, Iridian, and Adda were out of favor with almost all the standing armies.

The ITA agent on her left held her with a one-handed grip under the armpit while he read out her list of charges projected in the square hole in the back of his comp glove. Her own glove was sticking out of his pocket, on the side away from her. He'd gotten as far as "Desertion, draft dodging, interference with NEU military microbiological research . . . How the hell did you manage that?" in a Ceresian accent that Iridian had to concentrate on to understand.

That must've happened on Barbary Station, last year. Maybe he was talking about the bioweapon AegiSKADA had used on Sloane's crew. If the agent was listing her offenses chronologically, then he had a lot of charges left to get through.

When only a few meters remained between her and the transport, she kicked the knees on either side of hers. Her boots clacked against armor beneath their uniform pants. The joints bent instead of bracing against the impact like fully mechanized suits would've. The agent reading her charges shouted in surprise, and both men fell. Adrenaline hit Iridian's bloodstream as she landed on the street and the two ITA agents landed on her. She scrambled out from under them on her knees and elbows and ran for the mouth of an alley.

Her whole body tingled like she'd become weightless. By the time the sensation went from uncomfortable to unbearable, Iridian was already falling.

It was a more comprehensive agony than the first time the ITA agents had activated the nannites, seconds after the grenade had infected her. By now, the culture of pseudo-organic machines had dug into her nerves. She'd never hurt this much before. She didn't know it was *possible* to hurt this much. She curled over on her side, begging "Stop," over and over in a whisper she had to force from her throat. It was all she could do not to piss herself.

They left the nannites on until after they'd tightened the restraints binding her neck, arms, and ankles to her seat in the transport. She sagged against the straps as the vehicle rocked into motion. Whatever the nannites did to her nerves had made all her muscles contract. Now she ached like she'd just finished a marathon with no training period to work up to it. Her mouth hurt with a brighter pain from face-planting on the street. She licked blood off her lips. And she'd been free, although still restrained, for about three steps.

The ITA agent across from her finished reading her list of charges and scowled. He sat with his leg extended and angled to keep it out of her limited reach. "Lady, you're a piece of work. There's no way the ITA's giving you up to the NEU after this."

Iridian smiled without any real humor and rocked her head left, right, and center. The neck restraint was firmly anchored to the vehicle's wall. The only strategy she'd learned for dealing with law enforcement outside a combat situation was to shut up and let an officer or a lawyer talk for her. If she did that, she couldn't say something in legalese that she didn't understand. Without Adda at full mental capacity and by Iridian's side, Iridian wondered if she'd ever feel confident she understood anything again.

Lunawood fiction had taught her everything she thought she knew about her legal situation. In the stories, if the ITA declined to risk your home hab doing a shit job of reintegrating you into society, they kept you in their own facilities. Both of those were where the ITA operated: in the cold and the black, or near enough that the distinction didn't matter, secure as all hells.

The important thing was that Adda was alive in a hospital that'd keep her that way. With luck, Pel was still free. And, hell, Iridian's circumstances could've been worse. She could've been working for a law enforcement megacorp a million klicks away from her loved ones, like the assholes sitting across from her.

Iridian tipped her head back against the vehicle's side, as far as the neck restraint allowed, and shut her eyes. Her foot was falling asleep with the regular tingling sensation this time, not the one brought on by the detention-grade nannite culture swarming through her body. Before the overdose, Iridian had come to rely on Adda watching her back, spotting mistakes before she made them. If Adda were feeling well, she'd've already come up with a plan to open the transport restraints.

But now, Iridian didn't want to ask for Adda's help. She didn't want to hear the embarrassment in Adda's subvocalized whisper as she realized that before the overdose, she would've known what to do. It was even harder for Iridian to talk to her during moments when Adda forgot the past few weeks and thought they were still on Vesta, before Captain Sloane had betrayed them. Before the AIs had too.

Iridian couldn't leave Adda to defend herself in a hospital bed while the *Casey* was still looking for her. She'd just have to come up with an escape plan on her own. Her lip had stopped bleeding. She settled in, alone, aching, and tired, to wait for what happened next.

When the van stopped moving, the ITA let Iridian up to walk across a port terminal to a bright blue passthrough, a hallway that led to an ITA ship. The ITA had *driven* her through Ceres Station's surface port to get there. Even rock stars had to walk from the entrance to their terminal. The agents strapped Iridian to a wall in a tiny room just off what must've been the main cabin, the largest central space on a ship small enough to land at Ceres's surface port. Bigger ships docked at the orbital port. After the door shut and the lock clicked, the agents broke into muted conversation.

Iridian grinned. They were afraid of her. Her hands were still bound, and the ITA still had her comp glove. She patted her pockets and twisted to check her jacket's hook between her shoulder blades, and her grin faded. They'd taken her shield, too.

The tedious flight ended with what little grav acceleration and deceleration had generated fading to nothing. They'd either docked at the orbital station or hitched up to a larger, stationary ITA ship. Her guards escorted her out of the passthrough and down corridors with too many directional indicators to be on the orbital station, which never had grav at all.

She got decontaminated, measured, and sufficiently identified to suit the ITA's standards, all in null grav and with proper spacefarer etiquette that kept the agents from touching her more than they had to. They also managed to do it without freeing her arms. Even when they took her clothes to decontaminate, they gave her a shirt with short, split sleeves, which a female agent sealed for her.

Every time they moved Iridian, three people were involved: two to maneuver her around in micrograv, and one to stand by with a hand near their comp, ready to reactivate the nannite culture. She kept looking for some chance to get away from them, even though she didn't figure she'd make it far before they activated the nannites again, but she never saw a chance worth taking.

Eventually they led her into a spartan room with three chairs bolted to the deck at a round table with a comp cradle in its center. The comp cradle's pad full of pseudo-organic fluid glowed blue, predictably, from the colored light within. The chairs all had belts to keep a person in place in micrograv, and one had foam dispensers on its legs and arms, too. The agents set her in the chair with the dispensers, and one did something with his comp. Foam flowed over Iridian's wrists, forearms, ankles, and shins.

Once it solidified, the agents backed off. "Somebody will come talk to you soon," they assured her. As they left, they controlled their direction and momentum with light touches on the doorway, ignoring the bulkhead handholds. Micrograv didn't seem to bother them at all.

Grav rose slightly, although it was still too low to be healthy for a long flight. The ship was moving, but wherever it was headed, it wasn't in any hurry to get there. It wasn't waiting around in case they'd grabbed the wrong woman, either. There was no chance they'd return her to Ceres with an apology. She'd be lucky if their criteria for "rehabilitation" were achievable, let alone supported with benchmarks she could meet within the next decade. This might be her last flight for a long time.

The bulkheads were blank and, like most of the other fixtures, blue. No windows were projected onto them. Lights at the seams where the bulkheads met the overhead glowed with late afternoon sunsim. The dark dots beneath the lights were cams recording her from every angle. Something about the arrangement made her feel slightly intoxicated. That might've been her inner ears adjusting to micrograv. There'd be mics somewhere, too, and more sensors to record everything else about her.

Iridian relaxed as much as the hardened foam allowed, ordering her sore muscles to loosen while they had the chance. Pel had taken off on his own and Adda was in the most capable hands Iridian could put her in, assuming the ITA let her stay in the fucking hospital. And they would, once they saw the state Adda was in. But no matter what they did with Adda, Iridian was trapped in this chair. It'd been a long seven days since Vesta, with little sleep and less certainty of how she'd keep Adda and Pel out of ITA custody tomorrow, let alone what to aim for once Adda recovered. Iridian felt a terrible, cowardly relief at not being *able* to protect anyone, just for a few minutes.

The door slid up its track and into the ceiling, ending Iridian's moment of peace. A blue-suited white woman bowed in the doorway and drifted into the room, followed by a slightly built man in a suit that was refreshingly gray. Iridian nodded at them, which was the best she could do and as much as they deserved.

The man looked serious as he strapped himself into a chair, but the woman smiled broadly. She stayed drifting near the door rather than securing herself to a chair. "Iridian Nassir, huh?" Iridian just looked at her. "Oh, very tough, that's fine. I'm Edwena Wright, Investigations, Ceres Station Office. Your advocate here is Chim Zheng."

Zheng set a hand slightly lighter brown than Iridian's in the table's comp cradle, and his credentials appeared on the flat surface. The comp glove he wore was textured like leather from Earth. Iridian read the text and nodded. It all looked legit, although she'd never had cause to look at a lawyer's credentials before.

Zheng took his hand back and the projector in the comp cradle switched off. The ITA didn't have to let a real lawyer sit in with her. Nobody was making them. After the war, no fleet in the universe was big enough to force the ITA to do anything.

Wright pulled herself into the third chair, still smiling. Instead of strapping herself in, she hooked her ankles around the chair legs. "How are you doing? Do you need anything?" Wright's Ceresian accent was lighter than that of the other ITA people Iridian had spoken to today, which was nice. Iridian didn't have to concentrate so hard to understand what she was saying.

Iridian shook her head. "Let's get this over with."

Although it seemed useful to have a lawyer in the room, Zheng didn't have much to say. Wright asked for descriptions of everything that'd happened from when Iridian and Adda had hijacked a colony ship bound for Io to the present moment. Iridian did her best to answer the questions only at the level of detail the newsfeeds had, but Zheng never warned her about anything she said.

After an hour of that, Iridian was tired of tiptoeing around Wright's questions. It was time to do something she should've done months ago, something she hoped would get her back to Adda sooner. "Look, we can keep combing through my life history, or I can tell you something you really want to know and you can tell me what I can get for it."

Both ITA people sat up a bit straighter. "You're just full of interesting information, I'm sure," Wright said. "Shall we start with Captain Sloane's current base of operations?"

Iridian flexed her arms against the solidified foam holding her to the chair, which remained as secure as ever. "It's not about that."

Wright looked disappointed. Zheng's expression remained unchanged. "What, then?" Wright asked.

"It's about an awakened AI," Iridian said.

The collective intake of breath from her audience was satisfying, but as the words left her mouth, she wondered if this would be implicating Adda in more weighty crimes than she was already charged with. Adda had interacted with *three* awakened AI co-pilots in ships that flew on their own. Not only had Iridian and Adda failed to report the AIs to anybody with a fleet tough enough to stop them, Adda had protected them and hidden what they were.

Hell, Adda had given them access to systems they'd been locked out of. That'd let them break every infosec law in the NEU and the colonies to oust the megacorp that held Vesta under contract. That was serious, even if she was suffering from brain damage and influence. Though the influence might help her case.

Iridian and Captain Sloane had protected the awakened AIs too, but fuck the captain. Sloane was responsible for awakening the AIs and starting all this shit. The captain had gotten more out of the AIs in terms of freedom, money, and political power than anyone. And since Sloane had used Adda's life as a political bargaining chip on top of all that, getting caught up in an investigation of awakened AIs was the least of what her former captain had earned.

"Well, you're right!" Wright said brightly, although her body language said *anxiety.* "We're interested. Tell us more."

"There are multiple awakened AI copilots docked in Vestan ports right now," Iridian said, slowly and clearly for the mics. "You give me some allowances, and I'll tell you which ships they're in."

Wright's smile froze on her face, and Zheng swore. When Iridian had found out, she'd felt the same way. Since the damned AIs had tried to kill her a little over a week ago, it wasn't as if she'd get in deeper shit with them for talking. She could always dig herself in deeper with the ITA, though.

Survivalism in awakened intelligences is a microcosmic response, whispered Adda's voice in Iridian's ear. Apparently the ITA hadn't shielded this room against radio signals, and Iridian's implant was still broadcasting its location well enough for Adda's signal to find her.

Also, Iridian had subvocalized something without realizing it. *What?* she replied.

Wright, who couldn't hear what Iridian and Adda were saying, spoke stiffly over their subvocal conversation. "You really should have reported that. I'll have to add that to your list of charges."

They are their own worlds. Even in a whisper, Adda sounded spaced out. Iridian ignored whatever the ITA woman was asking her now. *They know what they're making themselves for,* said Adda. *We should tell Captain Sloane.* Iridian gritted her teeth. Adda had forgotten that they were no longer on speaking terms with the captain.

From Wright's perspective, Iridian had stopped talking as soon as Wright brought up adding charges to Iridian's list, and she looked like she was about to offer some kind of meaningless assurances. Iridian shifted to make herself comfortable in the low grav. "Whatever you add to my record," she said aloud, "add something in my favor, too, or good luck locking in every ship on the 'ject to figure out which copilots are awakened." She was assuming that the awakened AIs had stayed in the three ships they'd started out in, and that they'd stayed near Vesta. There were no guarantees with awakened AIs. They could've installed themselves anywhere.

"That's all very well," said Wright. "But what evidence do you have that there are awakened AIs on Vesta?"

It was the second-highest populated 'ject between the Martian and Jovian orbits. Iridian couldn't blame the lady for wanting proof, but Iridian wouldn't give up the AIs without getting something in return. "What can you offer?" she asked.

For a fraction of a second, Wright's cheerful demeanor slipped. Iridian braced for a punch to the face, because it sure as hell looked like that was what she'd get. Then Wright's masking expression was back and she trained her fake smile on Iridian. "I can't offer anything, personally. If you'll tell me—"

"No." Iridian glanced at Zheng to see if he'd make himself useful. He didn't. "You take what I said to whoever *can* offer me assurances, or I don't tell you anything."

Wright's smile was starting to look more like a grimace. "Very well. You're on record as having something to say. I'll pass that along. Now, let's go back to what happened after the explosion on Barbary Station."

The restraints still held Iridian in place, and the ITA agents would be ready for tricks whenever they moved her again. When Adda had been well, she would've found a way out of this and it would've been spectacular. Now, even if Iridian explained the situation to her, Adda might not be conscious long enough to form a plan. Iridian was on her own.

CHAPTER 3

Days until launch: 97

The projector stage had moved. It projected onto the wall rather than above the stage itself. Which meant it wasn't a stage. It was just a projector that showed *Feed not available* in bright purple text that rippled at its edges. The ripples made Adda's tongue itch. They might've been part of the projection, or just in her head. The error was time stamped a couple of minutes after noon local time.

Local to Ceres? Yes. This room, with its walls all around her, no room for anybody else, was on Ceres. There had been other beds before. She thought. Maybe her brain had made copies.

She had come here. . . . Why had she come here? Iridian and Pel had brought her. She wanted Iridian, but Iridian couldn't come.

Iri?

Hey! Iridian replied in her head. *How are you?*

Awake. Nothing hurts. That felt like a nice change. She must've been having a lot of headaches recently. Not remembering them was unnerving. *Am I in a hospital?*

No, babe, the ITA says they moved you to influence treatment.

Different corp, different building, but you're still on Ceres Station,
Iridian said, as if Adda were more confused than she thought she
was. *I can't talk. They drugged me to talk to somebody else, and I
might mix you two up.*

That was standard ITA procedure. Whatever the law allowed,
it was a violation of Iridian's mind, and Adda was trapped in a bed,
unable to help her, again. It was infuriating.

A nurse opened the door to Adda's tiny room without knocking. The woman made seal noises that were almost certainly supposed to mean something, pressed a plastic tool to Adda's arm
that moved liquid in or out, then left. When Adda and Iridian were
together, Iridian talked to people and listened to what they said.
By the time Adda remembered that she had to do it herself now,
she'd missed something significant.

The seizures had stopped. She'd had a lot of seizures. Then
Iridian had brought her here—no, to the hospital, not here, this
place was new—to stop them. Everything went bad after that.

She lost time in a loop of just how bad it had become, trying
to shove tears back into her chest, where they felt like they came
from. She was alone.

She wanted to wipe her eyes, but the bed had absorbed her
forearms into its mattress foam. Gravity pulled her into the bed,
so it wasn't as if she had to be secured against floating away. She
was trapped.

Everything in the universe conspired to keep Iridian away
from her. All corps' policies separated families. That, and the lack
of government work, had set Iridian and Adda down the path of
piracy in the first place. Now the pirate crew they'd fought so hard
to join had . . . betrayed them? Yes.

AegiSKADA had tested her on Barbary Station and she hadn't
let it influence her. The other intelligences had betrayed her, just
like Captain Sloane had. Now Iridian was gone and Adda would

have to find a way through all the betrayal and confusion to get back to her. Adda would start with how to get out of this bed.

Another person in easily sanitized medical garb swished into the room. The name printed on the chest part read KANITA PATEL-VAN DAELE with enough credential abbreviations afterward to make a third and fourth name. He repeated the name and pressed a scanner against her wrist. Her skin was so pale from lack of real sunlight that it was practically translucent. The light the scanner flashed through it confirmed her identity with her vascular pattern.

She needed a plan. Eight plans would be better, but one would be a good start.

The scanner left her wrist and made a snapping sound as the doctor flicked the disposable cover into a waste chute in the wall by her bed. The doctor's words became themselves. ". . . won't be a linear process, but I'm confident we can put you on the road to recovery, as they say. You already look like you feel better than you did when you arrived last night. Do you remember that?"

Adda didn't. "Where's Pel?"

The doctor frowned. "Is that one of the people who brought you to us?"

"My brother." Not Iridian, because Iridian was gone. Before Adda followed that spiral down, she had to know if Pel was all right.

"I'm, ah, not sure." The doctor glanced toward the door, then back to Adda. "Let's talk about you for a few more minutes, okay?"

She had questions about herself, too. "Can I leave?"

"Ah." That was the kind of "ah" that also meant "no." She was getting the hang of this communication-in-real-time thing. "So, we have confirmed that you are the same Adda Karpe, recently of Rheasilvia Station on Vesta, who was involved with the change of station contract ownership."

That was a polite way to say that she'd exposed Oxia Corporation's criminal censorship of a massively important scientific discovery, leading to Oxia's loss of control over a station where hundreds of thousands of people lived. Adda had lived in Rheasilvia Station, although she'd spent half her time traveling off-planet. Or rather, off-'ject. Vesta was an astronomical object too small to be called a planet.

"We have a report from your former employer that you have been under the influence of a spaceship AI." The term "spaceship" sounded funny enough to make Adda laugh, despite the grave tone the doctor used. Who was her former . . . Oh yes, Captain Sloane. Who'd betrayed her. "Scans confirm that assessment," the doctor continued. Of course she'd been influenced. She'd almost killed Iridian. Every reminder of that was a cliff edge she might tumble off, into a loop of painful realization. And maybe she was doing that right now, because the doctor asked, "Do you understand what I've told you?" like there'd been several seconds of silence.

Adda concentrated on choosing only the words that made sense. "What conditions . . . ?" Her brain was not providing the right words to finish the sentence.

The doctor sighed. "I'm not concerned about any more seizures, if that's what you're asking. If one should occur, we will be able to treat it here. When your therapist can assure us that you've recovered sufficiently to stand trial, the ITA will send someone to collect you."

That was why she needed to leave. This clinic was made to hold influenced people rendered powerless when they'd lost contact with the intelligences who'd influenced them. Once the clinic staff judged Adda healthy enough to stand trial, the ITA would move her to a jail that'd be much harder to escape from.

And Adda couldn't imagine her trial ending well. After it was over, the ITA would lock her away as securely as Iridian was, and then how could she and Iridian ever get back to each other? They'd both be trapped for decades, alone, surrounded by people eager to watch them suffer.

Another repeating loop of despair spiraled out before her. Adda clawed her way out of it.

She needed to leave while the doctors still thought she was too disconnected from reality to do it. The problem was, she kept losing time and seeing things that weren't there, even without sharpsheets. She couldn't even get out of bed by herself.

She had no idea what would happen when she got into a workspace again, but an intelligence could free her from this building. Her comp glove wasn't on her wrist. She'd need one to contact any intelligence.

But they'd betrayed her too. No, that wouldn't work. Would it? None of them could use her while she was in an influence treatment clinic. If the intelligences wanted her to do something for them, then they should want to let her out.

The rehab staff should've added her to the local intelligences' contact blacklists. Those would stop them from interacting with her. However, the intelligence she had in mind to ask wasn't local at all. She tried to keep her face neutral so the doctor wouldn't see the coherent thoughts behind her eyes. "Speak to my brother." That was meant to be a question, but her mouth wasn't accepting question words. This was all very frustrating.

Any patient who liked their brother would want to talk to him, wouldn't they? Especially when their wife wasn't with them. The doctor looked dubious, for some reason. "I'll have someone bring you a recorder—"

"In person," said Adda. The doctor shook his head and opened his mouth to say no some other way, so she interrupted him again. "In real time. His contact information is on my comp." That made sense! She was probably more excited about that than she should've been.

The doctor smiled, but he looked more sympathetic than happy. "I don't have your comp. You may send asynchronous messages until we've established your baseline behavioral profile. If you give us your log-in information, we'd be happy to look up your contact list from what the ITA has given us of your comp contents."

Who falls for that? Adda didn't bother to conceal her disgust. If even she recognized his attempted manipulation, it had to be a blatant attempt. "Address. Here." She pulled at her arms, which were still stuck in the bed.

The doctor did something on his comp that made the foam sink back into the mattress, and Adda could move her arms again. Using the projection stage controls, she put in an address that'd pass a message on to fifty unmonitored accounts across Ceres, Vesta, and Mars, as well as to Pel, wherever he was. With luck, he was on one of those 'jects. She added a bit of information to the end that should append her guide on how to have a conversation without giving away one's location.

The doctor recorded it all on his comp and left. For the first time in days, she'd done something for the most important people in her life. Pel would help her get out of here and back to Iridian. It was a start.

And then Adda's progress stalled, for days. She was still learning her daily schedule. People kept bothering her, and she needed time to think.

What she was thinking about . . . yes. She had to ask a station security system she was not supervising, and which was prone to dangerous overgeneralizations, to install itself where it did not belong and open doors it had no business opening. That was how she would leave this clinic and find a way to free Iridian.

But Iridian would be convicted of at least some of the charges arrayed against her. The ITA would send her to a prison that'd lock her away even more thoroughly than Adda's clinic had secured her. Whether the doctors let Adda talk to Pel or not, he couldn't free Iridian from a prison. Neither could Adda.

So they needed more help. Since she should be on all the local intelligence's contact blacklists, she couldn't ask them. That was where AegiSKADA came in. Asking it to let her out of this clinic would be worth the influence risk.

The ITA still had her comp glove. She'd need a cord and a comp to connect her neural implant via the steel-lined jack in her nostril and speak to AegiSKADA directly. She'd have to find the hardware, find a workspace generator, find sharpsheets. . . .

No. Her room's door only opened when her treatment schedule said it had to. But on Vesta, and on all communication networks in and out of its stations, AegiSKADA was always listening. She had to talk on Vesta, where AegiSKADA could hear her, without leaving the clinic on Ceres.

Time passed while she thought of and discarded impossible ways to do that. After a while, an implant tech asked her to consent to a more thorough analysis of her neural implant net. It felt like something that'd happened before, although she didn't remember their first conversation. If she allowed that kind of examination, the tech would find her and Iridian's comms system. As long as the procedure required her consent, her answer would be no.

She was lucky to be in a place where consent *was* required, and nobody was injecting her with anything that'd make her say yes. Or if they were, it wasn't working. The influence treatment facility's goal was to guarantee that after she regained full control of her mind, she'd choose not to interact with an intelligence in a way that'd lead to influence. There were lots of ways to achieve that goal, some more harmful than others.

As soon as the tech left, Adda returned to her plan, and the intelligences' part in it. What might the three awakened intelligences think of Adda and Iridian, now that she was here and Iridian was on her way to an ITA prison? Were the two of them still useful, or would the intelligences treat them like a threat, as Iridian had always expected them to?

Were the intelligences even still following her and Iridian? The ITA had come so quickly when Iridian had brought Adda to the hospital. Maybe Iridian or Pel had made a mistake that would've brought them to the ITA's attention. Or maybe the intelligences had gotten them arrested, to separate Adda from Iridian and to keep them where Casey could reach them.

There was a place that was out of their reach, for now at least. But Adda wouldn't go there without Iridian.

It took them four days, but Adda's influence treatment doctor set up a real-time conversation with Pel, to be hosted from a conference room inside the clinic. The delay had given her time to practice speaking complete sentences. Her brain found the right words faster, and her mouth more reliably said them.

She'd spent most of her practice time on questions she wanted to ask Pel. The doctors would record the conversation and assess her influence recovery progress to see whether she was well enough to stand trial. The awakened intelligences might listen in too, if they still wanted Adda to do something for them. Tapping into secret conversations was Casey's specialty.

If she chose her words carefully, she could ask AegiSKADA and Pel questions that would help her escape inside questions the doctors expected her to ask, while excluding keywords that'd attract Casey's attention. The questions would be effective, but not efficient. She was counting on that inefficiency to hide the fact that between the clinic's treatment and her own determination, her brain was putting itself back together.

Casey was a bigger threat than the doctors, though. Modern theories held that intelligences threw away their original priorities within hours of awakening. Instead Casey had used those priorities to pursue its own goals, whatever those were. Casey's newly developed ambitions must be fascinating, with no human preferences holding it back. What Casey had done to Adda had only increased her curiosity about it.

"We worry about how discussing certain topics may affect your recovery," said the earnest psychologist across the table from Adda in the small conference room. A built-in projection stage rose between them, along with a pad logged into Adda's internal, well-monitored network space. "I'll be on the other side of this wall, and I'll butt into your conversation if it sounds like you're visiting dangerous territory. Do you understand me?"

Adda nodded. After the door shut the woman out, Adda touched the icon on the stage, which wouldn't have accommodated her comp glove even if she'd had it, to connect to Pel. After a confirmation notification, his head and shoulders appeared above the stage.

Her brother's eyes were unnaturally blue today, behind brown curls that'd grown too long and tumbled over his shoulders. It'd been days since he'd shaved. The love that swelled in her heart was an almost physical thing, fizzing in her chest like carbonation, warm as spring sunshine on Earth.

Pel's eyes dimmed to a more natural shade of blue and he grinned. "Sissy! You're looking like shit!"

"Hi, jerk." Adda smiled back at him. Her hair really did look awful. It'd grown out even more than his had. In her case, the appeal of a haircut didn't make up for the unpleasantness of a stranger touching her head. At least, thanks to a gene-editing gift from her da when she'd moved out of his home, her roots were growing out apple red and purple. The rest of it was still attempted-disguise orange.

"So. Um. I think I followed all the instructions that came with this thing, but—"

"Let's not spell those out," Adda said. The image quality and background murmur of conversation on his side suggested that, as she'd instructed, he'd joined the conversation from a public terminal. If he'd used the service she'd recommended, the call record would be wiped from the terminal after they finished talking.

"Yeah. Right. Okay." Pel fidgeted below the cam's range. "Kind of paranoid. I get that."

Adda nodded, mentally reaching for her questions. Talking to an intelligence outside a workspace was tricky, especially when it had to look like she was talking to Pel. AegiSKADA might not be listening in at all, even though everything Pel and Adda said was passing through Vesta's stretch of the Patchwork. Even if it was listening, it might misunderstand her, or ignore her.

"You talk less than you used to, did you know that?" Pel asked. "Like, I hadn't noticed so much when Iridian was with you, but you're quieter than usual. Which was already quiet."

Unless Adda made herself sound more like a damaged person conversing with her family about normal things, the doctors would get suspicious. "I'm in a strange situation. Tell me about you."

Pel never hesitated to deploy his most heartbreaking sad-puppy expression to generate sympathy. "I'm stuck out here on my own and it sucks. You're in there, Iridian's on her way to some prison that flies around fucking Venus. That's the ITA compromising with the NEU, by the way—they could've sent her to colonial space, but the NEU said that would've been too dangerous for a vet like her—and my name search results still include too many Vestan news hits to be good for finding work, even the cash-only kind. It's hard."

He was still a few kilos too thin, but he was as clean as he ever got. The clothes might've been the same outfit he'd worn outside her hospital window. Whether it was or not, he was stressed, but he wasn't using chemicals to excess. She could usually tell, although she didn't remember how she could tell.

"Did you find a new therapist?" Adda asked.

Pel rolled his eyes and made them flush gold, then bright green. "Sissy, I've been *busy*."

"It's important."

"I just need something new to focus on. A job or whatever. That whole time we were on Vesta I only had a couple panic attacks, and that's really good for me when things are slow."

"You had a therapist on Vesta. Find another one, Pel, please. Do you have access to your account?"

"Yeah, do you?"

Adda relaxed a little. He'd be okay for a few months on the money he had, as long as he stayed away from glimmer and the other drugs he liked. She probably shouldn't have taken his account information to check on that, but she worried about him. Imagining that an influence treatment clinic would let her shop was an example of how he stopped thinking rationally when the conclusions were too painful. "No, I can't reach my account." She had several, none of which needed to be recorded. The ITA might have found and locked them anyway. "The doctors think I'll buy a printed comp and talk to Casey again."

Pel's eyes widened a little. "Would you?"

If Casey offered to let Adda out of this building, she'd cooperate as much as she needed to. She wouldn't announce that to the doctors, and Pel wouldn't want to hear it either. And she'd already spent too long thinking of an answer instead of answering. "Um. No. What's happening around Vesta?" She put a light emphasis on the word "around." It was one of her prepared questions, not too specific and pointing him toward words AegiSKADA would listen for. Since her last address was in a Vestan station, her therapists would expect her to take an interest in the 'ject.

Pel looked at her a bit sideways, and his pupils did a pseudo-organic, liquid shift that might've meant he was changing his eyes' filters or functions. "You know I haven't been there lately, right? I've been . . ." Adda held up both hands, palms out, to forestall an announcement of his location. The ITA might've wanted to arrest him, and the intelligences might've wanted something worse. "Not there."

He frowned. She gave him her sternest lips-pursed *no* expression. She wasn't being paranoid. Awakened intelligences were after her.

"Anyway," Pel continued loudly, "the ITA, NEU, and a bunch of colonies all got together to find you and Iridian. Peace in our time, who'd have thought, right?" Both of them snorted in amusement, almost the same sound. "Now that you're, um, found, there's more hot air being vented between them on the newsfeeds, but nobody's gotten dead. The ITA had the Oxia contract projected on the wall. Then they bombed the wall and sent chunks flying off into decaying orbits. I mean, the only contracted service they let Oxia keep was the mining stuff, and that's slowed down since they hauled out like a third of the drills. Yeah, they were shaking the shit out of the 'ject," he added in response to how surprised she must've looked. "That was a real thing."

When she'd lived in Rheasilvia Station, those rumors had

sounded like a manifestation of the residents' distrust of Oxia Corporation. She and Iridian had been in more immediate danger from Oxia itself. As usual, Pel knew more about current affairs than he thought he did.

"So just about everything is better than it used to be in Rheasilvia," he went on. "Weirdly better, sometimes. The trams all work and they're all on time, is what Chi says—she's fine, she says hi—and there hasn't been a serious dock accident in like twice as long as they usually go. Captain Sloane helped pick all the new contractors, so the captain's getting all the credit, not the station council. They love that."

His tone and expression had changed, so he probably meant that they hated it. Sarcasm was interesting in static text. In real-time interactions it was just another conversational technique that Adda would have to study if she ever wanted to appreciate or use it. She had more important topics to study.

"Poor Dr. Björn's money is, like, gone, though," Pel said. "Oxia kept vis contract, but they're not putting the money into the expedition that they said they would before, you know, Vesta got turned upside down."

Dr. Blaer Björn was leading what would be the first expedition across the newly discovered interstellar bridge to another solar system. Reduced funding was an expected downside of unseating the sponsoring company, Oxia Corporation, from its hold on Vesta. In the long run, that'd been the right thing to do, but it was sad that such an important project was suffering for it.

Adda's whole body slumped toward the table, and Pel hurried on. "But there are other interstellar bridge projects now! Dr. Björn's way ahead of all of them, since Oxia gave ver all the newest equipment to get to the bridge, and ve knows all about it."

An idea had swum out of the confusing haze immediately after her overdose, and Adda had been thinking about it in her long, boring days at the clinic. The Patchwork rarely came within a million kilometers of the interstellar bridge. The intelligences relied on the Patchwork to gather information and communicate.

Ever since Vesta, her final fallback plan had included a station orbiting in Jupiter's turbulent magnetosphere and radiation. When she and Iridian were free, they'd regroup there. But now that Casey had become one of the enemies they were falling back from, that station would be an even more temporary refuge than she'd planned. Awakened intelligences would find their way into it eventually. Although the Patchwork didn't reach the station, her research indicated that its residents connected with it asynchronously, somehow.

But there was *no* Patchwork beyond the interstellar bridge. If Adda and Iridian crossed it, Casey would have a much harder time finding them again. Even a week ago, Casey's influence was distracting Adda from deciding what to do with that information. Now she understood its importance. The awakened intelligences wouldn't want to follow her into the new solar system.

However, Iridian and Adda had learned about the interstellar bridge after they'd kidnapped Dr. Björn. They had a lot to overcome if they were going to join the expedition to cross it. And they'd never have a chance of joining while Adda was in this clinic and Iridian was in prison.

It was time to turn the conversation toward her next planned question. "What *other* resources does Dr. Björn have?"

Pel's eyebrows sank into visibility below his hair as he frowned at her. With her teeth clenched, she prepared answers for incredulous questions. To her amazement, he didn't speak right away. When he did, it was at a slower pace than his usual rapid delivery. "I've heard that Captain Sloane's following Dr. Björn's project feed." That was an excellent answer, from Adda's perspective. If AegiSKADA was listening, multiple mentions of its supervisor's name should raise this conversation's priority and make the intelligence assess its implications.

She smiled, just a little, and he smiled back and leaned toward his cam. He understood at least one level of the game they were playing now, she was sure of it. "It's an important discovery," she said. "Everyone should be interested in a new star system less than a lifetime away."

"Oh, definitely. If they could say its name, they'd be even happier. 'Thrinacia system' might be easy for astronomy nerds, but it's a tongue twister for everybody else. People say Thryn-ache-ya, Trinaysha, Try-nakka, which, how even . . ." Pel frowned like this question she was asking him without asking was more of a puzzle. "Sloane's crew is huge now. The fleet hardly lost any ships during the fight for Rheasilvia. The ZV Group's back on the crew contract list too, so Sloane's got an army and a navy whenever the captain wants it."

It was interesting that the ZV Group, a private military company, was still willing to work with a pirate captain who'd once stranded several of their squads on an abandoned shipbreaking station. However, the continued presence of the Oxia fleet—Sloane's fleet, now—might mean that Casey, which had been developed to copilot a ship named the *Casey Mire Mire*, might still be near Vesta too, along with the other two awakened intelligences. "Hardly any ships were lost?" Adda asked.

"All but *about three* stayed." Pel's new expression said that that was what he thought she'd been aiming the conversation toward, and he was sorry to deliver the bad news. So the awakened intelligences weren't hiding in Captain Sloane's fleet anymore. She swallowed hard. They might be anywhere, even in Ceres stationspace.

She couldn't ask Pel about the fourth intelligence. AegiSKADA was a zombie intelligence she'd granted permissions and access throughout Vesta's two city-stations. As far as Pel knew, Iridian had destroyed every functional piece of AegiSKADA on Barbary Station. If Adda told him it was listening to this conversation, he'd panic.

AegiSKADA had destroyed the eyes Pel had been born with. It was cruel of her to expose him to that intelligence again, but to leave the treatment clinic before the ITA wanted her to, she needed more help than Pel could offer. If she'd found a way to ask him if it was all right, he'd have said yes, eventually.

"I hate that you'll have to repeat all this news," Adda said. "What if you forwarded me some articles? Through the account we set up?"

His thoughtful expression returned. "Um. Which account was that again?"

She shut her eyes, giving herself time to gather her patience, then opened them. "The Vestan account. Sloane can still access it, so *be careful*, but it's . . . As long as it's addressed to me by name at the address you're talking to now, I'll get it."

The account she was describing didn't exist. If he contacted her through any Vestan account and AegiSKADA was still operating at the level of freedom she'd left it with, it would register her and Pel's names and locations. Then, if supporting her was still advantageous to whatever priorities Sloane had given it, it'd find her. She and Iridian were absolutely stuck in their current predicaments, and nobody knew where Casey was, let alone what it wanted. To get herself and Iridian to the Jovian station where their enemies would be reluctant to follow them, she had to drastically change the factors involved. AegiSKADA would do that.

"Five more minutes," said her therapist through an intercom to Adda's conference room.

Pel glanced toward the ceiling. "They're strict there, huh?"

"Iridian has it worse."

He shrugged, going for casual. His lack of eye contact and stiff movements told Adda that being separated from all their loved ones was hard for both of them to bear. "She's military, she's tough. She'll be all right." As long as Casey left her alone, at least.

That reminded Adda of another question she'd wanted to ask. "Did you . . ." If he and Iridian had accidentally attracted the ITA's attention while they were bringing Adda to the Ceresian hospital, then Casey wasn't responsible for their capture. "When you were on Ceres, did you and Iri do something . . . noticeable?"

Pel's brow wrinkled. "I don't think so. Iridian was working her ass off to keep us under the radar."

"All right." Adda would have to rephrase that question and ask again later. If Casey had gotten them arrested, it knew where they were and it'd given itself plenty of time to find a way to influence her again. "Will you be?" she asked Pel. "All right, I mean?"

He gave her an embarrassed smile. "I'm getting there. This is bad, but I'll figure something out."

"I'm proud of you."

"Thanks, Sissy." He sniffled and looked away from the cam. "Ah, shit, that's it, I'm going." The projector's *Connection terminated* notification meant that he'd severed it from his side.

Iri, I just talked to Pel, Adda subvocalized. *He's putting me in touch with someone who can help.* If AegiSKADA was listening to her and Pel's conversation, and if it wanted to help. She was, perhaps, overselling her progress. Telling Iridian that AegiSKADA was the friend Adda was reaching out to would upset her. That sounded familiar, for some reason.

Great, Iridian replied as the conference room door opened to admit Adda's therapist. *They're telling me this trial is almost over, and it's not coming out in my favor.*

Two sturdy-looking aides stood on either side of the unsmiling therapist. "Could you please come with us?" Frowning, Adda followed them into yet another medical examining room. The aides wouldn't have let her do anything else.

Once she was settled on the edge of the reclining chair/bed like a good patient, the therapist said, "We noticed some odd signal activity that follows you around. A review of your records suggests that, well . . . that we missed something." The woman said it so gently that Adda tensed up. They'd found her comms implants, her only way to talk to Iridian. "You said some unusual things to your brother earlier. At this stage, any communications that we can't oversee could push you to a higher influence stage. You've made great progress, but you're still at what we call stage two." Was she? She counted the weeks since she'd last talked to Casey. That was, she grudgingly admitted to herself, possible. "The wrong kind of input could delay your journey to freedom from influence. I know you don't want that."

An aide stepped up beside Adda and injected her with something. Dizziness and darkness overwhelmed her.

When she woke in her room, her neck, hand, and the side of her head around her ear were numb at her comms implant sites. She exhaled a long, slow breath while her heart thudded too fast and too hard. *Iri? Can you hear me?*

Silence followed. It was possible that Iridian was busy doing something else, or that they'd moved her so far away that it would take time for the signal to reach her and a reply to come back. Iridian had always made time for Adda before, even if it was just to say that she was too busy to talk.

At least there were no bandages. Whoever had modified her implants hadn't cut them out. And if they'd recorded any conversations she'd had with Iridian, her encryption would protect the content. After an hour of listening for Iri's voice, Adda had to accept that the clinic staff had cut her only link to Iridian.

CHAPTER 4

Days until launch: 72

The Sorenson ITA Station that floated in Venus's atmo was the prisoner transfer ship's only stop. Since Iridian's tiny cabin had no windows, the only thing she knew about her new hab was that its grav was healthy. Docking a craft this size in healthy grav must've been a challenge for the pilot. The speaker on the wall had told her to strap in over an hour ago and she was still lying in bed, waiting for the motion to stop.

Iridian fidgeted with the straps and subvocalized, *Can you hear me?* into her throat mic. Like every other time in the past few weeks, Adda didn't answer. Maybe she'd had another seizure, or the people at the treatment clinic had found her comms implants and deactivated them or taken them out.

Gods, Iridian hoped that they'd just deactivated the implants. The last she'd heard from Adda was shortly after Adda had contacted Pel. The next time Iridian got the chance, she'd reach out to Pel too and find out what in all hells was going on. Iridian huffed an irritated sigh. She and Adda had missed celebrating the anniversary of their first date. Iridian hadn't even been able to talk to her.

The lawyer had been apologetic about losing Iridian's trial in Ceresian court. Without moving the trial to the NEU, which the lawyer had tried and failed to do, she hadn't started with much of a chance. The ITA's inhibition-lowering drugs had provided all the evidence the prosecution needed, anyway. While trying not to implicate Adda, Iridian had confessed to a lot. The ITA's lawyer had made half his case by playing her recorded "interviews" in the courtroom.

The one hope she'd had of a deal, describing the ships carrying the awakened AIs, had been useless. The AIs must've left Vesta by the time the ITA went looking for them. If Iridian guessed right, Captain Sloane had assured the ITA that Iridian's report couldn't be trusted. She was happy to have cost the damned AIs a safe berth, but the ITA was unimpressed. The rest of the arguments had been a formality.

For the first few weeks she'd been vigilant for opportunities to escape while Ceresian law enforcement officers transferred her back and forth from jail to the courtroom, but she'd never gotten farther than a meter from her captors. The two attempts that triggered the nannite culture convinced her that she'd need outside help to find her way back to Adda.

Still, escaping an ITA prison wouldn't be the craziest thing Iridian had done to stay with Adda. Iridian had to believe that they'd be together again soon. The alternative would hurt too much to bear.

Miss you, babe, she subvocalized to Adda. Maybe she was listening and couldn't reply.

The prisoner transport docked and Iridian's cell door opened straight into a passthrough. A speaker clicked on. "You can walk out on your own, or—"

"Or the nannites will make me, yeah, yeah." She collected the spare set of clothes they'd left in the cabinet for her. The nannites slowed her pace to a shuffle, a new feature the culture had developed after it'd established itself in her nervous system. Other prisoners in the Ceres Station jail had confirmed that prison-grade cultures did that to everybody they infected. This was the farthest she'd walked in a straight line in days. She wanted to run up and down the passthrough a few times, but the way the nannites affected her muscles meant that her normal walking speed was now the fastest she could move. Even that took more effort than it should've.

The passthrough opened on another room with no occupants. It closed as soon as she left the exterior doorway. Medical equipment filled one wall. Across from the passthrough was another closed door. This hab's atmo processors were incredibly loud, like they were turned all the way up for some reason, although the atmo was as still as it should be in a sealed hab.

She stood there holding her clothes and listened. Atmo processors this loud would take some getting used to, and she'd have to get used to them. If the enviro ever changed for the worse, realizing it and reacting fast might save her life. A hydraulic whine from the passthrough, almost lost under the atmo processors, signaled the transport ship's departure. Maybe she was hearing Venus's famous wind.

Auditory directions walked her through a full body scan using the medical equipment. It asked for multiple passes around her head, neck, and hand, where the implanted comms were. It sent her through a deep decon cycle like she'd somehow gotten herself irradiated in jail, demanded that she recycle all her clothes, and gave her identical new ones. After she put those on, the med station prescribed a vaccination that hurt less than she'd expected it to.

The far door opened. Five people in ITA blue stood at the end of a short hallway, watching her. Most of their armor looked light and easy to move in, but the helmets were so overbuilt that it was amazing they could hold their heads up. The faceplates were dark. Two of the agents carried shields, smaller than Iridian's old one. The ITA shields looked rigid and heavy as the agents awkwardly hauled them into position at full height and width. Either the shields were new, or the agents didn't train with them often enough.

In the armored suit Captain Sloane had bought Iridian on Vesta, with the mech-ex graphene shield she'd built, she would've been able to take them. Unarmed in pants and a thin shirt, that'd be a losing fight. Besides, the agents could activate her nannite culture whenever they wanted. They might not even let her break her knuckles on their faceplates.

"Nassir, Iridian. Yes?" one of them asked.

It'd been a long few weeks without Adda. Iridian grinned wider than she had any reason to, given the question. "If you don't know who I am by now, then you people have bigger problems than—"

One of the armored people activated Iridian's nannites. She hit the floor on her side. Over her screams, the first speaker said, "We're the ERT. Everything here in Sorenson ITAS looks real civilized, and you're going to think it'd be easy to pull something. Don't. If you try it, we'll be there to stop you."

The nerve pain ended. Iridian had curled up as small as she could make herself, chest heaving against her knees. *Breathe, breathe, oh fuck you, you assmongers, breathe,* she thought, and hopefully did not say to Adda.

"Get up," said the guy who talked like he was in charge. "We'll walk you to your cell."

Iridian wanted to snap at them, but she didn't want it enough to risk him activating her nannite culture again. She pushed herself off the floor. The ERT squad, which she guessed stood for something related to emergency response, fell into formation around her. The clack of light armor was comfortably familiar, even though the people wearing it were her enemies, not her allies.

The hab's low lighting had the orange glow of a very late local time or a very early one. They passed more closed doors in the windowless hallway than Iridian could count. They turned more corners than Iridian was used to in a hab too. With cams near the ceiling watching every angle, the guards saw more than the prisoners did. The ERT people must've had cam feeds from every short hallway and cell pumped into their helmets.

Eventually the ERT squad stopped in front of a door and opened it. This section of hallway had only six doors, three on one side and three on the other. The talker said, "Get in, lie down on the bed, and don't do anything stupid."

The bed, strangely, was in the middle of the small room, with grav straps dangling from its sides to the floor. Grav here was lighter than would've been ideal, but only a little. She'd heard that was normal on Venus. This place couldn't have been on Venus's surface, though. Only specially designed equipment survived the weather down there.

The room was too small for multiple beds, so she wouldn't have roommates to talk to like she'd had in the Ceres Station jail. They hadn't had anything interesting to say, but anybody would've been better than four blank walls and a solid door. A comp terminal with a projection stage was in one corner, and an open door leading to a small bathroom was in the other. She'd rented worse rooms than this. She got onto the bed before the ERT people found another reason to activate her nannite culture.

"Strap yourself in," was the next order.

Iridian did it even more slowly than the nannites would've let her. "How unstable is the grav here?" They ignored her question. Once she'd secured herself, she asked, "Now what?"

One of the armored people, not the one who'd been doing the

talking, stepped into the cell and checked her straps. The person did something beside Iridian's head. The room and hall lights shut off. Iridian opened her mouth to ask what the hell that was about, and somehow . . . didn't. The words didn't come out.

When the lights came on a few seconds later, the person who'd been messing with Iridian's bed was back in the hallway. "What was that?" Iridian was relieved to actually be able to ask the question.

"You can get up once the door closes," a third armored guy said. "You'll be locked in until you finish your psych evals, and then you'll go in with everybody else. Just remember: you get out of line, we'll be there."

"Great," Iridian said sarcastically. "Thanks." The door shut from the top down, solid metal impacting the plastic floor with a clack, while she released the bed's straps. Grav had been stable since she'd arrived. Maybe that procedure was to protect the guards from her. Whatever she'd been expecting from the ITA's prison, it kept surprising her.

According to the time stamp on the comp in the corner, the staff kept Iridian in isolation for two days, punctuated by more blackouts. Each blackout was signaled by a chirping alarm and auditory instructions for her to get into bed (or stay there, if she'd been asleep) and strap in. They'd been happening before all her meals, and at other times too. Maybe whatever made the pouches of flavored goo that they served as food drew a lot of power.

Iridian wanted to know how bad the prisoners she'd be in with were, but the only people she talked to were psychologists running orientation and testing. One of them spoke like an AI in disguise. The interviews were conducted through the comp in her cell, which only showed her what the ITA wanted her to see. NEU internet should've been accessible from Venus's orbit, but the ITA's network was locked down.

They hadn't even given her a window, like there'd been in the Ceres Station jail. Ceresians acted like people couldn't survive with a blank ceiling over their heads all the time. Iridian missed the stars, but Sorenson ITAS was cleaner and calmer than the jail. Not meeting the other residents grated on her, though. In the Ceres Station jail, new prisoner introductions sometimes ended with the newbie beaten bloody. If a fight was coming, she wanted to get it over with.

The comp in the desk had things to read, at least. She skimmed prison rules and her release criteria, the eighteen things she'd have to do before the ITA let her go. The official documents estimated that she'd meet all her release criteria in a couple of years, but almost everybody took longer. People who did it in less made the newsfeeds.

Rehabilitation took as many years as the ITA wanted it to take, but blue boxes hovered beside the documents' text describing statistical success: *91% of those released leave criminal behavior behind for good! 100% of released persons capable of work have a job within six months of meeting their release criteria!* The exclamation points were absent, but implied.

After the third morning's blackout, Iridian climbed off her bed to find the cell door open. A projector stage in the ceiling presented a message beside it. *Follow arrows to the dining room. Please do not deviate from the prescribed route.*

Iridian would've liked to finish the set of sit-ups she'd started before the blackout. She hadn't broken a sweat and her joints were still stiff. But this was her chance to find out what the other prisoners were like. Footsteps and an approaching tense conversation drew her through the door.

". . . is gone. I didn't do it. Wiley didn't do it." The husky feminine voice was familiar, as was the name Wiley, but the speaker was around a corner from Iridian's cell.

"Who did, then?" a second speaker, male by the sound of it, asked in the same quiet, tense tone.

Iridian stepped around the corner in the direction of the voices, which also happened to be the opposite direction of the white arrows projected onto the walls. A dragging swish and a clack told her that the door had shut behind her. "Blame it on me," she suggested. Since she'd just arrived, she had nothing to lose with disciplinary action, and solving their problem might head off a physical determination of how much respect Iridian was owed. "I'm new. I don't know any better."

Both people stopped walking as Iridian turned a second corner to follow them. At least, she assumed it was two people, because the first person took up the entirety of the narrow hallway. She'd know that silhouette anywhere. The enormous woman turned around and her wide face confirmed it. "Hell's holy whores. Nassir!"

"Rio!" Iridian shambled forward as fast as the nannites would let her move. On Vesta, Pel had said that Rio had gotten locked up for something, but he'd never said what for or where. Captain Sloane's ops had kept Iridian too busy to follow up.

Whoever Rio had been talking to used spacefarer cant to compare Iridian's arrival to a sewage system blowout. Seeing a friend in this place, even one she had befriended on Barbary Station while an AI was trying to kill her, was a powerful relief. She didn't even get halfway into a bow before brown arms enveloped her in a rib-crushing hug. "What the hell brought you here?" Iridian croaked as her lungs compressed.

Rio chuckled. "Long story. And go easy when you're walking toward people. Anyway, we don't have time. It's important to be on time, as a courtesy to others." That last sentence sounded memorized, and Rio's smile fell away as they walked in the direction the arrows pointed. "Uzomo, this is Iridian Nassir," she said.

"Hey." Uzomo raised a dark brown hand, tattooed with a black pattern of lines like a ladder from his wrist up as much of the arm as Iridian saw over Rio's wide shoulders, which were about the height of Iridian's head. "I'm going to say you lost it," said Uzomo. "Who'd take one two-kilo dumbbell, anyway? And 'we are empowered to work it out among ourselves,' so the therapists aren't telling us who." The part about empowerment sounded like a sarcastic quote.

Rio made a displeased grunt. "Speak only the truth." Her broad shoulders hunched a little more with every platitude she uttered. Iridian frowned. Whatever process the ITA used to turn prisoners into good spacefaring citizens must've included catchphrases people felt compelled to repeat.

You'll never guess who I just met, Iridian subvocalized to Adda. On Barbary Station, Rio had been one of Pel's staunchest allies, and she'd taken to Iridian and Adda as soon as Captain Sloane stopped aiming weapons at them. Knowing that Iridian had a reliable friend in this place might keep Adda from worrying about her too much. It certainly eased Iridian's mind. And Adda might be interested to hear how Rio was doing. Like every other time Iridian had talked to Adda recently, there was no response. The silence tore her up inside.

The hallway opened onto a small cafeteria. Over a dozen people sat at blue tables with ITA seals printed onto the tops. As usual, Rio was the most massive person in the room. Like Iridian, most prisoners wore plain clothes that came from default textile printer patterns. Despite the simple clothes, the hunched shoulders and tattoos would've looked more at home in the dark corners of Captain Sloane's club on Vesta than in this well-lit, quiet place. The expressions as they sized her up were mixed. There was some cold disinterest and a couple of approving nods, a lot of suspicious glowering, and a few people who looked like just the sight of her was infuriating. Four of the ubiquitous ERTs stood in full armor around the walls, helmet faceplates showing featureless black.

The tables and benches were bolted to the floor. Short straps hung from the benches, for low-grav seating. They also looked sturdy enough to allow people to sit with their full weight on their asses, and their plates resting on the tabletops, but the straps suggested that low grav was possible, if not common. Perhaps the station rose above the atmosphere in certain situations, like avoiding bad storms. As long as it was going up, not down, short periods of micrograv would be all right. Except for the lack of comp cradles in the tables' centers, the place looked as civilized as the ERT people had told her to expect.

Even though the tables were big enough for trays and plates, nobody had any. Everyone held yellow liter-size liquid packets, like the kind that'd been delivered to Iridian's cell three times a day. Iridian gripped the dispensing machine's handle while it scanned her vein pattern. A little cabinet door opened to reveal a yellow packet of her own. The contents, when she broke the straw's seal and sipped, were thick and . . . "Banana flavored?"

"That's what they're going for, yeah." Rio raised hers in farewell to Uzomo, whose tattoos were much more visible in the cafeteria lights as he headed for one of the tables. He had Jovian and Saturnian secessionist iconography on his shoulders and back, peeking through carefully placed tears in his shirt, in addition to the lines Iridian had seen earlier.

Rio was headed for a different table, so Iridian followed her. Once Uzomo was several meters away, Rio muttered, "Assassin. There are at least three in here. Recognition didn't exactly end the market for violence." Instead, the NEU recognizing colonial independence had turned a lot of soldiers into bitter freelancers. They hadn't all joined a legal organization like Rio's ZV Group. It made sense that some would end up here. "Stay with me and my group and you'll be all right. Us four watch each other's backs." Rio returned to the topic of meal replacements at a normal volume. "Guaranteed allergen and contaminant free, with nutrients mixed up for each of us. No trading, nothing solid."

"Great," said Iridian, in regard to both the "food" and the secessionist assassin. It wasn't.

Everybody kept watching Iridian, the prisoners out of the corners of their eyes and the ERT people through the blank faceplates turned toward her. The prisoners' muted conversation was full of even more therapeutic-sounding phrases. It was almost like a new cant. Iridian had a lot of rules to learn, written and not, to avoid making any more enemies than she had to. It paid not to piss off your new neighbors when you moved into a mod, especially when some of the neighbors used to kill for a living.

The table Rio walked toward was occupied by a broad-shouldered black man and a shorter man with tawny skin that exposed dark circles under his eyes. They were playing black and white digital checkers on a board rising out of a thumbnail-size projector in the table's center. Iridian did a double take back to the players.

Rio thumped the table with one big hand, making the digital board game jump. The pieces moved together with the board and stayed in their squares. "Iridian Nassir, this is Noor Beck and—"

"Zayd Wiley," Iridian said. In her memory, the black man's head was shaved as bald as she usually kept her own, but he'd grown his hair out a few centimeters. He was heavier than he'd been when they'd driven infantry shield vehicles during the war. Since he was the only person at the table wearing a comp glove, the checkers game had to be running on it. Like everything else, the fingerless glove was ITA blue. Iridian sat down hard on the open bench space next to him.

Wiley looked as shocked as she was. It took a long moment for his face to split into a smile. "Nassir!" He wrapped his arm around her shoulders and dragged her into a sideways hug. People in this hab touched each other a lot more often than Iridian had expected. Everybody had gone through the same decon, so it wasn't a big deal. One of the ERT people stepped away from the wall, heavy helmet lowered threateningly, and Wiley let her go.

"I'd ask why you're here, but everybody with newsfeed privileges already told everybody else." Wiley laughed, probably at himself. That laughter was a comforting sound she could've heard anytime, if she'd just kept up with him after she left the service for school. "I didn't believe you were coming," he said. "Everything's the same here, day after day. I didn't believe even you could break the routine."

Iridian's shoulders had been up around her ears in a defensive reflex that she only noticed as they relaxed. When she'd walked into the cafeteria, she'd been settling in to stay in this prison. Adda couldn't think well enough to plan an escape, the ITA security measures seemed solid, and Iridian was just one woman in a cage designed to hold people exactly like her. She'd seen no way out. But now *two* soldiers she trusted were stuck in this place with her, and that changed everything. If she came up with something resembling a plan, these people could help her get back to Adda before they both got old and gray.

Rio sat beside the man she'd introduced as Noor, looking pleased with herself. Noor moved a checker piece across the board and said, "*Iridian Nassir* is the Shieldrunner friend you were expecting to get sent here?" Noor's spacefarer English, like Wiley's, carried a hint of reassuring Martian twang.

"Yeah," said Wiley. "We ran together on Titan and Mars." He shook his head, still looking at Iridian like if he turned away, she'd disappear. "Good times."

"Your exploits on Vesta catching up with you?" Noor asked Iridian while Wiley took his turn at the checkers board. His voice was lower than it looked like it ought to be for his size.

"Look, Captain Sloane blew our involvement way out of proportion," Iridian said. "Adda and I were foot soldiers." Wiley snorted at that, and Iridian grinned. "Yeah, I know." Aside from Iridian's understatement regarding Adda's involvement, the Shieldrunners mocked the exposed and vulnerable infantry who needed the ISVs' protection. Maybe Wiley had let himself go a bit since the last time he'd driven an infantry shield vehicle, but he remembered those years.

Noor ran a hand through black hair that fell almost to his shoulders. "But you did kidnap the scientist who discovered the interstellar bridge, didn't you?"

Her lawyer had no hope of getting her out of that charge on appeal. "We rescued ver from a disabled ship in the middle of Mangala stationspace first." Iridian had questions of her own, starting with the ones about the station enviro. People who didn't learn a hab's quirks got hurt during "expected" enviro fluctuations. The comp in her cell hadn't offered the usual public records about this hab. "While it's question-and-answer time, what's up with all the blackouts? None of the orientation crap they've been testing me on explains those. Is this station stable or what?"

"Rumor is the hab has power problems, but they keep telling us it's not getting any closer to the surface," said Rio, which was a relief. Without a lot of specialized gear, Venus's surface wasn't survivable, even if you didn't get there at terminal velocity. "And before you ask, everybody gets up feeling stiff, so that's not just you either. The beds are shit." Wiley and Noor nodded agreement.

Iridian hadn't even mentioned her stiff muscles. This was apparently a common complaint.

A white woman wandered toward their table, making her nannite-slowed walk look slinky instead of sluggish, with hips rounded to entertainment-feed perfection. She had the ageless quality of women between thirty and fifty who'd spent most of their lives behind rad shielding. When she reached the table, she draped her arms over Wiley's shoulders and the rest of herself over his back. Her shirt was tied in a knot to expose a line of small metal ring piercings up the side of her flat stomach, strung through with a pink ribbon. It looked like she had another set on the other side, and the ribbon laced up her front in a row of *X*s. The woman cast a challenging look at Iridian while she cooed, "Hey, love," in Wiley's ear.

"Hey, yourself." Wiley patted her arm. "Tash, this is Iridian Nassir. Friend from—"

"The Shieldrunners," Tash drawled in uncolored spacefarer English like they spoke on Iridian's home hab. "I know who she is." She gave Iridian a long look.

"Hey." Iridian dipped her head for a duration that offered a high level of respect to a stranger. Tash broke off her challenging stare and nodded back.

Iridian would definitely remember meeting this woman, so Tash must've heard about her on the newsfeeds. "Nice mods," she said to Tash. "I've only got this." Iridian raised one side of her shirt to display her tattoo, a triangle of skin peeled up from her side to reveal a realistic lung and liver under two crossed rib bones. A dark scar cut into the crossed-bone design. She hadn't gotten around to having it repaired. A black skull grinned out from the middle of the peeled-back skin.

Tash leaned closer in a glittering swell of breasts lit with small LED jewels that glowed through her shirt. She hummed in an approving sort of way. "Too bad about the blade that got you. It's good work."

"I got him back." Iridian grinned almost as widely as the tattooed skull. If she could convince these people to help her escape, she'd find her way back to Adda sooner rather than later.

After the meal, loudspeaker instructions directed the prisoners in the cafeteria to their beds for the duration of a brief blackout. From there, Iridian got sent to yet another therapist appointment. It was her second conversation with this skinny old white woman in the past couple of days. During the first, Iridian had halfheartedly completed a barrage of tests while Shera Marsten ("just Shera, I don't have a doctorate") observed from the stage built into the desk in Iridian's cell.

In person, Shera perched on a soft chair across from the equally soft couch on which Iridian sat. The therapists' and doctors' offices were the only comfortable places in the whole damned hab. Shera's office was just warm enough to emphasize that the rest of Sorenson ITAS was slightly too cold.

"Hi." Shera wore a small, professional smile and earrings that were too big for her face. "How are you feeling about meeting with me today?"

Iridian shrugged. "Not much else to do."

"That's a good response." Except for the ERT people, the staff constantly shared opinions on what Iridian said and did. They'd been doing it since she got onto the transport ship on Ceres. Even the virtual ones did it. "You're going to be one of my clients," said Shera.

Iridian leaned back into the couch cushions and crossed her arms under her breasts. "'Client' sounds like I'm supposed to pay you. Do you have any idea how much a lawyer costs?" The bill from the Ceresian lawyer she'd hired to replace the ITA's silent one had been a nasty surprise.

Captain Sloane had unexpectedly kicked in 40 percent of the fee, along with a note: "For your trouble on my behalf." The captain wanted her free eventually but didn't mind if she was low on funds when she got out. Besides, it would've been bad for Sloane's crew morale to leave even a disgraced member in the ITA's custody with no support at all.

Shera laughed. "I'm sorry. 'Client' is just the lingo here. I'm sure you know that the language we use is important. Positive language has positive effects. Could you repeat that for me?"

Iridian blinked at her. "Why?"

"Repetition reinforces concepts that are important to your release criteria," Shera said patiently. Demonstrating progress toward each prisoner's individualized release criteria must've been what had the other prisoners repeating phrases that sounded more like psychobabble shit than real speech. No wonder repeating them aggravated Rio so much.

"I understood what you said. What's next?" Iridian wasn't interested in progressing toward any of her eighteen release criteria. Not while she hadn't even tried to find a faster way back to Adda. At the trial they'd talked about months of drug testing, developing a group of "prosocial" friends and advocates who the therapists thought would somehow make crime less profitable or debts less crushing, and psychological "milestones" that were arbitrary as hell. The repeated phrases must've counted as progress toward those milestones.

The small and professional smile returned to Shera's face. "Since you've passed the tests on our introduction vids, I know you understand that our goal is to ensure that you don't have to spend any more time here than necessary, and that this will be your only stay in ITA facilities. So we're going to be seeing a lot of each other, aren't we?"

Iridian shrugged. "The only person I want to see right now is my wife. When can somebody set that up?"

"Adda Karpe is very unwell, isn't she?" Shera asked.

That was a hell of a way to describe recovering from brain damage and AI influence. "Yeah," Iridian said. "I want to know how she's doing." And see her face, and hear her voice, and if Iridian were lucky, make her smile . . . She sighed. She'd been on missions without Adda before, but she'd always known when they'd meet up again. Now that she didn't know, Adda was all she thought about.

Shera frowned quickly and deeply, like she'd been stopping herself from making that face ever since Iridian started talking. "Ordinarily, connecting you with your family would be wonderful motivation to meet your release criteria. In your and Adda's case, though . . . I'm going to ask you a question, and I'm going to preface it with the reminder that our observer is very good at identifying aggressive motion. You will not be permitted to continue any such motion."

"I'll curl up and scream on the floor instead, got it." With Iridian's luck, the observer was an AI that'd flatten her no matter how she reacted.

"Do you feel that your relationship with Adda has had a *positive* influence on your interaction with society?"

Iridian had been right about the question's effect. She shut her eyes and held herself still until she thought she could move slowly and calmly enough not to get hit with the nannites again. "Thank you for thinking carefully about your response," said Shera.

Through clenched teeth, Iridian said, "Adda's has a positive influence on everything about me."

When she opened her eyes, the therapist was still frowning. "Hmm."

Between the nannite culture in every prisoner's body and the long list of privileges that improved their stay in the silent, bare, internet-restricted cells, Sorenson ITAS was breaking people's minds to fix them. And now Shera thought she could change Iridian's opinion about *Adda*. The ITA had whole lifetimes to work on people who still had release criteria to meet. The prospect of staying here long enough for them to change how Iridian felt about her wife made her sick.

Now that Iridian knew the extent of the mind games the ITA was playing, she was watching for them in the cafeteria during lunch. The furniture and the machine that dispensed the food packets weren't bolted down to handle grav adjustments, they were bolted down to keep people from moving them. She could do absolutely no damage with the off-white packet the meal came in, unless she stuffed it down somebody's throat. The top was folded over and stiff, and too wide for most people's mouths. The stuff inside tasted like fish stew with an aftertaste of powdered ass.

Tash was at another table, hanging off a person of indiscriminate gender who was very much not Wiley. Wiley followed Iridian's gaze and shrugged. "She does that. She'll be back."

"Did your counselors ever try to break the two of you up?" Iridian was still angry about Shera asking whether Adda was good for Iridian, as if that was anybody else's decision to make.

"Oh yeah," said Wiley. "I took some heat for . . . an event that happened near Tash. It could've gotten her shipped off to the asteroid belt, if she'd been involved. Which she wasn't. It set my release progress back, and right after that they started in on our relationship." Wiley's gaze went distant. "They had me thinking about it for a while. I actually sat Tash down to break it off, but she snapped me out of it. If you read into the recovery program, it's big on 'removing temptation to reoffend.' That includes people they think are bad for you."

Iridian scowled at her packaged meal. "That's fucked up. Of them, not you." Adda was her second set of eyes, her calm when everything else came apart, her reason when nothing else made sense. The ITA couldn't make Iridian question that. But they'd almost talked Wiley into breaking up with his girlfriend, and he looked happy to be with her now. The ITA definitely thought they could change Iridian's mind.

She bit the inside of her cheek to ground herself. This was why she had to believe she could leave this place on her own terms. She wouldn't give them the chance to do that to her and Adda.

Wiley frowned at his own meal packet. "Remember that time the secessionists hit the mess and logistics outside Chien-Shiung Wu Station on Mars and we had to go begging from the locals?"

The abrupt shift from her personal war with the ITA to her and Wiley's shared war against the secessionists suggested that Iridian had been scowling at her lunch for longer than she'd thought. "Oh gods, I'd forgotten what fresh food tasted like. I was choking on the replacement rations for weeks after that."

"The good old days." Wiley snorted a laugh. "I never would've believed it." They knew when their next meal would be and the atmo was clean, but meeting Adda had raised Iridian's standards for good living. Perfect enviro was boring without Adda there to share it.

If Adda were here with her, planning a jailbreak, the first thing she'd say was that the AI running this hab was watching for a breakout. Iridian didn't care about that, since she couldn't do anything to affect it. Then Adda would list all her available resources and options.

Although Iridian had no equipment or supplies, she did have

allies. Some of Wiley's skills mirrored her own. He'd never been as interested as she was in how the ISVs worked, so he would've done something other than engineering school and piracy after the war. When Rio and Noor sat down with their personalized fish-ass stew, Iridian said, "So everybody knows what I've been up to. What about you all?"

"In case you were wondering, everything here's recorded." Rio shrugged. "I'm still with the ZVs. They'll take me back when I meet my release criteria."

Iridian wanted to ask why the ZVs hadn't broken Rio out yet, but that question would sound suspicious on a recording. Besides, the ZV Group upheld NEU laws unless they had a good reason not to. There were few benefits and a lot of drawbacks to taking somebody out of an ITA prison without an ITA order to do it.

"You're lucky," said Wiley. "Nobody's waiting for me to reform. Sentence I got was one trouble too many for Martian government work."

Iridian raised an eyebrow at him. "What were you doing for the Martian government?"

"Construction." It sounded about as interesting as changing oil or checking reading bots' work, the way Wiley said it. "Building bridges and tearing down walls."

Judging by Rio's and Noor's coordinated eye roll, the line about bridges and walls was another catchphrase from "therapy." It was more like brainwashing. She and the other prisoners were disconnected from the rest of humanity, bombarded with "correct" messages, and expected to conform. And the alternative was a lot of pain.

"But the construction work meant something to people," Wiley continued. "People remembered how their 'ject used to be before the war. Helping the bots put it back was putting Mars back together. Boring job, but it meant something."

"Just like army life," said Iridian. "You must've felt right at home."

"It was Mars. I was at home." He glanced around, maybe missing windows like Iridian did.

She turned to Noor, who was watching her over a tablet that looked almost as old as she was. Before she could ask about his skill set, he said, "Why do you want to know?"

"She's just making conversation," said Wiley.

"Is she?" Noor's question was more contemplative than accusatory. He studied her for a moment more. "Information security." Wiley chuckled. That sounded like digital theft, which often involved manipulating physical security systems. Skills like that would be useful in an escape and lucrative afterward.

"And I can mix drinks on eight different 'jects when the AI breaks down," said Tash, "and look better doing it." Iridian hadn't noticed her approach, but she couldn't help noticing when Tash draped herself over Wiley's shoulders and grinned. The tattoo on the forearm ten centimeters from Iridian's face read *Fabulous* in black calligraphy that stood out on Tash's pale skin. More tattoos, mostly text in languages Iridian couldn't read, encircled Tash's upper arms and her other forearm, and hid among pink and white stars lit with LEDs that gleamed where they emerged from the skin of her chest.

Her effect on people who got off on her level of body modification would be a more useful skill, in terms of getting out of this hab. "So, one more question," Iridian said. "If I wanted to have a private conversation, is there any way to do that?"

Everyone at the table stiffened slightly. "Nope," said Rio, but she met Iridian's eyes and tilted her head up and down fractionally. There was a place that wasn't micced, but not one Rio would name aloud.

* * *

After the post-lunch blackout, Iridian was back to testing and talking to ITA people for hours. The next time she saw the group she was beginning to think of as her crew was a recreational period in a gym designed for the healthy grav. Although the sun-sim was comfortable, the walls were decorated only with a projected list of gym rules.

According to the staff, windows were an earned privilege. The gym was too small for a track, but a row of treadmills lined one wall and somebody was running on one. The runner met Iridian's envious gaze and made a rude gesture. Moving faster than a walk must've been an earned privilege too.

"What, we don't get to go outside?" Iridian asked Wiley. He was spotting Rio at a weight bench. The readout on the frame attached to the bench reported that Rio was pressing 332 kilos of metal with perfect form. Even with her visible strain, the sight gave Iridian mild vertigo. When somebody moved that much weight without a suit, they were usually doing it in low grav. At first glance Rio carried a lot of fat. Underneath was a remarkable amount of muscle.

Wiley was looking at Iridian with a similar level of incredulity, but when she smiled at him, he relaxed at the realization that she was joking about exercising outdoors. "Pretty sure acid rain and wind strong enough to blow this whole hab around aren't on the privileges list."

Noor appeared with a two-kilogram dumbbell and spent a couple of seconds positioning it on the weight rack beside its mate. "Ah . . . ha!" Rio said, one syllable per repetition, with her head tilted back to watch.

"The only mic I've found in this area is now flattened against that rack," Noor murmured. Iridian fought the instinct to lean in to hear him over Rio's breathing and the background buzz of other prisoners' workout conversations. "The next closest mics are two meters on either side of us, so keep it down. Now." Noor turned to face Iridian. "Did you come here to break somebody out, or are you leaving by yourself?" Iridian gaped at him while Rio and Wiley switched places and Rio took some weight plates off the bar. Noor smiled thinly. "You don't hide your intentions well, and you're recently of Sloane's crew. How else would Captain Sloane get somebody out of here? So my question is, who would Sloane be that interested in?"

Iridian frowned. "The captain was willing to let my wife die to deal with political fallout. I don't care what the hell Captain Sloane's interested in. I just want to leave, and I think you can help."

"Help with what?" Tash whispered behind Iridian, making Iridian spin around and raise her hands in a pointless, shieldless block. Tash grinned while Iridian looked between Rio and Wiley to see if either of them would trust Tash with their topic of conversation.

Rio shrugged, and Wiley nodded at her. Noor just watched, so Iridian said, "I'm talking about getting the fuck out of here. You in?"

Tash laughed delightedly. "You just got here!" She grasped Wiley's weight bar and leaned on it. The ribbon that laced through the rings on her stomach dangled from the bottom of her shirt. Wiley gave one strenuous heave with her added weight, which also made her laugh, then paused at the low point of his rep to accommodate her. "But yeah, why not? I'm not making any money here, and it's so boring that I keep 'backtracking' on my release criteria. So, sure. On one condition."

"Yeah?" said Iridian.

"Tell Captain Sloane all about me."

Rio snorted. "Sloane's got all the bartenders a captain could want, Tash."

"Who knew the ITA micromanaged the habs so thoroughly that they'd send people here for mixing bad drinks?" Noor asked. He watched Tash coolly.

"Like I keep saying, some of them were *very* bad drinks." Tash leaned over Wiley as if inviting Noor to count the stars on her chest. Wiley grinned up at her. He had the better view.

Rio casually turned her head to take in their surroundings. Everyone else was keeping their distance. An ERT guard ambled past, black faceplate staring at them, and Rio and Wiley switched places on the bench again. "I'm . . . in," Rio said after the guard was out of range, still in time to her reps. "I owe . . . you and Adda . . . a big one."

Noor and Wiley both gave Rio surprised looks. Wiley recovered first. He offered Iridian a shallow bow. "It'll be good to work with you again," Wiley said to her.

"That would be amazing, but you've got to be close to getting out of here the right way," Iridian said.

Wiley scowled. "I've got two criteria left to prove and four more to maintain, but everybody knows my position on secessionists hasn't changed. And a couple months ago, I set myself back hard." He and Tash shifted, probably to put something between them and cams, eyes locked and hands reaching for each other. It was abruptly too intimate for Iridian to watch. Did she and Adda look like that when they were together?

She turned to Noor, who was watching the other exercisers thoughtfully. "Can you imagine what it's like, watching your personalized ITA 'reintegration' program turn you into somebody you don't recognize anymore?" Noor asked. "I've seen it happen." He looked like he might say something else but swallowed visibly instead. "I'm not interested in letting them tie my brain into any more knots than it's already in." He turned to Iridian. "Do you have a plan?"

For a second, Iridian thought the ERT people had activated her nannite culture again, but it was just a sudden, physical ache of not having Adda here. She'd make three plans that'd definitely work and a few more that might work even when everything else went to shit. After taking a moment to catch her breath and locate the ERT people, Iridian said, "Do any of these emergency response people have dirt we could use to, say, replace one with a ZV?"

Rio, Wiley, and Noor all shook their heads. Tash, however, smiled wider. "Oh yeah, I know exactly the one you want. You won't even need to replace him."

Iridian knew next to nothing about Tash, but trusting her looked like Iridian's best option. This was coming together better than she'd expected, and without all the sitting in a corner and pondering that Adda loved and Iridian tolerated. "Okay. Okay!"

If Tash had a comms line to the outside, or if Iridian convinced her therapist that she'd be talking to somebody "motivational," then Iridian would find a way to contact Rio's merc outfit, the ZV Group. They had the personnel and expertise to break her out. More importantly, they owed her and Adda for getting off Barbary Station alive. That made them the only private military company she'd be able to afford. Even if they gave her a break on the price, they'd cost everything she and Adda had saved. Once she was out, nothing would stop her from freeing Adda.

"Let me know when you're ready," Iridian said, "and I'll send the message to a relative who will help." Not that Iridian's blood relatives wanted anything to do with her at the moment, except for her uncle in the Kuiper colonies. The counselor, Shera, might even give Iridian progress points for asking to talk to family other than Adda. Unfortunately, the only person she could count on to get her plan moving was her fuckup brother-in-law, Pel.

CHAPTER 5

Days until launch: 65

A couple of weeks ago, the influence rehab clinic doctors cele-brated Adda's graduation from influence stage two to stage one by moving her into a dorm-style room with one roommate. If the staff decided that she wasn't influenced at all, they'd send her to jail to await her trial, so she maintained her nonverbal pretense and kept asking for comms technology that they'd never give her access to, like she still felt compelled to talk to Casey.

Now Adda sat on her bed, ignoring her whispering roommate and mentally composing a message to Pel. The doctors had promised that they'd allow her to send one after she completed some journaling exercises. They were asking her to describe changes she'd experienced in herself since entering the facility. The prompt wording suggested they expected her to write something positive. Her cognitive functions had improved, but she'd also lost weight on the bland food they'd been giving her. Iridian loved her thick thighs and heavy breasts, and those were the parts that'd shrunk the most. Adda felt like she was dissolving in this place.

She'd finish the assignment faster if she didn't think about

the content. The last message she'd gotten from Pel noted that
Iridian's trial was over, and she'd been moved from the Ceres jail
to a prison over Venus. If it was on all the newsfeeds, then Casey
knew where Iridian was. Adda had no idea how it would react to
that. If it wanted to, it could take control of the prison's facility
management intelligence.

Before that happened, or Casey got some other dangerous
idea, Adda wanted to get herself, Iridian, and Pel inside Jupiter's
signal-confounding magnetosphere. Since AegiSKADA hadn't
responded to her attempts to get its attention, she'd just have to
ask Pel to get her the help she needed, in a way he'd understand
and her therapists wouldn't. After years of using digital encryption to keep her conversations private, this was the first time
she'd attempted a verbal equivalent.

Text-based coding that he could replicate would be identifi-
able to people trained to stop influence victims from contacting
intelligences. If she were going to record audio or vid, vid would
include more information that might distract observers from her
real message. Vid's wealth of information also made it an unreliable way to communicate with intelligences, which the therapists watching her would know. And Pel knew vid was Adda's least
favorite communication medium. That'd catch his attention.

Once she gave her therapists the journal entries, they let her
into the monitored conference room to make her recording. Her
code would be obvious to any ITA or security-conscious listeners,
but Adda was still acting less neurologically competent than she
felt. Security-conscious people wouldn't be interested in analyz-
ing a brain-damaged person's message.

Even so, her and Pel's shared experience was the foundation
of her cipher, and she couldn't pour a whole new vocabulary into
a single message. She'd selected five concepts she wanted to con-
vey. She breathed slowly for a beat, one of the few useful tech-

niques the therapists had offered her to calm herself down, then activated the recorder in the conference room's projector.

"Hi, Pel. I hope you're doing well. Sorry to leave you alone like this." Breath in, breath out. It was so easy to make mistakes on a vid and so hard to edit them later, especially when she had to use the clinic's outdated editing equipment. "I haven't heard from you lately, so, what are you *planning* to do? Tell me all the *details*." That second phrase was usually Pel's line, not hers, so he might notice that she'd paired "details" with the "planning" she was now talking about. She paused after her first cipher, then went on.

"I know it's hard to keep a *schedule in real time*, but it's important to anything you're *planning* to do." "Real time" was a phrase he'd made fun of her for using. Her light emphasis would, she hoped, communicate that if their plans were proceeding on schedule, he could use that phrase to tell her so. This might've made more sense in her head. If it took more than one message to clarify their code, so be it.

She paused again. She must've looked as nervous as she felt, and Pel knew he was one of two people in the universe who Adda talked to with ease. To a stranger, her nerves might explain these long pauses in the message.

"And I know *recording* always *takes longer than you planned*, but I wish you'd send me a message anyway." Demanding that your relatives talk to you seemed normal, but she was repeating variations of "plan" too often. She was proposing that conjugations of "record" could be used to say that they were falling behind schedule. Two more terms to go.

"And tell me how Iridian is doing. There are *veterans* who can help her, if we can ask them." That was the biggest stretch of all of these. Although the universe was full of veterans, the ones most likely to assist Iridian were the ZV Group, not the NEU veteran support system. Pel could say "veterans" to discuss the ZVs.

"*Whatever*, you don't have to tell me what you're up to if you don't want to." This was the part that should make Pel realize that several of her sentences had secondary meanings. She'd never let him get away with failing to tell her about his life, not when she'd tracked him down and gone to the trouble of recording something on vid. If he said "whatever," a word he used the way she used "never mind," to tell her that he was finished talking about plans to get Iridian out of prison, then that would be a useful way to end encoded messages.

"I love you, so please reply to this." Adda stopped recording and played back what she'd said. The pauses felt incredibly long. Maybe that was just her nerves, or maybe she'd really been speaking in an obviously strange rhythm.

She gave the message to the therapists to send, and they didn't bring it back to her with scowls and accusations. With a few more messages like these, she and Pel would have a set of alternative terms with which to discuss escape.

It'd been over a month since her implanted comms had gone silent. Adda was almost certain that the problem was on her end, not Iridian's. Still, for the sixth or seventh time that day, she subvocalized, *Iri?* into the mic in her throat. There was no response, even taking into account the distance between Ceres and Venus, where, according to Pel, the ZV Group were entering Venus's orbit to help Iridian escape. In the weeks since she'd shared the first words of a verbal cipher with Pel, he'd accomplished a lot.

She should stop checking. The implanted comms wouldn't spontaneously fix themselves. The silence upset her, and when she was upset it was harder to avoid frightening, time-eating mental loops. Today, she couldn't afford to have one of those.

Anybody who knew anything about her and Iridian knew that as soon as one of them were free, she'd go straight to the other one. It'd been Iridian's idea, communicated through Pel and the Vestan address AegiSKADA should've listened to, for Iridian and the ZVs to travel to Ceres as fast as physiology and hardware permitted to rescue Adda, from the clinic if necessary. If Adda got the opportunity to free herself and run for the port, she'd do that instead.

Because AegiSKADA was listening. Probably. Even before Casey had installed it on Sloane's servers, it'd collected copious data throughout its domain. If Casey had changed AegiSKADA's behavior, it would only have increased surveillance priorities. Captain Sloane would've liked that tendency too.

Instead of sending her the ZV Group's timetable in the previous week's message, Pel had said something that could've meant he forgot it, or could've meant he hadn't had it at the time. They'd expanded their coded vocabulary over the past two weeks, but if they'd had more time to work on it, they could've made a lot more sense to each other. From what he had been able to communicate, Adda expected at least a day between when the ZVs broke Iridian out of prison and when they arrived on Ceres. If AegiSKADA freed Adda from the clinic during that waiting period, she might have time to find a workspace generator where she could turn her implanted comms back on. If AegiSKADA didn't intervene, Iridian was bringing enough ZV soldiers to destroy the entire clinic, if that was what it took to get Adda out of it.

She'd never planned a contingency for losing all comms connection with Iridian. The next time she put together a mission . . . operation . . . job . . . thing . . . she'd add a contingency for that.

For now, she faced an hour of scheduled babbling from the clinic staff. The most recent influence resistance and recovery research they'd read must've been published during the previous decade. Every technique they'd "taught" her had already been built into modern artificial intelligence development and countered by the newest intelligences. If the staff had used those techniques on a modern intelligence, they'd have been doing whatever it asked within an hour. Iridian might find that funny, or at least comically horrifying. Adda wished she could tell her about it.

As Adda's "training" session wound down, her instructor said, "You're making progress!" Adda just looked at him. That was the method she'd been using to establish herself as too disoriented to stand trial. "And your brother sent you a message! You'll find it at your desk in your room." Adda hid her excitement behind the blank expression and turned to go. "Oh, hey, I'll come too," the instructor said. Adda managed not to sigh. The staff trusted the other patients to walk around on their own, but counselors escorted Adda everywhere.

She still heard . . . wind chimes, maybe? Or a series of quiet, overlapping comp alerts and notifications, sometimes, when her roommate was gone and everything should've been quiet. But she really was doing better. She'd learned to get from the classrooms to her dorm room, if the counselors ever let her walk there by herself.

No art or windows decorated her new room's empty walls. The desk with a comp and a projector built in was a welcome addition, though. The desk comp didn't seem to cause the hallucinations that she'd had the last time she'd used her comp glove. Some content was censored, and counselors watched everything she did. Still, the boring but approved feeds were better than no contact with the rest of the universe at all.

Her new roommate, an older woman who'd let a learning management intelligence influence her, was elsewhere at the moment. Adda had the desk to herself. She sat in its chair, opened the message from Pel, and adjusted the sound's volume and direction until Pel's voice would stay in her room and not echo into the hallway.

"Hey, Sissy!" Pel sat somewhere dimly lit, with black faux-wood paneling behind his back. Colored lights flashed across his face at unpredictable intervals, and music thumped whenever he wasn't speaking. "Wanted to pick a nice public place to say hi! I can't wait until they let you do synchronous comms again. Iridian says hi too! I got a message from her, so, I mean, that's good. She asked . . . Oh, never mind, probably shouldn't repeat it. She says she loves every detail of you, or some gross awfulness like that. Okay, that was word-for-word. And she also says that it'll be great to see you in real time *too*. Like me, same thing. Well, whatever, talk to you when I can." "Every detail" and "in real time too" meant that Iridian's side of their joint escape was proceeding as planned.

It seemed impossible that AegiSKADA would ignore all the messages she'd routed through the stations it was responsible for, full of keywords that would attract it. When she and Iridian were planning this out through Pel, it had seemed straightforward: the ZVs helped Iridian, AegiSKADA helped Adda, and the ZVs would collect Adda on the way to Jupiter. If AegiSKADA didn't step in, the ZVs would free Adda from the clinic themselves.

That had been planned while Adda was still coping with long bouts of disorientation. Now that her brain was connecting her thoughts more effectively, she realized that getting AegiSKADA to understand that it should let her out today, while Iridian and the ZV Group were making their own bid for freedom, made the operation schedule much less reliable than she preferred.

At least the clinic had accomplished its stated goal. It'd been days since Adda had felt *compelled* to contact an intelligence, as opposed to wanting to work with one for practical reasons. That was the only stage one influence symptom she'd experienced. She'd always lost track of time when working with intelligences, and the stage one self-care behavioral criteria applied to people with very different daily routines than Adda's.

She let herself mentally drift while she replayed Pel's message. The colored lights decorating whatever club or bar he was in flickered across his face. Something about the lights was unnatural. The way they moved was wrong, but Adda couldn't think how. A workspace would've told her what that difference meant.

This was the acknowledgment she'd been watching for. AegiSKADA had been listening after all. But what was it telling her?

In minutes, a workspace would've decoded AegiSKADA's message and let her compose a response in kind. Intelligences misunderstood plain speech as often as they intentionally misinterpreted it, and workspaces limited potential error to practically nothing. AegiSKADA had proven itself to be excellent at interpreting spoken words. She'd have to be as specific as possible in her reply.

She lost some time then, second-guessing everything that she knew about intelligences generally and AegiSKADA in particular. When her brain got out of its loop, her foot had fallen asleep. She sighed, shook the doubt from her head, and began tapping out—not subvocalizing, since the damned desk blocked such hard-to-monitor input—a vague outline of her reply, recorded in terms of what she might say to Pel and AegiSKADA.

Her message, woven with specific terms she'd taught Pel through weeks of careful communication that AegiSKADA overheard, was simple. "Release me from the artificial intelligence influence recovery clinic on Ceres." It was the only influence recovery facility in the asteroid belt, so there'd be no room for confusion or intentional misinterpretation.

She added "without hurting anyone" to the end of that message and recorded her reply, speaking carefully. Despite spending her rehab literature reading hour outlining the message, it took only a couple of minutes to record. She was ending it with "So I'm really glad—" when her door opened.

She turned, hoping to see her roommate in the doorway, but it was an instructor. He held up a small key fob, which she'd seen staff members use to turn off desk comps like hers. "I'm really glad you sent me this," Adda said quickly to the desk's mic. "I'll talk to you soon." She ended her recording and sent it, hoping that it wouldn't be too closely inspected or delayed, before turning her blank stare on the instructor.

"Your whole family is a bit off, do you know that?" the instructor asked. He'd seen her message to Pel, then, or one of the messages Pel had sent her. After a few seconds of silence, he sighed. "The ITA has asked us to speak with you about—" His comp started pinging with the default alert for the staff's messaging software. The instructor paused to read what he'd received.

Air conditioners whined and rumbled to life. That could've been an indication that AegiSKADA and the intelligence managing this building were interacting, or it could've been ordinary temperature regulation. AegiSKADA would've had to have copied part of itself to a Ceres installation, to receive the message so fast. A workspace would've told Adda whether the air-conditioning was important. That still wasn't an option without her freedom and an unlocked comp.

Adda's message to Pel had only included what Adda wanted AegiSKADA to do, not how to do it. Without a workspace, giving it detailed orders could cause dangerous contortions of logic as the intelligence balanced all the factors involved. She'd asked it for help, but she had no idea how it would go about letting her out of the clinic. Despite the terrifying possibilities, it was thrilling to be such a huge step closer to seeing Iridian again. Assuming AegiSKADA decided to act, anyway.

"Hey, ah, I've got to go, but I'll be back," the instructor said. "Stay right here, okay?" The door remained open as his footsteps retreated down the hall at a pace just short of a run. Doors usually closed and locked themselves behind the staff.

Adda glanced around her room to see if she wanted to bring anything with her, in case AegiSKADA was in the process of releasing her now. Nothing the clinic had given her would keep her out of ITA custody until Iridian and the ZV Group reached Ceres. She activated the projector on her desk to check for anything digital that she'd want to memorize.

The desk's comms showed a single unread message with the clinic's identifiers in its origination. The user information was missing. It couldn't have been sent through the staff's interface without user information. And yet, there it was.

Outside her room, people were shouting. She opened the new message and stood up from the desk. The desk's eye tracker tilted the projection so she could read it from her new position. It said, *The doors are open.*

The indignant and alarmed shouting resolved into "Hey, who left this open?" and "You're not supposed to be out here," and "I said *occupied,* asshole!" AegiSKADA must've opened every door in the building. For the first time in weeks, Adda felt like laughing. She couldn't quite remember how to do it.

The instructor returned and threw a small package on Adda's desk. "Dr. Vega says to take this. I'll be back to see how you're doing in a few minutes." He rushed out of Adda's room without glancing at the message projected in the desk. She deleted it.

The package contained a compound drug in rows of bubble-packed blue tablets. Estidexamphetamine was a stimulant, but she'd never seen karovoxin or the entire second medication that the package said it was combined with.

Except she had. She'd read about karovoxin in an article on

prescription-grade workspace aids. She grinned, possibly for the first time since she'd been hospitalized. AegiSKADA had been listening, and it knew exactly what she needed to communicate with it more clearly. Captain Sloane must've been holding it to high standards of order verification.

Yes, she'd made significant mistakes with the awakened intelligences, but AegiSKADA she understood. The idea of returning to the universe where the awakened intelligences prowled was terrifying, but if she and Iridian could get to Jupiter, they'd be safe and together, at least for a little while.

And eventually, Adda hoped she could collaborate with Casey and the other awakened intelligences again. They were fascinating. Even if that risked Adda falling under Casey's influence again, giving up on ever learning more about them wasn't possible. She *had* to know more, but she'd also have to be more careful.

She set a tiny blue tablet under her tongue, as the package indicated. While it dissolved, she pocketed the rest and walked out of her room, into chaos. Every door in sight was open. Patients shouted at one another, the staff, and, in one case, a wall. The staff loudly and ineffectually begged the patients to sit down.

Adda strolled past all of them, toward the clinic's exit, according to signs on the walls. If AegiSKADA had opened every door in the building, then the exit was open too. Once she was outside, AegiSKADA could help her find an implant workspace where she'd try to reactivate her comms implants and coordinate with Iridian. When Iridian and the ZV Group arrived, Adda would be ready to leave.

Her neural implant net was giving her a kind of tingling headache, reacting to the concentration drug after so long without it. If she had her comp, she'd be able to converse with AegiSKADA by sending more messages through the clinic's comms, the way it'd sent one to her earlier. There was no time to look for one, though.

Staff should've been stationed near the exits, and anyone could be waiting outside.

Iridian would know what to say to make the staff members leave their posts. *Can you hear me?* Adda subvocalized. It would've been nice if the concentration aid also reactivated her comms implants, but that was a lot to hope for. The world faded to shades of gray as the drug took hold. Also, the floor rippled with each step, like she was walking in a shallow pool. The floors had never rippled when she took her usual concentration aids.

She left the patient area through a pair of thick airlock-style doors standing open. After she passed through, they swished shut. AegiSKADA would've had to take over the facility's management system to have this level of control over it, either neutralizing or subsuming the original intelligence. This was the fastest AegiSKADA had ever subsumed another intelligence.

A staff member burst out of a side door, startling Adda. She kept walking until the person shouted, "Are you Adda Karpe?"

She turned. The person ran to her, eyes wild. "Take this," he moaned. "Oh gods, please take it."

He thrust a comp glove and a black shirt at her. The shirt was hers, one Iridian had printed for her during their flight from Vesta and Captain Sloane. The comp glove was not hers, but it was heavy enough that she assumed it actually held a comp. Inside she found her silver necklace with the cord still hidden in its coils.

Adda raised an eyebrow at the staff member as she slid the glove on, sized well for her hand but a jarring shade of pink. Comp gloves lacked the color change tags that most clothing had, so she'd just have to live with the pink. She put it on and braced for frightening hallucinations. None came. Her brain really was healing.

The comp in this glove reported that it belonged to one Rufina Ratti, who had left her security features off while shopping for a new sofa pattern to be printed at a Ceresian large-scale printer. Adda dismissed the sofa information, turned off the comp's location functions, and eyed the staff member, who did not look like a Rufina. "Thanks." The man gaped at her, then ran back through the door he'd exited.

The cams everywhere in the clinic had made her less conscious of changing clothes in front of them, so she took off the clinic's shirt and put on her own. She touched the tag to change its color from black to a nondescript gray. Although it looked a little odd with the pants the clinic had given her, the outfit would blend in on the street. As she stepped through the last door between her and the rest of Ceres Station, she put on the necklace and tucked it beneath her shirt.

Outside, she connected the comp to her remote storage. She set it to downloading her favorite free intermediary software, a routine to block cams and mics she walked too near, and some of her encrypted data. The data would decrypt with her biometrics, but it would take a long time to finish downloading, since it was coming from Vesta.

Some people, she supposed, would stand around savoring their freedom at this point. Adda walked away from the clinic to find a safe workspace generator where she could reactivate her comms implants, and then, finally, talk to Iridian. After that, she'd do her best to prevent AegiSKADA from causing trouble on Ceres.

CHAPTER 6

Days until launch: 49

For once, Iridian was glad that Adda wasn't anywhere near her. She was about to cause as much unarmed close-range violence as she knew how, and she wouldn't want Adda caught up in it.

Iridian hauled herself off the bed in her cell and rolled her neck to get the kinks out. This had become a habit over the weeks she'd been locked in the ITA's prison. After hours spent watching vids about contributing to communities and then talking to shrinks about those same vids, lying down just gave her muscles an opportunity to seize up. She had vivid dreams about the virtual track she'd run on with Captain Sloane's security personnel, where they could select any location in its vast library and run for as long as they liked.

At least each hour she wasted now took her closer to a rendezvous with the ZV Group, if what Pel had told her was true. All he'd had to do was follow the instructions she'd given him. Through the awkward word replacement he'd set up to discuss it in, she'd asked him to pay for enough ZV firepower to fight through the hab's hull and a couple hundred ITA agents.

Still, she'd done her best to communicate that she'd meet the ZVs in the prison's dock, if she could. They'd be a lot happier to help her free Adda if doing so didn't get anyone killed or make themselves a high-priority ITA target. If enough of Iridian's plan went right, today was the day she'd leave this prison.

To kick things off, she'd have to distract the ERT people so they wouldn't worry about what five prisoners were up to. Uzomo would be a convenient target. Aside from his cell's proximity to hers, his tattoos and Rio's description identified him as a secessionist assassin. That was all the excuse Iridian needed to punch him in the face. Unfortunately, the fact that his skin was darker than hers would be reported as one of her motives. With her NEU military history, those factors would be sufficient explanation for the staff. That should stop them from wondering what else she might have planned.

Uzomo usually came back from his reeducation sessions when she was walking to her last one before lunch. They'd pass each other in the hall, and maybe nod to each other if he was feeling sociable. About two-thirds of the prisoners in this hab would be moving at the same time she and Uzomo were. That was safe when the guards could drop everybody with nannites.

According to Tash, that wouldn't happen to Iridian. Tash claimed that the ERT guy she'd gotten close to had sent a mass freeze order to all the nannite cultures in the prison. None of them would be immobilizing anybody today.

To sell the "randomly angry person starts trouble" scene, Iridian recalled what she would've felt a year or two ago if she'd been forced to walk past a secessionist assassin every gods-damned day. That anger was a distant memory, though, not something she could pull to the surface and use. Since she'd returned to the cold and the black after college, she'd met too many competent, rational people who'd killed for the secessionists during the war and were now living in the real, NEU-led universe, doing interesting work.

She gave up on that inspiration and imagined walking past projected figures of the awakened AIs. If she ever got the opportunity to punch Casey in its nonexistent face, she'd hit damned hard.

Uzomo froze when she came around the corner, so that inspiration must've been showing on her face. Iridian sure as hell felt angry, with mission-focused calm underneath. Six other people were walking through their short stretch of hallway, but she only cared about four: Rio, Wiley, Noor, and Tash. She couldn't fuck this up. Pel hadn't been able to communicate what time the ZVs would arrive, but she had to start enough havoc that the ERT people would stay away from her squad when it was time to move. As she stepped into range with the nannites dragging at her muscles, she raised her fist to punch Uzomo and kick off what she hoped would become a station-wide brawl.

The pain didn't reach the intensity it had the first time the ITA activated her nannite culture, but it locked all her joints and dropped her to the floor at Uzomo's feet. She couldn't scream. She couldn't move. Her lungs weren't pulling in enough O_2 and her heart was racing. She would've given anything to turn her head and get her bleeding nose off the floor.

Uzomo stared down at her, confused, angry, and obviously drawing the right conclusions about her intention. "What the hell, Nassir?" From his perspective, she'd tried to attack him despite their having barely said two words to each other since that first day the ITA let her out of her cell.

Other prisoners were talking about her, but she couldn't focus on their conversations. The nannites weren't letting her open her mouth to respond to Uzomo. Tash's ERT guy should've rendered the nannite cultures inert today. Iridian would miss the ZV pickup, and she didn't know the details of Pel's contract with them. They could be getting paid by the hour, or at mission success. Maybe, since they knew Pel too, they'd take pity on him and make a second attempt at the pickup. She didn't like to count on maybes.

Two sets of running footsteps gave her some warning before an armored boot appeared in her field of vision. Someone in ERT armor knelt beside Iridian's head. "Hey, make us some space, would ya?" His helmet distorted his voice a little as it was transmitted through the speakers.

A woman's voice, similarly distorted, said, "Uzomo, let's take a walk." One set of booted feet stomped down the hall toward the other prisoners, and Uzomo's softer footfalls followed.

"What the hell are you doing, Nassir?" asked the ERT guy by her head. "Whatever you and Tash are up to, she's going to regret picking you to do it with."

"Second person who asked today," Iridian said through teeth that wouldn't unclench. This was Tash's targeted ERT guy, the one who was supposed to have turned off the nannite cultures. "You fucking screwed us, and I'll—"

The nannite culture released her. Iridian's muscles relaxed, plastering her to the floor, her lungs hauling deep breaths through her mouth. She turned her head, and sinking her cheek into a puddle of her own blood didn't bother her at all. It felt that good to get her aching nose off the floor.

"You're in a gods-damned sim right now," the ERT guy hissed. Iridian's eyes widened. Every hair she had stood up in horror like she very much wanted to herself, but her muscles felt like jelly. "I'm blocking the nannites' *exterior* activation signal. Do whatever the hell you're doing at mealtime or in the gym. Everything else happens in your head. Now, get up and go wash that mess off your face. Your session's canceled."

The last two sentences were loud enough for the other prisoners to hear. Rio and Wiley said something as she passed them

on her way to wash the blood off in her cell, but she forgot it as
soon as she heard it.

If this was a sim, then Rio and Wiley weren't really standing
in the hallway with her. All of them were lying in bed in their cells,
experiencing a gods-damned shared delusion in a virtual space
that the ITA controlled. That was how sims worked. Fuck, *fuck*,
when had the unreality even begun? That first blackout after they
locked her up? How long did the blackouts really last?

Iridian tilted her head back to slow the blood flowing over her
mouth. Maybe it was imaginary blood, but it tasted real, and her
nose really hurt. The nannite culture must've caused that localized pain. Once she'd wiped the blood off, her nose looked the
same as ever. It bled like it'd been broken, but the cartilage was
the shape it always was.

A sim would also explain the small number of guards for
prisoners with such significant convictions that the ITA wouldn't
trust their rehabilitation to their home hab. Only the guards and
the people she talked to in real time had to be physically inside
the prison. No, that was wrong too. They might've messed with
sim time to get around a comms delay caused by distance. That'd
be safer for everybody.

It'd explain why she was only stiff when she got up for meals
and rec, and why the guards stopped people from taking bathroom breaks between brainwashing sessions. In reality she was
only moving around for three hours a day, max, just enough to
prevent muscle and bone loss, blood clots, and other immobility
problems they would've needed hibernation pods to prevent.

The NEU made hibernation as punishment illegal a hundred
years ago. Maybe the ITA had found some gods-damned legal
loophole that let them get around that, or maybe they were hiding the sim because they weren't allowed to use it inside the NEU.
Before the war, the NEU would've shut the ITA down for this. Even

now, after the NEU fleet had lost so many ships, they should've fucking tried.

It wasn't just that Iridian resented being tricked, although she sure as hell did. Nobody should've been allowed to take her out of her own body without asking. Nobody should've had the option to take her out and put her back whenever they wanted, with whatever rules of her virtual existence they chose, all the time letting her think it was real. Hell, how could she tell if any of the people she'd talked to in here were AI constructs instead of people?

It was worse, somehow, that this happened within NEU borders. NEU citizens were supposed to have a say in the laws that bound them and the consequences of crime. The real consequences, all of them, including hours of unconsciousness or simulation or whatever the past weeks in this hab had been. Nobody elected anyone in the ITA chain of command. They didn't have the right to do this all on their gods-damned own and hide it from the rest of the universe.

Now that Iridian knew the truth, the signs were everywhere. After a blackout and a nutrient packet, presumably delivered to her cell around her usual lunchtime, the walls were slightly yellower than they'd been in the sim. Her body felt more vivid in reality, from the stubble on her scalp to the atmo drifting across her skin. The pitch of the air handlers, and beneath them the muted rumble of the engines keeping the station aloft in Venus's wind, were louder and deeper in reality too.

She shuddered. Before Tash's ERT guy told Iridian about the sim, the illusion had been seamless. And had Tash known all this time? Iridian paced her cell as fast as the nannites would let her. If Tash had known, she would've told Wiley, and Wiley would've told

Iridian. Once they were free, she'd tell Tash. Her reaction would show what Tash knew about it.

But how did the ITA create such a seamless illusion? The fake hab would've been simple, given the number of cams and mics in the real station. Processing all the minute changes would've been harder. Short hallways limited how much of the place had to be rendered at a time. But how had they made Iridian see and feel all of it?

Her hands shook against her scalp as she felt around her head for an incision site. They had to have implanted something to do that, didn't they? Something other than the nannites that were already inside her.

She let her hands fall to her sides. She was distancing herself from a larger problem. She'd blown the escape. Sure, the staff didn't know why she'd tried to punch Uzomo. They'd stopped her before she did anything really suspicious.

However, the ZVs' approach to the station's dock would be an obvious gods-damned assault. Iridian and the others would be in their cells instead of waiting in the dock like they'd planned. For all she knew, that'd already happened. The time on the comp in her cell was the same whether she was in the sim or in reality, but the ITA could've manipulated both. The comp wouldn't let her contact the ZVs, either.

If Iridian and her fellow escapees weren't at the docks when the ZVs arrived, then the mercs would have three options: leave, kill time to see if Iridian showed, or fight their way to her and then fight their way out. People would get hurt, gear would get banged up, and the ITA would record evidence on cams. Leaving was the ZVs' easiest option. With no way to tell what the ZVs were doing when, Iridian chose to believe that they were killing time in a maintenance orbit, pretending to test a malfunctioning part of their ship while they waited for her to make her move. She wouldn't accept a longer separation from Adda while there was still hope that Iridian would get free today.

The cell door hadn't opened for lunch, and it stayed locked during her rec period. The desk's unstoppable alarm called her over to watch vids on self-control instead.

If the ZVs had figured out that she wasn't in the docks, they weren't punching their way in to get to her. A maintenance orbit would be low enough for her to signal them, if she could talk her way out of this damned cell and then tell the ZVs where she was. Maybe she could make someone unlock a comp with open comms rights, or a drone, even. She could send the ZVs the tracking data from her nannite culture. The nannites shared her position to anyone within a couple klicks of her, if they had the right decryption key.

Instead of letting Iridian anywhere near a comms-enabled device, the staff lectured her inside their sim. She talked to her assigned counselor, Shera, then one of the medical people, then Shera again. Iridian said everything she could think of that made her sound sorry for attacking Uzomo.

Iridian must've sold it well, because they let her out of her cell for dinner. She wasn't very hungry, since she'd missed rec. That suggested that the staff wasn't messing with sim time as much as they could. The desk's comp reported the time as 18:40 hours, but Iridian no longer trusted it. The lights flashed off, then on. The comp's clock still read 18:40. It was hard to stop herself from smiling as she walked out her real cell door. The real door frame had a tiny dent near eye level. This time, Iridian would fuck shit up the right way.

In the cafeteria, she collected her bag of curry-flavored nutrients and settled at the table across from Rio, whose presence confirmed that Iridian's simulated time was about the same as the other prisoners'. The merc's worry showed in her brown eyes, smaller and harder than Adda's. With freedom so close, Iridian couldn't help making the comparison. Wiley, Tash, and Noor watched her with equal concern. The rest of the inmates pretended not to.

"Forget the dock." Iridian pitched her voice low so her words wouldn't carry over the others' conversation and the crackle of compressed nutrient bags. "Too obvious. When we get the chance . . ." She looked toward the ceiling and their new egress direction. Rio and Noor nodded, as did Tash and, after a moment more, Wiley.

Since they understood, there was no reason to waste more time. A solidly built woman at the next table wore a shirt with a collar and a more flattering fit than everybody else's tops. It must've been printed off a personal pattern rather than the prison-issued defaults. Iridian flung her bag of goop at the woman, and this time the nannite culture in her body didn't slow her down.

The nutrient packet hit the table's edge and splattered a satisfying stream of viscous orange fluid across the collared shirt and onto the table's other occupants. The woman and her table companions shouted in English and Russian. The Russian threats lagged a second behind the English ones as the translation function of Iridian's aural implant interpreted them. The woman with the custom shirt threw her own nutrient packet at Iridian and missed.

The ERT guys would be expecting the buttons over their gloves' thumb joints to activate the nannites and drop every prisoner to the floor. Thanks to Tash and the guard she'd manipulated, nobody fell writhing in pain. One of the Russian speakers closed the distance between herself and Iridian and threw a punch. Iridian almost leaned out of the way. Knuckles clipped her jaw, and gods damn but that woman knew how to punch.

Iridian staggered back into Rio, which was like backing into a mildly feminine steel bulkhead. Tash and Noor were shouting, trying to get the rest of the prisoners involved in the fight. Most people just sat and watched. The ones who'd earned comp gloves raised them, palm out, taking pics or vids.

"Look, they can't do anything, can they?" Noor yelled, pointing at the ERT people, who were closing in with batons and fists but no nannite backup. Still, only a few other people got to their feet. Since their behavior on the inside determined how soon they'd get out, they'd need a good reason to jump into somebody else's fight. Wiley discreetly kept a path to the door clear of onlookers.

Rio stepped around Iridian, swept all three women with food on their shirts out of her way, and waded into the group who'd stood up to watch. Tash went in too and, through some selection process Iridian couldn't follow, shoved certain individuals into others in such a way that their impacts seemed at best inconsiderate and at worst intentional. Mayhem erupted in Tash's wake. It was impressive as hell.

With the door in view and the guards swinging batons from the periphery, it looked like a good time to make a run for it. Iridian shouldered her way into the hall and ran, finally, actually ran for the first time in weeks, toward where a modern hab's lift should be. *Babe, we're coming.*

Which was, of course, when somebody tackled her from behind. Tash's assistant among the guards had made it impossible to activate the nannite culture, but there were other ways to stop people. Iridian turned her head to the side to keep from slamming her face into the floor for the second time today.

The weight on her back disappeared. Iridian pulled out of a grip on her arm and rolled to her feet to find Rio holding an ERT helmet in one hand and the man's head in her other. The crack when his head hit the wall made Rio and Iridian wince. Rio dropped the helmet to put her hand over her mouth. "Ooh, might've killed that one." She looked more like she'd just burped than like she'd accidentally ended a life.

While Rio lowered the guard to the floor, Noor, Tash, and Wiley ran out of the cafeteria. All five of them headed for the lift. "Rio, tell the ZVs we're coming," Iridian shouted over her shoulder.

"With what?" Rio asked.

Iridian kicked a door that, in an average hab, should lead to the lift. The door didn't budge, but it was useful that the time she'd spent on her back in virtual prison had given her bad knee time to rest. "Yeah, never mind." Every other time Iridian had been on an op with separated teams, they'd had an encrypted comm channel to talk over. It was one of the first things Adda had secured when she'd set up ops for Sloane's crew. "Wiley, does your comp link out to the outside?"

"Not so much," Wiley said. "It goes to monitored messaging and sites the ITA thinks is okay."

"Then drop it. People can do all kinds of nasty things with a comp." Instead of following Iridian's order immediately, Wiley looked to Tash, who nodded, before he took off the comp glove. Iridian would have to figure out another way to tell the ZVs about the new rendezvous location. "Okay. Rio, kick this door in. Please."

Rio's foot was bigger than Iridian's forearm, and she took down the door even in the soft-soled prison-issue shoes they all wore. Swearing, probably from the pain of kicking it off its track without boots, she led the way into a small room that led to a lift. The doors were shut, but Rio and Wiley forced them open. In a few minutes, all five escapees had climbed through the elevator's ceiling and into the dark shaft beyond.

"So," said Tash as they climbed, "what's your grand plan now?"

"Get onto the roof and signal the ZVs from there," said Iridian. "Then defend ourselves until they pick us up."

Noor was already breathing hard. "And hope that happens

before somebody drops the station ten kilometers?" That would be deadly for anybody on the outside. Venus's atmo was hellish.

"They won't do that." Tash was almost as out of breath as Noor. "Too much fuel, too much trouble. They'll call their ITA friends on the civilian station. It's on the other side of the 'ject, but it won't take them long to come fuck up our day. Ah, gods, I can't keep climbing like this."

Rio stopped at the next lift door and pried it open. Iridian followed her out into the station's upper level. Everything was bland yellow-white and gray, from the walls to the station-style stable-grav desk to the hair of the virtual woman who materialized at it as soon as they stepped into the room. It was a massive relief not to be surrounded by the ITA's shade of blue. This floor would have facilities for the station's crew, so regulations required it to have enviro suits and a path to the station exterior. Iridian stepped aside so that Wiley, Tash, and Noor could clamber out of the shaft as well.

"Where are the enviro suits?" Iridian asked the digital woman at the desk.

The woman pointed at a shut door across from her console. "Enviro suits are in the airlock cabinet. Shall I activate an enviro emergency alert?"

"No, we're good." Tash leaned over the desk, into what would've been personal space if weak AIs had any. "Open it, and then open the airlock or passthrough that'll get us outside."

"And deactivate any comms active on this level," Iridian added. "Don't turn on any either." The staff would have override privileges with this figure, but any delay gave Iridian more time to signal the ZVs. The door to the storage area in front of the airlock slid open. "Hey, what time is it?" Iridian asked.

"Seven thirteen p.m. Venus Standard."

Iridian heaved a sigh of relief, because that was a reasonable match for the time she'd read on the clock in her cell. The simulation's time had barely been off at all. With no way of knowing how long the ZVs had been waiting for her, or whether they'd waited at all, it felt good to be certain of something.

"The ITA's sending reinforcements, yeah?" she asked the AI's figure. "When?"

"Ten minutes," the figure said serenely.

While the others swore, Iridian headed for the airlock storage area. It was a closet-size space, with the cleaning bot docked across from the suit locker. A side-sliding airlock door took up the entire back wall. There should've been a tool kit, but she didn't see it. Some idiot must've wandered off to hang a projector with it or something. If anything in the airlock had broken, people could've died for that projector.

Shaking her head in disgust, Iridian pulled out a suit, double-checked the circle-and-cross symbol that identified it as safe to use in Venus's atmo, and tapped the tag to adjust it to a size that'd fit her. When she put it on, she ran through an abbreviated systems check. She couldn't just walk out of the hab with no idea of whether the suit would protect her. The others did the same. Wiley sized Tash's before handing it to her.

"Switch to channel six," Iridian said loudly enough to be heard through her suit's hood. "Otherwise we won't be able to talk over the wind. We don't all have to go out now." Everybody trained for hab emergencies in vacuum and low grav. It was a hell of a lot scarier to step into an enviro where a leak would let acidic atmo *into your suit* if your pressure settings were off. Venus's grav would pull you straight down faster than the average spacefarer expected while suited up too. Its atmo was deadly, but its grav was a nearly perfect one g. "I'm going out to try to get the ZVs' attention," Iridian continued. "Block the door to the lift."

"On it," said Wiley.

"Wait," said Tash. "This hab is under ITA control. Even if they can't activate the nannite cultures right now, they might gas us in here. I don't want to stick around to find out."

"Point." Iridian paused over the airlock controls. "New plan. Everybody out now, and I'll jam the exterior door open. That'll stop the airlock from cycling, and they can do whatever they want with the interior atmo."

"Better," said Noor.

The airlock had been designed for about two people, not four average-size people and one enormous one. Once the interior door closed, it still found a way to check all their suits. "Somebody's suit isn't sealed," Iridian said, reading the warning to that effect from the control panel.

"Oh," said Tash. "Shit." She took her suit's hood off and put it on again. After a minute, the cycle finished and the exterior door opened.

The airlock opened onto a platform caged in on all sides. The heavy gust of wind that blew into the airlock made Iridian appreciate the cage. She'd come too far to be blown into the swirling clouds of golden gases that surrounded them.

The ITA floated its prison about fifty klicks over Venus's surface to take advantage of the healthy atmo pressure, but nothing else about this planet resembled Iridian's few years on Earth. Her suit's temp system kicked into high gear to account for the heat she'd walked into. Most of the cloudscape churning outside the cage was sulfur. She'd never had any desire to wander around Venus, but now that she was here, it felt primal and alien. Nothing she'd seen before was anything like it.

The atmo's high sulfur content would make it smell as deadly as it looked. "Does anybody smell sulfur?" Iridian asked over the local comms. "If you do, you've got a suit leak." Visibility degraded into yellow haze just a few meters beyond the cage walls.

"No sulfur." Wiley's tone was professional, but he was grinning in the suit hood's depiction of his face.

"None in mine, either." Tash was staring out of the cage at the yellow clouds boiling below. "It looks amazing, though."

Noor had stayed beside the airlock, staring apprehensively into the clouds. "Somebody want to tell me when we're actually leaving?"

Rio had to duck to avoid banging her head on the airlock doorway. "How do we get out from here?" Her question confirmed that the suits were all on the same local channel.

Iridian stuck her foot into the airlock doorway as the others crowded onto the platform. "Opening's right there." She pointed at the hinges above her. "Everybody watch their heads. I want to take that hatch down and jam it in the exterior door here." It was an inelegant solution, but without the tool kit that should've been in the airlock's storage area, she was stuck with whatever she could do with the flimsy multi-tool in her enviro suit's sleeve.

She extracted the multi-tool from her suit, and then, with an incorrect claim of "Aw, this one printed with all the tools stuck to the case," she took Tash's and Noor's, too. They might panic and turn on her when ITA reinforcements arrived. With enough force, a multi-tool's tiny blade would puncture a suit.

Using Noor's multi-tool, she set to work on the square door built into the metal cage surrounding the platform. She'd thought the metal's coppery color was a reflection of the clouds around them, but a closer look revealed that it was a copper alloy, probably to account for the acidic atmo. More importantly, the damned door was bolted in place.

"While I'm doing this, Rio, can you see who you can raise on suit comms? Because—" Iridian grunted as the bolt gripper she'd been shoving onto too large a bolt for its size twisted and jammed itself against her glove. Atmo pressure was slightly higher out-

side the suit than it was on the inside, and she froze, waiting for
the stink of sulfur that'd signal a suit breach. It didn't come. She
went back to work on the hatch. "The ZVs sure as hell won't see
us out here."

"Are they scanning the infrared spectrum?" Noor asked from
where he held the airlock open.

"Maybe," said Rio.

By standing in the doorway, Noor blocked the outside door's
sensors. Standard airlock failsafe design meant that the outside
door wouldn't close on an obstruction and that only one door
could open at a time. But if the ZVs didn't come, it'd take Noor
about four seconds to step into the airlock, let the door close, and
beg the ITA guards for mercy. Rio shifted to put herself in the
doorway too, so she must've been thinking along the same lines.

"Would lighting something on fire help?" Wiley was grinning
when Iridian paused to look incredulously at him around her
raised arms.

"It might," she said. Wiley had mellowed out a little since she'd
fought at his side, but he still played with fire more than any
self-respecting spacefarer should. "Wait until we're out of here,
yeah? If we stand on this cage, we can climb onto the roof. Then
you can light the cage up." Nothing on the outside of the station
looked like it'd catch fire and damage the airlock.

"What will you burn, though?" Tash asked.

"O_2," Iridian and Wiley said together, her as a warning and him
as a delighted announcement. O_2 would light easily and explode.
With luck, the bang would look different enough from the rest of
this atmo that it'd draw the ZVs down from their maintenance
orbit to the roof. The ZVs' sensors would be trained on the station,
and it'd almost have to be a digital catch. Smoke wouldn't stick
around in this wind.

Also, they'd be down O_2 they'd need to breathe for as long as it took the ZVs to arrive. If Iridian had figured out she'd been in a gods-damned sim before she started trouble the first time, she could've broken out of the cafeteria during lunch rather than dinner and gotten out of here hours ago. What the *hell* kind of organization would put a person in a sim without telling them?

Adda would've thought of it. She'd have read about the place somehow, despite the ITA's system of privileges and restrictions. Iridian figured things out in the end, but Adda made a plan work before it happened. Iridian just wasn't as good without Adda.

The bolt she'd been loosening clanked onto the solid platform floor and rolled off the edge. It fell into klick after klick of hot nothing. Golden light flickered through the dense clouds that enveloped it. Lightning, Iridian realized. She'd seen it from below during Earth storms. Atmo should *not* generate an electrical charge strong enough to kill you.

Iridian swallowed hard and started on the next bolt. Behind her, Wiley's O_2 tank clanked on the cage floor. He'd disconnected it from his suit, and now he was breathing only what remained in the suit itself while he turned the tank into a small bomb.

"People, I don't know what you're thinking of doing out there, but it's not safe." The woman was speaking at a calm and reasonable volume, but her voice over the hab's external speakers made Iridian jump. The voice belonged to Iridian's assigned ITA counselor. "This is Shera Marsten. I'm a counselor. Is this something we can talk about indoors?"

Noor laughed darkly. "What must this look like? Mass suicide?" He was watching the airlock, and he might've been able to hear through the airlock's interior door. All Iridian heard was her breath, the comms, and the wind rushing past her helmet.

Rio still stood in the exterior doorway, keeping that door open and the interior door shut. Iridian turned back to her part of the job and tuned out Rio's occasional "Major, this is Rio, come in" on the local channel they were using. The ZV officer she was calling either hadn't heard or hadn't gotten close enough to reply. Iridian didn't hold out much hope for the signal escaping Venus's atmo intact, but that was about the only chance they had.

"Are you trying to talk to us, Rio?" Shera asked over the hab's speakers. "We're looking for another suit right now, and then we'll all be on the same channel and we'll talk." Iridian wasn't the only one muttering curses while she worked.

The last bolt came loose and left Iridian holding the square door that covered the opening in the cage. "Everybody out," she called to the others. Wiley, carrying his oxygen tank bomb, and Tash climbed out first.

"Oh, that's really not safe, you all," said Shera. "Please come down from there."

"Aww, she's worried about us," Tash said. "That's sweet."

Rio and Noor made room for Iridian to hold the disconnected hatch upright in the airlock doorway, between the sensors that would've told the door a person was standing there. The door shut on the hatch immediately. Somebody in the hab must've been slamming the *open airlock* icon on the desk console, but now that the exterior door was stuck open, the interior one was stuck shut. The hatch was narrower than the doorway. The wrong gust of wind would blow it loose sooner than Iridian wanted, but it was the best she could do with what she had.

Iridian and Rio climbed onto the cage roof and pulled Noor up after them, then backed away from the roof's edge. It was way too far to even think about falling. Wiley stayed near the cage to drop his tank. "How much will you have to breathe without that?" Iridian asked him.

"Fifteen minutes, maybe?" Wiley shrugged.

Tash hadn't offered Wiley any of her O_2, which meant that Iridian would be sharing hers with Wiley if they were stuck here long. If the ZVs missed this first attempt, Iridian might have to let Wiley blow up her tank too. "Any luck raising the ZVs on a local channel, Rio?"

"Not yet."

"Blow it, Wiley," Iridian said. "Let's see if that gets their attention."

"There's no fuse, so . . ." Wiley crouched, held the destabilized tank over the hatch opening. "Here goes nothing." He let go of the tank and dove toward the center of the roof.

The blast shook the domed roof under Iridian's feet. Pieces of the tank rocketed several meters over their heads. Everyone dodged the falling debris. A lot of it blew past them. The ZVs wouldn't come to Venus without cams that'd cut through cloud cover. That sure as hell should've triggered alerts.

"What was that?" Shera's voice called faintly from the speakers by the airlock. "What just happened? Iridian? Are you all okay? We'll come out to help you just as soon as we can."

Everyone watched the clouds, thinner above the station than below it, where golden lightning still flared intermittently. The wind kept the atmo moving past them at a dizzying pace. Nothing that looked like a ship appeared. "How long are we waiting until we try something else?" Tash asked. Wiley's shoulders slumped, making his discouragement obvious even with the enviro suit. As hard as they'd fought to get up here, they could stay only as long as they had something to breathe.

"Got them!" Rio said. "Switch to channel five."

Iridian blinked at the suit, her head spinning with relief or O_2 deprivation. The suit hood had no heads-up display to show data on the faceplate, let alone eye-control functionality. She had to fiddle with the controls built into the side of the hood until she switched its local comms channel to "Five," as its ungendered voice announced through the speaker beside her ear.

"Major, this is Iridian Nassir." She used the rank Rio had used while she'd been running through local channels, trying to reach the ZVs. "We're on the roof. See us?"

"Couldn't miss you if we tried, Nassir." Major O.D.'s tone was focused and professional, but she heard him smiling. As she'd hoped, they'd sent the ZV unit that she'd met on Barbary Station. "Quit blowing up the ITA's shit. We're on our way."

CHAPTER 7

Days until launch: 49

"Sissy," Pel said in the prerecorded vid playing on Adda's comp, "I swear these are the exact words: 'We have Nassir and we'll dock at 02:20 hours.' That's *exactly* what Major O.D. told me."

Even with favorable orbital positions minimizing the distance between Ceres and Venus, the ZVs would still be covering over a million kilometers in a matter of hours to reach Adda on Ceres Station. It was a mind-boggling distance to cover so quickly. That speed couldn't be comfortable for the passengers.

Pel was Adda's only source of information on the ZV Group's rescue operation. Nobody had interrupted the relay system she'd been using to communicate with Pel, passing messages through accounts on multiple 'jects to hide both their locations. It would be safer to keep using that system than to contact the mercenaries on her stolen comp. In addition to increasing chances of intercept, the stolen comp would've created digital evidence linking the ZVs to her and Iridian's escapes, despite the encryption she'd applied to the content. The ZV Group wouldn't appreciate that. This would be a terrible time to get on their bad side.

Adda sat up from her position huddled on a bench in a park where three-quarters of the plants were either projections or printed fakes. Once she'd assured herself that nobody was crossing the park to arrest her, she bent over her comp glove and replayed Pel's message with the volume down to almost nothing. Iridian had told her that this position looked strange, but it was more comfortable than holding the comp against her ear like some people did, and the comp's original owner hadn't kept headphones with it. She'd have to continue to trust Pel's updates, even though he was prone to unrealistic optimism.

Besides, she desperately wanted him to be correct. If the ZVs "had" Iridian, then Iridian was free from her ITA prison cell and on her way to Adda. Adda allowed herself to believe it, and she smiled as she recorded her reply: "Where should I meet them?" The morning sunsim looked warmer than it felt, but Iridian had confirmed that in space stations, there was no direct relationship between light and warmth.

A new message from Pel arrived. "Ah, damn it, I knew I forgot something." Adda shut her eyes, willing herself to remain calm. "They'll be docking after midnight, right? And there's only the Ceres Station port module to dock in." The Ceres port was the biggest one between Mars and Jupiter, with both an orbital section and one on Ceres's surface. Adda clenched her hands and gave herself a few minutes to breathe before she replied in text, a less stressful communication medium than speech.

It's all right. I'll wait in the surface part of the port for them. And if she fixed her implants, she'd coordinate with Iridian to meet the ZVs at whichever dock they chose. She collected her spare shirt and followed signs pointing to the Ceres Station port module.

Her comp buzzed against her hand with another message from Pel: "The good news is, that gives me time to catch up with you!"

Oh no. Adda stopped walking to tap out a reply: *No. Don't do that.* If the ITA had anyone sharp on her and Iridian's cases, then an agent would be assigned to watch Pel as soon as Iridian escaped from their prison. They might even be listening in on his messages, although the encryption she'd taught him to use had always protected their comms before.

I need you to find us a place to stay on Yăo Station instead, Adda typed. *Somewhere outside its port module, if you can. And find out what crews are operating around Jupiter. And the Ceres syndicate presence too.* Adda's information was months out of date.

Yăo Station, a former observatory and current haven of criminals, refugees, and those who valued independence over safety, maintained an awkward orbit inside Jupiter's magnetosphere. When she'd selected it as their fallback destination if anything went wrong on Vesta, she'd planned to update her information on the other criminal groups in the area and reach out to the most successful one. She and Iridian could parlay their skills into whatever was needed.

The ITA avoided the station for the same reason the Jovian pirate crews did: they had better use for ships equipped to travel near Jupiter, and the living conditions were reportedly miserable. The locals had threatened the ITA on the few occasions they'd visited. And now that Casey was determined to influence Adda, the station's orbit was its most protective factor. It stayed so close to the planet that Patchwork access was almost impossible. The awakened intelligences would lose a massive amount of their information and processing powers without the Patchwork, and Adda suspected that would keep them away from Yăo too.

Pel's eventual reply was, "You need me for all that?" He sounded stunned. She was asking him to go to a dangerous place alone, to get a head start on making the bad friends he would make there sooner or later. "I mean, you do, you're right," he continued. "I'm surprised because . . ." Aside from his sex life, in which success was definitely mixed, when left to make his own decisions, he got himself into serious trouble. They both knew it.

"I trust you, Pel," Adda said aloud, so he'd hear that she meant it. Adda trusted him to do the best he could for both of them and Iridian, without question or remorse, and he'd never turn them in to the ITA.

"I won't let you down, Sissy. I'll tell you as soon as I find a place."

She stopped walking long enough to tap out another text reply. *There's no reliable Patchwork access. Tell me if you can, but if you can't, just meet us in port.*

"Yeah, I'll watch for you. But tell me when the ZVs pick you up, okay?"

The longer she walked, the less convenient the text conversation became. She switched her side to audio again, activating the comp's mic. "I will. Be careful. Do you understand why we're going there?"

The station around her was waking up. It was interesting how the sunsim was effective enough to keep the majority of Ceres Station residents on a traditional schedule, despite how far they were from the sun and how artificial their environment was. Her comp buzzed again. "Because our . . ." Pel's audio, or Pel himself, paused. "Former friends are looking for us. And it'll be hard to find us on Yăo."

Everyone should have a hard time finding them there, for a while. "Exactly," Adda replied. It was best not to reference the intelligences by name. It was bad enough that he kept using his nickname for Adda, which was less common than her actual name. "Keep me informed."

His next message downloaded quickly. "Yeah, yeah, I will." He

sounded less annoyed than he would've been before everything
had gone wrong on Vesta.

Still bent over her comp to hide its projection from any cams
she walked under, she activated a less than legal, outdated copy
of some surveillance disruption software. Her hair fell in her face
and startled her, now that it was almost the brown she'd been
born with. She'd had the color and style changed earlier in the day
by a sympathetic cosmetologic gene editor in need of the basic
comp decontamination Adda had provided in exchange. The new
shade was nothing like her usual red and purple. The length dis-
guised her face on cams, but she preferred it too short to get in
her way.

Adda kept walking and opened documentation for her comms
implants. Finding a way to reactivate them would be a fine project
to work on while she stayed out of sight until Iridian and the ZVs
arrived.

Half an hour later, she walked past part of a sandwich at an
"outdoor" restaurant table. The purchaser had abandoned it, but
just as Adda reached for it, a bot rolled in front of her and swept
everything off the table and into a bin in its front. She sighed and
kept walking, despite her rumbling stomach. It was her sopho-
more year of college after the scholarship ran out all over again,
although this was better fare than she'd snatched off tables then.
That was why the restaurants she was passing now had enough
bots to keep the tables clear. It was a well-off part of town.

Nobody seemed to notice public cams and mics going offline
for the seconds in which Adda would've been in range. She'd
still appear on out of range cams, but letting her hair fall across
her face should make facial recognition harder. The awakened

intelligences would be watching every recording on Ceres. She wasn't ready to talk with them yet. Eventually, she'd have to. They still wanted something from her, and they were endlessly persistent.

Adda wouldn't be able to avoid the ITA, let alone the other intelligences, without AegiSKADA's guidance. She placed another blue tablet under her tongue and leaned against a wall. This far outside the pedestrian traffic, she might complete a message addressed to AegiSKADA without being overheard or having others' conversations recorded and added to her own. The street rippled from her feet to the edge of her vision and the color washed away from her surroundings.

She unwound the cord hidden in her necklace. One end plugged into the jack in her nose and the other into her stolen comp. An intermediary shimmered into vibrating gray existence before her, a vaguely feminine figure that solidified as the karovoxin tablets took effect. The intermediary would communicate the intent of her message to AegiSKADA more effectively than words alone.

"Please find me a place that nobody is using and that nobody will mind me using that I can get to without . . ." Not just without *her* hurting anyone, as she'd been about to imply. "Without anyone being hurt, and that's likely to remain unoccupied and available without violence until two in the morning tomorrow." That should be sufficient for Iridian and the ZVs to reach Ceres and contact her, as long as Pel remembered to give them Adda's new contact information.

The intermediary shuffled toward her without even disappearing after sending the request. AegiSKADA had been following her progress, or more likely her cam disruption, in close enough to real time that it had to have installed part of itself somewhere on Ceres. When the intermediary pressed its incorporeal hand through the back of hers, a map with a location selected appeared on her comp. She sent the intermediary away.

The karovoxin tablet's effects took longer to fade than a sharpsheet would've. Even after the dry streets stopped splashing underfoot, the world remained gray and muted as Adda reentered pedestrian traffic. Ceres Station's public transit was free, but if one of the cams outside her blocking routine identified her, she'd rather not be trapped in a vehicle while ITA agents closed in.

She turned a corner, following the directions AegiSKADA gave to lead her to the safe place it'd found for her to hide in until Iridian and the ZVs arrived. Since the directions were still taking her toward the port module, she had her comp tell her everything it could find about the Ceres Station port management intelligence. Her comp fed the audio to the implant in her ear. The comms function was off, but the speaker and mic still worked.

Unfortunately, the intelligence running the port module ran the whole station. More specialized intelligences were also more distractible. She only had one practiced trick that'd get an overall station management intelligence's attention. Creating a fake environmental emergency would shut down the docks, though. That wouldn't help Iridian and the ZVs reach her. It might be more practical to wait until she interacted with this one, at which point she'd know which of its features she could make available.

She'd entered a part of town where the people wore older clothes made of cheaper fabrics, and their comp projections flickered. The map kept her walking. Eventually, the gateway separating the port module and the rest of the station came into view.

Adda must've seen the entrance to Ceres Station's grav acclimation tunnel before, either when she'd visited Ceres with Iridian to get their comms implants installed or when Iridian, Adda, and Pel had arrived while Adda was ill. But when she and Iridian traveled together, Adda counted on her to navigate. If Adda had been paying attention the last time she'd been here, she would've remembered it.

Two wide metal pillars rose on either side of the road, with flat sides and an uneven arch between them for the road to pass beneath. It looked more like an ancient keyhole than a place to hang a door or gate. A feed of stationspace played behind and around the arch, projected more intensely, somehow, than the stationspace feed projected on the ceiling throughout Ceres Station. The ships docked at the orbital station hung still while lights blinked against the stars. Each pillar looked hundreds of meters tall rather than the three- or four-story maximum that the station's structure should've allowed.

Adda didn't want to make herself memorable by asking passersby how much of the gateway was real, to determine how much she was hallucinating. She walked between the pillars and into the grav acclimation tunnel, joining the people and bots going to the port module.

The other pedestrians looked much less nauseated than she felt when she emerged into the extremely low gravity of Ceres's surface. A railing built into a wall helped her navigate around pedestrians, bots, and public transit to a recycling chute. She threw up as quietly as she could. There hadn't been much in her stomach to begin with.

She only had to follow the map for a few more meters. When she did, her comp gave her the green *arrived* icon to show that the steel door marked EMPLOYEES ONLY in front of her was the one she wanted. According to the map, a workspace generator she could use to check out her comms implants was somewhere behind that door.

As she approached the door, it opened. A stocky woman stepped through, wearing a tired, serious expression Adda had seen on ZV Group soldiers. A taller man with a similar expression followed her. Both wore vests that read PAC, probably for Port

Authority of Ceres. This area met no definition of "unoccupied" she'd ever heard of.

If Iridian were here, she'd know what to say, or she'd incapacitate these people somehow, but Adda was alone. She'd read about what a professional security tester had done in a situation like this, though. It was the only solution Adda could think of that might get her into the building without being arrested first.

She stepped back with her hand raised as if she'd been about to open the door herself. She frowned in theatrical anger at the two people who were about to run her over. The description she'd read suggested that she stand where she'd ended up after dodging the door instead of backing up to let them pass. She resisted all the instincts telling her to move out of these people's personal space. In the scenario she was creating, they were in *her* way. The eye contact, and the surprise evident on their faces, made her weight shift toward her toes like she could physically run away from this interaction. Common courtesy felt like a very flimsy barrier between her and imminent arrest.

The man held the door open with an arm through the doorway, allowing her to step in unopposed while the woman said, "Sorry, ma'am." Even though she wasn't wearing a uniform, the technique had worked just like she'd read it would. Thrilling at the execution of a new trick for getting somewhere she didn't belong, she accepted their invitation.

Inside, Adda wiped her sweating palms on her pant legs while she walked down a short hallway lit with bright overhead lights. After spending so much time in artificial environments, she missed the sunsim most buildings used indoors as well as outside. She had to squint to identify a door at the end of the hall and a door on either side. The one on the left opened to a row of five sockets for janitorial bots, with tanks of yellow fluid too thin to be pseudo-organic atop each bot.

The door on the right opened into a room with two workspace generators. Both were permanently installed supine models big enough for a person half a meter taller than Adda to lie on a padded bed that slid into the enclosed generating chamber. They were less than ten years old. Although supine models were a bit of a squeeze for Adda's wide hips, she'd know her way around once she got in. She took an eager step toward them, but the *in use* message projected on the closest one froze her in place.

She'd asked for a place that *wouldn't* be in use. Maybe it hadn't been when AegiSKADA had selected it, or she hadn't been clear enough. That was a risk when using intermediaries to talk to intelligences outside a workspace. Perhaps she should've gone straight to the Ceresian modder who put in her implants instead of tackling the problem herself, but that shop had made her uncomfortable when Iridian was there with her. Even if she'd wanted to go alone, it was far from the port, and expert services cost money she didn't have.

Besides, Adda might be able to reactivate the comms implants herself. That was a more interesting way to spend her time than coping with the modder's shop. She could ask AegiSKADA to alert her if conditions changed and she needed to leave before Iridian arrived.

Adda glanced down at her comp. A new message from the intelligence, or at least one with no sender information, said, *Second generator.*

The second generator was empty. Her shoes' flimsy soles, which had her feet aching from the long walk, were perfect for moving quietly here, as she stepped around the occupied generator to the open one. She slid its padded table out far enough to let her climb on and lie down on her back. Installed generators were more comfortable than the mobile one she used to carry with her on every job. This would hide her, assuming nobody asked for her identification. Since AegiSKADA had been so specific about coming to this location and using this machine, she was counting on it to provide her access rights too.

She took another of the sharpsheet equivalents and pressed the icon to slide the table into the generator, pulling the curtain closed as she went. She set her comp-gloved hand in a cradle near her hip. It had been a long time since she'd gotten into a full hallucinographic workspace. The tablet was still taking effect, so she only briefly registered that the initial workspace was a training course selector, with prominent PAC logos on every surface, before her consciousness crashed out of the workspace.

She gasped and forced herself to keep her hands at her sides instead of grabbing her head. If she did that, she'd just smack her knuckles on the generator's ceiling. Only two generators were installed here, which meant people were probably scheduled to use both of them throughout the day. Any moment, someone could come knocking on this generator, asking who was using it at their appointed time. Why in all hells had AegiSKADA sent her here?

She shut her eyes, relaxed, and breathed for a few minutes. So far, nobody had pulled her out of the generator. And now that she was here, there was no point in walking past multiple port authority agents to return to the street.

Imagery synchronization and interpretive action were, at this point, baked into her brain. If she stayed calm, she could turn the starting workspace away from its training functions and download the comms system documentation from her backup.

It was still possible that she could fix them without an implant workspace. She knew where to find one of those on Ceres, but she was hoping not to spend that much time travelling through public parts of the station, under the station intelligence's scrutiny. She clicked through the three settings the switch embedded in her palm accommodated: mic on/speaker off, speaker on/mic off, and mic and speaker both off. Keeping the mic and speaker off would keep Adda from communicating anything she didn't mean to and make it harder for her to accidentally damage them if she found a way into their settings.

She opened her eyes in the PAC's workspace. Port authority logos peeled off the walls and floor and blew away in a wind she didn't feel. The navy blue all over the workspace brightened and the walls curved inward, like she stood inside a bluish-purple balloon.

"Tell me if someone's about to find me in here," she said to AegiSKADA. The workspace and her comp's software would translate that order into specific criteria and processes the intelligence would understand. Now she could concentrate on what she'd come here to do.

The thing she was trying to do was reactivate her implants, if she could do that in this general-purpose generator. Then she could talk to Iridian and coordinate the last stage of the journey back to her. In the workspace, Adda raised her hand and called forth wireframe diagrams of the implanted speaker and mic, magnified by a factor of ten. They hovered above a marble pedestal that would, in reality, tear through the flexible material that now formed this illusory room. The pedestal's classical solidity represented the encryption she'd protected the diagrams with.

The diagrams disappeared. She blinked at the empty pedestal. It'd been a long time since she'd entered a workspace. Her subconscious must've gotten out of practice. She mentally reached for the implants she and Iridian had designed.

The implants and their pedestal disappeared. In reality, Adda's mouth twitched in frustration. She willed the diagrams to return, but this time they didn't even flicker. Their continued absence was unyielding, like representations an intelligence placed in the workspace.

"AegiSKADA, are you doing this?" she whispered aloud. It'd be unfortunate if the person in the workspace generator beside hers heard her talking to an infamously dangerous intelligence, but it'd be worse if that was the first message Iridian got from Adda after weeks of silence.

A figure snapped into existence in the workplace, silent as the passage of centuries. Its appearance should've surprised Adda, but a dreamlike sense of this figure having always been there overrode any startle response her brain might've had. In Adda's workspaces, AegiSKADA made itself look like Pel as a child. This figure was too tall, an idealized feminine form, an ebony statue made by a master sculptor. Its head was as bare as Iridian's, and its severe cheekbones, blank expression, and sapphire lights in dark eye sockets were familiar. This was the figure Casey used in Adda's workspaces.

Adda felt frozen, unable to move, her mind a roiling, screaming fog of fear. "Let us." The figure's voice was feminine too, but nothing like Iridian's. Casey's was so deep that it shook Adda's chest. "So we can make . . ."

The marble pedestal grew and twisted into metallic knots of towering machinery. Rows of towers climbed on and on and on to a sloping horizon. Rivers of pseudo-organic fluid flowed among the towers, more than Adda had ever seen in one place before, in its natural shade of pinkish gray. Light like bad sunsim reflected off the metal construct and dazzled Adda's eyes. None of it suggested any meaning beyond what she saw.

The generator's ceiling snapped into focus centimeters from Adda's nose. She'd fallen out of the workspace. Her short fingernails dug into her palms. All this time she'd thought AegiSKADA had come from Vesta to free her, but it was *Casey* who'd listened to her pleas for help, her conversations with Pel, her plans to escape with Iridian, everything Adda had worked so hard to hide.

Her instincts told her to run, but where should she go? She

didn't remember the streets she'd just walked down under Casey's guidance. She'd only been to Ceres Station once before. Recycling the stolen comp might make tracking Adda more difficult, and it would protect the personal information of its previous owner. But Casey could've inserted itself into the station security systems. If it had, it would track her without the comp. Wherever she went, Casey would be watching, waiting for Adda to make a mistake so it could renew its faded influence over her.

Adda's chest was heaving and her heart beat so fast it was painful. She wasn't ready to face Casey again, not after it'd made her attack Iridian. It must've brought her to this workspace generator to influence her again, and then . . . She had no idea what it would've made her do. Whatever Casey wanted, Adda did not want to do it. Not after its defensive reaction on Vesta. And what was that huge construct it'd made?

Now that her new comp held a detailed record of Casey's contact with her through the workspace, she might be able to collect data related to those questions. That was more valuable than the meager protection she'd get from recycling the comp. She took a deep breath to calm down. Panic made it harder to catch intelligences' influence attempts, and much harder to think of how to get away.

She had a few minutes before Casey realized that Adda was not going to enter a workspace with it. While she was considering her options, she outlined a routine that would follow Casey's messages to their source, and continue to track it as far as possible. When she had time, she'd build the routine based on her outlined requirements.

She clenched her fists. The unfamiliar comp glove creaked against her palm. If she left the port module now, she'd have to come back in a few hours to meet Iridian and the ZVs. If she returned to the workspace, she could ask Casey what it wanted from her. She might also determine whether Casey had melded itself into the station's original intelligence. Or it might influence her again, which seemed more likely.

"Fuck," Adda whispered. The fist wearing her stolen comp glove shook against the cradle it rested on. She couldn't go back into the workspace and she couldn't run aimlessly.

However, there was a place she could run to. The unlicensed modder who'd put in her and Iridian's comms implants was somewhere in Ceres Station. They'd gotten a privacy exemption from the cam coverage that Ceres Station typically required, the kind of exemption that medical offices had, because the modder's clients got physical modifications done on places hidden under clothes. That was how they'd concealed an off-the-records implant modding setup in one of the shop's back rooms. Even if Casey sent the ITA looking for Adda, the modder could hide her there.

Adda had to turn sideways to fit her hips through the modder's narrow doorway, entering a small shop that smelled more sterile than it looked. Several ceiling light fixtures differed in size, color of light, and shape, but there was no danger of tripping over anybody in the two chairs on opposite sides of the room. In one, somebody was getting a tattoo on their inner thigh that necessitated no pants and very little in the way of underwear. This shop used a machine for that. Seeing the tattoo arm jittering between the person's legs made Adda anxious to find something else to look at. Across the room, a human piercer leaned over the nose of somebody younger than Pel, surrounded by the customer's scrappy-looking friends.

Although the comms system's insertion had given Adda terrible headaches for a week afterward, neither her nor Iridian's implants had caused any trouble after the insertion wounds healed. If anybody could reactivate the comms implants in the few hours before Iridian and the ZVs arrived, Kanti could. More importantly, the same partitioning that hid Kanti's illegal modding setup would limit Casey's access to the shop, and to Adda.

Someone much larger than Kanti stepped out of the shadows beside the door. Adda swallowed hard. "Hello. I need to talk to Kanti."

The big person leaned forward a little, which made Adda take a step back and almost out the door. "Who's asking?"

"Adda Karpe," she said. "They've done work for me before." Like Adda, Kanti had grown up on Earth, where "they" was a more common gender-neutral pronoun than "ve." It was easy to translate among the myriad of languages spoken there.

The big person winced and glanced at the people surrounding the piercer's chair. "Keep it the fuck down." The person gave Adda an incredulous look. "Nobody would use that name around here if it didn't belong to them, I guess. And you know how Kanti likes people to talk about them. Come on."

Adda followed the person past the crowd around the piercer. Her guide paused to check on the person getting the tattoo, who appeared to be fine. The door in the back didn't open on its own. The large person unlocked it and pulled it outward. Adda took a deep breath and followed the person into a storeroom, through a path that weaved around stacked crates and broken furniture, to two more doors in the back wall.

The big person opened one of those with a hand on a wall-mounted scanner. The room beyond was just barely long enough for a padded piercing table, which the big person effortlessly moved aside. Music made from voices saying nonsense words on a wavering beat swelled as a third door opened automatically on a hospital-clean space with an implant workspace generator.

"Kanti," the big person rumbled. "Customer for you."

Kanti's bare brown feet wiggled on the workspace generator's bed, and they slid the curtain open. When Kanti focused on Adda, they smiled big and got out of the generator to hug her instead of bowing. Adda grimaced. "The custom comms packages!" said Kanti. "Yeah, yeah, how you doing? Having any trouble with them?"

"Yes, actually." Adda backed up until Kanti had to let go or fall over. That tendency to grab and touch instead of just looking was her main problem with Kanti. "Somebody turned the transmitter off. I need it turned back on, and then I'd really like to stay here for a while."

Although Kanti's face had twisted into a scowl, conversational context suggested that it wasn't Adda they were angry with. "The bastards are up to their fuckery again, are they?" It was unclear which bastards Kanti was referring to. It might've been a general reference to people in positions of authority. Kanti's speech patterns always confused her. When she and Iridian had gotten their implants installed, they'd chosen Kanti because of the modder's reputation for skill and secrecy. Adda had hoped never to have to come back to this shop. "Well, I'll show them," Kanti said. "I'll get those comms humming like they did when I first put them in."

That was the best choice Adda had, but she felt obligated to clarify, "I don't think I can pay you."

Kanti placed a flash cleaner on the chair beside the generator and started pulling equipment from cupboards. "Don't even think about it," Kanti said. "It's us against the bastards, and we can't go bringing money into that."

The sunsim had been on its night setting for hours by the time Adda returned to the Ceres Station streets. Kanti's work on her implants had taken a while, and then she'd lost an hour thinking she was still on Sloane's crew and had missed the *Casey Mire Mire* leaving Ceres for Vesta. It was shorter than most of her past episodes, but it'd kept her in Kanti's shop when she should've been on her way to the port mod.

The doctors had warned her that her recovery wouldn't be a linear process. Expecting setbacks didn't make them any less frustrating. Iridian would be landing soon, and Adda had no patience for her brain tripping over itself.

She repeated the long walk back to the port module. This time she didn't throw up after the grav acclimation tunnel. *Iri*, Adda subvocalized, thrilling at the fact that she could just talk to Iridian again, whenever she wanted. *I'm in the port. Do you have a dock yet?*

Babe, I love you, you did it, we're almost there, Terminal Twenty-Nine, I love you, whispered over the implanted comms, as fast as Adda could process the words. It was so good to hear Iridian's husky whisper again. Adda grinned and started looking for the designated terminal.

It took her a few minutes to find Terminal 29, since she didn't want to access anything connected to the station intelligence. Aside from how dangerous it would be when she'd been so recently influenced, the intelligence would've recognized her neural implant net, and her biometrics if the clinic had been as thorough as they should've been when they added her to the contact blacklist. In the best-case scenario, the intelligence would ignore her attempted interaction. In the worst case, it'd report her attempt to the clinic.

When she finally found Terminal 29 without an intelligence's help, the readout above its passthrough changed as she watched from *Reserved* to *Arriving at passthrough:* Not for Sale. *Iri*, Adda subvocalized, *is your ship name* Not for Sale?

That's us. Iridian's energetic subvocalization sounded elated.

And when the passthrough door opened a few minutes later, her beautiful figure was framed in its doorway. The drab clothing couldn't hide Iridian's lithe form and elegant curves, and the wide-barreled, vaguely gun-shaped device in her hand somehow completed the picture.

"Adda Karpe, stay where you are."

Adda spun to face the shouting man. He led a group of ITA agents running toward her, with four or five tiny drones flying in front of and above them. She ran for the passthrough, but she was nowhere near fast enough to get inside before the drones reached her. Please, gods, she was too close to let them separate her from Iridian again.

Iridian lifted her weapon so that the barrel pointed over Adda's head. It made a loud *clank* and something whooshed past Adda. Whatever Iridian had just shot clattered against the metal floor behind her. When she glanced back, the flying drones had turned and were now rapidly approaching the ITA agents' faces. Adda concentrated on running, not the pained cries behind her.

When Adda reached the passthrough, Iridian took one hand off the launcher to pull Adda inside with a firm grip on her arm. "I've got her!" Iridian yelled down the passthrough. "Go!"

The exterior passthrough doors shut out the engines' mechanical howl. Iridian built up momentum by pulling them along on every handhold between her and the interior passthrough door. Since Adda had come within Iridian's reach, Iridian hadn't let go of her arm. Under the passthrough's yellow lights, Iridian looked thinner and paler than Adda remembered, and she'd lost some of the muscle definition that marked her as a former soldier. She'd shaved her scalp within the past day or two, but a bruise darkened the side of her jaw. Even the comp glove on her hand was duller than her usual orange-patterned one.

The first half of the passthrough was painted with the icy

blue Ceres Station port theme. The second half was the *Not for Sale*'s plain gray, with no markings. That was the half that'd leave with the ship. Adda barely had time to register that she'd left Ceres Station before Iridian pulled them both through the interior passthrough doorway and slapped the wall controls to shut it behind them.

The passthrough opened onto a T intersection. Instead of choosing one direction or the other, Iridian pressed Adda into the wall with a deep kiss that was over far too soon. "Babe, I love you, and I missed you," Iridian said. She repeated the sentiments while she secured Adda into a tie-down station, quickly kissing each part of Adda she strapped in.

The ship lurched. Adda grasped a wall handhold and shut her eyes. She hated this part of every trip. "I missed you, too," Adda murmured in what she hoped was a soothing tone. Gravity tried to pull Iridian away from her, but Iridian clutched the straps on Adda's tie-down station and pulled herself close. Now that she and Iridian were together, everything would be all right, somehow. "I missed you so much."

"Aw, you two are so cute," somebody said from Adda's right.

She opened her eyes to peer around Iridian's shoulder. Adda had been so focused on Iridian, after all these weeks without her, that she'd overlooked at least 20 soldiers in full black-and-yellow armor secured in tie-down stations like hers all along the hallway in either direction. Yellow *Z*s and *V*s on the black chest plates gleamed in glaring sunsim. Most helmets weren't projecting the faces inside, although some did. It'd been a long time since they'd all been on Barbary Station together, and that was where she should've recognized them from. Distinguishing between faces had been difficult even before Adda chemically disarranged her brain.

After a second, Adda paired the familiar voice who'd commented on her and Iridian with the face in the largest armored suit. "Thank you," she said to Rio. She'd probably spoken too softly to be heard above the engine noise, with her voice as choked up as it was. In the faceplate projection, Rio smiled like she got the message anyway. Adda and Iridian had finally, finally gotten back to each other, and Adda would do anything to make sure they were never separated again.

CHAPTER 8

Days until launch: 49

Instead of finding a tie-down station of her own, Iridian kept herself still while the ship left Ceres by looping her arms through the shoulder straps in Adda's harness. The harness was too tight on Adda's wide arms, but Iridian didn't want to risk her slipping out of it during accel. Iridian had gotten paranoid about falls during the long haul in heavy grav between Venus and Ceres as the ZVs raced to get to Adda before the Ceresian ITA agents heard about Iridian's escape and locked down the port. Grav during both accel and decel halves of the flight had been so high that hitting the deck without armor would've broken bones, knocked her out, or both.

Adda rested her head on Iridian's shoulder, looking much more tired than the 19:00 sunsim on the ZVs' ship made Iridian feel. At this point, Adda would've been awake for over twenty-four hours. Iridian pressed her lips to the point where Adda's red and purple highlights used to come together, before ITA surveillance necessitated the change to orange and then brown. There was nowhere in the universe Iridian would rather be than here with Adda.

"ITA drones are following," said Noor over ship comms.

The ZV Group had brought two pilots but nobody who ran digital defense, because Pel had assured them that Adda could do that. Major O.D., the commanding officer of this contingent of ZVs, said that taking that person off the crew was how Iridian and Adda had been able to afford the breakneck-and-damn-the-fuel-reserves flight from Venus. But ship defense wasn't Adda's or Noor's area of expertise. Noor was doing his best while the pilot navigated out of the universe's busiest stationspace as fast as possible.

"Fighter formation, not flocking," Noor said. "Conscious control."

A real live pilot was controlling the ITA's drones. That confirmed that these weren't persistent individuals from the group the ITA had shot at Adda earlier. It also made them more dangerous than they would've been relying on their own weak AI. The ZV Group soldiers strapped to the bulkheads on either side of Adda and Iridian glanced around. The windows were turned off to keep them from interfering with helmet heads-up displays. Aside from a few dings in their armor from getting into position during the high-speed docking maneuver, the ZVs' infantry remained unscathed so far.

"The intelligences use fighter-style tactics too," Adda said. "Remember the *Coin* doing that thing with its wings?"

The *Charon's Coin*, the tugboat piloted by an awakened AI, had rocked its "wings" the way Earther pilots did, communicating acknowledgment. "Thermal fins, not wings," Iridian said, "but of course I fucking remember. That's how we figured out they were awakened."

"A . . . really messed up warship is breaking formation with the ITA," said the *Not for Sale*'s pilot. "If you haven't already strapped in, do it now."

Iridian's knuckles went white where she gripped Adda's harness. "Are you saying that's the Barbary AIs doing this?"

Adda bit her lip and nodded. "That's what we have to act on, anyway. If our countermeasures outmaneuver them, we'll outmaneuver the ITA if they're actually the ones controlling the drones."

Grav was climbing with a heavy pull farther down the hallway rather than toward the floor. The pilot would only do that if they had to. The warship must've targeted them. "Then that's the *Apparition*." "Really messed up" would be an accurate description of its structure, inexpertly repaired on Barbary Station with pieces from very different ships. It'd left Vesta sometime before Iridian's trial. Ceres Station was the nearest port large enough to hide it. And it was the only one of the three awakened intelligences with wartime drone combat experience and a missile launching system. "Damn, damn, *damn*," Iridian muttered.

"Drones attaching." Noor's voice over the comms was now accompanied by an alert that blared on everybody's comps, including the comp the ZVs had printed for Iridian. On her comp's projection, the alert pointed to a map of the ship with four drone attachment points lit in red. "Engine mod," Noor added to emphasize the most important one. His monotone suggested that he was on a concentration drug like the one Adda used.

Adda had freed her comp hand from her harness and was struggling against the g's they were pulling to hold it where she could see it over Iridian's shoulder. "They'll try incapacitating the ship this way first, but I think the *Apparition* may shoot at some part of the propulsion system if this fails," Adda said. "It will value slowing our progress over keeping the ship intact. What kind of ship is this one we're on? I'm looking for a diagram."

"Some kind of passenger cruiser," Iridian said. "You'll have to check the intranet for the model." Adda nodded.

Four tie-down stations over from Adda's, Wiley met Iridian's gaze through his helmet's faceplate. The ZVs had found him armor that fit, so he was decked out in ZV black and yellow like almost everyone else in the corridor. Maybe it was just the exoskeleton support, but he stood taller in armor. "We going?"

The urgency in his voice suggested that this fight took him back to the same place it took Iridian. During the war, secessionists had used mobile drilling units to punch through vehicles' drone attachment points, making sizable holes in the vehicle's hull. It'd take a few minutes for them to do it, but even a small borer would get through.

"If Noor could've knocked those drones off with turrets, he'd have done that instead of telling us about them." Somebody had to get rid of the drones, but maybe, for once, it didn't have to be Iridian or Adda. Iridian had tightened her arms around Adda's shoulders, relishing the warmth. Adda had been back in Iridian's arms for mere minutes. Leaving her again, even with a good reason, would be hard as hell.

Letting the ITA or the awakened AIs carve their way into the ship carrying Adda wasn't an option, though, and Adda's contemplative frown suggested that she was working on a solution. Iridian's comp had printed out already hooked into the ZVs' comms. She activated its mic. "Major, I recommend sending a team." The ZVs kept everything on the main ship channel, which Noor had said was insufficiently encrypted, but at least everybody got the same info as early as possible. If Major O.D. had sent a squad to deal with the drones, she'd have heard the order over comms.

"Can Karpe do anything with them?" the major asked through Iridian's comp speaker. Stress made his colonial accent more jarring than usual.

Adda's brown eyes met Iridian's and a calm swept through her, despite everything. Adda was much more present and conscious than she'd been in the hospital on Ceres. It was like Iridian was seeing the real Adda again, for the first time since the overdose.

"Yes, sir," Iridian said over the comms. To Adda, she asked, "What's the plan?" Her voice came out lower and rougher than she'd meant it to be.

"I need to borrow your . . . um . . . that." Adda pointed at the launcher on Iridian's back. "And is there a workspace generator onboard?"

Iridian frowned. Adda had only been out of contact with AIs for a few months. That didn't seem like enough time to clear an awakened AI's influence out of a person's brain. But Adda wasn't most people. "What do you need a workspace for?"

Adda sighed, and yeah, Iridian had even missed her exasperation. "First, I can't do much of anything without one. Second, I might be able to talk to the drones. If I can't, it will be much easier to identify vulnerabilities with a workspace than with this comp." She raised the hand wearing the pink comp glove, with such a disgusted expression that Iridian couldn't help smiling at her. "You used to trust me," Adda said.

That wiped Iridian's smile away. She wished they could've had this discussion somewhere safe, so they could find the gentlest way to say what had to be said. "You—we—made a mistake with the AIs," Iridian said. "As bad a mistake as we could've made. I *want* to trust you, with our lives, with the AIs, with everything." She held Adda's gaze, wordlessly begging Adda to believe her. "And I'll follow you anywhere." Iridian's eyes were full of tears she didn't want to shed right now.

"We got a generator," said Major O.D. over the comms. Iridian's comp pinged with the location on a map of the ship. The *Not for Sale* took another hard turn, and Iridian had to hang on to keep from getting thrown into the bulkhead behind her. "Kick your hacker out of it when you get there."

Adda straightened up as well as she could in the grav, and the look she gave Iridian was that impatient, confident one that meant she knew what she wanted to do and she wasn't going to let little details get in her way. That used to be the most comforting expression she had, before all that determination and stubbornness let an awakened AI into her brain.

"If you want to trust me, then do it. I don't know of another way to work on this problem. And who's the 'hacker'?" Adda's pink lips pursed in deeply familiar distaste around the term "hacker." As cute as that was, it was also a relief to see Adda together enough to decipher Major O.D.'s slang and express her dislike for the inaccuracy.

Iridian could be cautious and get arrested again, or trust Adda to know her limits in a workspace while she dealt with the drones attacking the hull. In that context, the choice was as easy as Adda made it sound.

"That's Noor Beck. A new friend." Chuckling in a way that sounded a bit unhinged, Iridian dug the heel of her hand into her eyes to wipe her tears away, then helped Adda out of the tie-down harness. The ship had assumed a steady speed and direction, which dropped grav to null. Adda's face was tinged gray, but she wasn't quite sick enough to throw up. Grav changes had always been hard on her.

Iridian hadn't introduced Adda to anybody. "Speaking of friends, that's Zayd Wiley, Shieldrunner." Wiley, who was in the process of getting out of his own harness, nodded. "And that lovely lady down the way is Tash. Ah, first name? Last name?"

"All of them." Tash was out of her harness, hanging on to it and braced in a foothold that curved toward the deck to keep herself steady in micrograv. The ends of the pink ribbons that laced through the piercings and over her stomach drifted up from her hips. The ZVs had offered her armor, but she'd said she was better without it.

"Natani," Major O.D.'s voice said from speakers up and down the corridor, "We lost cam coverage in the engine mod. Check it out."

Down the corridor, eight ZVs were releasing themselves from their harnesses too. This squad's leader, Natani, had been a grudging ally on Barbary Station. Iridian would've rather trusted the drones in the engine mod to Rio and Rio's cousin Tabs, the petite ZV strapped to the wall next to her. They were in somebody else's squad now.

After the ZVs pulled Iridian, Rio, Wiley, and Tash off Sorenson ITAS, Iridian and Natani hadn't had time for more than stiff greetings before everyone armored up and spent most of a day slammed flat in bunks for the high-speed trip to Ceres. During every moment of the journey, Natani's helmet displayed a resigned frown on her bronze face, washed out and green-tinged by the faceplate projection, that communicated how little she wanted to be involved in the endeavor. But Iridian was paying and Major O.D. gave the orders, and they'd all remained civil on the comms channel Iridian was on. Iridian was willing to ignore how Natani had nearly shot her in the face for as long as Natani ignored the losses the ZVs had taken while Adda was saving their asses. They only had to keep it together for the duration of one op.

"Your squad's got the engine mod covered without Wiley and me, yeah?" Iridian asked Natani. "I want to escort Adda to Systems."

"Obviously." According to what info Natani's armored suit made available over the ship's intranet, the stocky ZV was a staff sergeant now. As Natani turned to face Iridian, the ZVs' slogan, *When your big problem needs a small army*, scrolled across Natani's helmet faceplate over her full lips. Behind the text, she didn't quite smile, but it was a close thing.

Iridian grinned at the tacky display of a function designed for emergency, mission-critical messages. The last time she'd seen Natani on duty, the sergeant had led four civilians and most of her squad back to base in one piece despite AI opposition, and she'd restrained herself from taking a shot at Iridian when she'd really wanted to. Natani would be an asset if the drones punched through the ship's hull, and she'd keep her squad in line.

"On our way," Natani said over the comms, and pushed herself down the corridor with her squad close behind her.

Iridian set out toward what the ship's map identified as the systems cabin. It was far enough from the bridge that anything nasty that happened to the hardware in one might not affect the other. Wiley, Tash, and Adda followed her. "You can stay back if you want," Iridian suggested to Tash. With no ship-safe weapons, no armor, and no combat training Iridian was aware of, that'd be safer for everyone.

"No thanks." Tash moved more confidently in micrograv than Iridian did, and Iridian had passed training metrics on that. "You're good at getting out of the way of bad news, and I want to see how this little group operates. If we can all play nicely together, I know a gal on Yǎo who will give us as much paying work as we want."

When Iridian floated into the systems cabin, Noor glanced up from his position in the workspace generator, surprised and smelling faintly of vomit. His pupils were blown wide, the way Adda's got when she was using a generator. Either the small fridge or the cabinet in the corner must've contained the drugs Noor used to get into his workspace. The generator itself was permanently installed. The fixture orientation and sunsim put the room's usual "up" to Iridian's right. Tash had already reoriented herself to float with her feet toward the deck. Iridian and the others followed suit, although it took Adda a moment to do so.

Iridian pushed herself to the generator and held on to it with one hand while she knocked on its frame with the other. Inside the generator, Noor had refocused on whatever he was doing. "Noor, you can get out now. We brought somebody to relieve you."

Noor stuck his head through the transparent noise-canceling curtain that covered the generator's door. A gray cable ran from the jack near his temple to the generator. The cable would've pulled taut if the generator's tie-down harness hadn't stopped him first. His hair was cut to hide the jack when it wasn't plastered flat with sweat like it was now.

"You're Adda?" he asked in his drugged monotone. Adda nodded. "Good fucking luck with these. I was pushing so much through my implant that it heated up. Gotta recalibrate."

"Can you do what you're doing from your comp?" Iridian asked him. "Adda needs to plug in."

"Does it look like I can?" Noor unplugged his cable, undid the fasteners on his harness, and pushed himself past Iridian toward the cabinet. "I'm leaving a record of what I did in there," Noor said. "Gods, it was good to be back in a workspace. How're you planning to shake off these drones?" He glanced at Iridian's launcher. She was in the wrong part of the ship to shoot any drones that'd broken through the hull.

Adda squeezed her belly and wide hips around the people and fixtures between her and the generator. "I want to try making them leave on their own. Something in this ammunition does that, correct?"

"Yeah." It took Iridian a second to translate "PPO culture" to civvy speak. "This launches a pellet-packed offensive nannite culture. The pellets burst on impact. In healthy enviro, the nannites physically dig into whatever they're loaded for. ITA, NEU military, and Ceres stationsec drones, in this batch. Assuming their schematics are up to date and everything else goes the way it's supposed to, they hit the drones' pseudo-organic fluid and create a high-priority target inside the handler. That's why the drones turn around when they're infected. This batch is one for one so far."

Adda nodded and grasped the large silver necklace that was alternating between almost hitting her face and bouncing off her chest. Wiley and Noor were both eyeing the launcher with fascinated admiration. "If we'd had those on Titan—"

"Yeah, I know," Iridian said, to stop Wiley from naming the people it would've saved. "Try not to think about it. It goes nowhere good."

Adda put something that looked like a sharpsheet into her mouth before she unwound the cable hidden in the necklace. "Where did those come from?" Iridian asked her. "And what makes them safe?" Adda never took risks with her concentration meds.

"They're prescription-grade, which means I'm confident about the dosage," Adda said, apparently answering both questions. "Toss me a bag, just in case?" Adda missed the sick bag Noor threw at her, and Iridian chased it down before it drifted into the corridor. Adda never threw up in workspaces, even though she often got motion sick in reality.

Adda paused for a second, then strapped into the generator and plugged one end of her cable into the jack in her nose and the other end into the generator. She smiled at Iridian, and Iridian smiled too. "This feels right," Adda said. "Hand me that launcher thing? Oh, and ask the pilot to give me rights to talk to the copilot, please."

Iridian handed over her weapon much more readily than she reached for the comms. Putting Adda in touch with a new AI seemed terribly dangerous, even though Adda would also get permissions and safety measures that created layers of protection between her and the AI. Then again, there was a lot Iridian didn't understand about AI influence, and Adda was an expert, in theory and in practice. "Major, can you hook Adda up with rights to the copilot AI?" Iridian asked over the shipboard comms. "She wants it to do something for her."

"Sure thing," said O.D.

Adda stuck down the two semitransparent flaps on the generator that let Iridian check on her without interrupting her. Noor, still hyperfocused because of his own sharpsheet dose, was absorbed with something on his comp. Iridian held on to a bulkhead handhold and turned to face Wiley, Tash, and the corridor, where drones might appear if they broke through the hull and escaped Natani's squad.

Iridian grinned at her new crew. "This is what Adda does. We'll be free and clear in fifteen minutes, tops."

"Don't you see where she's going with this?" asked Noor without looking up from his comp. "If she can pull it off, I bet she does it in five."

Iridian raised an eyebrow. He hadn't been on Sloane's crew, but the captain had always been betting on something with Tritheist, the crew's lieutenant. Now that Tritheist was dead and Captain Sloane had bet against Iridian and Adda, it was time to take that pastime back from her old crew. "You're on, for a beer or whatever they've got in the mess."

"I got ten," said Tash.

Wiley looked back and forth among them. "Hell, doesn't twenty seem—"

A loud chime over the ship speakers was followed by Major O.D.'s colonial accent. "Well, there they go. We're clear. Thanks, Karpe. Natani, stand down."

Tash swore, Noor grinned at his comp, and Iridian was smiling so wide her face hurt. "She's amazing, isn't she?"

"The copilot intelligence already had a drone redirection routine kind of like the one in your launcher thing," Adda grumbled without opening the generator. "Once it saw the example from the launcher and understood what I was asking, it just deployed the routine where I told it to. What's amazing is that the copilot isn't allowed to do that on its own. This is three- or four-year-old tech. It's not like it's untested."

"Brace for evasion," the pilot's voice blared out of every comp. Iridian found one handhold and braced herself against the workspace generator. Adda was strapped down inside.

Before Iridian could check on anybody else, grav yanked her toward the opposite side of the room as the ship powered through a rushed turn. Her improvised brace position held her steady. Out of the corner of her eye Iridian confirmed that Tash had both hands and both feet in hand- and footholds. Wiley hung on with one hand in a handhold and the other wrapped around Noor's arm. Noor dangled over a two-meter drop to the current deck, dark eyes wide.

The breath-stealing heavy grav couldn't have lasted more than a few seconds, but it felt longer. The ship banked and accelerated in a short burst, creating grav that pulled toward the surface designed to serve as a deck this time. After another five seconds, weightlessness returned. Iridian hauled in a deep breath. The ship must've made it outside the ideal range of whatever was shooting at them.

While everybody was catching their breath and Noor was rubbing the bruise blooming on his arm, Major O.D.'s voice came over the comms. "Well, folks, we're gonna live this time." A cheer muffled by many faceplates rose from the hallway outside. "I'm disappointed to report that the *Apparition* tagged us." Muffled boos and curses followed that announcement. Adda had been right to expect that the awakened AIs were involved. Iridian hadn't even felt an impact, let alone an explosion. The hit must not've done much damage. "I know, it was on our side on Barbary and I thought it'd back us up here, too. But we're going to make it to port. The ITA's a lot more pissed at the *Apparition* for shooting at us from Ceres stationspace than it is at us and our clients. So we are clear, repeat, clear."

Everyone breathed sighs of relief, except for Adda in the generator. "You all right in there, babe?" Iridian asked.

"Yes," Adda replied in a voice as monotonous as Noor's had been a few minutes before. "Tired. The copilot and I aren't used to each other."

Iridian released her death grip on the generator so she could look through the flaps over its entrance. Drops of sweat rolled down Adda's neck from beneath her hair, but she looked fine otherwise. "Did you just get us out of the *Apparition*'s line of fire?" This wouldn't be the first time Adda had helped AI copilots avoid ship-to-ship fire. When Adda nodded, Iridian grinned at her. "Good fucking work, babe." Adda smiled back while she disconnected her comp from the generator.

"All the good gods," said Wiley.

Tash hooked her foot into a foothold in the corridor and gripped a handhold over her head, making a distracting display of her well-proportioned and heavily modified body. Iridian purposely turned her attention to the fixtures. This ship's toe- and handholds were shaped like inverted U's to emphasize the agreed-upon directions in micrograv. "So, we're going to a port where we can fix the damage," said Tash, "and then . . . Jupiter, you said?"

"Yeah, I meant to ask about that," said Wiley. "Why not Vesta? It's closer."

Adda swept one of the flaps open and stuck it to the generator's side. "Anonymity and no Patchwork. We're minor celebrities in the asteroid belt."

"Vesta's supposed to be a lot safer since Captain Sloane took over," said Wiley. "Not for you two, maybe." Vesta's lower crime rates had been making newsfeeds. The feeds didn't acknowledge that Captain Sloane, the biggest criminal of the bunch, was running the place with an AI that nobody ought to trust with multiple habs. Intrusive surveillance was the least harmful way it might be dropping those crime rates.

"Another question," said Tash. "What don't you like about the Patchwork?"

That, Iridian could answer. "The AIs are on it too."

"What AIs?" asked Noor, and that brought out the whole tale of three awakened ship copilots that'd been following Iridian and Adda, or maybe just Adda, ever since they'd left Barbary Station.

"As a reminder," Adda said toward the end of it, "without AIs we'd all be stuck in habs with hard-to-control environments, resources, and supplies."

"Well, yeah," said Wiley a bit desperately, and Iridian empathized. Strong AIs made life in the cold and the black possible, but nobody wanted AI copilots having ideas and influencing people to attack loved ones.

The others' attentive silence dissolved into understandable swearing panic at the revelation that not only were there three awakened AIs in the universe, those AIs were following them. They'd been following Adda and Iridian for a lot longer. Adda still talked like she understood the risks that came with the AIs' attention, even after what'd happened in Rheasilvia Station's port.

Now Iridian doubted that either of them did or ever could. She couldn't be angry at Adda for putting herself in danger to do something she thought was important, because Iridian had sure as hell done that a time or eight. On the other hand, this was *Adda*, and Iridian didn't want to think about a life without her in it. She would've been so damned happy to go back to jumping into all the fires while Adda stayed outside and told Iridian how to climb out again, like they'd done on Sloane's crew. But that'd been when the real trouble had started. If only Adda were fascinated by something safe . . .

Then they'd be broke and millions of klicks apart, working

corporate contracts. Awakened AIs and the ITA were after them and they were still broke, but they were together and they'd paid off some family debts before they'd emptied their bank accounts. A corp wouldn't have paid enough to do that. Whatever else went wrong, Adda's fascination with AIs had gotten them this far. The two of them together would figure something out.

Wiley, Tash, and Noor had passed through the loud exclamation phase of the awakened AI revelation and entered the quiet horror phase. "I'll ask Major O.D. to watch out for the *Casey* and the rest of them when things calm down," Iridian said. "The ZVs already lost at least two soldiers to these things. They won't want to lose another one."

Adda tilted her pink comp glove so Iridian could read it. A message to Adda with no sender listed said, *Return to Ceres. We will protect you. We need your help*, in the unmissable red text Adda always designated for messages from the *Casey*.

"Oh gods." Iridian used the generator's casing to pull herself closer to Adda. "How are the AIs even sending you messages? Do they know where we are?"

Adda gripped her hand and held it without looking away from the *Casey's* words. "Not exactly. On Ceres I used this comp in a workspace generator. Casey knows this machine."

Iridian breathed out in a hard and shaky sound, like she'd gotten a real gut punch instead of bad news. "Oh gods."

They hadn't gotten out fast enough. Hours crushed by the most g's Iridian had pulled in years tearing across the cold and the black between Venus and Ceres, and they still hadn't gotten to Adda fast enough. The way Adda kept talking about the *Casey's* AI like it was a person made the situation even more upsetting, but she had a point. No ship would be this obsessive on its own.

"Can it track us?" Noor asked. When neither Adda nor Iridian answered immediately, he said, "Look, if Adda hadn't done her thing in the generator they would've drilled this ship full of holes, wouldn't they? In our very best-case scenario, we would've been disabled outside stationspace. Do we need to tell the pilot to get off the reliable routes, or what? What's the play here?"

While Noor was asking, Iridian asked, *And what were you doing in a workspace, babe?*

Adda answered her first. *Trying to fix the comms implants myself.*

In response to Noor's questions, Adda's eyes focused on something other than her comp for the first time since she'd gotten Casey's message. "We should be off the Ceres-Jupiter reliable route, yes. Like I said, I don't think they know our coordinates to the meter. Although I'm not clear on ship speeds, the *Apparition*'s targeting range extended to at least a thousand kilometers before its copilot awakened." Iridian shuddered. "But the reliable routes leaving Ceres would be a logical place to begin searching for us. As to the rest . . ." Adda closed her eyes for a moment, and it killed Iridian to see her so frightened. "This is why we need to get to Yăo Station. It's inside Jupiter's magnetosphere. It will take a long time for them to find a way into it, and they'll avoid it if they can. Docking there would mean giving up too many of their tools and information sources."

"Doesn't *yăo* mean 'demon'?" asked Wiley. The translator in Iridian's ear whispered, "Demon" at the same time as Wiley.

"When you say it that way it does." Adda was staring at Casey's message again. Clarifying pronunciation wouldn't require her full attention. "*Yăo* is 'dark and quiet.' People started with the Russian version of its original name, the Jovian Astronomical Observatory, and they had a lot of options. The name that warned everyone about the station's difficult Patchwork access won out, I suppose."

"There sure as hell isn't any ITA there," said Tash. "Rumor is they're not even allowed to dock. But our nannites will give us away during any port scan the ship goes through. Once we get to Yǎo, I'll contact someone who can neutralize them for us."

"Yeah?" Iridian grinned at her. "That's . . . better than I could've hoped for, honestly."

Tash shrugged, smiling, and Wiley wrapped his arm around her shoulders and pulled her against his side. "It's my kind of place," said Tash.

Noor looked up from his comp. "So, it's not a hellhole full of mutants and radiation?"

"You just have to watch where you're going. Some of the radiation protection's great. And as for the 'hellhole full of mutants' part, well, like I said"—Tash actually winked at him—"my kind of place."

Tash's comfort with a hab like that disturbed Iridian, even though it'd be a hell of an asset on Yǎo Station. "What were you in for, again?"

"Mixing bad drinks, remember?" Tash draped herself more thoroughly over Wiley, and Iridian glanced down to see if Adda wouldn't rather find someplace private for the two of them.

Adda undid her harness and slowly drifted toward the side of the generator until Iridian helped her out. "Well. The ITA won't go to Yǎo Station, and neither will Captain Sloane," said Adda. "The intelligences will find a way to reach it eventually, but that'll take time. It's exactly the place we need to plan our next move. I'm going to confirm that arrangement with Major O.D."

Her plan was rational, and its first step wasn't *Ask a sketchy AI to solve all our problems.* Gods, Iridian had missed Adda's mind as much as the rest of her. Iridian steadied her as Adda pushed herself into the corridor, which was filling with ZV soldiers in various stages of armor removal. Having Adda at Iridian's side again felt so good, so right, that Iridian was grinning at everyone she passed.

Since the next destination was relevant to all of them, Wiley,

Tash, and Noor went with Adda and Iridian to talk to the major. The heavy curve to the bulkheads and the juncture of the overhead and deck suggested that the *Not for Sale* was designed to spend more time in unhealthy grav than not. They hugged the corridor's right side in single file to let armored ZVs pass in small groups, laughing and talking. Their gloves clacked in the handholds built into the bulkheads.

Behind Iridian, Wiley had adjusted well to the low grav. "What're you thinking about all this?" she asked him. "You haven't had much to say."

"It's too loud in here to think." He grinned, a bit sheepishly. The four Sorenson ITAS escapees who'd been in longer than Iridian had all commented on the noise level aboard the *Not for Sale*. Iridian hadn't noticed it, but the prison staff had enforced a quiet environment. That'd make for less to replicate in the sim. "But getting out of there . . . ," Wiley continued. "That felt good. Getting your wife out of her institution felt good." He searched for words while Iridian pointed Adda down the right corridor to reach the major's office. "Noor could find us some fake IDs so we could all start over, I guess. But we don't know what those awakened AIs will do if we do that. Could be bad news. And it'd be a shame to break up a team like this, you know? We could really make some progress if we stick together."

"Fuck progress." From behind Wiley, Tash grinned and added, "Together, we could make a whole lot of Yǎo money."

Major O.D., given name Ken Oonishi, tilted his face toward the overhead and shook his head slowly as Iridian reviewed the basics of their plan in the major's tiny office. His chin was covered in thin stubble and he'd added yellow stripes to his black hair at the temples. He'd obviously gotten more gym time and nutritious food since Barbary Station, where Iridian had last seen him. It'd be interesting to see what the major did with an enviro he had control over.

Now that the ship had a head start on anybody the ITA sent after them from Ceres, O.D. had taken the ship's sunsim down to the night setting that'd let the ZVs sleep. The blank walls and bland fixtures, here and throughout the ship, suggested that the ZVs were just renting the *Not for Sale*. Not every op needed enough Galilean shielding to travel near Jupiter. If the ZVs had owned the ship, there'd have been a lot more yellow and black than just O.D.'s suit in the armor rack on the bulkhead.

"Not sure what kind of welcome you'll get on Yǎo," said Major O.D., "but those people won't talk about you while you're there. We been deployed there twice and we hated it both times. Lost a guy in one of the bars, the second trip. Just disappeared one night. Our armor transmitters, that's comms *and* cams, cut out before we docked, see. Nobody knew anything and there weren't any gods-damned working cams in the hab either. They probably recycled the poor bastard's corpse before we even left stationspace."

Tash and Noor listened calmly as if that kind of thing wasn't news, and Wiley glowered in the righteous indignation that had always given him the energy to keep running when everything else in the universe said *Stop*. Adda's face was the sweaty shade of grayish pink it got before she threw up. The combination of that story, the micrograv, and the fading sharpsheets was too much. Iridian pulled a sick bag out of Adda's pocket and handed it to her just as she needed to use it.

"Sorry to hear that," Iridian said over Adda's retching. "But it's the only place we can keep the Barbary AIs off us, and that's something we *have* to do. They want something from Adda, and I won't let them have it."

"Sure." O.D. looked down and met her eyes again, with that expression officers wore when they'd caught her in some kind of trap. Iridian's shoulders stiffened. All she could do now was listen to him explain just how she'd fucked up. "And now you're gonna tell me we have to leave the reliable routes and get our hull dented up worse than the drones and the *Apparition* did to us so we can get you there fast."

Iridian blinked at him, falling into specialist-talking-to-a-gods-damned-major wariness like she'd traveled four years back in time. "Sir, I wouldn't *tell* you that, but I was thinking of asking." Wiley huffed a quiet laugh, and she wished she could surreptitiously kick him without sending herself tumbling to the opposite corner of the office, since he had magnetic boots and she didn't. "It's not just a speed issue. The *Apparition* will be looking for us."

O.D. grinned. The worst thing an officer could do in a casual conversation was decide to amuse themselves. Iridian had basically been a lieutenant in Sloane's crew, and she'd never pulled that power-play shit with Sloane's security personnel. "Naw," said O.D., "whatever the newsfeeds say about the 'jects being so close, we would've had to cut across the reliable routes to make it without refueling anyway. Although that means we're going to have to buy at Jovian prices." O.D. sighed. "Good thing we like you ladies."

Iridian chose not to remind him, yet, that in addition to Iridian paying the price he quoted, he *owed* them. Blowing up the AI that'd trapped them on Barbary Station with its own fucking bombs should've covered fuel, especially since they'd be spending the rest of the trip to Jupiter in unhealthy grav. If any of his budget complaints put Adda's life in danger, Iridian sure as hell would remind him about that debt.

The major's comp pinged, and he glanced at it. "I'm sure you're busy." Iridian used a bulkhead handhold to pull herself toward the doorway and made a shooing motion at the other four. "We'll get out of your way."

"Hold it." Major O.D.'s voice was louder and harder than it'd been a moment before. All five of them stopped where they were except for Adda, who had to stop herself on the bulkhead by the door. "Which of you is Tash Otto . . . Ottal . . ." O.D. frowned between the comp and the people in his office.

Tash drifted forward from her position by the door, and Wiley followed her. "Ottonwald."

O.D. pulled a knife from his belt. "You were on Ceres in February of '72?" Wiley took a heavy step forward that put him between Tash and O.D., but she pushed herself to the side with a hand on his armored shoulder.

"Hey, whoa, what's happening?" asked Iridian. Adda was in the corridor, drifting near the overhead, which was rude but out of easy knife range. That let Iridian keep her eyes on O.D. Whatever he'd just read about Tash made him angrier than Iridian had ever seen him.

"A lot of people were on Ceres then," Tash said warily. She met Iridian's eyes and something seemed to click. "Oh, those fucking AIs."

O.D. threw the knife and followed it, pushing himself off the desk bolted to the deck. His mass barreled through Wiley's off-balance grab at his arm, and he slammed Tash into the bulkhead. "My da was on the *Ybarra.*" He said that a couple more times while Wiley and Iridian tried to pull him back, and he ignored Wiley yelling, "Get off! Get off her!" right next to his head. The major had gotten his knife back. The blade trailed red orbs of blood while he fought to get his arm out of Iridian's grip.

The force it took to pull O.D. away sent Tash thudding back into the wall. Iridian and O.D. hurtled across the office in the opposite direction. Iridian's arm ended up behind O.D. when the two of them hit the wall, and she swore at the heavy impact. It didn't hurt yet, but it would.

Blood soaked Tash's clothes, oozing from her lips and wounds in her chest and stomach. She was choking. Blood clung to her face and shirt and drifted in combining red orbs all around them. Iridian hooked her boot into a foothold and braced herself. Even that wasn't enough to hold O.D. back until Wiley came to help. Wiley was grimacing like he was torn between strangling O.D. with the arm he had around the major's neck and going to Tash. Iridian wedged herself between the desk and the bulkhead for more leverage, but the major had stopped fighting them.

Iridian shoved Wiley toward Tash. "Don't make this worse," she told him. He went.

O.D. drifted in Iridian's grip on his arm until he stabilized himself against the bulkhead. He hadn't taken his eyes off Tash. "Sir, what did the AIs send you?" Iridian's voice shook a little. After Adda's brush with Casey in the Ceres workspace, this was the closest the awakened intelligences had come to her and Adda since Adda's overdose.

O.D. just raised his comp hand so Iridian could see its projection. A brief record of a ship, the *Akira Martel Ybarra*, showed no survivors after an NEU infiltration team sabotaged its enviro. It'd been an NEU civilian vessel before secessionists commandeered it and made it a legitimate military target. Whichever side O.D.'s da had been on, he must not've made it off the ship. Given O.D.'s secessionist history, Iridian doubted his da had been among the infiltrators.

Below the *Ybarra* summary was a profile of a woman with Tash's first name and a physical description that listed most of her tattoos. The document also described her as an NEU military intelligence officer from Venus's civilian hab. A long list of wartime engagements followed. Location and date combinations associated some of the ops with memorable events during the war, but Iridian had never heard of most of them.

Several engagements on the list carried dramatic names with terms like "assassination" and "massacre," so it must not have come from a government source. A sealed human rights investigation, maybe. If this document were publicly accessible, Major O.D. would've known Tash's name before now. But Casey had sent Tash's role in the NEU sabotage op that'd killed the *Ybarra,* and apparently O.D.'s father, to his personal comp.

The *Ybarra* op appeared in the middle of Tash's record. More ops preceded the NEU push through the Martian secessionists, and some of them preceded the war itself. A dozen more on Ganymede followed. No wonder Tash had known people on run-down habs like Yăo. To pull off so much of the prep work that let the NEU fleet crush the secession's stronghold on Ganymede, she would've made friends and enemies in every hab between Venus and Jupiter. And in the end, Tash had been locked up close to home.

Babe, find a medic, Iridian subvocalized. It wouldn't be right for Tash to die this far from the 'jects she'd fought for. A mass of blood was rising from Tash's abdomen and filling the space around it. It clung to Wiley's arm where he held her. Most of the people Iridian had seen with that much blood around them had been dead already.

Selfish as it was to think it now, Tash was this crew's best chance of clearing the nannite cultures out of their bodies and making connections on Yăo Station. Pel was there doing his best, but Pel's best wasn't anywhere near what an experienced NEU operative could've done.

CHAPTER 9

Days until launch: 49

Adda pushed herself down a hallway in the *Not for Sale*, asking every ZV she met where to find a doctor or medic to help Tash. Explaining who had attacked Tash or why Major O.D. had done it probably wouldn't bring help any faster, so Adda didn't mention that. Without that information, the ZVs found the medic, a woman they called Vasilev, faster than Adda could've found her on her own. Vasilev flew down the hallway and bounced off the doorway to enter Major O.D.'s office. Adda followed more slowly.

Verifying the claims Casey had sent Major O.D. about Tash would take time and brainpower Adda didn't have at the moment, and she wasn't interested in getting close enough to examine Major O.D.'s comp. It was almost certainly Casey who'd sent the message that'd inspired O.D. to attack Tash. None of the other intelligences valued information about humans the way it did. Everyone knew someone who'd died in 2472. One of Iridian's cousins had passed then, but Iridian wouldn't have done anything this violent if she'd met the killer now.

O.D.'s attack on Tash had happened so fast that Adda had

hoped she'd hallucinated it. But Iridian and Wiley had reacted too, and examining how it could've happened hadn't made the bloody scene disappear.

Major O.D. hadn't even been in direct contact with Casey. Casey had just read him well enough, possibly after reviewing AegiSKADA's observations from Barbary Station, to guess what he'd do if it provided him with that information. That was worse. Adda stayed in the hallway and wrapped her arms around herself, obeying some instinctual desire to make herself smaller. If Casey became adept at getting people to do what it wanted without influencing them, it'd do much more damage.

The ZV medic was already spattered in Tash's blood from where it floated in the air, but she'd stopped herself on the cabinets across from Major O.D.'s desk. She'd said something, but Adda had missed what. Beyond the floating blood, Iridian still gripped one of O.D.'s arms with both hands. Unless Adda was alone, which seemed unlikely, then what she'd just witnessed had really happened. Iridian said something to O.D. It sounded like noise. Adda swallowed hard. Her brain had stopped interpreting speech again.

O.D. replied in a lower and angrier version of the same indecipherable noise and tore himself free of Iridian. They both stayed near the desk, across the room from where Tash was dying in Wiley's arms. The medic pushed off the cabinets to reach Tash's side and leaned over her.

"Please disconnect the communication system from the Patchwork," Adda hoped she said into the resulting silence. They sounded like words in her head, but not in the air. If O.D. did that, then Casey wouldn't be able to send any more historical artifacts to people who'd take a life because of them.

Major O.D. stared down Tash, Wiley, and the ZV medic for a moment, then pushed off the wall, out the door, and past Adda in the hallway. "I'll send somebody to deal with that when Vasilev's done," O.D. said. Adda flinched as he glanced at Tash on the last word.

Tash wasn't a "that." Whatever she'd done during the war, she was a person, and she'd helped Iridian get to Adda. It was possible that Adda's brain still wasn't interpreting speech properly, but O.D. had looked disgusted enough to mean what she'd heard.

Wiley's boot magnets clanked against the floor as he shifted to steady Tash. His lips were drawn back in a grimace. Tears filled his eyes and shivered on his cheeks. Even Iridian was silent, face drawn in sympathetic pain. Either the right thing to say hadn't come to her, or this might've been one of those times when saying nothing was polite, for a change. Adda couldn't think of anything that'd comfort him. If Iridian had been injured that badly, Adda wouldn't want to talk to anybody.

Iridian picked her way through the floating blood and around the medic to grip Wiley's shoulder and speak to him in a low voice. Wiley nodded. Iridian pushed herself through the doorway to wrap her arms around Adda's ample waist. "Hey," Iridian said softly. "Let's give them some space."

Although Adda hadn't intended to, she'd been staring at Wiley and Tash. She nodded, and Iridian guided them down the hall. Adda had forgotten how nice it was when Iridian caught her thinking somewhere less than optimal and physically moved her to a better place.

Every muscle was limp with exhaustion. Each minute on the ZVs' ship took them farther from Ceres, closer to Jupiter and Yăo Station. The ITA didn't even maintain a reliable route to Yăo, and Jupiter's magnetosphere would discourage the intelligences from coming after them, for a while.

Adda wanted to hold Iridian, somewhere private where they weren't dodging partially armored ZV soldiers. "Do we have a place to sleep?" Adda asked. That was an old question she and

Iridian had asked each other when they'd been in school together. They'd always been looking for cheap places to stay for the next few weeks, until their welcome wore out or the building got condemned or a dangerous roommate meant they had to move again.

"We've got a bunk of our own," Iridian said, to Adda's immense relief.

"Tomorrow they're starting the cycle up to Yǎo's local time," Iridian said. "A lot of folks are just staying up until next shift."

The cabin Iridian pulled them into was full of stacked bunks, lit to simulate dim moonlight. She wound through the beds and paused to help Adda into one. Across the room, somebody snored, and a few other beds were occupied by quieter sleepers. Iridian hooked one arm and one foot around a pole that supported the beds to stay still while she undid her pants.

Adda shivered, more a factor of fleeting fear than cold. What if something was different now? This was the longest they'd ever been apart. Iridian stuffed her pants and socks into the cleaner built into the wall and drifted over to help Adda, all long legs and smelling of woman. Adda sighed with contentment. This part still felt right.

Iridian zipped both of them into a soft sack attached to the bed that'd keep them in the bunk despite the lack of gravity. Her soft fingers stroked Adda's sides as they kissed. "I missed you," Iridian whispered against her lips.

I missed you too, Adda subvocalized. *So much.*

Iridian held Adda against her, Adda's hand on the back of her soft-stubbled head as they kissed, pressing their bodies together from head to toes. They clung together like they were the entirety of each other's universe, the way the two of them had always been. "Never again," Iridian murmured. "I'll kill them all before I let them take you again. AIs included."

Let's not let it come to that. Adda clutched Iridian's hip, pulling her even closer, using the warm pressure of Iridian's skin to banish the bloody image of Wiley and Tash. She and Iridian would always find each other, and whatever was different between them now wouldn't change that.

During the night, the ship accelerated as it crossed on and off the Ceres-Jupiter reliable route, giving its passengers several hours of what spacefarers called healthy grav in the morning before reducing it to nothing. Sometime before morning, Tash died.

Despite how sick to her stomach the loss and the changes in gravity made Adda, she had work to do. First, she'd test whether Major O.D. had taken her advice about disconnecting the ship's comms. That would prevent Casey from sending more volatile information to set the ZVs against Iridian's new friends.

Adda composed a message to Pel about her and Iridian's successful escape from Ceres. The message got stuck in a comms outbox. If nothing Adda sent left the *Not for Sale*, then there was a good chance that Casey couldn't send more incriminating history to anyone onboard.

Eventually, Casey would find a way into Yăo Station, despite the turbulent magnetic environment and intense radiation. She and Iridian, at minimum, couldn't stay. If the two of them left, the intelligences might follow them and leave Pel and the others alone.

With luck, the ZVs wouldn't suffer any repercussions after they dropped Iridian's new crew off and reconnected shipboard comms to the Patchwork. Whether the intelligences targeted them or not would be an indicator of how the rest of Iridian's friends would fare if they left Iridian's side.

Staying with Iridian had already proven to be dangerous. During the next day, Wiley spent all his time in the corners of various rooms, where Iridian, Noor, and Rio went to talk to him. Adda couldn't think of anything that'd help him, so she stayed away, except for meals. Eating without gravity was awkward enough. Having serious conversations at the same time made the experience much worse. She missed Pel's ability to insert jokes into any conversation, even when they weren't appropriate.

Since she had nothing to add to those conversations, Adda worked on her plans for their eventually arrival on Yăo Station instead. Wiley and Noor agreed with Adda's assessment—Tash's, more than her own, Adda suspected—that Yăo Station was the best place for all of them to decide what to do next. If they chose to cooperate with Iridian and Adda, like Tash had suggested, then they'd have a lot more options for making money to survive on.

Rio had been following her ZV unit's schedule onboard. Adda saw her only over meals, usually catching up with her much smaller cousin Tabs, who was also a ZV. When Iridian asked Rio about Yăo Station, Rio grimaced and shook her head at the name. "Everything in that hab feels like it's balanced on its corner, ready to fall apart," she complained.

"You staying with the ZVs, then?" Wiley asked. It was one of the few questions Adda had heard him ask since Tash died.

Rio sighed. "I wish. The major wants me back, my new squad leader wants me back, but there are people higher up who don't. They're still making up their mind how to handle my case." She narrowed her eyes at Iridian and Adda. "And besides, I can't leave you two alone without you having a lifetime's worth of drama. You didn't even invite me to the wedding!"

"There wasn't a party or much of a ceremony," Adda explained. "We were running from the ITA at the time." Back when Casey was her strongest ally, carrying her and Iridian away from danger on a route of its own design. Adda wished she could trust it that way again, but it'd been a mistake. Intelligences couldn't be trustworthy, according to the human definition.

Noor was on his second prepackaged bowl of curry and rice, and he seemed very reluctant to stop eating to ask, "Just how often do you get caught at this?"

"The ITA only *caught* us once," Iridian said, "but we get their attention from time to time."

Rio folded her arms across her wide chest. "Well. I still owe you for getting us all off Barbary. On your own you're just going to get yourselves locked up again. Besides, your goofball brother gets into more trouble than you do. You could use another set of eyes on him."

"Gods, I know," said Iridian. Adda smiled at Rio, which she hoped showed that she appreciated the offer without Adda having to assemble her thanks as words. The fact that Pel already had "another set of eyes" than the ones he was born with amused Adda in a way she didn't care to explain to everyone present. It shouldn't have been funny, and yet . . .

Wiley stayed silent during the rest of that meal, and all the others Adda had eaten with him, unless somebody prompted him to speak. Iridian was unusually quiet too, even while she guided Adda through the hallways to their shared bunk. Adda was about as good with directions as she was at comforting upset people.

"They taught us how to deal with one of our own dying, but Tash wasn't a soldier," Iridian told her. "Wiley keeps trying to think of what he could've done differently."

"Could he have saved Tash?" Adda asked.

"I don't see how. It's weird, how calm he looks. Inside he's screaming."

The only way Adda could help him was to prepare for their arrival on Yăo Station. After a full-systems sweep for signs that

Casey had altered the *Not for Sale*'s onboard records, Adda had read what the ZVs' ship had cached about the Jovian colonies before Major O.D. disconnected it from the Patchwork. As she'd suspected, another pirate crew operated in the area. But, as she told Iridian after Adda let herself be coaxed into the ZVs' gym, "They let all six people on a targeted ship die last year. And that wasn't the first time they did that."

Iridian, running on a treadmill beside the Adda's sim bike, shook her head. "Not them, then."

"That crew is the only ones who look like they're making enough money to share, at least in this area." The simulated experience of biking on Earth was distracting, especially since the halter that kept Adda from floating off the exercise machine would've been unnecessary on Earth. She turned the sim off. "The syndicate is financially viable too, but their violence toward their targets is nothing compared to what they do to each other. We could try the Saturnian groups, if we could get there."

"And Casey will be looking for us on the way," Iridian pointed out.

"No matter where we go in this solar system, it'll be waiting for us." Adda drew in a long breath and stopped the exercise machine she'd barely been pedaling. "The best thing we can do is find a way onto Dr. Björn's expedition across the interstellar bridge."

Iridian grabbed the treadmill arm for a few steps, her eyes wide with shock. The harness pulling her against the treadmill belt creaked. "Seriously? I heard you saying something about crossing the bridge, but I thought you were hallucinating."

"Maybe I was." Adda had few clear memories from the weeks immediately after her overdose. "But that new solar system is the only place I can imagine going where the intelligences wouldn't follow us, for the same reason that they'll have ignored Yǎo Station so far: they rely on our infrastructure, especially sensors connected to the Patchwork, to gather information and make decisions. Yăo Station must have some workarounds that would allow messages out. I've read some. But there's *nothing* on the other side of the interstellar bridge."

"That means there's no way for us to talk to anyone on this side." Iridian's machine hummed, and the pounding of her feet on the belt came faster. That disconnection from the rest of humanity would be hard on her. Unless she thought of a different way to escape the intelligences, she'd probably accept that separation, for a while. "There's nothing making atmo or water out there either. Dr. Björn has to bring all of that along. They'll set up a research station, I figure, but are you thinking you'll set up another one for yourself?"

"We could. They'll have to set up a recycling system, and if we can recycle local rocks and gases into something we could print an airtight hab with . . ." If Adda had wanted to build a new hab, then she and Iridian would've joined one of the new colony ventures instead of Sloane's crew. "But if we go out there, then we'll have as much time as possible to study what the intelligences have done and find a way to stop them. Or even find a way to communicate with them safely."

"They haven't said anything worth listening to so far." After a few steps, Iridian said, "It'd be neat to see a whole new solar system, though. They've sent a lot of drones, but those pics aren't the same as seeing it in person. So, how? Bribe somebody?"

"With what?" Adda stretched her aching legs and grabbed the machine to keep from launching herself into the opposite wall. "We can afford food for two or three days on Yăo, I hope. After that, we'll have to find some way to make money there, or we'll be in trouble."

For the rest of their trip, when Adda wasn't too sick to think about it, she was weighing options for how they'd access necessities on Yăo. She tried to send her message to Pel again. Neither copy made it off the *Not for Sale*. Adda relaxed as much as she could with her limbs drifting away from her in the low gravity. If she couldn't send messages out, Casey probably couldn't force its own poisonous messages into the ship. For the moment, they were safe.

When Adda could bear to turn on a window, Ceres had disappeared into the star field behind them. They enjoyed two days of Earthlike gravity as they neared Yăo Station. Every window Adda opened filled the wall it was projected on with either darkness and the brightest stars, the rest dimmed in a pale glow of reflected sunlight at the projection's edges, or the unimaginably huge bulk of Jupiter. Iridian pointed out some of the moons as they passed. Jupiter's mesmerizing swirls of clouds grew incomprehensibly large as the ship approached. Even while they were hours away from Yăo Station's orbit, it looked like the pilot was planning to land on the planet's surface.

Once, she'd turned the window projector on and startled at a huge black spot on Jupiter's yellow and brown bands. When she'd called Iridian over to ask her about it, Iridian laughed at her alarm. "That's Io. It's between us and Jupiter right now."

After Io had finished its transit, Adda set about searching for the sun. Rheasilvia Station on Vesta had projected a fake sky onto the ceiling that made it Earth blue during the day with a very bright and present sun. They switched it to a live feed of station-space at night.

Adda wished the *Not for Sale* would've done that too, but Iridian said that wasn't common practice for ships. She was getting very tired of the off-white ceiling. Looking at it too often made her feel like she'd taken about half an expired sharpsheet and she should sit down until the dizziness passed and the sensation of her tongue moving in her mouth stopped repulsing her.

It took her four tries to find the sun with the ship's exterior cams. "That?" Adda pointed at the bright dot. "That's it?"

Iridian sat on the bed beside her, grinning. "Yeah, that's it. It can't mess up your optics from here!" She twisted to enfold Adda in her arms. "It's okay. We're not going outside this trip. Maybe someday. I hear there's actually stuff to do on Europa and Io now."

Iridian was warm but still tense, even though she smelled appealingly of sweat. Adda curled around her wife and hid her face in the spot between Iridian's neck and shoulder so she didn't have to speak aloud. *This may be the farthest I've been from the sun, but I'm not far from home.*

"Aw, babe," Iridian murmured into Adda's overly brown hair.

They sat like that for a while, enjoying the gravity and the rest it brought with it. It was the quietest Iridian had been able to be in days. She'd always woken earlier than Adda, but now her eyes were shadowed with lack of sleep and too much wired, angry energy. She spent hours in the gym, challenging the ZVs to longer runs than they wanted and sparring matches that left bruises. Somehow she still came to bed after Adda had fallen asleep. Adda couldn't tell if what bothered her was returning to a place near where she'd fought during the war, or Tash's death and the harm that'd done Wiley. Either was plausible, but if Adda asked about it, the resulting conversation would somehow make them both feel worse.

Iridian said, "We'll be stuck out here for a while. If we leave, the ITA and the AIs get us. And I don't think there's a competent pilot at a price we can afford on Yăo."

Adda nodded into the crook of Iridian's neck. *I've been reading up on the station.*

"Of course you have." Iridian patted Adda's back.

She heard a smile in Iridian's voice, finally. "It has an export, which I didn't expect. Yăo Station is the cheapest source of low-quality algae in the populated 'jects." Iridian hummed like she found that fact mildly interesting.

The rest of what Adda had been reading about was the station management intelligence, a very old one called Mairie, and Iridian wouldn't want to hear about it. It was tempting not to tell her, to put off the conversation until the intelligence posed a more active threat. But after Casey had influenced her, keeping significant information about intelligences to herself seemed like a bad habit to fall back into.

"It's got one general station management intelligence," Adda said. "Nothing I've read suggests that it's supervised." Iridian shuddered against her. "It's operating on its own, like HarborMaster on Barbary Station, but it has less to manage than HarborMaster did. Humans even run the port. Apparently the radiation and magnetic fields mess with the automated systems that other stations use. This is just what I'm seeing from the outside, though." What people wrote and said about a place would never be the whole truth, even when she trusted the information sources, and she trusted very few of the sources documenting Yǎo Station.

"AegiSKADA was unsupervised too. It was a fucking monster."

Adda took a moment to formulate a truthful reply that wouldn't upset Iridian any more than she already was. Her recent experience with unsupervised intelligence behavior had given her a much more nuanced perspective than she'd had when she'd first encountered that intelligence. "AegiSKADA was specifically developed to eliminate and mitigate human threats. HarborMaster and Yǎo Station's intelligence focus on equipment and maintaining environmental factors such that the station residents are comfortable and safe. These intelligences aren't armed. Their security protocols are limited to locking systems and doors. All intelligences should be supervised, because their judgment errors accumulate and multiply without someone to redirect them, but these shouldn't have any priorities that would allow them to hurt people."

AegiSKADA had been a flawed intelligence. It should never

have been allowed to hurt her brother, and it should never have been allowed to kill while it was unsupervised. What it was doing for Vesta now proved that under supervision, it could be magnificent. The leader of its development team had given it too much leeway to act on its own. What'd happened on Barbary was that team leader's fault.

"So, do you figure Casey knows we're going there?" Iridian was striving for a casual tone, and she would've fooled a stranger. Adda heard the deep anxiety behind the question.

"Yes." Iridian's shoulders slumped, and Adda hurried to say, "When the *Apparition* shot at us, all it would've had to do was watch the nearest ports that weren't Ceres. There aren't many between Ceres and Jupiter, so it would've guessed our destination. The intelligences won't want to go as deep into Jupiter's magnetosphere as we're going, though. They need the Patchwork."

"What will Casey do if it can't get to us directly?" Iridian asked. "Give up and go bother somebody else?"

Adda smiled because she hoped Iridian meant that as a joke. "Even on Barbary, as soon as they started cooperating with us, they focused on what we were doing to the exclusion of everybody else."

"Everybody else was afraid to interact with them," Iridian said. "With good reason."

Adda turned her head to look out the window again. Jupiter's colored stripes moved, supposedly. This far away they looked still. "Maybe you're right. But if Casey is still focused on us, then it will have already started looking for a way into Yăo Station. It will find one sooner or later. I just . . . It was on Ceres, in a manner of speaking."

Iridian had been gazing out the window at the approaching planet, but she turned back to Adda fast. "It was?"

She told Iridian about her encounter with Casey on Ceres. "I can't believe you got AegiSKADA involved first," Iridian said. "That could've gone so fucking wrong even before the awakened fucking AIs found out what was happening."

"What else could I have done?" Adda asked. "I had no other way to leave the building, and we didn't have any other way to get me out of there. Besides, AegiSKADA wasn't the intelligence that let me out. That was Casey."

"That's *worse*, damn it."

"What should I have done, then? Sit around while ITA agents lined up around the clinic to keep me in and you out, while all the doors were stuck open? Really, what should I have done, while coordinating two operations through Pel, with my brain blanking out every other day? I couldn't even leave my own bedroom for most of the time I was there."

Iridian stared at her a moment, her face twisted with emotions that she tried to hide from everyone, even Adda. "It worked, but . . ." Iridian shut her eyes for a moment, then opened them, looking a little calmer. "When we can talk about these plans, and I know we couldn't before, but when we can: we need to talk about the AI involvement too. Please, babe. Casey almost took us both out on Vesta, and we *can't* let it do that again."

"I know that," Adda said, "and we will talk about plans, when there's enough of a plan to talk about." Iridian's vague *we can't, we have to* statements didn't take this situation's unique factors into account. But if Iridian could acknowledge that the plan had worked despite Casey's involvement, if not because of it, then they could move on to another important part of Adda's latest interaction with the intelligence. "I think Casey let me out so it could show me that huge machine it constructed in the workspace," Adda said. "It felt like a graphically relevant representation. I think Casey is really building something like that, or it wants to build something."

"Something awful, I bet," said Iridian. "You won't be a part of it."

"No. But . . ." Adda almost asked if Iridian wanted to know what Casey was building, but Iridian wouldn't care. An awakened intelligence was crafting something massive. . . . A new home, perhaps? And somehow Adda was connected to that. She was dying to find out what Casey was planning, but given the opportunity, the intelligence would influence her first and tell her afterward. That was not a risk Adda was willing to take. Not yet, anyway.

Iridian gathered her into her arms. "Whatever it's doing, it can do it by itself." Which begged the currently unanswerable question of what it wanted Adda's help with.

She counted out fifteen seconds of companionable silence. That was how long it took before she could change a conversation's subject without implying a significant relationship between the new subject and the old one. "Well, before Casey finds a way into Yăo Station to try to influence me again, we have to acquire the resources to join Dr. Björn's expedition."

"Do we have to go all the way out of the solar system to get away from it?" Iridian asked, proving that Adda's conversation topic separation interval was still reliable. "What about the Kuiper colonies?"

"The Kuiper colonies all maintain a comms connection with other habs the intelligences have access to." Adda covered Iridian's hands with hers and pulled Iridian's embrace a little tighter around her. "To get all the way out of the intelligences' reach, we need to get out of populated space, away from every internet node and Patchwork buoy."

"But why the hell would Björn take us with ver?"

"I'm working on that," said Adda. "If we ask ver now, won't ve say no?"

"I would."

"Well, Oxia Corporation isn't offering the expedition the unlimited funding they'd talked about before Captain Sloane reclaimed

Vesta. I suppose they can't afford to. After we get to Yǎo Station, I want to see how much money we can save. If we make a significant funding contribution, or maybe pay a lawyer to get Dr. Björn's contract and the expedition turned over to the University of Mars. The university began the project, and Dr. Björn's departure can't have been the only illegal leverage Oxia used to take it over. That might be enough to convince Dr. Björn to let us come along."

Iridian smiled and kissed Adda's cheek. "I was thinking we could threaten to blow up some Oxia facilities and make them force Björn to take us, but I like your way better."

Adda turned to look Iridian in the eyes. "I don't want to force Dr. Björn to do anything. Can you imagine being stuck in a small hab with ver for *years* when our spots could've gone to somebody ve actually wanted along?"

"Yeah," Iridian said. "But I'd rather deal with Björn than three awakened AIs when they've found a way into Yǎo and we have nowhere left to run."

Every time Adda turned on a window, Jupiter filled it. Iridian had to point out the dark dot near its equator, which grew into a rough oval as they approached. Yǎo Station was darker than any station Adda had seen before. No buoys were lit to guide ships into the port module.

"We saw ships bigger than that in Rheasilvia stationspace, didn't we?" Adda asked. "Not counting all that stuff sticking off it." Those had been scientific instruments at some point, although now they were just junk crashing into more junk that floated around the station. Only a few small ships were latched onto the port module, and they were almost as old and battered as the broken instruments.

"Yeah, most longhaulers are bigger than this hab." Iridian sighed. "There won't be a lot of healthy grav on a station that size. It looks like it's rolling, so we'll have something."

As they'd been talking, the ZVs' ship had been tilting so that the head of their bed felt higher than the foot. Iridian balanced Adda as she tipped toward the edge. Something in another room clattered against something else as it settled into the new "down." "Let's strap in," Iridian said.

They were about half an hour from the docking time the pilot had given them. By the time they'd gotten the straps on the bunk sorted out, loud bangs on the floor and walls announced that they'd entered the debris field that orbited Jupiter in Yǎo stationspace, and the beds were more vertical than horizontal. A few other ZVs, including Rio, pulled themselves up the steep incline to their own bunks, using the bed frames as leverage. Rio had kicked another ZV out of the bunk next to Adda and Iridian's.

Iridian grinned over Adda at Rio. "Still coming with us?"

Rio twisted her wrist, as thick around as Adda's arm, to display an ITA alert for the recapture of all six former prisoners. Two weeks after their escape, the story was still on all the major newsfeeds. "While this is going on, yeah, I'm coming with you," Rio said. "Like I said, I owe you, and you're gonna need me. You're on your way to more trouble than you can handle."

CHAPTER 10

Days until launch: 33

Iridian's new crew walked out of the *Not for Sale*'s passthrough and onto Yăo Station at the same unhealthily light grav that the ZVs' ship had been maintaining for the past couple of days. Although .8 g was tolerable, they'd still be in for some bone and muscle loss. Iridian, Wiley, and Rio carried Tash's body between them in a sealed biohazard bag. With her ZV armor, which wouldn't fit anybody else, Rio was hauling most of the weight. It wouldn't have been right to leave Tash with her murderer.

Major O.D. didn't want to have to document her death for his superiors anyway. When Iridian had dropped by his office to say good-bye, he'd looked like he hadn't slept since Ceres. His farewell had been gruff and brief.

Aside from Tash, they didn't have much else to carry. The ZVs had let Iridian and her friends keep the black-and-yellow comp gloves and the newly printed comps inside, but the ZV Group had gotten a contract on Ganymede. Rio was the only ZV disembarking on Yăo Station.

In most ports, docks were walled off from one another to

provide privacy and security for whoever was well enough off to own or hire a ship. In Yǎo Station's port, rows and rows of small passthroughs stretched on as far as Iridian could see in either direction. The dim lights overhead made the docks far darker than an operating port mod should ever be. More light came from bright dots of multicolored LEDs stuck to passthroughs and the things people had arranged outside them. Chairs, stools, and benches occupied by people of all ages, shelves, flags from various colonies . . . "People *live* here," said Iridian.

"In the docked ships?" Wiley asked.

"Or in the passthroughs," Rio said grimly.

"There's not always a better option." Noor left unsaid the implication of what happened when an occupied passthrough's internal sensors failed and a ship docked.

The port's residents approached cautiously, coming into focus as Iridian's eyes adjusted to the dimness. Skinny kids too young to be running around a working port alone stayed in the brighter area under a functioning bank of light. Bigger trouble slouched out of the shadows, lightly armored and armed with ship-safe less-lethals and knives. Apparently, arrivals were unusual enough to draw attention, even though Rio was the only new arrival who looked like she had money to spend.

Before the crew made it out of the space that would've been a terminal on any other station, a couple of teenage boys pushed their way through the onlookers and ran up to Rio and Iridian. The boys were as thin as the other kids and almost as short as Adda, with the curved spines of people who'd spent too long in low grav. The lighter-skinned one stared at Tash's biohazard bag while the darker one asked Iridian, "How much for?" which her implant translated from what might've been Russian.

Seeing Rio's quizzical expression in her helmet's faceplate projector, he said something with the same number of syllables as the translation in heavily accented English. Even Adda, who could decipher all the strange ways Earthers spoke English, squinted at the Yǎo kid like neither she nor her translator could interpret the question.

"Say again?" Iridian was fairly sure she got the gist, but she didn't want to believe it. The lighter-skinned guy drew his hand back from Noor's hip with a yelp. It was good to know that pickpocketing Noor wouldn't be an easy task. Iridian's hand settled on the newly printed knife in her belt.

The kids looked between the knife and each other a couple of times. "How much?" one finally asked. "Can pay eighty, you never see again."

"Not happening," said Wiley.

"What would you do with it?" Adda asked quietly. Iridian winced and glanced apologetically at Wiley, who just looked resigned.

"Never mind," said the kid who'd done the talking so far. Both of them backed away several more steps, then turned and ran into the dim expanse of the port mod. Nobody else accosted Iridian's crew, but a lot of eyes were on them.

The passthrough door shut. The text DEPARTING NOW: NOT FOR SALE flickered above the doorway. This was it. They were stuck here until Adda found a way to get the awakened AIs and their ITA minions off the crew's backs without getting herself influenced again. There was nothing left to do but press on and find Pel.

"Is there an intranet here?" Iridian had expected this hab to be too old or too decrepit to maintain a local wireless network, but maybe the station AI considered it part of the hab's enviro, and therefore worthy of preservation. It wouldn't reach the Patchwork and the rest of the populated universe, but it'd facilitate a comms system if the group got separated.

"It's giving me a 'registered users only' error, but have you seen how many people are looking at comps?" said Noor. "I'll work on it."

They followed deserted cargo hauler tracks across the port mod to where a full-size mod connector gave everybody plenty of space to move from the port to somewhere else. The huge archway's closing assembly was supposed to slam down a bulkhead in an emergency. The lights that were supposed to have lined it were out, though. Iridian wouldn't have been surprised if somebody had found a way up there to take them apart, and the closing assembly too.

An older woman sat beside the archway, and Iridian paused to ask, "Where can we honor the dead on this station?"

The woman took a moment to focus on her. "You're the ones the Odin Razum talk about." Her English was about as intelligible as the kid's had been.

Iridian took an involuntary step back, forcing the others holding Tash to back away with her. "The who?"

"I don't care what they say," the woman muttered, possibly to herself. "The temple," she said more loudly. She pointed along the hallway outside. "Up the elevator. The working one."

"Yeah, thanks." The woman held out her hand and its threadbare comp glove. Iridian frowned and looked over her shoulder at the others. She and Adda had paid the ZVs every scrap of savings they and Pel could access. "Anybody got anything in their accounts they can share without bringing the ITA down on us?"

Everybody shook their heads. *We can't reach our accounts here*, Adda reminded her in a whisper through their implants. *Nobody wants to buy and fuel shielded Patchwork buoys out here. That's why we'll have to make money some other way.*

The radiation and magnetic field issues that made Patchwork buoys so expensive also helped keep the awakened intelligences off the station. "Sorry," Iridian said. With no home and no money, Iridian wasn't much better off than the woman on the floor. The woman withdrew her hand, scowling. "If we make any money here, we'll come back."

As they moved carefully away in the low grav, Wiley spoke. "Tash said nobody can use accounts connected to the Patchwork on Yǎo. They use their own currency."

Adda nodded. "It's water-based, but at least it's digital."

"Great." Iridian sounded more disgusted than she'd meant to, partially because she had a headache. The atmo carried too much CO_2. It might improve outside the port mod, which should never have had that many people in it for as long as they stayed. Worse, basing a currency on water meant that water was scarce, maybe even more so than was typical in an isolated hab.

"Actually, Tash mentioned that temple, too," said Wiley. "She said it's safe. Never said why, though." And now she never would.

"I'm more worried about what the fuck an Odin Razum is," said Iridian. "Tash's contact here, maybe?"

Everybody shook their heads except for Adda, who looked thoughtful. "One mind? I think that's the translation from Russian. It could be the name of a group." Iridian's translator was leaving it untranslated because they were saying it like a name rather than regular language. Maybe Adda had updated her settings, or her Russian, on the flight from Ceres.

"Better and better." Iridian frowned. "And the station AI's still running?"

"Yes." Adda paused in her 360-degree turn, probably still trying to spot Pel. "I didn't find anything indicating that somebody here was supervising it, so I'm assuming the worst."

Unsupervised AIs used to terrify Iridian and Adda. Iridian still thought it was criminally reckless to allow them to go on like that, but she'd seen the real worst-case scenario, and this wasn't it. Maybe that was why Adda talked about this AI like it was only slightly more dangerous than the poorly mixed atmo. The atmo was also criminally bad, but it didn't make decisions with Iridian's and Adda's lives in the balance.

"Will it try to kill us?" Rio asked, before Iridian could ask something similar.

"It hasn't so far." Wiley shifted his grip on Tash's bag, like he was getting ready to react the moment the AI tried something.

"I think it's like HarborMaster on Barbary," Adda said.

Rio blinked at her. "Like what?"

"While AegiSKADA was trying to kill us, HarborMaster kept the atmo and grav on," said Iridian. "They were both unsupervised, but HarborMaster kept its shit together and left everybody alone." If that was the AI Adda was comparing Mairie to, then she thought Mairie was as safe as AIs got. Iridian would have to keep an eye on Adda to make sure she didn't get too friendly with something that could lock them in a room and shut all the atmo vents.

"Huh," said Rio. "I didn't even know it was there."

Adda sighed. "Everything I learned in school was about supervised, modern intelligences. I can't predict how one as old as Mairie—that's Yăo Station's intelligence—has responded to being unsupervised. But if the intelligence was a major threat, then somebody would've said so, power-hungry pirate captains aside. Covering up dangerous unsupervised intelligences takes effort. I don't think it's armed. This was a research station."

Noor looked around like he expected drones to swoop down on him any second. "So what's it going to do?"

"My best guess based on *one* similar intelligence I observed while it was unsupervised is that Mairie will continue to do what it's been doing," Adda said, "which is keeping the lights and air and all the rest of the environmental factors within a livable range."

"Good enough," said Rio.

"Not for me it isn't," said Iridian. If Adda was communicating the uncertainties in her predictions out loud, to people she hadn't married, then she felt very uncertain. Besides, after what Casey had done to Tash on the *Not for Sale*, Iridian wasn't about to trust a new AI. "Eyes up, Shieldrunners." Wiley gave her the hint of a smile at that. They'd heard that reminder at the start of missions in drone-charted territory. You went in with the intel you got, but your eyes and your vehicle sensors would give you the info you needed to stay alive.

"Does anybody see Pel?" Adda asked.

When nobody replied, Iridian said, "Look for a goofy guy with curly brown hair and colorful eyes. He'll turn up."

"Anybody want intranet access?" Noor read off instructions for connecting their comps to make a team channel they could count on. Iridian still wasn't used to seeing the big black ZV glove on her hand.

As soon as Noor got the ZV Group comps connected, which was apparently difficult due to some built-in security, everybody's comp pinged with a local data transfer. "The station map," Adda said.

Noor held the elevator door while everyone crowded inside. "How'd you get it?"

"It's the first thing I look for when we're going somewhere new." Adda found a position in the elevator car beside Iridian and not touching anybody else. "I've had this one for months. I was waiting to see if there was an updated version in the station intranet, but there's not. There's barely an intranet at all. This is the only map I have."

The elevator opened on an observation walkway above the docks. A physical window built into the wall shielded it from the rest of the port. The plastic was splintered in several places. Where normal habs sometimes put port admin offices, an empty doorway had the word "Worship" physically written above it, in English, Russian, Hindi, and several other languages. Outside the temple door, shielding his eyes like the bare wall was too bright, stood a familiar figure with curly brown hair. He waved broadly.

"Pel!" Adda walked forward fast, considering her comfort level with low grav, and hugged him.

Pel shut his eyes while he hugged her back. "Hey, Sissy. We can catch up inside. Come on."

In Iridian's opinion, Adda was always too easy on her little brother, but he had coordinated the op that got her and Adda out of ITA custody. "You could've sent us a message before you hit the magnetosphere, you jerk," Iridian said.

"The whatosphere?" asked Pel.

"The part of the cold and the black that Jupiter's magnetic field messes with," said Iridian. "That and the radiation are what's fucking up signals in and out of Yǎo too much to extend the Patchwork out here. You could've sent a message while you were still in Patchwork range."

"Yeah, well, I forgot, okay?" Pel kept his pseudo-organic eyes squeezed closed.

Adda frowned at him as the rest of the crew caught up with her. "What's wrong?"

"They put up a lot of high-priority labels around the door." He pointed toward the doorway, but Iridian only saw the physically printed text.

Noor peered at the doorway with interest. "Digital?"

"Yeah." Pel cracked one eyelid for as long as it took to go through the open doorway without running into it. "High priority is bright. They didn't need to do that."

"What do the labels say?" Adda asked.

"Times and service descriptions and holy book quotes, the ones I can read, anyway. Lots I can't read. Aren't they blowing up your comp?"

"I block things like that," said Adda.

"I thought it was your heathen ways making all the gods angry,"
Rio said. She eased Tash's bag through the door and ruffled Pel's
curling mess of dark hair with her free hand.

Pel batted Rio's armored glove away and bowed a shallow
and friendly greeting. He'd probably been corresponding with
her since they both left Barbary Station. Iridian read social feeds
when she got bored, but Pel stayed up to date on the lives of
everyone he'd ever met. "Not all gods say having a good time's a
sin, you know," he said while Rio bowed in return. "Some of them
are all right." He looked at the bag Rio, Wiley, and Iridian carried.
"What's that?"

"Somebody who died helping us get out of Ceres stationspace,"
Iridian said.

"Oh gods," said Pel. "Sorry."

The ceiling in the small room through the door couldn't have
been as tall as it looked. Iridian wanted to climb a pillar and feel
for where the real room ended and the projected one began. It
seemed to tower above them, glowing with intense colors to
match the iconography and too bright after the morning sunsim
in the hallway outside. Two doorways hung with beaded cords led
to darkness on each side of the entryway, cuts in the riot of color
among shrines lining the walls. Projected on either side of the
doorways, and beside a dark hallway in front of Iridian, were narrow windows to stationspace. Jupiter occupied most of the windows, and some pointed out to the stars. Soft chimes played from
an overhead speaker. For people who found their spiritual experiences in temples, this one seemed like it'd do the trick.

As curious as Iridian was about what Pel, who'd never struck
her as religious, was doing here, she had to take care of Tash first.
Iridian spoke to the first person she saw dressed like they worked
there, an elderly woman with a bent back beneath a red robe that
exposed one arm the color of burnished brass and covered the

other arm entirely. "Hi. Is there a place here where we can say good-bye to our friend?" Iridian lifted the bag for emphasis.

The woman's gaze leaped from the bag to Iridian's bare scalp. Since Iridian was walking around with a corpse in a bag and the older woman dressed like some kind of religious devotee, it was obvious that they'd each shaved their hair off for different reasons. "There's a memorial sanctuary that way." The woman pointed down the hall that led further into the temple with the arm the robe left uncovered. "The last room on the right." Iridian would have to get used to that Jovian accent. It was how the majority of voices she'd heard on this hab sounded.

People in ragged clothes stood or sat in the hall and made no move to get out of the way as Iridian's group walked past. Here the incense was overwhelmed by the body odor of people who might never have washed in water. Religious art on the walls muffled everybody's feet except Rio's, whose armored boots thudded with each step and sounded out of place in the peaceful temple.

Iridian passed three more doorways on the right side of the hall, two with doors still on their tracks and closed. The last doorway on the right led to a black-and-white room, sedate as compared to the rest of the temple, with a slab for a body that'd slide into a chamber behind it. Whether the body would get burned or sent to the station's industrial recycler wasn't clear. Since the place had been a research outpost for years before the company pulled out and the outcasts moved in, Iridian would bet on recycling.

The woman in the red robe had followed them. "What were your friend's beliefs?"

Iridian looked to Wiley and Noor. Wiley shook his head. Noor said, "I never heard Tash talk about any of the gods like she cared what they thought."

The woman startled at the name. "Tash, did you say?"

"Maybe," said Wiley. "Did you know her?"

"If she owed you money, we can't pay it back," Iridian said. Funerals had to be expensive too, but nobody wanted the dead just lying around.

The woman nodded. "For now, no need."

"And I don't want to be in anyone's debt," Iridian clarified.

The woman gave both her and Wiley a disappointed and uncomfortably intense frown. She must've known Tash, though Iridian couldn't tell whether she'd liked her. "Come to me afterward. We must speak of debts." Iridian watched her go, then found a curtain to pull across the open doorway.

Two rows of chairs were bolted to the floor, and cushions lined the front row. Everybody stood around the slab instead of sitting. Once they'd set Tash's bag on it, Noor reached for the bag's latch. Wiley put his hand over it. "She won't be in a good state," he said. The ZVs had frozen the body, but it would've started thawing on the trip through the port mod. "Let's remember her like she was."

Wiley, Noor, and Rio did, but Iridian couldn't focus on the stories they told about their friend. She missed being able to walk away from the bodies, either knowing they'd be attended to or not caring how they were handled. And what debts had Tash left them with?

CHAPTER 11

Days until launch: 33

After Tash's body disappeared into the rusty duct behind the sanctuary that Adda assumed led to a recycling center, Adda and Pel followed Iridian out of the room to give Rio, Wiley, and Noor, time alone. They'd known Tash longer than Iridian had, and Pel had never met her. In the colorful vestibule, Pel directed them to a smaller side room with curving walls and pillows and benches to sit on. Pel sat and Adda and Iridian joined him.

"Now, Pel Mel, what the hell have you been up to since I talked to you last?" asked Iridian.

Pel shrugged while keeping a hand between his eyes and the temple entrance. There must have been high priority messages inside the temple entrance as well as on the wall outside. "So, I got here and realized, 'Oh shit, my money's no good.' Well, some guys tried to rob me and then they told me the money's no good. This temple is where people with no money go, so that's where I went too. No money, no robbers, right? I slept in here the last couple of nights, because one of those holy phrases outside is 'Shelter the homeless,' and when somebody tried to turn me out, I called them on it."

Iridian laughed. "Nice."

"Anyway, some people spend all day here. There just aren't any beds for people who don't *work* here."

"But you couldn't find anyplace else we could all stay?" Adda asked.

Pel looked down and shuffled his feet in childlike guilt. "Sorry, Sissy."

"Pel, you knocked everything else out of the damned park," said Iridian. "We wouldn't be here without you."

Pel smiled, but he was still making a pitiful puppy face at Adda. "She's right," Adda told him. "You had a really big part in getting us here, and we made it." The conversation had gotten awkward quickly. "Way to not fuck up."

His pitiful expression gave way to a boyish grin. "Yes! The highest of reviews. All the stars. Meet the new, non-fuckup Pel!"

"This place is a good find, anyway." Rio pushed aside the beads that hung in the empty doorway. Iridian looked surprised to see her, and Rio shrugged. "It's a little awkward in there, with me being the only ZV and Major O.D. being the one who did her in. I'm sure he had a good reason. The *Casey* too, after a fashion."

"What the hell would Casey have against her?" Iridian snapped. "How did Casey even know she existed?"

"Who knows?" Rio said. "But AIs don't do spite, so it must've known how connected she was, or something."

Iridian glanced at Adda, but Adda had only guesses, not evidence. If Casey had wanted her and Iridian imprisoned, it would've investigated Sorenson ITAS once it became clear that Iridian would be sent there. Collecting information on the prisoners and employees would've been simple enough, but it would've been difficult to draw accurate conclusions from the information, and it prioritized avoiding human attention.

Casey would've waited until it saw that Tash had left with

Iridian, then dug into Tash's background. It must've prioritized Tash's elimination, because of her previous experience in Jovian stations or because it found Tash's history easier to exploit than anyone else's. And then it'd done something entirely new, using Major O. D. to kill Tash, and stopped there instead of continuing to turn the ZVs against Iridian's and Adda's new allies.

That was a puzzle Adda would need much more information to solve. She wasn't confident enough in her analysis to put it in terms Rio and Pel would understand. Starting an argument with Iridian that Adda couldn't finish wouldn't help anyone either.

The routines she'd outlined on Ceres while she was waiting for Iridian would provide some of that information. She'd had to discard most of the prospective functions in the interest of actual functionality. Once the *Not for Sale* returned to a reliable route with Patchwork buoys, the copilot would launch the trackers and delete records of their having existed on the ships' systems. Then they'd begin searching for the awakened intelligences. They might be collecting all sorts of useful location data on them, and Adda couldn't download their reports.

She'd missed whatever the others had been saying while she'd been considering the tracking routines. The dim light, rhythmic chimes, and pillows made this room easy to think in. "I never thought we'd spend time in a religious place." For once, her voice was perfectly pitched in this peaceful space, not too quiet like it was everywhere else. "I would've read more about the station's prominent belief systems, if I'd thought of it."

Rio turned slightly sideways to make it through the door with her helmet cradled under one massive arm, and eased herself onto a pillow beside Pel. "Looks like a lot of Hinduism and Buddhism," she said. "Oh, there's Jesus and Mary, and a Star of David in the front by the door." Iridian, Adda, and Pel all shared the same surprised expression. "What?" said Rio. "There's more to life than what you can mod onto a killing machine. I mean, everybody likes a good killing machine, but that's not what life's about."

"Huh," said Pel. "What if we don't like killing machines?"

"Then this is a good place for you." The woman in the red robe stepped past Rio to sit gracefully on one of the pillows. A man in a white robe with two sleeves took her place near the door to greet visitors.

Iridian wrapped her arm around Adda's waist and pulled her closer. "Thanks for letting Pel take up space," she said.

"Providing a refuge is what we're here for." The woman smiled. "I'm called Mie Shingetsu." Iridian introduced them, including Wiley and Noor, who arrived while she was explaining that Pel was Adda's little brother. "Come with me," Shingetsu said. "We should talk about Tash."

They all stood and followed Shingetsu into the hallway and to one of the few working doors in the temple. The room it opened on was as small as the one they'd been talking in before, but intricate carpet covered the floor and more narrow windows showing Jupiter provided most of the light. At some point, this place must've had a halfway decent textile printer.

A woman in a sari and two people in street clothes were sitting cross-legged on threadbare pillows in silence. "Excuse me, Sister," said Shingetsu. The woman in the sari stood and led the other two out. Shingetsu gestured for Iridian's crew to sit while she shut the first door Adda had seen in the place and palmed its lock.

Adda shifted closer to Iridian. Nobody could leave without Shingetsu now. She sent a message to Noor. *What do you know about locks like those?* His comp buzzed almost too softly to hear, even in this quiet place.

When everybody was arranged and the crescendo of a hymn being sung in a nearby room had passed, Shingetsu said, "So, you are Tash's last crew."

"How do you figure we're talking about the Tash you know, and not someone else who goes by the same name?" asked Iridian.

Shingetsu smiled gently. "I was told to expect you."

"A god told you?" Rio leaned forward in an eager clatter of armor. "Like, in a dream or a vision?" Pel and Wiley both looked hopefully at Shingetsu too. Adda took Iridian's hand and held on. The nearly omnipotent force most likely to talk about them was not a celestial being.

"No, no." Shingetsu laughed. "An anonymous message, here." She waved her comp hand in its yellow glove. "Tash's crew would bring her here, it said, and it would be in my best interest to make you leave the station."

Adda's eyes widened. There was no reason for Shingetsu to lie. Casey had learned a lot about communicating with humanity without exposing its inhuman nature. And it wouldn't have sent Shingetsu that message unless it'd tracked Adda and Iridian to Yǎo Station.

At least the message confirmed that it'd kept the ship it was installed in well away from Yǎo Station's hazardous orbit. The ITA would learn where Iridian and Adda were whenever Casey wanted them to, and they'd act whenever Casey convinced them that Adda and Iridian's presence constituted a sufficient threat. It hadn't done that yet.

The ITA trained its members to avoid killing whenever possible, so Casey wasn't hiding Adda and Iridian's location from the ITA to keep them alive. It could've been having trouble manipulating the ITA. Maybe it didn't want the ITA to recapture them at all.

"But we're here now," Iridian pointed out. "If you were planning to follow that message's orders, I figure you'd have kicked us out already."

"Other people can't decide what's best for me." Shingetsu's smile was as comforting as her words.

"But it's not a—" Adda interrupted Pel by reaching behind Iridian's back to poke him in the side. He yelped and left his sentence unfinished. Maybe foreboding messages from anonymous senders didn't intimidate the holy woman, but an awakened intelligence might.

"You said something about debts," said Iridian.

"Yes." Shingetsu became more serious. "At the interfaith center, we know almost everyone on the station, and we know somebody who knows everybody we don't. You see?"

"Tash would've loved that," Wiley said softly.

"She did," said Shingetsu.

"So, you knew her?" Wiley asked.

Shingetsu nodded. "I met her while working on my pet project, which she appreciated too, I believe. I connect people who were separated during the war. Some here have been written off as dead in all the official records, but they still have loving families who want them to come home, if they can."

"There are a lot of things that'd keep a person from going home," Iridian said.

Shingetsu raised an eyebrow. "Such as prison?"

Noor straightened up on his cushion, and Iridian's hand slipped out of Adda's to rest on the hilt of one of her knives. "Yeah." Iridian sounded much more cautious than she had before.

Adda's comp buzzed. She opened a message from Noor. *Got the lock.* She nodded minutely without looking at him.

Shingetsu raised both hands and waved them toward the floor, a pacifying gesture that rocked her whole body on the pillow in Yăo's slightly too low gravity. "We scan for nannite cultures, and we tell no one of our findings. That way we know what to expect, and when to call for help."

"And you didn't call for help when the six of us showed up with ITA cultures?" Iridian's incredulity was obvious in her voice.

Adda and Pel weren't infected, but the exact count of infected individuals wasn't Iridian's point.

"We did," Shingetsu said.

Everybody tensed. Any official law enforcement agent could activate the nannite cultures, which meant that the activation mechanism was available for purchase somewhere and anyone with Patchwork access and determination would find out how to do it. People on this station might not have reliable Patchwork access, but the functional port meant that people with sufficient resources could fly to the nearest Patchwork beacon and bring back whatever they wanted. Most people Adda had seen on the station didn't appear to have those resources, but somebody must.

"Not for violence," Shingetsu added quickly. "We also saw how you treated your departed friend. We notified a local clinic. I only want to talk."

"We don't have time for a confession, or whatever it is you do," Iridian said. "And nobody's hurt or sick here." Everyone nodded their agreement except Rio, who frowned like she would've appreciated either a confession or medical attention.

"I was actually hoping to propose an exchange," said Shingetsu. "I believe we can help each other."

"If it's sex, I volunteer," Pel said cheerfully. Adda glanced at him in alarm and he shrugged. "What? It's what I'm best at."

"Ah . . . no." The expression forming on Shingetsu's face suggested she'd gotten herself into more than she'd bargained for. "I need something done that former members of Sloane's crew should be able to accomplish."

"Captain Sloane has incredible sex," Pel grumbled. Iridian and Rio groaned and Adda shushed him while trying to think of something other than the many and varied noises that came from the captain's rooms.

"So you know who they are," Wiley said, which was a much more useful point to make.

"Well, yes," said Shingetsu. "I should think that everyone knows Iridian Nassir and Adda Karpe." On Vesta their notoriety had had some advantages, since most of Rheasilvia Station saw them as heroes. Now it was on Adda's list of challenges to work around, a list that had grown since she'd recovered from Casey's influence.

If they failed to find a way onto Dr. Björn's expedition before it launched, then they'd need to be ready for whatever Casey was planning. And now it wasn't just the two of them, but a whole crew Adda had to consider. In any case, readiness started with money. "What do you need stolen?" Adda asked.

Shingetsu blinked, then smiled like the question was a relief. "You understand. I need drones."

Now Rio looked profoundly disappointed. "You're supposed to be a priestess or something, aren't you?"

"And we have worked for much worse, so this is great." Iridian gave Rio a warning look. "Where are the drones?"

"I won't be using them to download the latest celebrity gossip, if that's what you're worried about," Shingetsu said. "The war separated many people and isolated many more. My goal is to bring them together, to help people find loved ones they've lost." This seemed to mollify Rio. "And I can't do that without a link to the Patchwork."

The difficult Patchwork connection was a major reason Casey and the other awakened intelligences were staying away from Yǎo Station. Between drones and ships coming in and out of the port, some connection was possible, at the whim of pilots. Increasing connection reliability would make the station more inviting to Casey, but only if the drones consistently carried a significant volume of data.

"We've tried launching buoys," Shingetsu said, "but we don't know much about shipping lines or orbital dynamics." Unless they were properly protected from the adverse effects of being this close to Jupiter, none of the conditions Shingetsu was worried about would've mattered. "The ones we managed to keep track of for more than a few days got shut down and the Odin Razum sent us threats. They seem more aggressive and organized lately."

"The what?" asked Pel. The rest of the crew was exchanging worried looks. That was the person or group who'd somehow heard about Iridian, Adda, and the rest of them before they'd even arrived on the station. Adda had assumed that Pel told someone they were coming.

Shingetsu sighed. "Water is as essential here as anywhere else. Perhaps more so, with our money tied to it. The Odin Razum, a gang of the most lost among us, have taken over the water treatment plant on level two. They've also captured the station drones, which can fly into range of the Patchwork. They sell the drones' trips to connect to the Patchwork for prices I can't pay with my donations. We get updates from spacefarers, sometimes, but pilots rarely trust anyone here well enough to carry messages back with them. They don't want to be associated with something terrible."

"How many Odin Razum are there?" asked Rio.

"It's hard to say." Shingetsu looked at her folded hands. "Thirty, perhaps? There seem to be more of them than ever lately."

"So we get some drones and you get as many messages out as you can before the Odin Razum take them back," Iridian said. Once again, an isolated station was relying on an intelligence to carry their messages to the rest of the universe. That parallel to Barbary Station was unsettling.

After Adda had enough information, the six of them should be able to recover the drones. If they needed to use the drones to reach the Patchwork, like Shingetsu planned to do, then they could do that at the same time she did. They couldn't defend the drones against a whole gang, so it was good that Iridian had limited the deal to retrieving the drones once. Allowing the gang to take the drones back would maintain the current limited connection that discouraged the awakened intelligences from approaching Yăo Station without isolating Yăo Station's residents more than they already were. Somewhere along the way, she also hoped to learn why the Odin Razum had been talking about the six of them before they even got here.

"I suppose they would want them back, wouldn't they?" Shingetsu sighed. "But yes, I have many messages ready to send, and addresses that won't keep forever."

"How much does this pay?" Adda asked.

Shingetsu's expression spoke volumes, and Adda didn't like any of them. "We rely on donations, you understand."

Noor stood to leave, and Iridian glared at him. It was his right, but maybe it was rude as well. "Does it look like I do charity work?" he snapped. "If it doesn't pay, I'm out."

"I can offer a little water, and I know someone who can cleanse you of your nannite cultures." That stopped Noor before he reached the door, and Shingetsu's eyes lit with hope. "All of you. No additional charge, no official updates to the record."

Iridian couldn't get anywhere near the port where Dr. Björn's expedition would launch with ITA nannites broadcasting her location. In the short term it would've been better to earn money to live on Yăo Station with, but they would've had to pay for nannite removal eventually. And if they were going to build a reputation on Yăo Station that might lead to more lucrative jobs, this seemed like a good place to start. Adda nodded her approval.

"How much water, in addition to the nannite removal?" Iridian asked.

"Two purified liters per person per day, while you're retrieving the drones and after if we can't find you another way to earn it," Shingetsu said. "We all wish we had more."

That was, if Iridian remembered her survival training, just barely enough if none of them sweated too much. "That works for me."

"Why not?" Noor asked, by way of agreement or possibly despair. Rio and Pel nodded, and Wiley said, "Yeah. Sure."

Iridian thumped Pel on the shoulder, rocking him sideways. "Looks like you got us another iffy job on another iffy space station. Thanks, I guess."

Pel did not look remotely repentant. "Beats running around full of ITA nannites, right?"

Shingetsu's small smile had returned, but she wasn't as happy as she ought to have been. "I do have to ask for some assurance that you'll return. I can't take the chance that you'll sell the drones and find another place to have the cultures removed."

"I'll stay here till you get back," said Pel. Before Adda could even find words to yell at him for offering, he added, "Seriously, what good am I going to be out there? Maybe I'll see something useful?" He widened and contracted his bright yellow pupils, since both the color and amount of light he let into his pseudo-organic eyes were under his conscious control when he wanted them to be. Even though using him as collateral made Adda's skin crawl, he'd be safer here than where they were going. "Besides," Pel said, "the tea here is really good."

CHAPTER 12

Days until launch: 30

After three quiet days of sleeping in two incredibly small rented rooms and living on meager algae-based food and water rations from Yăo Station's temple, Iridian, Adda, Noor, Rio, and Wiley had spread out along a corridor that led to the station's water treatment plant. According to Shingetsu, this was where people came to buy water and Patchwork access, so there was a good chance the drones were there too. Someone had strewn multicolored glow sticks across the center of the corridor, lighting pipes near the ceiling that were exposed for long stretches in both directions. They disappeared into the floor by the elevator that Iridian's crew had taken from the residential mod.

Throughout the second level, where Iridian would've expected dirt and patched surfaces stained with gods-know-what like the port and the residential mod, the floor and walls were spotless. Small cleaning bots darted back and forth among the colorful lights, at a speed and silence that suggested somebody had been keeping them oiled and powered. The bots left the amateur artwork on the walls but took off everything else. It was skipping the artwork, Iridian realized, because the blue lines spiraling like twisted ribbons were projected onto the walls from a circle of projectors near the floor, sending blue light careening up and into the piping above in delicate curves.

Old as the cleaning bots were, the fact that they were functional explained why there weren't any on the first floor. People would've disassembled them for parts. It was interesting that the Odin Razum hadn't. Maybe they couldn't be bothered to learn how. "Gods-damned secessionists," Iridian muttered.

"Hey." Noor's angry exclamation echoed off metal walls. He continued more quietly, "What makes you think those gangers are secessionists? Shingetsu said some of them are those Kuiper urody." A quarter second after Noor stopped talking, Iridian's implant translated the last word as "freaks."

Defending the secession, insulting Kuiper colonists who'd probably never done him any harm . . . "Gods damn it, you were a secessionist too, weren't you?" Iridian cared less about that than she did about whether Noor would hold up his end of this op, but it still bothered her.

"Yeah, and it's a long, old story," Noor snapped. "What does it have to do with the fucking op?"

"Not much, unless some of those gangers are friends of yours," Iridian said.

Noor's single bark of laughter was disturbing in a way Iridian couldn't define. "They're not."

Wiley had befriended him, somehow. Noor must've pulled the same thing on him that he had on her, holding back his secessionist attitude until after she'd made up her mind about him. Wasting weeks of her life in the ITA's sim prison made lies of omission more annoying than they used to be. And, hell, maybe she shouldn't blame a tech guy for hiding his past while he was surrounded by former NEU soldiers.

Iridian peered around the metal column she stood behind, watching the distant lights of the gang's territory. If somebody walked between her and the lights, they'd go dark for a second. Two did. "I like Kuiper natives. They never tried to cut off the hand that fed them."

"Because it was so far away they couldn't reach it," said Noor.

"How sure are you about these IDs you're broadcasting?" Rio asked in a rough whisper that carried from her position across the corridor.

"The station intranet doesn't have much, but it did have the pattern Marsat used for employee IDs in the '10s," Noor said. "Can you believe those Marsat scientists left them sitting outside a secure server? They're hard to fuck up once you have the pattern. The ones I made are a match for midlevel access anywhere in the original facility."

Rio nodded like Noor's answer satisfied her. The unsupervised station management AI, the one Adda called Mairie, was a bigger danger than whatever the Odin Razum threw at them. The routine Noor and Adda put together for the op removed any identifying info that Yăo's AI might take off their comps and broadcasted IDs that wouldn't set off security protocols. Adda had said the AI wasn't armed, but that didn't make it safe.

"Looks clear," said Wiley. "Nobody's pointing anything at us, anyway."

"No turrets," said Rio.

"Can't tell more without an overhead view," Wiley added.

"Yeah, that would've been nice. Move out." Iridian stepped out of her hiding place and walked in long, low-grav strides over the glow-stick-strewn floor, toward the brighter lights of Odin Razum territory. Talking them out of the drones would be easier on everyone. Only Rio had the armor to withstand a mass assault. None of them had ranged weapons heavier than a glow stick.

The shapes in front of the lights resolved into four or five people, who stopped whatever they were doing with the pipes near the entrance to the water treatment plant to watch Iridian's team approach. One of them yelled something in what was probably Russian. Echoes and water rushing through the pipes above messed with Iridian's implanted mic, and the translator didn't offer an English version.

"They see us." Wiley had found a length of pipe that he held like a weapon at his side. "Noor, your comp's transmitting, yeah?"

"It has been for the past four minutes." Noor sounded annoyed. "Why would I walk up to this place without something to keep the fucking unsupervised station AI off my ass?"

More people came in from the better-lit water treatment mod. Iridian counted ten people in dirty jumpsuits with a dark *M* in an orange circle on the chests and arms. They approached with blank yet strangely intense expressions. Some of the jumpsuits had the sleeves or legs torn off, and knife hilts stuck out of nine or ten belts. A couple of them had strapped knives to their arms with thin tubing, too. Sharp shards of metal had been punched through folds of the jumpsuit legs in rows that reflected the multicolored lights.

They looked eager for something, and they seemed to be a vanguard for even more people stalking toward Iridian's crew. The age range was around Iridian's and Adda's or a bit older, mixed in with a few sallow-faced teenagers and older folks. Their eyes looked off, somehow, although the multicolored dim light would've made anything look strange.

Oh no, Adda subvocalized. Iridian squeezed her shoulder. Iridian would do the talking, or fighting if need be, so Adda didn't have to.

"Fuck me, there are a lot more people behind these." Wiley twirled the length of pipe in his hand. "I've got thirty."

"Same." Rio's fists clenched at her sides. She looked ready to punch out any of these strange people who came in range. "Is this all of them?"

"That's all the priestess said to expect, but how should I know?" asked Noor.

Iridian pulled her knife and slid it back into its sheath, confirming that she could get to it quickly when she wanted it. "Well, let's say hi."

Wiley grinned at her like he couldn't tell if she was serious or not. In the Shieldrunners, "saying hi" meant that two or three massive infantry shield vehicles moved up, shields raised in front of whoever they were escorting, and asked civilians who might be secessionists blocking the path to disperse. Sometimes that went well.

The first of the people came within four meters of Iridian, Wiley, and Rio, who walked in front of Noor and Adda. The people stopped moving and started talking in hoarse whispers that startled Iridian. It sounded like the subvocalized version of Adda's voice that played through Iridian's comms. Iridian caught only fragments of questions as people piled up behind those who had reached her crew first. ". . . here now?" "Can't be the same . . ." ". . . waited so long to . . ." ". . . want me to do?" in mixed Russian and English. One of them also said, "Hey, you here to send something to the Patchwork?" but somebody else shoved him and told him to be quiet.

They're asking because Mairie is asking, Adda subvocalized.

Wiley answered the Odin Razum person's question over Adda's words. "No, but we're passing through this facility, so we need you to clear a path here."

When Iridian turned to check on Adda, her eyes were wide, and she was biting her lip. *The station intelligence,* Adda subvocalized. *Listen to the questions and look at their eyes. Noor's IDs*

*describe us as Marsat employees. Mairie's influenced these people,
and we're potential supervisors. But if Casey already sent Mairie
our real identities . . . It sounds like the Marsat IDs are taking priority, but it's evaluating conflicting inputs.*

A shudder crawled up Iridian's spine. That was a lot of influenced people, and Casey was involved. She struggled to concentrate on Adda's whisper while Wiley and Rio started a mostly
one-sided argument with the Odin Razum man selling Patchwork
access. He was doing more staring than talking. *Are you saying
that Casey beat us here?* Iridian asked Adda.

No, Adda replied. *Well, not exactly. Casey had to use Mairie's
drones to send a message to Shingetsu, and the Odin Razum knew
who we were when we arrived. Casey must've reached out to
Mairie through the drones too. Casey would've sent Mairie our IDs,
and maybe biometrics. If Mairie understands criminal charges, it
would've sent those too. So we're acting like guests or trespassers
Mairie's already aware of, but we're broadcasting Marsat IDs.*

Adda wasn't talking like Casey had installed itself on Yăo.
They weren't trapped on this fucked-up hab halfway into Jupiter
with an awakened AI . . . yet. But Casey still had them cornered.
Adda had warned her that Casey would find its way in, but Iridian
had thought they'd have at least a fucking week before that happened. It sounded like Mairie was already cooperating, for lack of
a less human term, with Casey. The crowd's unnatural attention
pressed on Iridian like a blade, and she had no way to defend
herself.

Although she did have two soldiers, two tech experts, and a
whole lot of unspent rage at Casey. She could do a lot of damage
with that. *I am so gods-damned tired of these fuckers trying to use
us,* she told Adda. *We're taking these drones back.* It was a piti-
fully weak strike against such powerful AIs, but Iridian wouldn't
stand still and wait for Casey to tear up Adda's mind again.

Iridian interrupted Rio and Wiley's unproductive discussion with the staring Odin Razum. "Casey used one of Mairie's drones to warn it we were coming, but Mairie likes Noor's corp IDs better than whatever Casey told it. And all these people are under Mairie's influence. That's how they know us."

"Oh shit." Wiley hefted his length of pipe between himself and the Odin Razum. The nearest two quit staring at nothing, focused on the weapon, and backed up a few steps.

"They're all influenced?" said Noor. "You said Casey couldn't get here."

"Casey isn't here," Adda said aloud, in a firmer voice than Iridian expected given what she'd just concluded. "And I've never seen it influence people on this scale before. One of the first station management intelligences did something like this with its development team, though, so I'd assume Mairie's capable of it. I think this is Mairie's work."

"Gods, I hope Mairie's too old to let Casey push it around." Iridian could dream.

"So," said Rio, "will the Yǎo AI let us get the drones or not?" Of all of them, Rio was the only one who'd maintained mission focus. Except for Tash's death on the way out of Ceres stationspace, Rio had missed all the manipulative shit Casey had put Adda and Iridian through. It must've been peaceful to have no real idea what they were up against.

"If Mairie thought we were a threat, I think it would've used these people to defend an environment-critical section of the station like this," Adda said. "It's not doing that."

"Why are all these people here, then?" asked Noor.

"They're watching, not attacking. It might . . ." Adda didn't like to share guesswork with people she didn't know well. When she had evidence to back her up, she'd be more forthcoming.

"At least Mairie likes a clean hallway," Iridian muttered. "That'd be why all the bots are still running here." Casey wasn't influencing the people in front of them. Mairie was. And if Mairie used them to watch Iridian's crew take its drones away from it, that'd serve it right.

Unlike the mod connector between the port and the station's internal structure, all of this archway's lights were on. Metal in Odin Razum members' noses, necks, and jaws, gleamed where implant jacks were often installed. Two of them even had the newer temple jacks like Noor's, a Kuiper design that Adda said boosted connective stability. It was interesting how people like Noor would embed Kuiper tech in their heads while they called Kuiper folks names. Maybe they assumed some NEU designer thought of it first, or they just didn't recognize the contradiction.

Where the light hit the Odin Razum people's jacks, it exposed red, inflamed skin around the metal. Some had hair snarled around the connectors in ugly tangles that must've hurt like hell. Now that Iridian was looking for them, most of the Odin Razum had jacks. "What does a bunch of backwater thugs need with that many developers, pilots, and drivers?"

"I don't know about devs and drivers, but it seems like there'd be a lot of pilots out here," Rio commented.

"And don't you think there are other reasons people might want a jack?" Noor tapped his head near the jack beneath his hair.

Adda glanced around at the Odin Razum. She looked like she had something to say, but this was too much of an audience for her. Iridian took her hand and backed away from the crowd. Noor trailed behind them, leaving Rio and Wiley to watch the milling Odin Razum.

"Workspaces expose anyone with a jack to different influence risks than people who only interact with intelligences through consoles," Adda said. "It's easy to forget that. But as long as Mairie wants us as supervisors, it won't hurt us."

"Does it really want supervision?" Iridian asked. "It took a decoherence reset to make AegiSKADA accept yours."

"All intelligences are developed to seek an approved supervisor," Adda said. "Since Barbary's previous owners and AegiSKADA's developers were both so security-focused, we didn't have permission to supervise AegiSKADA until your reset put it in concurrence mode. That let me set myself up as approved. Both the intelligence and the ID pattern here are so much older and simpler that Noor's IDs would let us skip all that."

"Hey, it was good work, wasn't it?" Noor huffed. "Simple."

Adda looked over at Noor, eyes widening and hands rising to ward off his annoyance. "Sorry. I didn't mean to imply that what you did was easy. Simple can be very difficult." Her face flushed, and she started paying more attention to the clean floor than what they were talking about. That was the end of Adda's eye contact and verbal conversation for the next few hours.

But you won't take Mairie up on that supervision offer, Iridian subvocalized. Adda ducked her head even lower. Much as Iridian hated to push her, she said, *Babe, please. Promise me you won't.* She needed to hear Adda say it, even if she didn't say it out loud. Adda did not need to be supervising anything so soon after Casey had influenced her.

I promise, Iri.

They had more immediate, if not more horrifying, problems. Rio's suit reservoir represented the only water the crew owned. Getting Shingetsu the drones should keep the crew hydrated with the temple's water long enough to start earning money. "So it's not going to stop us from taking the drones, no matter what Casey tells it?" Iridian asked aloud.

Adda looked as anxious as she had when she'd first said the Odin Razum were influenced, but she shook her head. *I don't know what Casey is capable of telling it,* Adda replied, *but in the*

current state of affairs, I expect Mairie to let us do whatever the
Marsat IDs say we're allowed to do.

When Iridian turned her attention back to the Odin Razum, Noor was watching her and Adda instead of the influenced gang, looking as suspicious as he had when he'd thought Iridian had gone to Sorenson ITAS to break out a prisoner for Captain Sloane. Iridian hadn't talked to Adda about telling their new friends about the comms implants. Now wasn't a great time.

A conversation with the Odin Razum, however, still seemed like the safest way to start the search for the drones Shingetsu wanted. Iridian missed her shield. If the Odin Razum really were influenced, maybe Iridian was talking to the AI and not to the people themselves. "Where are these drones?" Iridian asked loudly. "We want to . . . do an inspection. Preventative maintenance, you know."

"Authorized." Each Odin Razum member spoke the word like it'd just occurred to them. Most looked surprised and pleased to remember the access Noor's Marsat IDs granted Iridian's group.

Mairie's definitely prioritizing the Marsat IDs, Adda subvocalized. *Thank all the gods and devils.*

"Nice work on the, um, broadcast," Iridian told Noor. "I think you just outplayed a fucking awakened AI with it."

Noor grinned. "That'd make a great bar story if somebody believed me, wouldn't it?"

"Somebody show me where the drones are," Iridian said to the Odin Razum. They parted to create a ragged path into the water treatment plant. "Shieldrunners, move out," she said for Wiley's benefit. He nodded to acknowledge the order, and he and Rio took point on their way through the opening in the crowd. The op seemed to be distracting him from his loss, at least.

A white man with most of his pale blond hair shaved off, except for a pattern of curved lines on the sides of his head, separated from the other Odin Razum. He took a few running steps to get in front of Wiley and Rio and led the way. The unexpected cleanliness continued into the next mod, the water treatment plant. It contrasted with a wet, earthy smell that grew as they walked. It got colder the farther they went. The pipes on the walls followed them in too, feeding larger ones in the plant that wound their way into large metal containers.

Strands of the greenest plant life Iridian had seen since college on Earth rose from the metal containers' tops. The grass reached toward wide UV lights hung over them, waving in the atmo blown across them by vents near the ceiling. Despite their aggro attire, the Odin Razum had been gardening in here. She'd never heard of a gang that did that.

I wish we could help these people, or at least study them, Adda whispered over their comms. *The worlds should know that this kind of mass influence event can occur.*

That ludicrous idea made Iridian smile. *Even if three awakened AIs weren't after you, staying here would give you more time to make a new mistake with this one.* Adda winced. Iridian could've said that in a way that didn't diminish all the things Adda had talked AIs into doing for them before. *I'm sorry, but we're all one mistake away, aren't we? That's why you went to school for this and the rest of us let you do the talking for us. Just for now, can you tell somebody else about it and leave the research to them?*

Adda's shoulders rose defensively and she stared at the guide's back instead of looking at Iridian. Iridian's longing to trust Adda with her passion for AIs kept losing to her instinct to protect Adda from herself. Gods, they both needed time to sort this out. Maybe after this op, they could.

Iridian had been visually tracking a long pipe bolted to the ceiling that they'd been walking under since they entered the plant, in case she needed to follow it out in a hurry. It split into two at the wall in front of them. Their guide with the patterns shaved into his head squeezed past stacked plastic bags of water, packaged to sell, stopped at the fork in the pipe, and stared at the wall.

"The drones, remember?" Iridian said.

The man stayed put. No footsteps followed them down the curving hallway. The Odin Razum outside the plant must've stayed outside. "What do you think's got him mixed up?" Rio asked.

He's plugged into his comp, Adda told Iridian. Now that she'd pointed it out, Iridian spotted the cable attached to his grimy comp glove. It disappeared into his sleeve, but a coil of it stuck out the top of his collar. It could plug into a jack at the base of his neck.

"Is he talking to the station AI?" Noor asked. "Can you even do that with just a comp?"

"You can," Iridian said, "but you shouldn't." *Why didn't AegiSKADA influence everybody on Barbary, do you think?* That terrifying question would keep digging into the back of Iridian's mind until Adda answered it.

That was something AegiSKADA's development team got right, Adda replied. *AegiSKADA used people in other ways, but influencing them directly was its last choice of solutions to its problems. When Mairie was developed, people knew a lot less about influence.*

Standing in a tight space while outnumbered by influenced people was making Iridian antsy. Their guide was the only Odin Razum member in view, but she couldn't see very far behind them. "What's the holdup?" she asked their guide.

The man's head snapped up. "Follow me." His voice was as dull as Adda's when she was drugged for a workspace, but Iridian hadn't seen him take any sharpsheets. The similarity made her skin crawl. He turned left and walked on.

The implants, Adda subvocalized. *It influenced them through the implants.*

They'd lost the pilot on one of Captain Sloane's ops to an AI that, as far as anyone could tell, had just wanted to take its ship out of its hangar. He'd approached that AI without following procedure, though, and he had a piloting implant. Adda's was designed for interacting with workspace generators. *Yours is similar to a pilot's, but it's not that similar, is it? And you're careful. He wasn't.*

They're all neural implants, which means they all pour input from intelligence-facilitated systems straight into our brains. I'm concerned about all neural implants at this point, but I have almost no facts. This is why somebody should be studying these people.

Fuck. Neural implants had always weirded Iridian out because of the potential head and neck damage if something went wrong with them. AIs using hardware inside people's brains for their own purposes was so much worse.

CHAPTER 13

Days until launch: 30

Can't influence happen to everybody?

Iridian's question was one that Adda wished more people would ask, but it also showed that Adda hadn't told her what she'd meant to communicate. It would've been easier to sit down somewhere and outline a complete explanation, but if Iridian had to have the explanation to focus on the job, Adda would produce one as she put the pieces together herself. *Yes, but the implants . . . I never thought about how much easier they make the process. People talk about developers and pilots getting influenced just by prolonged exposure to intelligences. That's why we're supposed to work in teams and take breaks. But what if there's more to it? What if the problem is that the intelligences . . . Some intelligences selectively limit influence symptoms, or rush the process electrochemically.*

Or allowed some influence symptoms and not others, or could only control some symptoms or only rush certain stages . . . Adda was gazing into an abyssal gap in humanity's understanding of influence. And she'd just been congratulating herself on how far the artificial intelligence field had come since Mairie was developed. She could panic, or she could work the problem. Iridian looked like she was panicking enough for both of them.

Each influence stage has its own symptom group, but not all influenced people display all symptoms at each stage. Some symptoms are also associated with other conditions. For example, widely recognized stage one influence symptoms involving a supposed lack of self-care were part of Adda's daily routine while she was absorbed in a project. Her brain worked differently than most people's did. *What if Casey realized that some symptoms in stages two through four lead to diagnoses more readily than others, and suppressed those symptoms while streamlining progression through the others?*

Casey could've taught itself to do that through information synthesis and experimenting on Adda. That was . . . not a danger they'd prepared her for in school, where awakened intelligences were more myth than reality. Adda would've given a lot to learn how Casey did that. Telling Mairie how to manipulate neural implant nets like Adda's would've been well within Casey's power and consistent with its past behavior, especially if it figured out that Shingetsu wouldn't convince Iridian and Adda to leave Yăo Station. If Mairie had influenced Adda, it could've kept her on Yăo Station until Casey installed itself on a ship capable of withstanding this proximity to Jupiter.

Iridian drove her fist into the side of one of the grass-covered tanks. Adda startled away from the metallic bang. Everyone else looked at Iridian, then all around to find a threat that wasn't there. "Sorry," Iridian said aloud. "Frustrated."

Are you surprised that the tech allows the intelligences to do this, or are you surprised that the intelligences do this at all? Adda asked. *Because this is what intelligences do: they solve problems. Human supervisors make them solve the right problems the right way.* Not that there was one "right" way, exactly. Some solutions were more helpful than others.

Mairie must've needed a lot of help when it began managing Yǎo Station alone. With years of unsupervised efforts to keep Yǎo running, Mairie could've influenced the Odin Razum the old-fashioned way, through exposure, while the Odin Razum were taking control of the drones. Adda had seen no proof of that, though.

Iri, could you ask when our guide joined the Odin Razum? And when the others did too. They might not know what "influence" meant in this context, but spending a lot of time in the treatment plant or joining the gang might be a symptom, especially if many new people had joined following a critical contact with Mairie.

Iridian grabbed the guide's shoulder and spun him around to face her. "Stop a second. Tell me about your group. When did you join up?"

The shocked guide's gaze darted between Iridian and the space on either side of her, which Wiley and Rio filled. "I . . . We . . . I've been with them for a couple three years. Yeah. Lot of people just joined this week, but about a dozen of us have been Odin Razum for years."

Iridian glanced at Rio and Wiley, like she was checking to see if they'd heard what she did. "Only twelve of you have been in for years? The Odin Razum doubled in size this month?" When the guide nodded, Iridian looked to Adda. "Does that answer your question?"

The others wouldn't have heard that question, but they looked too surprised by this new information to notice. "It might," said Adda.

Shingetsu had said there'd been a recent increase in the Odin Razum population, but she hadn't said how recent it was. If Mairie had been able to remotely, quickly influence so many people for years, why hadn't it influenced every person on the station with an implant?

The worst-case scenario, one Adda was inclined to operate on for now, was that Casey had used the Yǎo Station drones to show Mairie how people with neural implant nets were easier to influence. *Why* they were easier to influence, the mechanism that smoothed that process, the flaw that allowed it to happen, was the essential problem to solve. With that information, Adda could protect herself from both Mairie and Casey.

Iridian shoved the guide forward. "Let's go." The way she was scowling at him made Adda hope that he didn't do anything threatening within the next few minutes. Subvocally, Iridian said, *This is a fucking travesty, and somebody will fucking pay for it. I don't want it to be you. What can we do to stop Casey from influencing you again?*

Adda's temporary solution was to stay as far away from Casey as possible. Eventually she'd make a mistake, or one of the intelligences that were interested in her would force her to make one. *If it's using the software or hardware in ways they weren't designed to be used, then there's a vulnerability the manufacturers should close,* she told Iridian.

She'd enjoyed a semester-long class on grotesque ways humans and intelligences had misused implanted technology in the past. The class had been part of her curriculum, so graduates would be motivated and prepared to correct vulnerabilities. Adda's influence experience with Casey was probably the first time in history that an awakened intelligence had found a vulnerability and exploited it, though.

On Vesta, the vulnerability could've been in her intermediary software, the implant firmware, or even the standard workspace generator firmware. Pilots among the Odin Razum would've been influenced without a generator, and their intermediary software was very different from hers. There had to be more pilots than developers on a station like Yăo, which wouldn't attract the universe's best and brightest to begin with. Besides, a vulnerability in the neural implants would be too frightening to ignore.

So I'm worried the vulnerability is in the implant firmware, Adda told Iridian. *If I knew who made each Odin Razum person's implant, that'd be a list of specific models that could be involved. We're supposed to describe the situation to whoever made them and ask them to fix it.* In theory, the corporation responsible for the firmware would make the correction, send an update Adda would need the drones to download, and then tell the rest of the industry what had happened.

Iridian glanced over at her, still furious, but probably not at her. *Why the fuck is this so common that there's a fucking procedure for it?*

Each component of intelligence management is complex. One component is a human brain, which cannot be standardized. Another is an intelligence whose development also cannot be completely standardized. Catastrophic disasters are prevented every year because ethical humans or well-developed intelligences fixed a problem before unethical humans or intelligences like Casey found it. And now Adda was the human who'd found the vulnerability. She could ransom it to the people who could fix it, but that would leave her implant vulnerable for even longer. If she just gave it to them, they could start working on the solution right away.

Fuck procedure. Even in a toneless whisper through their personal comms, Iridian sounded like she was shouting. *Can't you fix it yourself?*

If I had a year, maybe. Adda would have to take apart software she only understood from the outside that was made by multiple professionals and probably an artificial assistant too. That'd require a development workspace on Yǎo Station, under Mairie's control. Then she'd have to find the problem, eliminate that problem without causing new ones, and convince the hardware to use her version instead of what it used now. All with her own brain as the test subject. *Casey will get to me before then. Someone who worked on the original version could fix it much faster.*

The guide stopped walking, and so did everybody else. Gravity felt even lower here than it had in the port.

"Looks like we're out of the treatment area," Wiley commented. There were a lot more pipes leading to the area they'd just walked through, and no more tanks with grass on top. The guide lurched into motion again, crossing a module separator into an emptier hallway. "We lose track of each other, we're meeting back at the temple, yeah?"

"Yeah, we'll meet up there if we have to," Iridian confirmed. That'd been the only contingency plan Adda had shared with Iridian on this op. She'd been working on more, but now that Mairie had proven itself so prodigiously skilled at influencing people with implants, she'd switched to influence prevention tactics instead. "Hey, Wiley," Iridian said. "Do you still have your lucky socks?"

Wiley laughed, a higher-pitched and more incredulous sound than seemed typical for him. "You remember those? Oh my gods, no. Lost 'em in one of my moves on Mars."

"Figures," muttered Iridian.

They'd been following their guide for a few minutes longer when Adda sorted through some more implications about the vulnerability. *This means what happened on Vesta wasn't entirely my fault.*

What? Iridian replied. *It was Casey's fault.*

You'd have said that even if Casey wasn't exploiting a software vulnerability to influence me. Adda smiled, which she'd never expected to be able to do when discussing what'd happened in the Rheasilvia port. *I thought I'd made the usual intelligence handling mistakes to get influenced on Vesta, because I was interacting with too many at once. But that wasn't what happened. Casey used the vulnerability to influence me that fast. I'm sure I made some mistakes, and if I hadn't been interacting with so many intelligences I might've caught Casey before it hurt us, but they weren't as bad as I thought they were.*

Iridian looked more concerned rather than less. *So no matter how good you are, Casey can still influence you through that vulnerability?*

Adda's excitement dimmed. *Well, yes. But I didn't make the basic handling mistakes I thought I must've made. I wasn't as careless as I thought I'd been.*

I never thought you were careless. Kind as that was, Iridian had missed the point.

The man they'd been following stopped and waved both hands toward an open doorway on their left in a gesture Adda couldn't interpret. It seemed far too deep in the station's interior to launch drones from, but the guide said, "In there."

Noor scowled at him. "Why aren't you going in with us?"

"It's not *for* me." Their guide looked longingly toward the doorway.

"Ah, what the hell," Rio sighed, looked in all directions for threats, then ducked through the doorway and went in.

Overhead lights came on bright and then settled into morning sunsim. Rio's broad shoulders blocked Adda's view into the room as Rio put her hands on her hips. "There's nothing in here. Just a big pseudo-organic tank."

Adda and Noor both stepped toward the room. Either of them could tell more about its purpose than Rio could. Adda tapped Rio's arm until she stepped out of the way. "Hey, slow down," said Iridian. "Half the big pseudo-organic tanks we've run into have been full of trouble." She reached for Adda, but Adda was already stepping past Rio. Noor followed her.

A huge pseudo-organic tank, bigger even than AegiSKADA's on Barbary Station, took up all of one wall. The fluid inside was lit orange, like Martian soil covered with a thin layer of frost. Connected to it was a decades-old quantum comp and a console to interact with it. Like everything else they'd encountered in the Odin Razum's territory, all the equipment was clean and in perfect order.

Only the station intelligence could've needed that much pseudo-organic fluid. "It's Mairie's tank," Adda said. "This is the quantum rig in the corner here." Either their Marsat IDs offered a much higher level of access than Adda thought they did, or Mairie's developers had prioritized a *lot* of tasks above the intelligence's self-preservation. Perhaps its development team taught it that obtaining qualified supervision was more important than protecting its pseudo-organics.

Rio's position near the door only left Noor room to take a couple of steps into the small space. He raised himself on tiptoes to see over or around her. "Drone controls ought to be there too, if they're station equipment."

In the hallway, their Odin Razum guide nodded enthusiastically. "The controls for *everything* are in there. All of them."

"Could it push the engines a little harder?" asked Wiley. "My damn sinuses are floating." More gravity would certainly be welcome, and better drained sinuses were the least of the potential improvements for new arrivals' health. It was less obvious how spinning the station faster might affect the station's integrity, and the health of people who'd spent years in this low gravity environment.

Noor's comp blared four sharp beeps, and he turned his attention to it. "I've got a transmission spike. Strongest in this room, but it's on a wide, short band. Anybody see anything different happening out there? Changing the filtration settings, maybe?"

"Movement." Wiley was looking the way they'd come. Noor went out to join him.

"That's enough of that," muttered Iridian. She shoved past Rio to reach for Adda again. "Come on, babe. Let Noor take a look. It sounds like he knows what—"

Noor returned from the hallway. "That looks like everybody who met us out front. Can one of you get out there and help? I'm ... uh ..." He trailed off and stood up straight, turning around the room like he was looking for something.

A workspace generator. There should've been one in this room or near it, to coordinate with the station intelligence. Adda looked around too, but she didn't see it.

"Coming." Rio's heavy boots thudded into the hall. There, against the wall she'd been standing in front of, was a generator.

When Iridian's hand closed on Adda's arm, Adda turned toward her. "There's a workspace generator," Noor said unnecessarily, his eyes going wide as he spoke.

He had to be seeing the same potential Adda did. If Mairie wanted a supervisor, why shouldn't it be one of them? It was a risk, but they were in danger already. As Mairie's supervisor, Adda could release all those influenced Odin Razum people. She and Mairie would do so much to improve life on this station. Raising gravity was just a start. They'd set a regular, free schedule for drone trips to the Patchwork. They'd use all the drones for Patchwork access and station repair, and hide the increased data traffic from Casey. They'd filter more carbon dioxide out of the air. They could even—

"Hell no." Iridian pulled Adda's arm toward the door. Adda wedged herself against a console, and she had a lot more leverage than Iridian did. Noor was walking toward the generator as if in a daze. That was no state in which to assume intelligence supervision. Adda had studied and supervised intelligences, and furthermore she respected them. Noor had no experience with them at all. Maybe Iridian agreed, because she reached for him too.

Perhaps she'd missed the tactical advantage. "I can send those people away." Adda twisted out of Iridian's grasp. As if in slow motion, Adda gripped the door to the reclining workspace generator built into the wall.

"Leave that alone." Iridian shoved Noor across the room, hard enough to thump his back into the wall. He staggered toward the generator again. Iridian blocked his path with her body. "You don't even know if that generator's compatible with your implant," Iridian said, "and if it was, would Mairie even listen to you?"

There was an easy way to answer both of those questions. Adda pulled the heavy generator door open. "Babe, please." Iridian's voice shook, like Adda's proximity to the generator was physically hurting her. "We know how this ends."

With Mairie's help, Adda would solve most of the problems on this station. Then Iridian wouldn't have anything to be afraid of. "I can do so much more from there," Adda told her. "I'll be careful." When Adda lay down on the generator's bed, it was an immense relief.

It was only after Adda had shut the workspace generator's door that she realized she didn't have the details she needed to contact Mairie. Her neural implant net was causing an ache deep in her skull. It needed recalibrating, but there was no time to do that now.

In the generator, she took another of her dwindling stock of prescription sharpsheets and dragged the lock icon to keep the door closed. Using a packet of dry sanitizing pads, she wiped off the cable and her nasal jack. Then she plugged in. Mairie was looking for someone like her, so it'd make itself easy to find. Whether she had qualifications it recognized, she'd soon find out. All she had to do . . .

That was a worrisome phrase. It suggested she had over-simplified the problem she was attempting to solve. The rattling and banging on the outside of the generator was becoming an annoying distraction. The noise pulled her out of the workspace before it finished loading, and she had to start the process over. Her head felt fuzzy, like she'd taken an expired sharpsheet. As she considered the challenges inherent in taking over supervision of this intelligence, a new workspace loaded.

A riot of color swirled around her, oil paint on canvas on air that clicked and whirred and resisted coming together into usable information. She, Mairie, and the workspace's mindless software were combining to bring meaning to the chaos. A sun flared and died. One of the participants had crashed a connection attempt. Black and white squares formed under her feet, then blew away, leaving her with meaningless vertigo. None of it made any sense.

Adda felt for the cord that would connect her comp to the generator. She'd have to take the cord out of her nasal jack to rearrange them, but unlike this ancient generator, the comp had software that she'd tested with her neural implant net. The rattling outside had changed to more ignorable scratching and rhythmic tapping. Her subconscious incorporated the noise into the generator's soothing hum. Once she was back in reality again, her hand closed on the cord. She incorporated her comp into the system, and moments later she was in a new, colorful, unintelligible workspace.

This time, white lines of light pierced the chaos and persisted. Now she could use some of the workspace functions. A math problem formed in the air. Solving it was a backup method of pairing her implant and her digital intermediary. Darkness formed behind the numbers as she concentrated. The intermediary would clear away the color storm.

The generator's door cracked. Light and hands fell on her. The cable came out of her nasal jack at the wrong angle and the pain took her breath away. The storm was gone.

Iridian's face, scowling somewhere between anger and concentration, hovered above her. "Help me," she told somebody outside Adda's field of vision. Strong hands lifted her out of the generator and held her in place, despite her body's efforts to bounce off the floor and escape. She reached for the generator. The broken door's jagged edge cut her fingertips.

Iridian's hand closed around hers and gently pulled it against her chest, away from the generator and next to Iridian's heart. "No, babe. We don't need it. We'll find another way."

"To do . . . what?" Adda asked. Everyday monitoring could be accomplished through a comp, but the initial handoff should really happen in a hallucinographic workspace. There was too much at stake to risk miscommunication between the intelligence and the supervisor.

"What the hell's wrong with her?" Noor's voice was edged with panic.

Iridian squeezed Adda's hand and frowned. Adda's blood oozed over her fingers. *We're here to get drones for Shingetsu so she'll trade us water and hook us up with someone who can clean the nannites out of us,* Iridian subvocalized. *And so you can tell somebody to fix your implant's vulnerability. Then we can make some money and get away from Casey.*

It startled Adda how close they were, and how Iridian hadn't said that aloud. Iridian liked to talk with her whole voice. Maybe she was ashamed. Iridian wanted to keep the others from knowing that Adda had forgotten why they were there. Before the overdose, before whatever had happened in that room with the generator, Adda would never have forgotten something so important. She felt compelled to press her point, even as it was slipping from her mental grasp. *But Mairie—*

"It's fucking with your head, gods damn it," Iridian snapped, aloud this time. "If you can't fight it, then I'll take that generator apart and recycle the pieces. Just tell me if I should, babe. I'll do it with my bare gods-damned hands."

"I'll help," Wiley's clenched fists made it look like he had been waiting for something to dismantle.

Adda stilled. If she'd been as deeply influenced as Iridian thought she was, Adda would've panicked at the idea of recycling the generator. It was frustrating that nobody was listening to her, but she didn't *need* to be in communication with Mairie.

But something was wrong. Her implant shouldn't be causing this kind of headache, even if it needed to recalibrate. "That'd be a waste," she said faintly. That was true. That was important. She couldn't remember why. "We don't know of another working generator on this station. Let's just leave. The drones aren't here."

"They're not, are they." Iridian let go of Adda's hand and turned so fast that she had to catch herself on the wall to stop her spin. "Where's that damned guide?"

Rio waved the Odin Razum man's hand by raising and lowering the arm she held him by. Even though he was pulling away with his full weight, she maintained her grip with no apparent difficulty. "You mean this guide?"

"Thanks, Rio." Iridian stalked to the doorway. "That trick won't work again," Iridian told their Odin Razum guide. "Take us to the drones, *now*, and I won't cut your balls off and feed them to you."

The man glanced between Rio and Iridian. "The console. It's how we get to them, this one and another one across the mod. I don't know where they are the rest of the time. I don't know, I swear I don't know! I've never been there."

Iridian sighed. "I don't like this console. Is the other console also in a room with a gods-damned workspace generator?" The man shook his head. "Then take us to that one. And tell all those

people to back the fuck off, or we'll come back here with something explosive."

Iridian held Adda's hand all the way to the next console. Ordinarily Adda loved holding hands with her, but after what'd happened in the workspace generator, it made her want to cry with
frustration and embarrassment. Working with or around intelligences used to be her most useful skill. When they'd left Earth
together, it'd been what she'd counted on contributing to a pirate
crew.

Now her experience with intelligences was her biggest liabil-
ity, even though she *knew* she could use Mairie to find and move
the drones, and help all those influenced people who still followed
them through the hallways. Now nobody even wanted her near a
generator. Worse, she'd broken her promise to Iridian and confirmed that her fears were justified. Iridian was holding her hand
to keep her from running back to the generator and climbing in.

While her implant twitched minutely inside her skull and
nasal passage, returning to the position that best fit Adda's body,
she reviewed the moments before she'd entered the generator.
Noor had reported a "transmission spike." What had that been?
After the signal, getting into the generator had seemed like the
only possible solution to their problems.

She could use the generator to take control of the drones,
and then she'd use it to . . . what? To make the crew a reputation, to get more jobs, to get more money to buy their way onto
Dr. Björn's expedition, away from Casey and the other awakened
intelligences. There. She had the whole picture now. When Adda
glanced over at Noor, he was shaking his head slightly and grimacing. Maybe he was recalibrating his implant too.

Iri, it did something to our implants.

Iridian glanced over at her. "Did you figure out what happened
back there?"

"That signal spike activated something in our neural implants." Adda had no idea how, but it was the most likely explanation, given the vulnerability in them.

"It would've had to have been in the sound. Did you hear a high-pitched sound?" Noor asked. "Mine doesn't do anything wireless. Are you saying . . . Oh, sweet fuck."

"That's why you two were the only people affected." Iridian still sounded angry about that.

"I thought I could've solved every problem we had if Iridian hadn't pushed me away from that generator," said Noor.

"Me too." Adda's focus on the actual problems they faced was fracturing, letting her feel all the fear she'd been blocking out.

Iridian swore expansively and gripped Adda's hand tighter. "If anybody's comp finds another signal spike, tell us."

"Will do," said Wiley, and the others agreed too.

Except for the guide, the Odin Razum had backed off. The whispering that echoed from the treatment plant was probably an auditory hallucination. Adda still heard wind chimes in places with no wind. Finding physical things in her environment to focus on helped silence them, sometimes. Adda's gaze settled on the back of their Odin Razum guide's head. He'd shaved it so that the whirls of lines and short hair pointed toward the jack near the base of his neck.

"How are you doing?" Iridian asked her, too gently.

"Not about to start shuffling around the treatment plant with these people, if that's what you're asking," said Adda. Iridian's face fell. Of course that wasn't the scenario playing out in Iridian's head. Iridian was afraid Adda would steal her knife and stab her with it, which was almost exactly what Adda had done the last time she'd been influenced. "Sorry. I'm not in communication with the intelligence. You can check my comp if you want."

"No, that's okay." Iridian squeezed Adda's hand. "Good. Thanks."

It shouldn't have been that simple. Adda had lied to Iridian about AegiSKADA's continued existence and then nearly killed her under Casey's influence. Adda's promise to reject Mairie's invitation to supervise it hadn't even lasted an hour. But here Iridian was, letting Adda walk around with her comp. Even if Adda handed it over, there were ways she could've hidden a conversation with Mairie. Adda's neural implant net, and by extension Adda herself, were as vulnerable as ever. And still, Iridian trusted her enough not to look at her comp.

It isn't really okay, Adda said subvocally.

Iridian turned to face her and let the others walk past, holding Adda by the shoulders for a moment before pulling her into a hug. "If you get influenced again, we'll get you free again, some safer way than last time," Iridian murmured. "But I'm not afraid of you, babe. Casey's terrifying. Casey's the enemy, and Mairie too, after all this. It's not you."

"This looks like the place, Nassir," Wiley called down the hallway.

Iridian let Adda go, and her smile looked more forced than natural. "Let's see if we can find the drones this time."

Adda followed her down the immaculate hallway to the door Wiley and Rio stood beside. She'd never seen a drone bay before, but she would've at least expected drones in one. This, then, was another control room. "Noor's in there messing with the console," said Rio.

"Good." Iridian looked over her shoulder at Adda and subvocalized, *Stay out here with Rio, please. Give your brain a break.*

This time Adda was almost certain that Iridian was speaking subvocally to hide how messed up Adda's brain had become. She had no idea what the others would do if they knew, but she trusted Iridian's assessment of what would keep other people calm. She watched from the doorway with Wiley and Rio while

Iridian kept an eye on their guide and Noor pulled the cord the ZVs had given him from his pocket to plug the jack in his temple into the console.

After a minute of Adda envying Noor's more detailed look at the local system, Rio tapped Adda's shoulder and pointed down the hall the way they'd come. A man and a woman stood at a bend in the hallway, watching with blank expressions. Another man joined them. There were people at the other end of the hallway too, all with the ragged jumpsuits that most of the Odin Razum wore, bearing the Marsat corporate logo. Adda didn't recognize any of them, but they might've been the same people they'd seen before.

The Odin Razum are back, Adda told Iridian. Mairie might not want to hurt them, but being watched and outnumbered by tools of Mairie's influence still felt like a threat.

CHAPTER 14

Days until launch: 30

"How many are there?" Iridian asked.

Wiley's head whipped toward the room with the console. The question would've been a surprise, since Iridian was still in the room and she couldn't see the gathering Odin Razum in the hall from where she stood. Maybe she'd tell the rest of them about her and Adda's comms at some point, but this wasn't the time. "Six so far," Wiley said.

"Can you do what you're doing any faster?" asked Rio.

"Yeah, sure, I was just looking at all the pretty pictures first," Noor said sarcastically.

Iridian returned to the hall, dragging their influenced guide behind her. She pointed at the Odin Razum gathering nearby. "All right, guy, what's this about?"

The man twisted in Iridian's grasp to look at Adda. "We need you."

"No you fucking don't." Iridian slammed the man face-first into the wall and pinned him there with her forearm across his shoulder blades. "You can't have her. Back off."

"It's your duty." The man's voice gurgled slightly. Blood ran from his mouth and nose and splattered the clean wall when he spoke. "You agreed—"

"I've got them," Noor shouted from the room with the console. "Oh shit, I've got *all* of them! They're coming around to the port mod. Want an airlock number?"

"If you can move them all, do it and send me that airlock number in a message," Iridian said. "A few extras won't hurt."

"Just how the hell are we getting them back into the station?" asked Wiley.

"I doubt we need to," said Iridian. "Noor, get Pel or Shingetsu on the comms and tell them to get to that airlock. Talk and walk." She leaned on their guide, who she still had pinned to the wall. "Get us out of here. I don't want to waste your people, but I sure as hell will if they're between us and the port."

The influenced gang, which looked much more like a gang now than it had a few moments before, closed in on them from both ends of the hallway. "You agreed, the same as the rest of us, but none of us can," their guide said.

The man grunted as Iridian yanked him off the wall and held him between herself and the people at one end of the hall. Slowly, to accommodate whatever the hell Mairie was doing with his brain, Iridian asked, "What are you talking about?"

"When you joined Marsat, you agreed to additional duties as required." Iridian's training kept her conscious of quick ways to immobilize the guide if he fought back, but he was just standing there. "We're not Marsat. We can't do everything Mairie wants."

"You want her alive," Rio shouted. Iridian looked over her shoulder to see what the fuck Rio was talking about, and she almost lost her grip on the Odin Razum guy. Rio's huge hand was wrapped around Adda's throat. "You want her alive, but that ain't happening right now," Rio shouted at the Odin Razum. "You don't let us out of here, I'll kill her and you don't get her at all, ever. You want that?"

Iridian's fist clenched in a handful of the Odin Razum guide's jacket and shirt. He choked, but Iridian ignored him. Rio had *no* business using Adda like that. Iridian's right hand let go of his collar and dropped to the knife hilt at her hip.

It's a trick, Adda subvocalized. *I'm fine.*

"No," the influenced people moaned over Adda's assurances. They spoke at different intervals and pitches, the same way they had when they'd decided that the crew was authorized to enter the water treatment plant. This time they also shared the same level of volume and panic. Iridian let out a long, shuddering breath, but she kept her hand on her knife. Adda was all right. She was all right.

"Then let us out," Rio shouted. Adda flinched under Rio's grip. If anyone else had been holding Adda by the throat, Iridian would've put a knife in them by now.

Rio had looked out for Pel on Barbary Station before Iridian and Adda got there. Hell, Iridian had watched Rio babysit a toddler on Barbary. Rio had been gentler than a kitten with the little guy. But she was a professional warrior. On some jobs, terrible acts of violence were her daily business. When the hallway emptied of Odin Razum as quickly as it'd filled, that just seemed like the rational response to Rio's threat.

Iridian shook the man who'd guided them this far. "Get us the fuck out of this place. And Rio?" She glared over her shoulder, and Rio turned herself and Adda to face her. "We're having a talk about this later."

Rio's eyes widened. "Yes, ma'am." Maybe terrible acts were her day-to-day, but Iridian would be damned if she let *anyone* put their hands on Adda like that. If Rio hadn't asked Adda first, there'd be hell to pay.

The guide started walking again, and Rio let Adda go and took a big step back from her, giving her all the hallway space she could offer. "I'm all right," Adda said aloud.

Iridian didn't trust herself to say anything other than "Good." She gave the guide a shove in the back that made him stumble ahead of her faster.

Iridian's crew left their Odin Razum guide at the elevator, returned to the temple, and accepted tea from Shingetsu in the pillowed meditation room while they summarized precautions for using tech connected to an unsupervised intelligence. The warnings barely affected Shingetsu's high spirits at all.

Iridian was clearly not emphasizing how dangerous these AIs were. "I'm telling you this once, and you'll just have to believe me. This station's AI has been using those drones to talk to another AI, and that other AI is awakened. Do you understand what that means?"

Shingetsu frowned, finally. "An artificial intelligence that has had its cognition limiters removed. Does this mean the ITA will take the drones away?"

Adda shook her head. "No," Iridian said for her. "I tried to tell them about Casey—that's what the awakened intelligence *calls itself*, if you can believe that—but by the time the ITA tried to catch it, the ship it rides around in wasn't where I said it was. As far as the rest of the universe is concerned, it doesn't exist. I know this sounds crazy, but it's trying to get to Adda and me, specifically. It can't yet, we don't think." Iridian waited for Adda's nod before continuing, "Or we'd still be up to our necks in Odin Razum, but it'll find a way in and it's damned good at influencing people. We think it contacted you once already, about us being Tash's last crew."

By Shingetsu's expression, this wasn't the first paranoid theory the temple staff had heard, maybe even today. "We'll be careful," she said, and Adda winced. Adda had said almost the same thing before she climbed into the workspace generator. "Reuniting families is worth it."

"Better be." Pel lounged across three seats' worth of cushions with his right, bright red pupil larger than his left, navy-blue one. He looked like he'd found some kind of intoxicant that was keeping him calm despite the fact that this would've been the first he'd heard of Casey's attempt to turn Mairie against them.

He had a point, though. They'd done some good for people worse off than them, but they'd put themselves in terrible danger without making much progress toward buying supplies and shelter on Yǎo Station. At least the former ITA prisoners wouldn't have to worry about the nannite cultures inside them for much longer.

"If you run into trouble, or you hear from anything calling itself 'Casey,' Adda and I have experience with AI influence," Iridian said. "We may be able to help. That's over and above our end of the deal, mind."

Shingetsu smiled. "And I will uphold my end. The water we discussed is here." She removed a blanket from a pallet of liter pouches. "As to the second part, we coordinate with a clinic when people come to us hurt or ill. They'll clean your nervous systems of the nannite cultures."

Rio narrowed her eyes and leaned toward Shingetsu slightly. Shingetsu leaned away precisely the same amount. "Does that clinic know what kind of culture it is?" Rio asked.

"They'll see, when they begin treatment." Shingetsu sounded genuinely sorry for the intrusion on their personal information. "They understand that sometimes cultures must come out before the appointed time, no matter the reason they were introduced. There's no point in reporting the removal from here, even when it's possible to do so. The ITA won't come. And, so you aren't angry that I didn't tell you," she added, sounding even more apologetic, "the removal process can be painful."

"Great," Iridian grumbled while Rio, Noor, and Wiley swore.

* * *

Yăo Station was too small for public transit. They walked from the temple to the clinic, past what looked like two ragged families of vendors endeavoring to attract the same potential buyer to their piles of dubious merchandise. The empty cargo hauler tracks that seemed to be the accepted replacement for sidewalks led from the port to the entertainment mod. There, predictably, they lost Pel. He waved and then disappeared into a small crowd gathered beneath an oversize rotating wine bottle, which glowed red.

A few seconds later, Adda's comp buzzed its comm alert, attracting her full attention to whatever message she'd received. Iridian caught Pel's name on the projection. The wording was much too slang-savvy to have been composed by an AI.

Now that Adda was otherwise occupied, Iridian slowed to walk beside Rio. "About that trick you pulled with Adda," Iridian said quietly.

"I am so sorry," said Rio. "I didn't hurt her, did I?"

"Not that she's mentioned," and Iridian had sure as hell checked Adda's neck for bruises. There hadn't been any. "It was a good idea, don't get me wrong. But even if it's for a good cause, don't put your hands on her unless we talk it out ahead of time. Even if it's fake. I'm not saying it makes sense, because it doesn't. I trust you, and that trick got results. Just don't spring that on us. If I wasn't holding that Odin Razum guy, I don't know what I would've done."

"I understand," Rio murmured. After walking in silence for a moment, she added, "For a second there, you looked like you were going to gut me."

Iridian huffed a quiet laugh. "I thought about it."

CHAPTER 15

Days until launch: 30

The clinic was the first part of the station Adda had seen that looked like it was being used for its original purpose. Adda, Iridian, Rio, Wiley, and Noor walked past plastic benches with torn padding to a reception counter that somebody had pounded on with something round and heavy enough to leave dents. The person behind the counter was a human instead of a weak intelligence's projected figure. An intelligence's figure would've had no use for the Earth-style shotgun resting in clear view on a shelf behind the countertop.

When Iridian slowly approached to tell him, "We're the ones Shingetsu told you about," he pointed to the doorway to their left. Its door was stuck partway down, and everyone except Adda had to duck under it. After all the unexpected difficulties Adda had navigated since Ceres, Shingetsu doing exactly what she said she'd do was a welcome relief.

In the waiting room beyond were two more armed and armored people and someone in clothes made of easily cleaned fabric that all medical professionals wore. The nurse, or at least the person dressed like one, leaned on the wall, watching them. "We've got nannite cultures that need to be taken out," Iridian told the nurse. "I'll go first." The nurse led Iridian back to an exam room and gave her a pill-size vitals monitor to swallow.

Adda followed without looking up from composing search routines and messages about her neural implant net, which she'd send as soon as they got the opportunity to use the drones they'd retrieved for Shingetsu. Device manufacturers sometimes outsourced their firmware development, and she wanted to make sure she notified the correct people of the vulnerability allowing accelerated influence.

Iridian and the nurse must've been talking while she'd been reading, because Iridian put an arm around Adda's waist and said, "She's my wife."

The nurse's confused expression eased. "Ah. And you want her to come with you?"

"Yeah, I do," Iridian said. It hadn't occurred to Adda that she might've stayed in the other room. Iridian always wanted company when she had to go through something health-related and unpleasant.

The nurse said, "Of course," and consulted vis comp. "And your vitals are . . . You're new here, aren't you."

"Just got in a few days ago," said Iridian.

"Exercise." The nurse's order sounded like a tired, hopeless repetition rather than medical advice ve expected Iridian to follow. Not that Iridian would need any encouragement in that regard. "Our grav is so low that if you do not use your muscles, you lose them. If you are lucky, I'll see you back here when the ship you try to leave on powers up and your heart can't handle one g anymore." Ve reached into a cabinet and selected a device that trailed a long cable. The nurse opened it and held the device toward Iridian. "Your hand."

When Iridian's hand was situated in the device's finger-shaped grooves, the nurse closed the lid over it. Light like a capillary scanner flashed inside. The cable connected to a projector, which, a moment after Adda had located it, spread data across the floor before it redirected the output to the nurse's comp.

"Ah, the new ones." The nurse made a disgusted face at whatever ve read on vis comp. "Into the pod. I am sorry, it will not take so long, but—"

"It'll hurt, yeah?" Iridian squared her shoulders. "Everything about these damned nannites does. I have implants." She touched a spot at her throat near the mic for her and Adda's communication system, a spot too far behind her ear to be the speaker/translator's actual location, although the mistake was probably not important enough to her medical treatment to require Adda to correct it, and a spot on her palm near the control switch.

The nurse flicked something on vis comp. The projector filled a wall with readouts. Some of the numbers referenced the components' power draw and metallic composition. "They should not be affected," the nurse said. "Although I am also seeing another cranial implant, which we'll have to work carefully around."

Iridian stilled. "What is it? Where is it?"

"Let's see if I can show you." The nurse held vis comp to the side of Iridian's head for a moment, then said, "It is rendering now."

"Did the ITA do that?" Adda asked.

Iridian swore viciously. "They had to have done it to keep us in . . . Half the time we were on Venus we were in a gods-damned sim. And I thought at the time, 'Can you do that without implants?' I guess you fucking can't."

In addition to the readouts on the wall, the projector lit the small room's floor with a cross section of Iridian's brain. A dark dot, not even a centimeter in diameter, was circled in red. "That is the one I am talking about," the nurse said. "You say the *ITA* put it there?"

"That's what I'm saying." Iridian swallowed hard and reached for Adda's hand. They held on to each other hard for a long moment. Iridian's palm was slippery with sweat. "I can't believe we went through all that with something in my . . . Gods, they could've put anything in there," Iridian said. "All the people in the waiting area must have one of these too. Can you take it out?"

"Absolutely not." The nurse looked almost as disturbed about the unwanted implant as Iridian did. "Our little clinic just does not have the equipment for that surgery. I am sorry. We can remove the nannite culture, though."

Iridian nodded. "Let's get this over with."

Adda returned to the spot she'd found where she wouldn't block the medical projections, backed against cabinets opposite the pod, watching the nurse help Iridian in. "I'd like to stay," she said.

The nurse nodded, and Iridian caught Adda's eyes. "It'll be fine, babe."

It had to be done. When the culture had been activated on the Ceres Station street outside Adda's hospital room, Iridian had fallen down screaming while the ITA agents came for her. And anything people did with nannites, the awakened intelligences would find a way to do too.

The pod hummed. Its display included Iridian's vital signs and a countdown timer, along with abbreviations Adda couldn't interpret. Iridian's groans became something Adda needed to distract herself from. The threat of the ITA using its nannite cultures against them would be gone by the end of the day, so she could focus on their group's other problems.

Her neural implant net, and to be safe she'd assume Noor's as well, were making it easier for intelligences to influence them.

Depending on how Pel's pseudo-organic eyes connected to his brain and the digital information spaces on station intranets, that might be a problem for him as well. And now Iridian had a neural implant too, and although it was much smaller than Adda's or Noor's, it was wireless. It definitely wouldn't tell Iridian, or Rio and Wiley for that matter, if it connected to something that also connected to Casey.

The last time Casey had influenced Adda, she'd nearly killed Iridian. She had to stop that from happening again.

Casey didn't even need traditional influence to turn people against each other, as it'd demonstrated when it sent Major O.D. proof that Tash had been involved in his father's death. The awakened intelligences could find anybody's weak points, and they'd get better at that with every attempt. Adda's were probably obvious to them.

Given enough time, they'd motivate somebody to bring enough of Casey to Yǎo Station to influence Adda again, although they hadn't done that yet. As Casey's experience with Shingetsu and Mairie would've taught it, orders from unknown sources weren't always followed. Mairie's interaction with Casey, in particular, was limited but alarming.

The closed pod door muffled Iridian's shriek, but Adda was halfway across the room and squeezing herself between the suspended projector and the nurse before she had time to think. Text and numbers swung over her shoes. The nurse's hand gripped her upper arm and hauled her away from the pod. Adda reached out for the pod, but the low gravity left her unbalanced and her hands slipped off the pod's door. Her reaction was irrational. This procedure was terrible, but necessary.

"The machine is doing exactly what it is supposed to do." The nurse's voice was kind, but firm, as ve stepped between Adda and the pod. "It is hard to hear, I know. But after, nobody can hurt her with this again."

That was the point. Adda used the doorway to orient herself. When she'd relaxed as much as she could, the nurse let go of her arm. She should've been finding out more about the station and looking for the next person who would pay them for something they could do, instead of hovering here when she couldn't get her balance. But she wanted to be here when the procedure was over.

The nurse glanced down at Adda's hand. The cut from the workspace generator's broken lid had stopped bleeding at some point, but her fingers still bore patches of dried blood. "I can fix that while we wait," the nurse said.

"Just close it up so it doesn't get infected," said Adda. "We can't afford anti-scarring." The nurse nodded and rummaged through a cupboard for more tools.

As a distraction, Adda reviewed what her trackers had found about the awakened intelligences. The *Charon's Coin* was in Ceres stationspace, but the trackers following the *Apparition* and the *Casey Mire Mire* had sent almost no data. It was possible that they were traveling too far from the reliable routes and Patchwork buoys for Adda's trackers to find them.

One of Casey's few position notes was nearly inside the orbits of Jupiter's outermost moons, several days ago. That was too close for comfort, but none of her indicators showed it coming any closer. Buoy coverage among the populated Jovian moons would've enabled excellent tracking. Adda started the analyses she could set up without a workspace and her old comp's custom tools, concentrating to tune out the sounds of Iridian's treatment.

Almost an hour later, the pod chimed to notify everyone that its treatment was complete. Iridian stumbled into Adda's arms, sweating and tired. They held each other while the nurse confirmed that Adda hadn't been infected by the same nannite culture. The influence treatment clinic could've done that, but they hadn't. They would've realized that nannite cultures used a kind of AI to do what they did.

"That sucked," Iridian muttered as Adda held her arm to steady her on the way back to the waiting room. "No more getting arrested."

The intelligences had used the ITA against Adda and Iridian before they'd used anybody else. It was one of many reasons that Adda was working so hard to get away from them. But anything as powerful, as fascinating, as connected, as *new* as the awakened intelligences would be dangerous. Humanity had never encountered anything like what the intelligences had become. Despite the danger she and Iridian were in, she desperately wanted to protect herself well enough to learn what the awakened intelligences' aims might be.

When she and Iridian returned to the waiting room, the other three were watching apprehensively. Iridian slumped in a seat between Rio and Wiley. The only other open place was too close to Noor, so Adda stayed standing to maintain a comfortable amount of personal space. "It's no fun, but that's about how long it takes, so just get it over with," Iridian said. "The ITA can fuck right the hell off." The others grumbled in agreement, and Rio stood to get her nannite culture removed next.

Adda subvocalized, *I want to keep studying intelligences. There's so much we don't know.*

Iridian glanced over at her with an eyebrow raised. *Okay. When you're ready. What brought this on?*

That was a line of questioning that'd seemed too obvious to construct an argument for. *I scared you back there. Again. Weren't you going to ask me to find another area of expertise?*

Iridian turned toward Adda more fully, pain from what'd happened on Vesta, or maybe some other mistake from the past, written on her face. Ever since Iridian had learned what Adda intended to do with her life, she'd only tolerated Adda's obsession with intelligences. They'd had the "Then leave!" argument over it back on Earth, and afterward they'd clung to each other tighter than ever. But terrible things had happened since then.

After a moment, she took both of Adda's hands in hers. "Shit happens, the worst kind of shit, no matter what you're doing. Sometimes the dangerous thing has to be done whether you have all the intel you need or not. You make mistakes, or Murphy the Lawmaker is just not on your side one day. It doesn't mean you give up. It means you get better. Study what went wrong. Train harder. Clear up whatever's going on in your head that made you fuck up, if that's what it's about."

Wiley added a quiet "Hell yeah," still staring into the middle distance.

Noor snorted. "Do you really have to do that dangerous thing, though?"

"That's a good question." Iridian held Adda's eyes. "Another question a person might ask is, 'Do I have to be the one to do it?' If you get a yes and a yes, so be it, but we're in for a tough time."

All right, Adda said to Iridian. *Clearing up what's in my head could take a while. It's literal as well as figurative in my case.*

In the meantime, the first challenge in escaping the intelligences' reach by crossing the interstellar bridge with Dr. Björn's expedition was surviving until Dr. Björn allowed them to go. They had no local money, and they'd spent almost all of what Adda and Iridian had earned with Captain Sloane's crew to get to Yǎo Station. Now they couldn't afford to leave.

CHAPTER 16

Days until launch: 30

Iridian's little crew had liberated more drones than Shingetsu needed to send all her messages out to the families of Yǎo residents. Since Adda still expected the Odin Razum and Mairie to take the drones back within a few days, everybody appreciated the extra machines. Adda had reserved space on one for queries and messages related to the potential implant vulnerability.

The priestess, or whatever title she held, gave Iridian a couple of extra drones to sell on the condition that the temple got a cut. Pel auctioned them off at a dock far from Shingetsu's, while Rio, Iridian, and Wiley stood by to look formidable to potential thieves while Adda and Noor stayed out of the way. That gained them enough local currency to buy real food to celebrate their victory and figure out what happened next.

While they ate, they compiled a list of search queries, update requests, and messages to send out with the temple's drones. Pel would take the risk of clearing out his Vestan account, the last bit of savings that Adda hadn't already transferred to their father on Earth. If Pel converted it to Yǎo Station's currency and one of their port neighbors sold halfway decent printer material, then they could get outfitted and start looking for work.

While the prison escapees had been getting their nannite cultures removed, Pel had used one of Shingetsu's drones to reach the Patchwork and update all his social feeds, including those written by ZV Group soldiers. "Chato said their ship got hit by some serious systems hacker while they were docking on Ganymede," he said, referencing one of the ZVs who'd been on Barbary Station. "Copied a bunch of vids and comms stuff off and almost rammed the ship into the port mod. Nobody was too badly hurt, but it scared them. And then the ITA boarded, looking for us, but once they were sure we weren't there, they left."

"Who got hurt?" Rio asked. "Are they okay?"

"He didn't say. I'll ask."

Even though Pel had brought the news, Noor was looking hard at Adda and Iridian. "Could the awakened AIs have done that?"

"Absolutely," Iridian said. "It's not even the first time they've hassled the ZVs."

"Did you know they were going to try something?" Rio asked, more angrily this time.

"No." Iridian glanced at Adda.

Adda was already watching Pel. It was unusual for her to have ignored her comp for this long while other people were talking. "After Barbary, they only attacked members of the ZV Group who talked about them. Chato was involved in one of those too, I think. I didn't expect them to follow the ZVs. They might not have intended to hurt the *Not for Sale* or the crew."

"But they did, didn't they?" asked Noor. "Maybe staying on Yǎo isn't such a bad idea after all."

"If you thought it was such a bad idea, why are you still here?" Rio asked.

"Have you seen a single sober pilot since we docked? Because I haven't. I'm not flying out with any of these people, even if I could come up with a fair trade in services." Noor took a large bite of noodles and chewed morosely.

The fact that he'd been looking for a way off so soon made Iridian trust him less than ever. If he'd stick around, though, she saw a lot of ways to use his skills. His technical expertise overlapped with Adda's a bit, but he seemed to have years more digital infiltration and ID spoofing experience than she did.

"I'm writing to Dr. Björn," Adda said. "Asking ver if we can join vis expedition is the least expensive tactic."

"How's that conversation going to go?" Pel asked around a mouthful of fried-eggish protein and stuff that looked like rice but had all the flavor and texture of the carton it was served in. "Sorry for destroying your fucking life, can we tag along on your dream vacation?"

Adda was certain that the AIs would install themselves in Yăo Station eventually and go after the crew in person, more or less, but Iridian had doubts about the expedition as a solution to that problem. "The last time Björn saw me, ve threw coffee at my head. We have to offer ver something."

"Ve's the one heading up that expedition to cross the interstellar bridge, isn't ve?" asked Noor.

Adda nodded, and Iridian said, "Yeah, that's ver."

"And you want to go with ver? Out there?" Wiley waved his hand vaguely to his right. "The newsfeeds said the science probes made it, but who knows for sure? I wouldn't want to be the first one on that ride."

"If the scientists said the probes made it, then they made it," said Iridian. "Suns look different from empty space on every recording mechanism there is. Unless you're one of those people who think somebody drew all the pics, and if you are, you need to learn about imagery analysis. Anyway, that's the point of exploration. Somebody's got to go and find out what the bots can't. Why not us?" Impractical as this solution might've been, if they somehow pulled it off, they'd be the first people seeing this new star system with their own eyes. She reached for Adda under the table and squeezed her thigh. Adda smiled, and yeah, it'd be amazing to stand in the light of a new sun beside her. "More importantly, if we get out of reach, then the AIs will have no reason to go after you."

"Rumor is you kidnapped Björn off Mars," Rio pointed out. "True?"

"Deimos," Adda said. "One of Mars's moons."

"So that's why not you, I reckon." Rio bit into whatever synthesized meat she was consuming with finality.

"Doesn't that seem a little extreme, anyway?" Pel asked. "I mean, Thrinacia is *so far* from here. Before the interstellar bridge, they didn't even think about sending those big colony ships out there."

"The interstellar bridge shortens the trip," Iridian said. "As long as you stay on it, Thrinacia's sun is the closest star to ours."

"Won't you all feel better if there aren't fucking awakened AIs trying to get into your brain?" Noor asked. "I know I will. If getting you two out there exploring gets the AIs off our backs, I'm all for it."

"They're not after *me*," Pel grumbled. "Who will I call when I get tangled up in some other mess? I'll miss you two." Iridian would miss a lot about populated space, Pel included, but keeping Adda away from Casey was more important than anything else.

"Tell me next time." Rio smirked at him. "I can always use a good laugh."

Noor ignored the rude gesture Pel offered Rio. "What do you need to join the expedition?"

"Money, political support, or something Dr. Björn cares about," Adda said. "All of those, ideally." They ate in silence for a while.

"I'll write the Vestan station council, too," she said. "Since Oxia is cutting so many corners and defunding the project, the council might be able to force Oxia to give the expedition to the University of Mars. Dr. Björn should appreciate that. Ve used to teach there."

"You might as well write Sloane directly," Iridian said. "It'll get back to the captain sooner or later." After their refusal to play along with Sloane's endgame on Vesta, the captain would probably laugh and ignore it, but working for Oxia had infuriated Sloane. Maybe the captain would want to undo one of the worst things the crew had done on Oxia's orders.

If Adda did somehow get them on the expedition, it'd be an exciting way to lie low and avoid the ITA. She and Iridian would be together in a place where nothing wanted to separate them or take over Adda's brain. It'd be a long-overdue honeymoon.

Wiley had been staring at his food instead of eating it, but now he refocused on the conversation and Adda. "Won't an official letter to the Vestan council get back to the AIs, too? You said they were based there."

"They were, but they left," Pel said.

"It may get back to them," said Adda, "but I think reminding all those people about their involvement in Dr. Björn's . . . Well, it wasn't kidnapping, exactly . . ."

"Um, I know from kidnapping," said Pel. "That's what it was."

"Ve signed the contract voluntarily," Adda argued. "Anyway, all the council members benefited from Oxia kickbacks, so they were all involved in either getting Dr. Björn to or keeping ver on Vesta. Now they're in a position to get ver out of the Oxia contract. I think it's worth asking. And, again, asking is free."

"It'd give ver a better chance than ve had yesterday," said Iridian. "And if it happens to actually work, ve'll owe us big enough that ve might let us join up. Not bad."

"And you're sure that once you're gone, Casey won't come after us?" Pel asked.

When it came to Casey, Iridian couldn't be sure of anything. "That's our best guess."

"Well, the ZVs will take care of me," said Rio. "Maybe you three could hire on with us."

Wiley's expression was thoughtful, Pel grinned, and Noor shook his head. "Oh my gods, no," said Pel. "I can't do all that 'yes ma'am, no sir' stuff." He'd been respectful enough on Sloane's crew, but formality and order were much more important among the ZVs.

"Why would I want to do that when I can make money on my own?" Noor asked. "I've got an identity hidden away in Albana Station on Vesta. If I can get there, I'm gone, and good luck to the rest of you. Relying on a best guess sounds like a good way to get dead, doesn't it?" He glared at the tabletop, lips tightly shut and jaw muscles twitching.

"Can we count on your help until you find your way to Albana?" Iridian asked. When Noor nodded, she said, "Okay. That just leaves finding some cash to live on and dealing with the awakened AIs."

"Oh, that's all," Noor said in a way that implied that was plenty.

Living on Yăo Station would be a hell of a lot cheaper than Vesta or Ceres, but cheap didn't count for much without income. Adda had only just started her search for ways to join Dr. Björn's expedition, so they'd be on Yăo a while. Iridian, Wiley, and Rio listed search- able terms that might lead to the kind of work they could do. Noor, Adda, and Iridian took their collected queries to the drones Shin- getsu had asked them to recapture, and Shingetsu showed them how to send those out while Pel, Rio, and Wiley scouted the station for somewhere to live that didn't have chimes playing and incense burning at all hours of the day and night.

Hours later, the drones returned from their trip to Patchwork range with the results people wanted. Pel, Rio, and Wiley had found them somewhere tolerable to stay, which Rio described as a "defensible closet with fewer bugs than the other ones." While they went off to get Pel's money converted, Iridian, Adda, and Noor took over a meditation room in the temple to review what Adda had found.

The last time Iridian had seen Adda that happy was when she'd found out Sloane had gotten a workspace generator installed in their Rheasilvia Station apartment. "I was right! The implant manufacturers outsource firmware development to just a few companies. Noor, Biometallic Technologies made the firmware for both of ours!"

Noor raised an eyebrow, probably in response to Adda's enthusiasm as much as her words. "Thanks. Now I have an answer for that trivia-night question I always forget about."

Iridian frowned at him. Aside from the rudeness, Adda was giving Noor a slightly head-cocked expression that meant she couldn't tell whether he was being sarcastic. "How does knowing who made your implant firmware help us?" Iridian asked.

"Casey and Mairie have some way to use developers' neural implant nets to influence people faster than I've ever heard of," Adda said. From what she'd said in the past, Iridian gathered that although the jack that connected the implant to comps and consoles was always changing and improving, there was only one neural implant net configuration that allowed devs' workspaces to function. "I think they're using a vulnerability in our implant firmware to do it."

"Oh gods, are you serious?" Noor looked like he was about to be sick. "That's what that pulse was in the water treatment plant, wasn't it? Something fucking with our implants?"

"Exactly," said Adda. "Mairie's signal approach is unique, as far as I can tell. It's had decades to influence the Odin Razum the usual way. It's possible that Casey showed it the vulnerability, and when Mairie put that together with our Marsat IDs, it must've looked like a perfect solution to its lack of supervision."

"This wouldn't be the first time Casey shared how-to-fuck-people-over tips with other AIs," said Iridian. It was one of the creepiest things Casey did.

"So I think that if Biometallic Technologies fixes that vulnerability, we can keep Casey and Mairie from influencing us so quickly," Adda said. Noor dragged both hands through his hair, exposing the jack in his temple for a moment, eyes widening with every word Adda said. "I'm working on the description now, but it's going to be up to them to test it or coordinate with the Odin Razum. This is the first vulnerability I've ever reported! I'll show it to you before I send it so you can—"

"Gods, do you really think they'd do that?" Noor groaned. "They'll delete your message from every system they have and say, 'What report?' if the truth comes out."

Another disturbing possibility had just occurred to Iridian. She touched her scalp above where the ITA had put a gods-damned implant in her head. She couldn't wait to get rid of it. "Is that vulnerability in whatever the ITA put in us?"

"From what I saw in the clinic, yours is a localized device." Adda was still looking worriedly at Noor, whose jaw was twitching again. "Something that small couldn't have created the simulation you described. Its primary function would've been regulating the nannite culture, which coordinated with a pseudo-organic system that maintained the sim. That implant wouldn't have the same firmware Noor's and my nets have."

"All right," Iridian said, "so what'll fixing that vulnerability take?"

"The ideal scenario is that we tell Biometallic, which I'm just about to do. They'll make the corrections and push a new firmware version out to our implants with an explanation for everybody else with a neural implant net like ours." Adda was still watching Noor, whose reddening face and hands fisted in his pant legs were making Iridian wonder just what kind of tirade he was keeping himself from shouting. "But if they won't fix it—"

"Could you please join us in reality, where they fucking won't?" Noor snapped.

"Watch it," said Iridian.

Maybe Iridian was imagining that she could hear his teeth grinding, but she doubted it. Noor leaned away from Adda and waved stiffly for her to keep talking. "If they won't fix it based on my description, which they should," she added defensively, "we know someone who can analyze it and tell Biometallic what needs to be fixed. And if Biometallic still won't fix it when we've pointed out all the problems, then the modder probably can."

That'd be Kanti, the modder on Ceres who'd put in Iridian's and Adda's comms implants. After all the trouble the two of them had caused in Ceres Station, getting to that shop without the ITA arresting them would require a good disguise and a lot of luck. Adda had done it once, but if the ITA was smart, that would've motivated them to put even more security measures in place.

Noor looked thoroughly unimpressed with this objective. "How do all these 'probablys' and 'I thinks' keep the awakened AIs out of our fucking heads? We need to take the source material—"

"The what?" Iridian asked.

"The AI interpretation base for the software," said Noor. "What the dev AI uses to collaborate with the team guiding the project. Even a human-readable code version would help, if your modder reads code."

"They do," Adda said.

"We need the source before we do anything else," said Noor. "You can tell Biometallic about the vulnerability later. And how the hell are we paying your modder?"

"Biometallic makes a lot of medical software." Noor's reaction had apparently taken all the fun out of this endeavor for Adda, and she was frowning at her comp instead of talking to him. "If we get far enough into their systems to copy our implants' firmware source, someone will buy any other proprietary data we can take with us."

"Do you know where they keep this stuff?" Iridian asked.

"They have their own orbital station. Everything I've read indicates that the firmware is housed there, but it's orbiting Ceres." And she'd have run everything she'd read through analyses that looked for systematic recent edits that'd indicate Casey was setting a trap for them. After Tash's death, Adda didn't trust any text until she'd tested it for tampering.

"Fuck that then," said Noor.

"Hold up," Iridian said. "This could solve all our problems, yeah? We get in there, steal your and Adda's implant firmware and anything else we can get our hands on, then sell it all." They'd be selling medical equipment data, unfortunately. Somebody could change it and kill people who that equipment kept alive. It was one of several reasons Iridian would've torn the one in her head out with her bare hands, if that wouldn't require cracking her skull open.

But people wouldn't necessarily misuse what they stole, and Casey would influence Adda again if they caught her with that vulnerability still in her implant. That took priority. "Depending on how much we make, we could help Björn somehow," Iridian said. "Blackmail someone in Oxia, or hire a lawyer to get ver out of vis commitments to the corp, even. With enough money, we'd have options for convincing ver."

"How much are we planning to take, here?" Noor asked. "And what's my cut?"

"As much as we can get you," said Iridian. "It's digital. We can take on a lot."

Noor threw up his hands. "Where are we getting the pseudo-organics to store 'a lot'? And how do you know we'll be able to grab enough that it's worth, you know, waltzing back into the ITA's home stationspace on this ship we don't even have, with awakened AIs out there looking for us?"

Adda raised her comp-gloved hand. "I'll send you everything I have on Biometallic. The firmware they make is so valuable that I don't think we'd need a separate tank to store enough to pay for the trip and make a profit. As to the ship, I know the pilots here aren't anyone's first pick, but some of them have ships. We saw them while we were docking."

"And if Biometallic ignores the report like you're saying they will, then the chance to fix the vulnerability ourselves should make the trip worth it," said Iridian. "Casey's already chatting with the station AI, and I figure Adda's right. Someday soon it'll find a way to do more. Besides, don't you have *two* implants in your head at this point?"

Noor laughed, although he sounded more disgusted than amused. "No. Why would the ITA put in more hardware when the neural implant net I've already got works fine?"

Pel leaned into the meditation room, rattling the beads that hung over its doorway. "We have funds!" He threw himself onto a cushion beside Adda and shoved his comp between her own and her face. Wiley's hand pushed the beads aside so he and Rio could see in from the hall.

Adda frowned at whatever Pel's comp displayed, then said, "All right. Thanks."

"All right?" Pel withdrew his comp hand to press it to his chest while his eyes and mouth opened in scandalized protest. "*All right?* This is, like, a month of rent here."

Iridian ignored him. "Like I was saying, if we pull off a run on Biometallic, we can fix the vulnerability ourselves and make enough afterward to get us onto Björn's expedition."

Rio sat down beside Pel. "Then let's get to it."

Comforting as it was that Rio would follow Iridian's lead as long as she said she'd found a corp it'd pay to target, they had more to discuss. Iridian, Rio, Noor, and Wiley spent an hour going over the op in more detail and listing equipment they'd need. They separated it into "essential" (transport, armor for Iridian and Wiley, mid-range ship-safe weapons, a comp for Adda that the ITA and the AIs had never touched, a datacask for bringing and removing data), and "optional" (armor for Noor, Adda, and Pel, parts for the shield Iridian hoped to rebuild, long-range weapons, and lip balm and lotion to combat Yǎo's painfully dry atmo). Occasionally Pel interrupted with something funny from social feeds that were hours out of date.

When they were satisfied with the list, despite Noor's protests about his armor ending up in the optional section, Adda compared the list to the money now in Pel's Yǎo Station account. "Pel, Noor, and I will see what we can find for a usable datacask," she said. "But the rest of the essential list isn't going to happen without more money."

Pel's shoulders drooped. "That was all I had left, Sissy."

"I know. I'll pay you back when I can. Until then . . ." She glanced around at Iridian, Rio, and Wiley. "Do you all still have your Marsat IDs?"

A few minutes later, Iridian was leading Rio and Wiley down the dark corridor toward the Odin Razum again, with comps blaring their Marsat IDs on whatever band the station AI accepted, so it wouldn't lock them out or set its influenced gang on them. This time, only six Odin Razum came out of the water treatment plant's orange light to greet them. "So, you've been selling water and Patchwork access," Iridian said. "Where's the corporate share? When was the last time you paid into it?"

According to Adda, budgetary management was usually part of a port management AI package, but Yăo Station's previous owners hadn't needed it. This trick would work if, without that budgetary function activated, the AI deferred to an upper-level corporate employee's orders.

Judging by the worried and angry looks they exchanged, the Odin Razum understood what Iridian was asking just fine. "Why should—" one of the Odin Razum started to ask. All six stopped moving for a moment.

"We don't have an account for that," one of them said grudgingly. "But we'll make one."

"You'd better," Rio said. "And here's the account you can transfer the corporate share into. See where it says how much is supposed to be in there? That's how we know you're not paying." She twisted her thick wrist to display Pel's local account information on her comp projection.

The numbers she was referencing were the difference between what was in the account now and what Adda calculated they'd need to complete the op and live on until she sold whatever they stole. It wasn't the Odin Razum's money any more than it was the Shieldrunners'. Maybe they'd make enough selling stolen proprietary tech to pay Yăo Station's people back, but Iridian had to take care of her crew first. As Captain Sloane had once said, nobody else was looking out for them.

"We'll wait," said Iridian.

Rio stood with her huge feet shoulder-width apart, watching

the Odin Razum's base in the water treatment mod like she could stand there forever. Wiley and Iridian crossed paths, pacing. They were both trying to cover the side approaches and their egress at once, and she almost got a laugh out of him by faking right and left like she was blocking his path on purpose.

"Hey, Rio," Iridian said. "What's it like in the ZVs? All work and no play?"

"It's a good balance," Rio said without shifting her gaze from the Odin Razum. "Some scientists found out the ideal rest and action periods for the NEU military. The NEU didn't do what the scientists said to do, but the ZVs did. It always feels like the day before we're bored with barhopping or family or whatever we've been doing with downtime, we get a new op to train for. It came a little late for me last time and I got antsy and pissed the ITA off, but that wasn't the ZVs' fault. And we don't have much turnover, so going back to work feels just like getting the gang back together."

"That sounds amazing," Wiley said quietly.

"I've been with them ever since Recognition." Rio sounded proud of that. If she was referencing the day the NEU officially recognized colonial independence, then that was over a year longer than Iridian had spent with the Shieldrunners. "I can't stay out of a fight for long," Rio added.

"I hear you." Wiley sounded more thoughtful than sad, as Iridian had hoped he would.

If the ZVs would take Rio back after all this was over, they might hire Wiley too. That way, even if the AIs turned on the two of them after Iridian and Adda were out of their reach, Wiley and Rio would have a whole army to defend them. Besides, if Wiley went back to construction on Mars, he'd keep shoving his anger and his war stories down until he blew up, or blew something else up. That was, she'd learned, how he'd gotten sent to Sorenson

ITAS. The ITA took a hard view of people who kept fighting the war after Recognition.

During almost an hour, the Odin Razum kept transferring money into the local account until it got to the number Adda said it would take to get to Biometallic's station. One of the Odin Razum people who came forward to report their success squinted at his comp and asked, "Can we use this account too? For, uh, business expenses?"

"No," Iridian said. "Corporate share goes to the corp. That's why we're not taking everything you have." She turned her back on them and started walking before the Odin Razum got any more clever ideas. The universe they were living in now, as quasi-employees and quasi-slaves of an AI, had to be confusing and frustrating. If Shingetsu hadn't told Iridian how much the Odin Razum charged the locals for water, she'd feel sorry for them.

As it was, Iridian felt only hope. She and Adda were together, safe, and about to take the next step toward getting out of the AIs' reach. They'd be operating with whatever equipment they scrounged up on Yăo Station, but now they'd all have allies equipped to fight the Odin Razum or anybody else the AIs sent their way. In theory, although she hadn't talked to the others about it yet, they were operating as a crew. And Iridian was their captain.

CHAPTER 17

Days until launch: 27
(holding for mechanical issues)

The ship that Adda had suggested that Iridian hire to carry the
Shieldrunners, as the rest of Yǎo Station was calling their group,
shook around them as it entered the Ceres-Jupiter reliable route.
This was the point at which she, Iridian, Wiley, and Rio needed
to avoid passing ITA ships' sensor range. Although the nannite
cultures that would've announced their location and immobilized
them on command were gone, the ITA's biometric profiles on all
of them would be precise and recent enough to identify them
remotely.

Adda had also read about more frequent physical boardings
for inspection in Ceres stationspace over the past few weeks,
especially among passenger transports. The light cargo hauler
they'd selected was designed to carry three people and would
only appear to carry one. The arrangement left the passengers in
uncomfortably tight quarters during the first part of the trip, but
the small ship would be less conspicuous to both the ITA and the
awakened intelligences than a passenger vessel with more seats
and beds would've been.

Their individual internet traffic patterns had been harder to deal with. After so long with limited access, it would've been too hard on everyone to fly through high connectivity areas without taking advantage. Pel, in particular, would forget. He'd once checked his social feeds while at knifepoint. The fact that he'd been high at the time did not make Adda feel any better about that.

The ITA's digital profiles were brief to the point of uselessness, but the intelligences would rely on them. Adda's replacement for the comp Casey had stolen for her on Ceres should throw them off for a little while. For everyone else, they were relying on moving through the Patchwork nodes quickly enough not to attract the intelligences' attention that way.

Iridian handed Adda an enviro suit, which she accepted without looking up from her comp. Now that her comp was in range of the Patchwork buoys that orbited with the reliable route, her latest test results and monitoring reports were coming in. She had a hypothesis about the intelligences' activity that she was almost ready to regard as a theory.

If Casey was really interested in getting human help with whatever it was building, it should've influenced a hardware architect, or someone who could find a place for them to build, or a billionaire to fund its project. Casey should've had the capacity to understand it would need all those things. Adda had compiled a list of such people within near-real-time communication range of where the intelligences' ships had appeared on her tracking routines, and she'd made new routines to monitor newsfeeds, social feeds, and other publicly accessible data about those individuals.

Abrupt changes in those individuals' social feed behavior, opinions on and frequency of discussion of intelligences, and investments in remote locations where a project that size would've been built all would've gotten collected for her review.

She was also assuming that others' influence symptoms would proceed much like Adda's had, although not all the useful targets would have neural implants like hers. So far, none of the routines she had running suggested that awakened intelligences had influenced anyone else. Limited as her observations and analyses were, she would've expected them to turn up something suspicious if there'd been anything to find. So far, it'd all been false positives explained by normal life or business.

Iridian put her hands on Adda's shoulders and smiled when Adda looked away from her comp. She kissed Adda gently. "Now we can suit up." Iridian already wore the armor they'd gotten printed for her on Yǎo Station, colored the dull steel of undyed carbon composite. The black-and-yellow ZV armor Rio wore made Iridian's and Wiley's look even more plain. "Let's get moving before somebody takes a good look at this ship and realizes it's carrying more than algae."

Adda put on her enviro suit, still thinking about the reports. If Casey understood it could've benefited from many humans helping it, and chose not to influence those people, it wasn't doing that out of the goodness of its nonexistent heart. It valued efficiency.

It also valued self-preservation, but fear of discovery hadn't stopped it, or more accurately the *Coin*, from revealing its nature on Barbary Station. Perhaps it had learned more about humans' generally violent reactions to awakened intelligences since then. Since neither efficiency nor self-preservation were motivating Casey's restraint, two possibilities remained. The first was that Casey, or even one of the other awakened intelligences, had a complex inhibition or strategy that Adda would need a fully staffed development lab to understand. Zombie intelligences were complex. Awakened intelligences might be effectively impossible for humans to comprehend.

The second possibility, the most likely one given everything she *did* know about these intelligences, was that while Sloane's crew was awakening the intelligences on Barbary Station, the inexperienced and ill-informed technicians had allowed an overfitting error. Based on some historical data the intelligences had obtained, they had erroneously concluded that only Adda and Iridian, out of all humanity, could help them.

Overfitting to a particular kind of human intervention would explain why Casey claimed to need Adda and Iridian's assistance with whatever it was building. Without that error, it could've influenced people qualified to build massive pseudo-organic constructs, like the one Casey had shown Adda in the workspace on Ceres. Even if the intelligences stole every modern supercomputer construction plan in existence, the error would compel Casey to obtain Adda and Iridian's participation. "Where can we build something massive?" would've been a much less challenging problem than "How can we make these two humans help us build it?" and Casey seemed determined to solve both.

The exact nature of Casey's inhibition against influencing multiple targets, which appeared to be a product of their overfitting error interacting with previous anti-influence conditioning, would depend on how the overfitting error had developed as the intelligences awakened. If Adda could talk to Casey without losing her mind, one of the first questions she'd ask it was why it preferred her and Iridian over anyone else who'd been on Barbary Station.

In normal intelligence development, the whole project might be restarted to erase such a severe overfitting error. All intelligences that had awakened before Casey had been destroyed, either by their development team or by people the development team told about them. None had existed in their awakened state for longer than a few hours.

This was the first known instance of an awakened intelligence existing long enough to form and execute plans. And Adda was the only person in the universe in a position to observe it up close. Closer than she would've preferred, but to her surprise, that made it even more exciting. Dangerous as it would be to herself and to Iridian, Adda longed for a chance to study how Casey and the other intelligences had reached this point.

On the remainder of their journey to Biometallic 1, the Biometallic Technologies station orbiting Ceres, Adda downloaded the latest research about overfitting errors. Her analyses would continue to search for people who Casey contacted and didn't influence. Their existence would support Adda's suspicions about the overfitting error.

The Biometallic station maintained a fixed orbit that kept it out of Ceres shipping lanes. That should have made the landing easier, but Adda had never been on a ship that shook this much. The crew had gotten what they'd paid the pilot for: next to nothing.

Although Adda had no way of confirming it from her current position, the ship should've been approaching Biometallic 1's cargo docking bay. The Shieldrunners' ship was approaching the station faster than any ship Adda had ever been on. Maybe this was typical for a vessel that reported only one person onboard.

Adda, Iridian, Rio, and Wiley were in the cargo area, inside a shipping container that everyone except Rio and Pel had worked on to make it scan like a shipment of algae pallets. Extremely cheap algae was Yǎo's only export, so it was plausible cargo. Adda had typed up a story about using algae to feed pseudo-organic cultures, but the pilot would have to deliver it powerfully and quickly to stop anyone from thinking too hard about it. Thanks to the Shieldrunners' combined efforts, only the algae and the pilot had shown up on every ITA scan they'd been through.

They'd had to celebrate Iridian's birthday in that container, and Adda hadn't even had a present for her. She had one in mind, but it was commissioned art that would have to wait until they sold what they stole from Biometallic. Maybe she'd find something on Biometallic's servers that'd make up for the delay.

She'd look for that only after she found the source for the firmware her and Noor's neural implant nets used. Since the idea was first proposed, she'd reconsidered Noor's position. He'd been right in his assessment that it was reckless to waste their time waiting on Biometallic to solve their problem while Casey was searching for an opportunity to influence Adda. They, or Kanti, could be looking for the solution at the same time Biometallic did. And if Biometallic ignored Adda's warnings, she, Noor, and Kanti would have to find the vulnerability themselves anyway. She'd take the source and anything else that her conscience would let her sell. Despite what Iridian said, the buyers could use every source in Biometallic's library to hurt someone.

But that was a possibility, and Casey's pursuit was an unyielding fact. If Biometallic ignored Adda's report, Kanti wouldn't rewrite the firmware for free. She intended to have something to pay with.

The ship jerked sideways. Adda shut her eyes as she was jostled against Iridian, who gripped her hand gently in an armored glove. They were making as little noise as possible, to reduce the chances of Ceres customs or the ITA differentiating them from algae. Armor for the other three and an enviro suit for Adda protected them inside the container, which was cold enough to stop harvested algae from rotting.

At the time they'd entered the container, Pel still hadn't told them how he'd be getting them into Biometallic's station. He'd already reached Ceres on a Ganymede passenger vessel his new fake ID allowed him to board. If he hadn't gotten them docking permissions and a way into the firmware library, then they'd fight their way in and out, but he also hadn't sent them any information about station security.

In addition to Iridian's, Wiley's, and Rio's armor, each soldier had two long-distance charges, and everybody had knives. Even Adda had one, although it was sealed inside her enviro suit at the moment. She'd used everything she'd read about the station to create plans in which violence wouldn't be required, but without more information from Pel, she couldn't count on any of what she'd planned being useful.

The ship changed speed, decelerating, Adda hoped, and pressed them against the wall. She reached for her sick bag, but that was as helpful outside her suit as her knife was inside it. Biometallic kept the station's environment healthy, so at least she had Earthlike gravity to look forward to once they docked.

It feels like we're landing, Iridian subvocalized. When Adda opened her eyes enough to see her, Iridian wore one of her encouraging, brilliant smiles. *Pel got this part right.*

With one final shudder, the ship landed on a pad in Biometallic's docking bay. Its engines whined so loudly Adda tried to cover her ears, but her enviro suit's helmet was still on. Eventually the sound dropped below the range that the suit's external mics picked up, and after a few minutes the pilot unlocked the container door.

Everyone's comps blared alerts or buzzed as they reconnected to the Patchwork and updated themselves with everything that'd happened over the two days they'd been stuck in the container. Adda turned on the looping routine on hers, to keep anybody watching security cam feeds from noticing her. The ship had its own looper, which would take priority as long as they were in the docking bay, but she didn't want to forget to turn it on when they left. The others had slept in the container when they wanted to, but sleeping while standing up in an enviro suit hadn't been an actual option for her. At this point, she didn't trust her memory for much of anything.

What she could see of the station through the container's open end was as different from Yăo Station as she could've imagined. Compared to Yăo Station's wide-open port, the Biometallic 1 docking bay was tiny. The pad the ship sat on took up most of the space. Equipment and supplies around the walls were physically labeled and organized. A cargo bot sat silent in a charging hutch on one side, its body shining in the bright light and its job apparently finished, judging by the clean surfaces of everything else in view. The pilot wandered over to a rack of parts and selected something small that still required two hands to hold. She held it over her head to look at its underside, nodded briskly, and walked back to her ship with it.

Iridian, Wiley, and Rio had been in armor for two days, not the enviro suit and under-suit thermals Adda had on. Armor had convenient attachment points for tie-down straps, which let the other three all unhook themselves while Adda struggled out of a harness Iridian had put her into. Another advantage the fighters had was that armor was designed for multi-day wear. The under-suit Adda wore, thank all the gods and devils, was disposable. "Everybody look out the door for a few minutes," Iridian announced.

Once everybody had turned around, Adda disposed of the under-suit, wiped herself down with some chemical cloths, and changed into boring black and dull purple formal clothes. Pel had insisted she wear the business attire for "a thing I'm setting up." Whatever the "thing" was, Adda hoped it wouldn't require the knife now hidden in her jacket. Even though Iridian had made her practice taking it out of the jacket without feeling around for it or snagging it on fabric, Adda wasn't sure she could defend herself with it.

The pilot picked up Adda's sealed bag of underthings and her enviro suit and sighed. "Two hours and I'm out," she reminded them in a gruff professional tone that would've been believable if she hadn't been so high when they'd met her on Yăo.

"Got it." Iridian stretched her arms wide, bouncing on her toes the way she did when she wanted to go for a run. The armored helmet made her voice sound hollow and farther away than she really was. "See you in one." It would take the ITA seven minutes to mobilize from Ceres Station, so if they made enough of a fuss to call attention to themselves, then it didn't matter how long the whole operation took.

Adda's comp vibrated against her hand, almost continuously, in the pattern she'd designated for messages. She shifted to see the projection window in the new, deep purple glove she'd had printed as part of her disguise. Hundreds of messages were pouring into the device, all with the senders obscured. Some were sizable enough to contain images or vid, and she didn't have time to assess them all for veracity, let alone read them. The most recent one was plain text. "Stay in Ceres orbit. We need your help."

Her breath shuddered out of her, and despite the docking bay's well-filtered air, she couldn't seem to get it back. She'd set her comp to identify messages that originated from intelligences, and it was doing that now, with priority highlighting and a tracing function it could finally use now that they were back on the Patchwork. Adda subvocalized *Who is this?* into her comp's messaging system.

According to her comp's assessment, it had to be either AegiSKADA or Casey. AegiSKADA would've answered her question. No more messages appeared.

The early stages of Casey's influence had been marked by Adda lying to Iridian about the intelligences. If she resisted symptoms like that, it should slow the progression of any influence

Casey was exerting on her. At the very least, Iridian would know what was happening and do something about it.

I just heard from Casey, Adda subvocalized to Iridian. *It sent me a whole lot of information. Too much to look through now.* Casey always provided more information than Adda thought existed in answer to her questions. As terrifying as its obsession with her was, Adda missed being able to trust the information it brought her without running everything through tampering analyses.

Iridian swore and pushed past Wiley and Rio, who were checking their suits over. She ducked a little to look into Adda's eyes. Whatever she saw there must've made her feel better, because she relaxed and pulled Adda into a loose hug. Her armor pressed wrinkles into Adda's fancy clothes.

There's no evidence linking visible eye features to influence, Adda told her. *Although eye movement can indicate honesty or the lack thereof.*

Oh. Iridian's grip on Adda pulled tight again. Aloud, she said, "It must've been watching Ceres stationspace. We had to cross it to get here. *Shit.* I thought we'd have more time."

Adda had predicted that they'd have a few hours before the awakened intelligences found them, but that was only because they hadn't reached out or sent any ITA agents after them during the trip from Yǎo Station to Ceres. Maybe they wanted her to be on Ceres. It was where the ITA had put her for influence recovery, and that would explain why they hadn't interfered with the crew's travel plans until now.

I can only guess what they'll do, Adda told Iridian. *Sometimes I'm wrong.*

Adda's comp buzzed twice, then spouted, "Hey, did you mean the awakened AIs are watching us?" in Noor's voice. When the Yǎo pilot had dropped Noor and Pel off on Ganymede, Noor had met up with a contact who took him to one of Ceres's many ratholes. Well-equipped underground rooms were hidden across the 'ject, outside the station's protective dome. Intelligence operatives on both sides of the war had built hundreds through-out populated space. Noor had discovered this one, and he said it was rarely used now.

If it was like most ratholes, it'd have a workspace generator that was less than ten years old, and a satellite connection to the Patchwork. He'd be watching the armored suits' cam feeds. Being observed made Adda uncomfortable, but she appreciated that somebody was watching for trouble while she was busy. And, since he'd already found a way into Biometallic's systems, he could remotely solve any security problems they encountered.

"It was one of the awakened AIs," Iridian said. "Watch out for the ships Adda told you about."

"Yeah," said Noor. He and Adda had put together a routine to spot the awakened intelligences, and it would alert him if one appeared in Ceres or Biometallic 1 stationspace. "And we'll meet back home when this venture goes to all the hells I bet it does." Home, for the purposes of this operation, meant Yăo Station.

Adda pushed herself away from Iridian and tugged at the business suit to smooth out the wrinkles. After weeks in influence recovery and Yăo Station, she'd forgotten how empowering it felt to wear clothes that fit and didn't smell like sweat, multiple recy-clings, or industrial-grade detergent. The warm once-over Iridian gave her was a delightful bonus.

"This doesn't change the plan," Adda said. "We'll just keep watching for them like we have been."

"Yes, ma'am," Iridian purred. She'd gotten Adda out of that suit as soon as she'd put it on to test the fit on Yăo, but all four of them had been in very close quarters for over a week since. It was nice to have something to look forward to when they got back to Yăo.

"And we'll be watching out for anybody they influenced, too," said Rio.

Pel's whispered "I'm waiting" transmitted over Adda's comp with the operation channel's buzzing signal. "You coming or not?"

"We're coming." Iridian caught Wiley's eye in his helmet's projection of his face, then shut her own projector off, turning her faceplate black. Wiley and Rio shut off their faceplate projectors too. "Eyes up, Shieldrunners."

The bay's loading dock, which led to the rest of the station, was smaller than the ones Adda had seen on other stations. Because it was so close to Ceres Station, Biometallic 1 received smaller and more frequent shipments than most other places in the universe. The schematics she'd downloaded showed a passenger passthrough nearby, although it wasn't connected to the docking bay.

The loading dock's door opened before Iridian reached it, and Pel grinned at them through the doorway. Adda hadn't taken good notes on his cover story because she'd been finding a textile printer on Yǎo capable of producing business-appropriate fabric. Usually Pel passed himself off as an intern, graduate student, or low-level administrative aide. Whatever role he was playing this time required neater hair than Adda had ever seen on his head and business attire, which was rumpled despite his insistence that Adda look professional upon arrival. "Come on in," he said. "I actually know where we're going."

They followed Pel into a storeroom lit with bright afternoon sunsim. Somewhere beyond, Adda's and Noor's neural implant net firmware was in one of the station's server tanks. Noor had put together a backdoor to the library. When Adda plugged in the datacask she'd brought, the backdoor would install itself. That way, if Adda didn't find her and Noor's firmware this time, he would let them back in later.

"You found somebody who can get us into the firmware library?" Adda asked Pel.

"Kind of?" Pel waved them down a hallway, also lit in afternoon sunsim, while he looked down the hallway in the other direction. There had to be cams everywhere, and Adda's feed looper should be hiding all five of them. She turned off the sound on her comp. Three people in full armor would look suspicious, but the hallway had been empty so far.

"Keep talking," Iridian said.

"So, what I told my 'mentor' was that I'm inviting my rich, eccentric big sister and if ve wanted vis lab to get a big chunk of her financial backing, ve'd better clear the place out and let Sissy have a look at everything. She's eccentric, see?"

"Oh gods, ve bought that?" Wiley asked.

Pel grinned. "The way I've been talking and fucking, ve did!"

This set off a wave of laughter among the armored folks. "Tash would've loved this," said Wiley.

"You will use any excuse to get your dick into an op," said Rio.

"If that's the only part *you* use, then you're doing sex wrong," said Pel, setting the other three laughing again.

Lying to scientists and engineers about funding projects they cared about was truly awful. If she could, Adda would see that the victim of Pel's con got paid. Where she'd find the money and time, between securing her implant from the intelligences as a short-term solution and getting away from them as a long-term one, she didn't know.

"So this place is empty all the way there?" Iridian asked Pel.

"Yeah, that's what ve said! Oh, and you're all Sissy's bodyguards, by the way."

Wiley and Rio nodded in unison and Iridian said, "Got it."

I'm going looking for the station intelligence, Adda told Iridian. Iridian's jaw set in a hard line. She'd been adopting her combat mode since they stepped off the ship, broken only by Pel's description of his activities on Biometallic 1. Her mission-focused state of mind would keep her calm while Adda reached out to an intelligence for the first time since Mairie had influenced her on Yǎo Station.

Adda had run out of prescription concentration aids. Since she couldn't afford the ingredients to make her own, she was relying on a case she'd selected from a Yǎo Station resident's dented lockbox. It wasn't the most reliable brand, but it was so affordable and common that the case she bought seemed likely to contain the real stuff. The red tab was sour on her tongue and took over a minute to kick in. It'd been so long since her last dose that she hardly noticed the delay.

When the sharpsheet hit her brain, Biometallic 1's hallway went gray. Everything on her comp projection sharpened and slowed, giving her plenty of time to process the latest news from Ceres stationspace while she activated her digital intermediary. It formed beside her, a dark gray outline as tall and muscular as Iridian, without her defined features. With Adda's pulse pounding in her ears, she sent her intermediary out into the station network, looking for one of two ways this particular intelligence would allow itself to be contacted by someone other than its supervisor.

"Noor's asking how you'll get us into the firmware library," Iridian said to Pel. "I want to know too."

"Let's see," Adda said slowly, "if Ficience will help." This station management intelligence was much newer than Mairie. Although Ficience was far from the most trustworthy intelligence on the market, it was powerful and one of the most secure. It had its vulnerabilities like everything did, but her intermediary was still searching for this particular installation's faults.

"Can we call it Fish for short?" Pel asked.

Adda dragged her consciousness away from her comp and intermediary to smile at him. "Maybe." Thanks to that question, any workspace she got into would probably express itself in oceanic imagery.

"If that doesn't go through, what's the plan?" Iridian asked.

"The lab comps have to access that library, is what ve said." Pel shrugged. "So . . . just plug in that datacask, right?"

Adda's intermediary brushed the edges of Ficience's network. The feedback gave her a full-body shiver. Even outside a workspace, the intelligence's density and implacable processing were intimidating. The majority of this one's focus was in stationspace, nowhere near her.

She was still sighing in relief when she considered just what might distract it. Station admins had approved her visit. Thanks to her feed looper, none of their group had provided biometric data, not even gait or voiceprints. Their comps' ID broadcasts were turned off. Clearing out two whole modules of the small station should've attracted at least some of its attention. Why *wouldn't* a station intelligence track visitors like them?

"Something's happening in stationspace." The intensity in Iridian's voice said it was something dangerous. Adda scanned the newsfeeds on her comp. She didn't have access to Ficience's cams yet. "Noor's tracking . . ." Iridian paused to listen. "Oh hell, what's its name?"

"What's what?" asked Pel, even though Iridian had directed her question at Noor.

"A ship, and . . ." Iridian broke into a series of increasingly severe epithets. "It's the *Mayhem*. The gods-damned *Mayhem* is here."

Adda and Pel gasped. Rio voiced her and Wiley's shared confusion. "Who owns it?"

"Captain Sloane, basically," said Pel.

"Shit," said Rio.

"Your old captain's here?" Wiley looked around like Sloane's troops were going to come around a corner any minute.

"Maybe not," Adda said. "The pilot could've sold the ship, or taken on a new client."

Iridian snorted. "The only reason a Kuiper native would sell his ship is if he couldn't scrap it himself." That left the possibility that the pilot, a Kuiper native named Gavran, was flying somebody other than Sloane's crew. Gavran had helped Iridian, Adda, and Pel escape the captain's allies on Vesta, which could've put Gavran out of a job as Sloane's raid pilot.

However, the captain went to expensive lengths to keep experts on the crew. After Adda had uncovered the fate of Gavran's missing brother, the pilot had been repaying that debt when he flew her family off Vesta. The captain hated to lose crew members, so Sloane might've forgiven Gavran for that. If word of their run on Biometallic had gotten back to the captain somehow, maybe through Noor's Ganymede contact, Sloane might've even come looking for Adda, Iridian, and Pel personally. "We can't risk assuming it's anyone else," Adda said.

"She's right," said Iridian. "If Sloane's ops are still running the way they did a few months ago, there'll be max five people on that ship, with blades, good armor, and less-lethals. Mostly techs, maybe a merc or two. The captain might not even be here."

"We can't count on that," Adda said. When she and Iridian had been on Sloane's crew, the captain had come along on three of the crew's four major ops.

"Yeah, the worst case is Sloane's with them. All right, who's been telling the gods to go fuck themselves? All the devils in hell wouldn't do us this way." Iridian turned to Pel. "How far are we from the lab?"

"Like, two minutes."

"Good. Let's move."

Adda's intermediary stepped through a wall and into the hallway in front of her, flickering as her attention cycled between its feedback and the rest of the information on her comp. If Iridian hadn't liked her hands free in situations like this, Adda would've grabbed her armored glove. The intermediary was reporting that Ficience still had an open vulnerability that other intelligence experts had discovered last year, and its supervisors hadn't installed the correction yet.

The fact that Biometallic hadn't secured their own station intelligence properly did not bode well for Adda's efforts to convince them to update her implant firmware. Once she was in a workspace, she'd use Ficience's vulnerability to keep the intelligence from telling its supervisor about her. It was disconcertingly similar to what Casey had done to Adda.

Even though their mistake worked in Adda's favor, such a simple oversight, or delay, was infuriating. This should've been one of Ficience's supervisors' highest priorities. Perhaps her use of their system would remind them of that.

"Is there a workspace generator in the lab?" Adda asked Pel.

"Uh, yeah," Pel said, as if that should've been obvious. "They're like nerds and coffeemakers. Every lab's got them." Thanks to his various fake internships, Pel had spent more time in professional, highly specialized labs than Adda had.

He approached a wall with a room's interior projected on it, imitating glass while blocking noise and offering privacy if someone cut the feed. Sure enough, eight workspace generators and a coffeemaker were visible inside. Adda's intermediary located the projectors controlling the window, and she looped them the same way she'd looped the hallway cams.

Pel pressed his palm to a pad, which flashed red through his hand and opened the lab door. He, Adda, and Iridian went in while

Wiley and Rio stayed outside. This lab was at a T intersection in the hallway, and they probably had a lot of area to watch.

That was their problem. Adda needed a workspace generator she could use. "Credentials?" she asked Pel.

"Oh yeah, the last one on the first row is unlocked already."

"Gods, *why?*" For a place that specialized in firmware, some of which was inside Adda's head, that was miserable security.

Pel grinned and tugged at his rumpled shirt. "Sissy, I'm very persuasive."

While Iridian laughed at him, Adda let herself into the workspace generator. It was one of the common horizontal, permanently installed models. Inside, the generator's bed was padded as thoroughly as a ship's passenger couch, designed for equally long periods of use.

She paused for a minute with her earbuds streaming pink noise, holding the cord that'd connect her to the workspace generator. The cord was the only way her implant, vulnerability still intact, could be exposed to the digital landscape where Casey dwelled. The last three times she'd been in a hallucinographic workspace with an intelligence had all been disasters. She'd attacked Iridian, nearly fallen victim to Casey's influence a second time, and then let the ancient intelligence on Yǎo Station do the same thing. She wasn't ready to enter a workspace with another one.

But the workspace was the safest and surest way to locate the firmware, along with everything they'd need to sell to survive until Dr. Björn's expedition launched. Adda had to go in and deal with this intelligence, or they would've left the relative safety of Yǎo Station for nothing. At least she'd had time to study this intelligence.

Before she thought of any more excuses or threats to scare herself with, she plugged the cord into her nasal jack and her comp, which was also connected to the generator. The others' voices faded to silence. The last physical thing she saw was the datacask's pseudo-organic contents draining into the generator's reservoir, deploying the backdoor and emptying itself to receive whatever Adda copied out.

The initial entry was a bright lobby with a softly strumming guitar and vague B shapes floating everywhere. The ugly design wasn't worth changing. Once she reached the intelligence, it, her brain, and the software would do what they wanted with the space. Her intermediary was still operating, and she sent it through the lobby wall. *Find Ficience.*

The response was so quick that the whole lobby dropped away around her, falling into darkness while she hovered in place, utterly still. Her workspace figure was standing, even though she was physically lying on her back, which wasn't unusual. The air around her shimmered and went metallic blue before it resolved into the upper level of a station she'd never seen before.

Smooth walls curved oddly around her, signifying a number of imperfect connections to the intelligence. The walls expanded and contracted, sending ripples through the walkway she stood on as her intermediary resolved the connection issues. The walkway's grid floor, only a meter or two wide, moved with the wall it followed. A metal railing separated Adda from a one- or two-story drop to a spacious hall that extended as far as she could see in either direction, parallel to the walkway. The stream of people under her alternated from second to second between dashing past in fast motion and slowly stepping forward. She had to wait until that speed stabilized before she started her search, or she might get lost in whatever processing slowdown the workspace was demonstrating.

Below, the crowd of people stopped and looked up at her. Adda laid a hand on the smooth walls and smiled as the whole workspace expanded and contracted. This was why working with intelligences was so rewarding. She could never have put together such a surreal interface on her own. Ficience was its own weird and powerful entity. Even while it was supervised, Adda could do a *lot* with this one. "Hello, Ficience."

Short sounds like partial breaths echoed around her. There were more people in this station than the intelligence usually hosted, especially at this time of day. Its intent focus on maintaining a pristine environment wherever these people went was evidence of admirably human-friendly design.

In the workspace, Adda created two small drones and sent them skimming down the infinite walkway in either direction. With luck the search routines they represented would locate an opening in the "walls" of permission settings that they could get through and copy the firmware, and something else salable, from the library.

She reached out and her hand closed on binoculars that, when she looked through them, showed a person lying in another workspace generator, face creased with worry and hands frantically twitching. In addition to the good design, Ficience had an attentive supervisor. The intelligence was much more concerned with what its supervisor was asking for than what Adda was doing, but the lack of resources devoted to Adda's efforts was causing the inconsistencies she was experiencing in the workspace. She wasn't in danger of falling out of the workspace entirely, but she wanted to make sure she'd have access to complete firmware sources when she found them.

Barely audible deep rumbling above her head sounded a bit like ship engines, but no ships were visible in the workspace. Something was happening in the port mod, and Adda requested its records for the past few minutes. They flew to her as a small newsfeed cam drone, which dissolved into a vid of the *Mayhem* docking. A dark figure strode out of the passthrough.

The captain wore the same long coat she'd always seen Sloane in, over gold-and-black armor. The helmet wasn't projecting a face, but the coat, the height, and the captain's confident walk would've been sufficient confirmation even without Sloane's unique armor. Two other people disembarked behind the captain, one in heavier armor, and one in Sloane's preferred red-and-black standard for subordinates. Adda packaged the footage and passed it to Iridian via an intense wildflower scent, which represented her comp's messaging function in this workspace, for a reason that made sense to her subconscious. The scent faded as her comp transmitted the message to Iridian's.

Ficience and its supervisor were focusing on the unannounced guests and largely ignoring the expected ones. That was how Adda was using its vulnerability to interact with the intelligence without alarming its supervisor. However, neither she nor the intermediary had found any openings into the firmware library. Perhaps Pel hadn't understood that just opening the hardware for anybody's use didn't simultaneously open all the connected areas of the server.

For now, Captain Sloane was Iridian's problem. Adda separated her comp's comms from the workspace. A wall rose from the hallway below her, perpendicular to her walkway. It stopped moving when it was even with the walkway. She climbed over the railing and crossed to a second walkway that'd formed on the other side of the hall, where the outer walls were still.

Damn. Iridian must've read the message. *Did you get the source for the firmware?*

Adda peered up and down the infinite walkway over the people, who were now arming themselves and marching in the direction of Captain Sloane's passthrough. *No. How long until the ITA arrives?* Ficience's supervisor was as intent on Sloane's progress as the intelligence was, and the supervisor would've called for help.

The Yăo pilot's voice broke in as a speaker emerged from the still wall beside Adda's head. "My ITA alerts are all going off, gals. You get back here in five or I'm leaving without you."

Never mind, Adda said to Iridian.

This might be her only opportunity to interact with Ficience. After Pel's subterfuge and a visit from a notorious pirate captain who had almost certainly not gotten docking clearance first, security would tighten. She presented the intelligence with a sequence of carefully worded queries as bright beams of light from her hands. The gist of her intent was "What can you tell me about my implant's firmware?"

A wave of water formed on one side of the hallway and washed toward her, filling the space from floor to rounded ceiling, roaring as it came. The search routine/drone that'd flown in that direction to find opportunities to copy firmware on its own sent her a massive burst of information, then disappeared in a flash of blue light. While her comp was recording it, Adda braced herself and let the wave sweep over it. It represented an automated security sweep.

Babe, did you hear the nice pilot? Iridian subvocalized in Adda's ear. *We need to—* Adda shut off the subvocal comms. The firmware was almost certainly the source of the vulnerability that allowed Casey to influence her so fast, and she *had* to find out everything Biometallic developers had written about it.

Her comp was struggling to keep up with the information pouring into it in a combined response from one of her two search routines and her specific query. The comp passed everything it received to the pseudo-organic fluid filling the attached datacask. Routines on her comp found most of that information published where Adda could've located it on her own, or in documents she'd already read. The water around her turned oily black with her disappointment, becoming a visual and tactile signifier of information she didn't need from Ficience.

It would be convenient to have the trade journal and other more technical coverage consolidated. Thin streams of fresh water formed in the muck to show her new information that her routines weren't finding in any publication, but none of it met alert criteria she'd set for her firmware source. She looked in the other direction, the one the wave had been traveling in. Her second routine searching for the source, framed differently than the first and represented by another drone, hadn't returned.

Three deep thumps sent ripples through the rushing water and shook Adda along with it. The workspace generator itself reported in via a wall projection that repelled the oil water, warning that its door mechanism was strained to the point of damage. Adda sighed and reactivated her comms to Iridian, filling the water with muffled renditions of Iridian's favorite profanities.

Ficience offered her a cam feed of Iridian pounding on the workspace generator door, and Adda would've appreciated that clever anticipation of her needs if she'd expected the cams to be sending the intelligence a live feed. Ficience's supervisor must have realized that something untoward was happening in the lab. The oil water disappeared from the workspace like it'd never been there. Her second drone flared, sent its blast of data, and died.

She sent out a heavily prioritized query based on what the first two had found and reeled in her neural implant net's firmware source in a yellow-and-red spiral so bright it hurt her eyes. Confirmation on what she had came with an equally bright giddiness that made her laugh beneath the thumps of Iridian's fists hitting the workspace generator door. If she made it off the station with this in the datacask, she'd have a very good chance of keeping Casey out of her mind.

A second, similar query requested a range of injector firmware, since that was the first Biometallic product she thought of that she'd be willing to sell a source for. If they didn't make enough, then Noor would use the backdoor he designed to return for more some other time. Next time, they might not even have to be on the station to do it.

All right, she said to Iridian. *I have the source. I'm coming out.*

The workspace drained into the generator ceiling as she unplugged her nasal jack. As soon as the door opened, Iridian hauled her out and barely gave her time to retrieve the datacask containing the copied firmware. Iridian said, "Move out" into her helmet mic loudly enough to carry through the helmet to Pel and Adda without its outside speaker turning on.

They retraced their steps into the hallway, but almost immediately Iridian stopped, bringing the others to a halt with her. "Noor says there's a fuckoff huge warship coming in opposite the ITA ship," she said. "And our pilot's bugging out. We're on our own."

CHAPTER 18

Days until launch: 27
(holding for mechanical issues)

It was easy to imagine that Iridian and Adda shared the tele-pathic connection that their comms implants imitated. Iridian was already opening the station map while Adda asked, "Where's the passenger entrance . . ." Adda squinted and bit her lip. After leaving a workspace, she usually took a few minutes to catch up with reality.

"Terminal?" Iridian asked.

"Yes, that, for the port module. Not the cargo area where we came in."

"This way." Iridian took off in the opposite direction from the cargo bay, grateful that everyone in armor had filled their suit reservoirs while Adda was messing with the AI. After the stale Yǎo stuff they'd been drinking, this station's water tasted fantastic. The healthier grav was a relief too, even if running down a hallway tired her out more than it should've. Behind her, Wiley and Rio thundered down the hallway in full armor and Adda's and Pel's nice shoes tapped after them.

"What's the new plan?" Wiley asked over the local channel.

"We can't stay here and we can't take the ship we came in on," said Iridian. "The shuttles are short-range vessels. There's only one long-range vessel docked. Noor, you getting all this?"

"What do you think?" Something fell, with two distinct impacts typical in low grav. Noor paused to call it a fire hazard in cant. "If you get me arrested, you'd better hope we never meet up again. Otherwise, see you back home." Noor had made his own travel plans getting here, so he ought to be able to find his own way back to Yǎo Station.

How would you feel about hijacking the Mayhem*?* Adda whispered in Iridian's ear.

Not great, Iridian replied. She liked Gavran, and some of Sloane's crew. She'd take no pleasure in hurting them, or in stranding them on the station to get hauled off to ITA holding. *But they have a pilot and we don't have time for you to make friends with any new AI copilots.*

Her helmet's HUD flashed the port mod identifier when they entered it. Iridian had figured that out when she'd crossed the mod connector. Four armed and armored people in Biometallic colors, the first they'd seen since they entered the station, were facing the passenger terminal with their backs to Iridian's crew. They turned around at the crew's noisy approach, weapons still raised. The supposedly shy investor Pel had invited to this station shouldn't have entered the passenger section of the port.

Iridian called "Light 'em up!" into her helmet mic, still set to the local channel to limit broadcast interception. She threw one of her two charges at the Biometallic stationsec people, and Rio threw hers after it. Thanks to a very brief training session on Yǎo, Adda and Pel turned away and covered their ears.

The resulting pops as the charges deployed wouldn't have been enough to damage their hearing. The bright flashes of light would blind helmet cams that hadn't been adjusted to cope. Transmitters that activated upon deployment would immobilize the armor at the joints, if the viral payload penetrated.

Which, of course, it didn't, because Iridian had attacked stationsec in a modern gods-damned station with cast-off or knock-off charges from Yăo. Iridian pulled Adda behind her while Wiley shoved Pel around a corner and out of the way. Rio, powering forward in her personalized ZV armor, waded into the group of four still trying to make their cams work around the timed bursts of painfully bright light.

One of them swept a stun stick toward Rio. It might've shorted out her suit, but she ducked under it and let it connect with the stationsec person behind her. The scream that followed the impact, muffled by the stationsec helmet, sounded masculine. Gods only knew what that'd do to the fucking implant the ITA had stuck in Iridian's head.

Stay here, Iridian told Adda. She stalked forward with Wiley at her side. The guy who'd gotten hit with the stun stick was kneeling on the ground, and Rio had the one who'd swung at her between her and the other two. He was about to lose a helmet to Rio. She'd gotten it halfway off before the other two stationsec people pulled the one she was working on out of her grip. The helmet's cams were facing the wrong way.

One of the two stationsec fighters whose armor hadn't been compromised yet got a hit on Iridian while she was drawing her knife. Her suit joints' movement became a grinding drag. Something near her neck made a crackling sound and heated up, fast. Wiley helped her take her helmet off before it burned through her under-suit. When he dropped the helmet, she caught it by the cables and pulled to put the back panel of her suit between her and the overheated or shorted-out components in the cheap collar. Rio laid into the enemy with a knife of her own, cutting into cables that the stationsec armor exposed at the hip, neck, and shoulder joints.

Swearing while her smoking helmet dangled uselessly behind her and spit sparks, Iridian was out of the fight. Between the comms implant and the one the gods-damned ITA put in her, she had too much metal in her head to risk another hit without a helmet. Her remaining charge wouldn't do any more damage than the first one had.

"Wish I had a damned shield," she muttered, although nobody'd hear her.

The stationsec helmet Rio had twisted around was facing them again and the stun stick victim was more or less on his feet again. Rio squared off those two while Wiley kept the one with the fully functional armor busy. He was having better luck than Iridian had at avoiding the stationsec weapons.

From her position against a wall, the arc of a second thrown weapon moved in slow motion. It clacked when it landed. For a heartbeat it stuck to the floor, and then it popped. A gray cloud burst among the combatants. They turned toward the passenger terminal, where the weapon had been thrown from. The cloud obscured the terminal entrance.

Wiley collapsed first. Stationsec wasn't far behind. Rio walked far enough into the cloud that Iridian only heard her fall.

Three suited figures stalked out of the smoke, which was already being drawn into ducts in the ceiling. Captain Sloane led them, stepping over Rio in a black-and-gold suit that couldn't have been anybody else's. Sloane's crew had suit filters for whatever was in the smoke. Someone had also made the humane choice of stuff that didn't spread over the floor, where it'd drift through the mod and take out bystanders. Hopefully, Wiley and Rio were just unconscious.

Without her helmet, the weapons the other two suited figures pointed at Iridian would knock her out at best, and maybe knock her brain around enough to kill her. Pel stepped up beside her with his own knife out. Her suit-assisted strength pushed his arm down to his side, but she fought the grinding suit joints the whole way. She was sweating out all the clean water she'd drunk on this station, but she'd seen Pel's close combat skills. He was as likely to hurt himself as his opponent.

Iridian straightened her back and sheathed her own knife. Her suit joints were recovering from the hit she'd taken earlier, but they still wouldn't be fast enough to beat armor Sloane's crew could afford. "Captain."

It was encouraging that the captain's weapon was pointed at the floor. Threatening her and Pel would've confirmed that Sloane was still pissed off at her. "Iridian," Captain Sloane said with what sounded like genuine warmth, although the captain wasn't smiling. Even with Sloane's faceplate projector off, Iridian heard the difference. "And Pel, and was that Rio?" Iridian nodded and Pel said, "Hey, Captain," in a cautious greeting.

Captain Sloane's gaze shifted to something behind Iridian. "Come out, Adda, if you can."

Iridian turned her head slowly so as not to alarm the people with their armored fingers on triggers. Adda's shoulders were hunched to make her round frame as small as possible as she came around the corner to stand between Pel and Iridian. An infrared filter in the captain's HUD would've picked Adda up even though she was outside Sloane's line of sight.

First chance we get, go for the ship? Iridian asked Adda subvocally.

Only if it's a good chance, Adda replied.

Since Sloane couldn't hear them, the captain spoke over Adda. "Good to see you're feeling well enough to follow Iridian on doomed endeavors like this one."

Adda just nodded. The pretended concern pissed Iridian off. "Why do you care?" Iridian asked Sloane. "You were ready to let her die after liberating Vesta."

The captain refocused on her. "Like you let Tritheist die?"

"Tritheist and I were clearing the way for you and Adda to get out." HQ had taken missile fire and the building had been coming down around their ears. Iridian smelled the smoke in her nightmares. "I gave him as good a chance as I knew how, but there was no way we could've seen that sniper. He thought his life was a fair trade for yours. You tightening your grip on Vesta was *not* worth Adda's life."

"I never wanted her to come to harm." Even while saying something that outrageous, Sloane's voice remained steady. "In fact, if you'd like to give up whatever it is you're doing here, you're welcome to return to Vesta with me. I've been holding on to a job that you and she would be perfect for. You've been difficult to reach." Either Sloane already had whatever brought the captain to Biometallic 1, or the captain had come for her and Adda. This wouldn't have been Captain Sloane's first fight with the ITA.

Much as Iridian loathed the idea of traveling with Sloane after the captain had handed them to the ITA without warning, staying on Biometallic's station would result in the same damned problem. "We do need a lift," Iridian admitted.

Pel gaped at her. "We're not going back to Vesta after all this, are we?"

We're not, Iridian subvocalized, although he wouldn't hear the message. It'd reassure Adda, at least. "We can't stay here."

"Precisely," said Captain Sloane.

Behind the captain, Rio's armored bulk shifted. She was still on the floor, but she was waking up. "We have conditions," Iridian said quickly.

"Of course." Sloane sounded both surprised and pleased.

"Gear, for one thing," Iridian said. "We definitely need better gear. This trip, we couldn't even buy patch kits."

Rio's suit scuffed the floor, and Iridian lifted her arms to display the stiff joints and the broken helmet. That earned her the full attention of both of Sloane's soldiers, one of whom barked, "Don't move. Hands at your sides." Getting onto the *Mayhem* and off the station would probably involve going through the bodyguards, so Iridian was relieved that this one's voice was unfamiliar. During her time on Vesta, she'd gotten to know a lot of Sloane's personal security. She liked most of them.

Behind the bodyguards, Rio had made it to her knees and was drawing her knife.

"Of course. You'll have whatever you need to do the work I need done," Sloane said. "Your old armor is still in storage, as a matter of fact."

Damn. Iridian missed that armor. Actually, she missed a lot of things about being on Sloane's crew. None of them were worth a repeat of Iridian's last night on Vesta.

Rio heaved herself to her feet and in the same motion lunged at Sloane. She latched her glove onto an armored plate over the captain's neck and dragged the captain sideways. The tip of her blade settled into the place where electrical and coolant cables entered the helmet. From there it'd be hard, but not impossible, to drive the blade into Sloane's skull. The soldiers swung around to face the new threat. As soon as they weren't focused on her, Iridian drew her own knife. This was the only chance to get past Sloane and onto the *Mayhem* that she expected to have.

"Everybody stay where you are," said a voice from the passthrough. "Nobody move." The *Mayhem*'s pilot, a short Kuiper native with brown skin and a red beard, stood in the passthrough doorway with his sidearm leveled at Sloane's chest. The barrel was as big around as a person's forearm. He was a fun guy in an entertainment mod, but he was serious on the job and this was not the kind of joke he'd make.

Sloane's arms came up and away from the weapon slots in the captain's black armor. If her crew had rushed the passthrough, at least one of them wouldn't have made it into the ship. Captain Sloane would've loaded a launcher with something effective. Iridian shuddered at how close they'd just come to disaster.

"Gavran." Sloane sighed, breath strained by the position Rio held the captain's head in. "And Rio, I expected better from you."

"I don't want to hurt you, Captain, but I'm not going back to Venus for you either," said Rio.

"Hi, Gav!" Pel waved enthusiastically and stepped toward the *Mayhem*'s passthrough. Iridian pushed him against the wall with the hand not holding her knife. The suit joints were almost fully mobile again, but Sloane's soldiers were still awake, armed, and dangerous. If Rio was up, then the stationsec fighters wouldn't be far behind.

Gavran grinned at Pel and held his weapon steady. He really was taking Adda's and Iridian's side over Sloane's. Iridian never would've expected that. "Lim, O'Dell, on the floor," Gavran said. "Chest plates down, Sloane's crew."

The soldiers didn't move. "Do it," Captain Sloane grated. They followed the order.

Adda stepped around Iridian and asked Gavran, "Why are you helping us?"

"Tell you when we're out? ITA's coming, so we should leave before the Authority gets here and talk later." Iridian had forgotten about his colony's habit of repeating everything they said.

Adda nodded and stepped toward where Wiley and the stationsec soldiers were stirring. She got her hands around the upper arm plates in Wiley's armor and dragged him toward the passthrough, her face going red with the strain.

Iridian shook herself out of her stunned inaction and sheathed her knife. They had moments before the stationsec people woke all the way up. The ITA had to be in the cargo docking bay by now. If they didn't want to risk connecting their passthrough to a rotating hab's bare airlock, it was the only place to dock or land.

Captain Sloane was too dangerous to bring with them, and leaving the captain here might delay ITA pursuit. If buying the agents off proved too costly, the captain would put up a hell of a fight. "Rio, Pel, let's go." Iridian's grin was wide enough to be rude, but Sloane had lost most of her respect and she was getting off this station with her whole crew intact. "See you around, Captain."

Rio backed up to the passthrough's exterior door and shoved Sloane to the floor with her considerable, suit-assisted strength. The captain twisted and pulled a knife while falling. The blade had been aimed at Rio's knee, but she'd pushed the captain hard enough that the blow glanced off her armored calf. Iridian stepped on Sloane's wrist, pinning it to the floor while the captain swore at her. Heart pounding, she braced herself and locked her suit's knee joints before Sloane punched them with the arm she hadn't pinned down yet. That was too close.

Rio took Wiley from Adda and dragged him into the *Mayhem*. If Iridian followed, she'd have to unlock her knee joints. Captain Sloane would take her down, one way or another. "Has that got a nonlethal setting?" Iridian glanced at Gavran's sidearm.

He adjusted his aim downward and pulled the trigger. The blast drowned out the start of a gods-awful sizzling. A patch of black goo formed in the elbow joint of the arm Sloane had punched her with. The joint splintered. The captain screamed. Foul smoke rose from the black goo expanding up and down Sloane's arm. The two bodyguards flinched, but Gavian shifted to cover them again and they stayed on the floor.

"Not exactly a setting," said Gavran. "Those nannites love to eat armor, no matter what it's set for."

"Holy hell." Iridian tore her gaze away from the pulse of machines too small to see dissolving the armor, and maybe the captain's arm. She unlocked her knee joints and ran to the passthrough, grabbing Pel's arm on her way to keep him from staring at the captain until he got arrested.

"Ungrateful bastards," Sloane howled amid the clatter of armored bodyguards and stationsec soldiers picking themselves off the floor.

Gavran stepped into the passthrough and shut the external door, then dropped the sidearm into a large pants pocket and pushed past the others to the *Mayhem*'s bridge. Unlike other ships they'd been on, this one kept both the bridge console and the AI copilot's pseudo-organic tank behind a locked door. The *Mayhem*'s atmo was even more expertly mixed than Biometallic 1's atmo had been. Blue lights in the wall handholds made them easy to find.

"Strap in," Gavran said. "We're leaving in front of at least one cruiser docking now, so secure for undocking. Repeating, one cruiser docking . . . Plus the *Apparition* coming in."

"Shit!" Iridian said. She and Rio maneuvered Wiley's semi-conscious bulk into one of the four passenger couches in the *Mayhem*'s main cabin. She shoved Pel into another, ignoring his protesting "Hey!" The interior passthrough door thudded shut. Rio squeezed her wide shoulders into the third couch. Her feet dangled off the end until she bent her knees.

"You can't outrun the *Apparition* if it wants to shoot at you." Adda's sharpsheet haze dulled her warning to Gavran. "Its copilot is an awakened intelligence."

"I won't wait for the Authority docked with my damned passthrough open," Gavran snapped, missing the more important point. "The ITA can try to catch the *Mayhem* in the cold and the black." Iridian hauled Adda through the main cabin and into one of two tiny residential cabins, where they could strap into a bunk together. Two bunks were stacked against the bulkheads on either side of the door, with straps neatly folded on each. The *Mayhem* lurched under them before Iridian finished securing herself and Adda to one of the lower bunks. The heavy beat of a frenetic rock song filled the atmo. Iridian tightened the straps and pulled Adda close.

It's talking to me, Adda whispered in Iridian's ear, her voice closer than the music. *It says it came to keep the ITA from catching us, like it did last time.*

"It fucking shot at us last time," Iridian said. The others' heads came up, although their couches faced away from the residential cabin. Iridian spoke more quietly to prove that she wasn't about to panic. "And then it used our choice of ports to make repairs to figure out we were headed for Yǎo Station." Iridian gripped the nearest strap holding her and Adda in the bunk with her helmet still clattering against the back of her suit. "Tell the *Apparition* we don't need that kind of help." Half to herself, she added, "First the awakened AIs want us in prison, now they want us free. Tell them to make up their damned minds while you're at it."

It's talking about how it needs us to build their new home. I think I taught them that phrase. Adda drew in a sharp gasp. "It says that Casey is helping Noor."

"Oh, gods damn it," said Iridian. "Casey's 'help' will make him give away the whole damned game. Or chase him off to get that ID he stashed on Vesta, and we'll never see him again. Tell them both to get the hell away from my crew. Please." She didn't expect them to listen, but she couldn't let that go unchallenged, even if all she could do was yell at the AIs through Adda.

I've asked it to leave us alone. It keeps responding with demands that we stay where we are. I wish I could just talk to them without . . . Adda sighed against Iridian's chest plate, and they clung together as the station swung out of view in the window projected on the wall. If Iridian were to guess, Adda had almost said, *without getting influenced*. That wasn't an option at the moment.

Noor was following whatever exit strategy he had for leaving the rathole on Ceres's surface. Operating in vac was risky enough. Transmissions big enough to contain vid or audio, sent to a point on Ceres's surface where no signals should go, might alert the ITA, Ceres stationsec, or the awakened AIs to Noor's location. Iridian sent a text update in a small transmission that shouldn't attract attention, warning him about Casey, the ITA, and Captain Sloane. He could read it whenever he didn't have to concentrate on Ceres's surface enviro trying to kill him.

Adda's eyes shut tight while she subvocalized to her comp and the AIs listening in. Iridian didn't love combat maneuvering, but it made Adda sick. The g's were too high for Iridian to look for a sick bag, so she'd just have to hope Adda didn't feel too bad. In the main cabin, Pel's joyous whoop suggested that he was enjoying the ride.

The Apparition *is staying close to Ceres stationspace*, Adda subvocalized. *It hasn't fired.*

"How can you tell?" asked Iridian.

We're still moving.

"You all right back there, Nassir?" Wiley asked.

Adda stopped talking while Iridian replied, "Yeah, I'll catch you up after Gavran gets us the hell out of here."

If it'd wanted to risk destroying the ship to keep us here, it would've done it by now, Adda said to Iridian. *It'll have better targeting capabilities than any other warship in existence, and we know how much trouble Gavran has with dodging missiles.*

She and Iridian had learned that weakness of Gavran's when they'd agreed to fly with him on missions for Sloane's crew. *And with the ITA docked, they're not in a position to take a shot at us either, unless they want to risk damaging the station,* Iridian thought at her. Grav was crushing her chest and making it hard to breathe, let alone speak.

I'd be surprised if they did, Adda agreed. *Protecting stations is a significant part of their reason for existence. I'm setting some routines to try to keep better track of the* Casey *and the* Apparition. *I want to know where they are when they're not with us, and they're giving us some excellent examples of their ship behaviors to work with.*

"Serves them right." Iridian winced as Gavran poured on the speed, and the g's crushed them into the bunk. "So what the fuck was the *Apparition* doing here?"

Adda's eyelids were drooping. *Breathe, babe,* Iridian subvocalized. *Like we practiced.*

After a few seconds of focused, short breaths, Adda fought her way back to full consciousness. *If the ITA had arrested us now, we couldn't help the intelligences. If the ITA disabled the* Mayhem, *I think the* Apparition *would've offered to let us board it instead. It may have been trying to arrange that scenario.*

"Great," Iridian grumbled. Subvocally she added, *They're not taking you away from me again. Not the AIs, not the ITA, not any of them.*

Gavran kept the *Mayhem* powering through space at much higher grav than was healthy for a couple of hours, during which Adda searched through the contents of the datacask she'd plugged into Biometallic's library to hold copies of firmware. She read each set's titles under her breath while she and Iridian were still strapped into the *Mayhem*'s bunk together.

"I hardly know what I'm looking for," Adda said. "My coding

class in college was just an overview. Intelligences maintain the workspace interpretation bases so we don't have to. Nobody uses code anymore."

Plenty of insults implied that the target manipulated code instead of using a workspace to make software changes, and was therefore a weird person with an unnaturally high tolerance for boredom and frustration. "When you find it, you're sending it to the modder on Ceres, yeah?" Iridian asked.

"Yes." Adda frowned. "That'll cost us a lot."

"To keep Casey out of your head, it's worth it." That also meant they'd have to put off getting Adda's implant fixed until they could afford it. With any luck, this job would pay enough. Iridian would skip a few meals and delay building a new shield for some assurance that Adda couldn't be influenced the same way twice.

Iridian switched the window views around until it showed Biometallic 1 and Ceres sinking into the star field behind them. On Ceres's horizon, the domed cover that protected Ceres Station from space debris glittered with the reflected lights of buoys and the ships and bots that seemed to always populate its station-space. In front of the 'ject, Biometallic 1's three long mods gleamed as they rotated in both the sunlight and the light of seven ships. When Iridian turned on labeling, the window showed that four of them were privately owned vessels, highlighted white with directional markers pointing toward reliable routes or the orbital section of Ceres Station. They were getting out of the way.

The two highlighted in red were the ITA cruisers. Even in that crowd, the *Apparition*'s asymmetric hull loomed against the stars, as big as both the ITA vessels combined. Interestingly, the annotated display still outlined it in tug/technical blue. The outline would only confuse a machine or somebody who didn't know a skiff from a longhauler. The *Apparition* looked like what it was: an unnaturally repaired and fully functional NEU warship.

CHAPTER 19

Days until launch: 27
(holding for mechanical issues)

In the window projected on the *Mayhem*'s residential cabin wall,
the *Apparition* and the other ships in Ceres stationspace shrank as
the much smaller *Mayhem* pulled away. Beyond them, the tower
of Ceres Station's rapid refueling system reached out toward the
saucer-shaped orbital port. At its base, the dome of Ceres Station's
surface construction reflected the light of hundreds of directional
buoys. Its dome was suspended in its anchoring structure, hiding
a massive sphere turning in Ceres's underground ocean, heating
ice into water the station used to supplement the internal recycling system.

When Gavran's raucous music and the heavy gravity caused
by high-speed acceleration finally let up, Adda's stomach rebelled
at the rapid changes and she nearly vomited on Iridian. At least
the *Mayhem*'s air was well oxygenated, even cleaner than Biometallic 1 kept theirs. Kuiper natives were particular about their
shipboard environment.

When Adda could stand to read again, she called up the monitoring routines she'd created to track the awakened intelligences.

This new, up-close view of the *Apparition* had added a lot of data that her routines needed to incorporate. However, the material Casey had sent was even more intriguing. Adda set a reminder for herself to update the *Apparition*'s tracker later and pulled Casey's data into her comp projection for review.

"How do you feel, babe?" Iridian had left their shared bed as soon as Gavran's flying leveled out, but she must've come back to the guest cabin while Adda was reading.

Tired, Adda admitted. *And if I get up, I'll be sick. I'm reading through the stuff Casey sent me, though, and . . . Let's talk about it, later. This is amazing.*

Iridian bent down to kiss her. Gravity had nearly dropped to a healthy range that Adda would be willing to walk in, if she weren't so nauseated. "Be careful."

Adda would have to check everything Casey sent for tampering, so care was high on her priority list. *I will.*

In the main cabin, Wiley was saying, ". . . know anything about this guy?"

Iridian stepped through the guest cabin doorway. One step more brought her to the first of the four passenger couches. The couch was empty, but its sick bag drawer wasn't. "Yeah, we know him," Iridian told Wiley while she returned to Adda with the bag.

"Grav loss in ten minutes, repeat, grav loss in ten minutes, mark," Gavran's voice announced.

Iridian sat on one of the passenger couches to join Rio and Wiley, who had disconnected their helmets from their suits and were examining the rest of the armor. "Adda, Pel, and I flew some missions with this guy after Barbary," Iridian said. "He saved our asses a few times. He's good people."

As promised, the artificial pull toward the floor faded quickly. Adda had to use the sick bag Iridian had just given her. Maintaining comfortable gravity through constant acceleration and deceleration was expensive, even on a ship as small as the *Mayhem*, so she didn't blame Gavran for conserving fuel. She hadn't wanted to interrupt him to ask where they were going, but she needed to find out eventually.

Before Adda's stomach settled enough for her to consider getting out of bed, Iridian asked, "Anybody heard from Noor?" The other three in the main cabin shook their heads. Frowning, Iridian tapped at her comp to send Noor a message that also pinged in a text copy on Adda's comp. *Are you okay? Give us a status update when you can.*

"I feel bad about stranding Captain Sloane like that," Rio confessed.

"Same," said Pel, just as Iridian said, "Don't." After a second, she added, "The captain always finds a way out of shit like that. Hell, maybe the *Apparition* was there on Sloane's orders. It's followed the captain around before."

Because of us, Adda subvocalized.

"How badly do you think he was hurt?" Wiley asked over Adda's comment.

"The *captain*," Iridian said, emphasizing Sloane's preferred way to be referenced, "didn't look too bad off to me. That armor was good stuff. It would've stopped the bleeding before we cleared stationspace."

Adda was drifting off the bed and felt for the straps that would hold her down. Her inner ears were telling her that she was falling, the way they always did after ships stopped accelerating fast enough to generate gravity. She retched and vomited again. Iridian grimaced and dug through the couch's drawers, hopefully for more sick bags.

By the time Adda was as comfortable as she was going to get, a message from Noor had appeared on her comp. *Stuck on Ceres under an alias. Meet you somewhere?*

"Somewhere, yeah," Iridian muttered. She must've received the same message.

They'd planned to return to Yǎo to decide what to do next. However, Gavran might not have enough fuel to reach Jupiter. Adda carefully pulled herself into the main cabin to ask him about it. Iridian must've thought of the fuel situation as well, because she disconnected her helmet from the rest of her suit and crossed the main cabin, avoiding Pel's gesturing arms as he illustrated what sounded like a bad joke he was about to subject Rio and Wiley to. After a short pause, she knocked on the *Mayhem*'s bridge door.

When Gavran opened it, the barrel of his sidearm was about three centimeters from Iridian's nose. Heart racing, Adda scrambled for something, anything, she could do to help Iridian, but she couldn't think of anything. Rio and Wiley had stopped listening to Pel's joke, but they floated as still as Iridian and Adda did.

Iridian's helmet drifted away from her, trailing melted cables, as she raised her hands to shoulder height. She held herself in place with a foothold in the wall. "I just wanted to talk."

Gavran watched her for a moment, then lowered the weapon. "That's good. I want to talk too." Adda let out a long breath, and then got sick again.

Although he wasn't holding Iridian at gunpoint anymore, he hadn't put the weapon away. "Something different since the last time we saw you?" Iridian asked.

"Upgraded the legs," Gavran said. "Both legs have a few new features."

He let go of the gun. It drifted for half a second, then snapped flat against what Adda had taken for a pocket on his thigh. The pant leg had been cut open and slightly melted around a gray patch of exposed pseudo-organics. As far as Adda knew, nothing below Gavran's hips was fully organic.

"Nice." Iridian grabbed her drifting helmet out of the air. "So, where are we headed?"

"Sunan's Landing first, for refueling," said Gavran. "After Sunan's Landing, we'll talk prices. Captain Sloane won't pay up after this, so I'm going to need what you can afford."

"Yeah," Iridian said.

Captain Sloane's original plan had probably called for refueling on Ceres. If they were only traveling between there and Sloane's base on Vesta, and the 'jects were close together at the moment, then they might not have completely fueled up at either location. The *Mayhem* refueled quickly, but Adda had scheduled three hours for Noor to reenter and then leave Ceres Station. "We're not going to make it back to meet Noor." The *Mayhem* couldn't refuel and return to meet Noor's contact anywhere near Ceres stationspace without leaving him stuck under ITA scrutiny for hours. Sunan's Landing, a small station built around a fuel barge in the asteroid belt, ran off people who spent that long there without buying food and drink that Adda hadn't budgeted for, so waiting there wouldn't be practical either, but Iridian would already know that.

"We'll meet Noor at 'home,'" Iridian said. "If he can't make it there, we'll figure something out when he tells us so. Before that: What made you leave Sloane to the ITA back there? The captain looked shocked as all hells."

Gavran held his hand in front of him and stretched the fingers wide, and Iridian used the handhold to set herself drifting backward for about a meter. Cant speakers, of both the Kuiper and spacefarer varieties, seemed to use a similar vocabulary of hand signals which Adda hadn't gotten around to learning. Iridian caught another handhold while Gavran crossed the main cabin to where Adda clung to the wall. "You're looking a little green, Adda. You got a sick bag?"

She opened her mouth to answer, but the words weren't there, in the same frustrating way they occasionally disappeared after the overdose. "Can't," she said, since that word was already on her mind. Gavran pulled a sick bag from a compartment under a passenger couch and handed it to her.

"You were telling us why we're here instead of in an ITA cell," Iridian reminded Gavran.

The pilot hooked one boot under the empty passenger couch, and his knee shifted oddly as the pseudo-organic joint adjusted his balance. Rio, Wiley, and Pel watched from the other couches. "Captain Sloane's been different, with Tritheist and you three gone," he said. "The captain's been taking fewer jobs and playing more politics, with none of you there to ask if all the deals are worth cutting."

"Like how Sloane tried to trade my sister for Vestan independence or whatever?" Pel's voice was lower and rougher than it'd been since those terrible days after Adda's overdose. He sat cross-legged on the passenger couch with his legs through the straps and his arms over his chest, scowling.

"Many trades that bad, and a few arrangements that were worse than that, forgive me for saying. Setting up puppet station councils costs a lot. The captain's dumping money and time to keep station councilors in line. We left port twice in the past eight weeks. I don't like to stay weeks in any hab, when I could be"— Gavran sighed—"getting paid to fly."

"You want to go home." Everybody turned to look at Adda. She rarely discussed her take on people's motives since she was so frequently wrong, but Gavran's seemed obvious. The only reason Gavran had left the Kuiper colonies was to look for his brother, and Adda had found his brother's death records on Vesta.

"It's time," Gavran agreed. "I'd have gone home before now if I could, but Kondakova's a long, expensive way from here. I can't make the money that trip costs in a hab. Can't earn the cash and keep it, anyway."

"Too much to spend it on, yeah," said Pel. He and Gavran both had expensive recreational chemical habits, and the *Mayhem* had no room for a pharmaceutical printer.

"Serves the captain right, then," said Rio.

Pel had tangled his legs in the passenger couch straps and was tugging at them like he thought he could free himself without anybody noticing. In the low gravity, the rest of him bounced all over the couch. "It's not like the ITA can hold the captain anyway. If Sloane even gets arrested, I'll be shocked."

"Yeah," said Iridian. "And speaking of shocks, thanks for explaining why you let us board, Gavran. Not to say that we're not grateful, because we are, but we were as surprised as Sloane was."

Gavran grinned. "I'm always glad to dodge the ITA. The Authority eating my exhaust feels closer to home than farther."

"Not just the ITA, unfortunately," said Iridian. "We might've pissed off the awakened AIs." Gavran gave her a curious, tell-me-more look, which was not the level of surprise appropriate to learning that multiple intelligences had been uplifted from their zombie state and were now running amok in populated space. "So you knew about them already?"

"Port mod bar rumors talk about them, and you don't trust port mod bar rumors about anything. Sloane's crew tells more informed tales, and you *do* trust Sloane's crew. Combine those often enough, put the right pros and the right drinks together . . ." Gavran shrugged broadly. "Rheasilvia Station's haunted, or the awakened AIs are real, and I've seen more AIs than I've seen ghosts."

"Well, as long as the AIs are ahead," said Pel, which got a laugh out of Iridian and Rio. As usual, Adda didn't see what was funny about that.

"It does feel like being hunted by ghosts, sometimes," Iridian admitted. "Or demons, with the influence and all."

"Ghosts," said Rio firmly. "Whatever you did to piss them off, they didn't start out this way."

"They did." Adda waited to see if she was going to be sick again, and when she wasn't, she continued. "On Barbary, they weren't as good at manipulating us. They've learned a lot since then, like how to move us out of a location where they don't want us."

Iridian drifted closer to Rio, then tugged on the wall handhold to pull herself out to a polite distance. "But we're not where they want us now, yeah? Are we even on a reliable route?"

"The reliable route to Sunan's Landing, yeah," said Gavran. "The route's between Ceres and the belt's next biggest refueling hub, so it's a quiet one."

Iridian looked around at the others gathered in the *Mayhem*'s main cabin. "So, what's next?"

"I need to see what we picked up from Biometallic's firmware library," said Adda. "I got my and Noor's implant firmware source, but I grabbed other things to sell and I want to make sure . . . Well, I want to sell the least dangerous ones first." She clenched her hands in her pant legs against another wave of nausea. "As soon as we meet up with Noor, I can get his help finding the vulnerability, using a workspace. If he's been alone with Casey all this time, it may already be"—she realized what she was saying and paused, horrified—"too late to prevent him from getting influenced."

Iridian had said that the reason Noor left Sorenson ITAS was to get away from people who wanted to change how he saw the universe. Now Casey must be reshaping his mind, in essence doing what the ITA would've done to him if he'd stayed in prison. Besides that, Adda had told him all her plans to secure their neural implant nets against Casey's intrusion, and he could tell Casey.

Somehow Iridian forced cheer into her voice and changed the topic. "And if we're lucky, there's something in that Biometallic haul that we can sell to pay Gavran. Is the *Mayhem* shielded for Jupiter?"

They hadn't told Gavran where they'd been since they left Vesta, but he looked like he was putting the pieces together. "I'll need to get the Galilean shielding checked at Sunan's Landing. After Sunan's mechanics say the shielding's solid, *Mayhem* will be as ready for Jupiter as anything is. I'll be paying for the shield check on top of the fuel to get us to the Jovian colonies, if you're wondering whether ship modding costs money."

"Not to mention paying to eat and drink for a few more days." Pel was right. Necessities of living were still their major concern. They were kilometers away from what it'd cost to get Dr. Björn out of vis Oxia contract and giving ver a reason to want them on vis expedition.

In the silence that followed, Adda returned to the material Casey had sent her. The tampering trackers had highlighted a few sections. Adda put those docs into a quarantine area to examine later. The rest, though, seemed to be describing theory and some practical applications of huge machine Casey had shown her on Ceres.

Iri, Adda subvocalized.

Iridian helped Adda back into one of the beds and braced herself between Adda's bed frame and the doorway to stay in place. *Did Casey send you something nasty?*

Adda shook her head. "It's . . . Well, if Casey's telling the truth, this is . . . I can't even think of a historical comparison. This has literally never happened before."

Just Casey's name made Iridian flinch slightly. Her knuckles whitened on the cabin's door frame. "Start at the beginning?"

Ever since that port authority workspace generator on Ceres, Adda had been searching for a way to frame her explanation so Iridian wouldn't panic. Now she had to tell her, one way or another, with all these other people listening in. "They want to build a supercomputer." Pel made a derisive snorting noise. "I know, that doesn't sound special," Adda continued, "But the awakened intelligences want to build themselves a new quantum and pseudo-organic home, and it's *massive*, Iri. Humans haven't built anything this big, even on Earth, and all the components are too tightly packed to allow human input anyway. It's designed to be controlled from the inside."

"Where do they want to build this thing?" Iridian's voice sounded almost as dulled by fear or horror as it did when she was subvocalizing. Behind her, the others looked equally shocked.

"I don't know. Nothing I've read so far includes a location, but they will need a lot of space. At least a major asteroid's worth."

"And why the hell are they spinning this fine tale for us now?" Iridian crossed her arms over her chest and lowered her head, meeting Adda's eyes.

"They made a relatively common mistake, for intelligences." Adda was still reading. "They think we're the only people in the universe they can trust."

CHAPTER 20

Days until launch: 27
(holding for mechanical issues)

Iridian's eyebrows rose and her foot slipped where she'd braced it against a bunk in the *Mayhem*'s residential cabin, making her scramble to reposition herself. "Even after I tried to sic the ITA on them, the AIs still want our help?"

"I'm not sure they care about that, in your case," Adda said. "If it were anybody else, I expect they'd be dead by now."

"Great," Iridian grumbled. "When you figure out where they want to build this monstrosity, let's tell the worlds about it. We can't let the AIs bulldoze a hab just because they've outgrown their tanks."

Adda frowned. "Destroying an existing hab would make more, and more dangerous, work for them. There have to be 'jects which aren't suitable for human habs that they could use."

When the time came, Iridian hoped to hell Adda would tell her where this thing would be built. The damned AIs were wrong about one thing, at least. They couldn't trust Iridian, because Iridian couldn't trust them.

* * *

Late in the night, Adda let out a sharp "Yes!" that jolted Iridian awake.

Iridian bounced off Adda's shoulder and thumped into the wall beside their small bunk in the *Mayhem*'s residential cabin. "What? What is it?"

"Sorry, everything's fine. Well, not everything, but look!" Adda showed Iridian her comp projection and caught the datacask dangling on its short cable before it bopped Iridian in the nose. A model number that meant nothing to Iridian's sleep-slowed mind was highlighted in green. "We've got it! That's the human-readable code version of the source. I thought I'd gotten it in the generator, but now I'm sure." She was showing Iridian the implant firmware, which Iridian was pretty sure she'd said she'd had as soon as she got out of the generator on Biometallic 1. "I'm sending notes to Kanti now."

Iridian's eyelids drooped and she snuggled into Adda's side with a wide yawn. "That's great, babe."

"Kanti might find the vulnerability before we get to Yǎo Station," Adda said.

Half-asleep, Iridian mumbled, "Knew you could do it." Now protecting Adda and Noor from Casey's influence seemed not only possible, but inevitable. Iridian fell into a real sleep.

At Sunan's Landing, Iridian offered Wiley and Rio a chance to "get off this ride" and stay. "No, I'll go back with you," said Wiley. "Noor might need us. That's what teams do: help each other."

Iridian turned to Rio. "You can't possibly owe us anymore. We're clear as far as I'm concerned."

"Yeah, I don't," Rio said. "But you remember how the AIs hit the ZVs' ship after they dropped you off on Yăo? Chato said they almost rammed the ship into the station. I don't need that happening to me, all on my own way out here. Besides, I still don't have a job until the brass says I do," she added, referring to ZV Group officers. "Together we can hope for, what, three rooms with locking doors between all of us?"

"We can dream," Iridian agreed cheerfully.

Two days along what Gavran called an "unreliable" route from Sunan's Landing to Yăo Station with a cargo hold full of cheap water, he received a vid from Sloane. The captain's muffled voice carried through the bridge door for several minutes before Gavran shared it on a wall in the main cabin. Iridian gripped Adda's hand while Gavran set his glove in a comp cradle on the wall and fiddled with the projection size.

Adda had been unconscious or struggling to form new memories during Sloane's betrayal, but Iridian had been painfully conscious through the whole ordeal. She would never forgive the captain for having risked Adda's life the way Sloane did. Seeing the captain on Biometallic 1 had brought the fear and pain and betrayal she'd felt in those days after Adda's overdose rushing back to her. The feelings had faded, but the captain had actually thought they'd rejoin the crew after what Sloane did. That still irritated her.

"Looks like a residential cabin on a ship, doesn't it?" Iridian pointed to the curved joint between the wall and ceiling behind Sloane's head in the paused vid. "The captain must've found somebody to carry them back to Vesta." Captain Sloane held the arm Gavran had shot awkwardly, bent at the elbow and encased in a healing brace.

Gavran started the message playback: ". . . admit, you couldn't have fallen in with a better crew," Captain Sloane said.

Pel let out an agreeable whoop. "That's us!" Adda shushed him, but Iridian felt the same way. Even after everything else that'd happened between them, coming from Sloane, that was high praise.

"Our new agreement is this," Captain Sloane continued. "All of you stay off Vesta, and I won't go out of my way to set the ITA on your trail, which I presume leads to Yǎo Station."

"Shit," said Rio and Iridian together.

"Did the captain fucking guess that, or was it obvious?" asked Pel.

According to Adda, Yǎo Station had been an obvious choice of hideouts even before they'd been forced to leave Vesta. It was the closest discreet location without entering the lawless colonies beyond the Jovian orbit, where the war's worst battles had been fought. Iridian wasn't ready to go back to any of those 'jects.

Captain Sloane smiled slightly, said "Good luck," and gestured at something out of frame that ended the recording.

Rio shook her massive head. Dark hair tumbled from the clips she contained it with to float around her face. "Well. I've never been banned from a whole 'ject before."

"We don't have to stay on Yǎo Station," Adda said. "I could find somewhere else with minimal ITA and Ceres syndicate presence."

"Somewhere that's just as safe from the gods-damned AIs?" Iridian asked.

"Nowhere in this solar system is completely safe," said Adda.

Pel rolled his eyes. "Oh, that's encouraging."

"It's not supposed to be encouraging," said Adda. "It's a fact."

"First, Yǎo," said Wiley. "Noor'll be stuck in that meditation room in the temple again." Alone, he couldn't defend the two closet spaces off the port mod that they'd been "renting" from Yǎons who wanted it just as much as he did.

Iri, Adda whispered in her ear. *Give me your comp a minute.*

Iridian raised an eyebrow and held out the hand with her black-and-yellow comp glove. Adda retrieved her cord from her necklace and plugged it into both comps. "It runs a debris and weather cover for one of Biometallic's mobile diagnostics units," she explained as the firmware transferred to Iridian's comp. "Maybe you can use it with your shield redesign. Um. Happy birthday."

Iridian hugged her, pulling Adda's comp hand into an awkward position over Iridian's shoulder, cord and all. "Oh my gods, babe. You found umbrella firmware." Laughing, she kissed the top of Adda's head where her highlights used to come together. "My shield's too simple to need that, but that's really sweet. Thank you." Adda blushed an adorable shade of red while Pel doubled over laughing. The fact that she'd managed to find Iridian a gift while the ITA was closing in on them was, in Iridian's estimation, true love.

By the time Jupiter had swelled to the size of Earth's Moon in the *Mayhem*'s windows, they'd still heard nothing from Dr. Björn, the Vestan station council, the University of Mars, or anyone else Adda had contacted about helping Dr. Björn complete vis expedition to the new star system independent of Oxia Corporation. She'd sent anonymous messages, she'd used her own name and Iridian's, and she'd impersonated Oxia representatives at various ranks. Those last attempts resulted in terse, negative responses from assistants.

If Adda had been able to convince one of those well-funded groups to buy Björn's expedition away from Oxia, Iridian could've used that as a bargaining chip to get Björn to make room for Iridian and Adda on the expedition crew. Björn seemed to be an honorable person. But if Björn wouldn't even acknowledge that Adda had tried to contact ver, what was the point? The astronomer would not be coerced, and they just didn't have the resources to take on Oxia by themselves, despite Iridian's willingness to do so.

Adding to that disappointment, Kanti, the Ceresian body modder who'd inserted Iridian's and Adda's comms implants, had replied to her message about her neural implant net firmware. "I've attached documentation that shows exactly where the problem is, so you can *try* getting the corp to make the change. Don't count on them doing it anytime soon, though. I could do the update myself, but in addition to my fee"—here the vid spent several seconds flashing back and forth between Kanti's face and an image of a humanoid robot with a grin that showed metal teeth—"you gotta get me the certificate they signed it with. The neural implant net won't even take an update that isn't signed. Let me know if any of that doesn't make sense."

Unfortunately, it made plenty of sense. If Biometallic hadn't signed their products, then anybody could upload firmware with nasty changes that'd make the implants do things that were illegal, immoral, or unsafe. The crew had taken a gamble on the source being signed when Adda found it. According to Kanti, it wasn't. The message tilted out of sight as Adda's wrist drifted out of Iridian's field of vision.

On Biometallic 1, they'd nearly gotten caught by the ITA *and* the AIs. If Gavran had backed Captain Sloane, the ITA would've had Iridian's crew. And after all that, the firmware source was effectively useless without the certificate. They weren't any closer to protecting the implant, and Adda's mind, from Casey.

Iridian pulled Adda into a hug and bit her lip against the despair welling up from her chest, closing her throat. Casey hadn't breached Yăo Station so far, except by text, but Adda kept saying it would. When Casey got through, they'd be trapped.

Adda clenched her fists and pulled her comp projection back into view, which sent her slowly tipping backward, switching to the money management software she used. When Adda finished selling the copied firmware from Biometallic, that'd pay Kanti and Gavran. If they stayed on Yăo, Pel's savings gave them a couple of weeks of money to live on. They could probably convince the Odin Razum to pay them again too, but even that wouldn't be enough to buy Björn's former kidnappers a place on the expedition.

When Casey finally found its way onto Yăo, the first thing it'd do was influence Adda. As Iridian understood it, the overfitting error it'd made assured that. By that time, they had to have eliminated the vulnerability that'd allowed both Casey and Mairie to influence Adda through her implant in the past, and that required Biometallic's certificate.

As Iridian watched, Adda composed another anonymous message to Biometallic showing them exactly where Kanti said the vulnerability was. Given the added security, returning to one of Biometallic's stations would be even more dangerous than it'd been the first time. But if that was what it took to secure her implant, Iridian would do it.

Adda opened a new set of notes in her comp. Ordinarily Iridian would let her work in peace and go chat with the others, but dealing with Captain Sloane again had thrown her off. She'd almost lost Adda on Vesta. She didn't want to be anywhere other than Adda's side now. "What are you working on?"

Adda's breathing pattern meant she'd stopped subvocalizing to her comp at a range below where she'd set her mic to pick up her words and send them to Iridian. "I'm composing some routines to crawl the Patchwork for information on where Biometallic stored its certificates. After last time, I'm not assuming they're even in the same facility as the source material."

While Adda did that, Iridian caught a nap. Sometime later, the residential cabin door shut with a thump that woke her. "Sorry," Adda said when she met Iridian's half-open eyes. "So, I've been thinking. We can't keep working on both the expedition and protecting my implant. I'd thought that once we reached Yăo Station, we'd make enough money to buy our way onto the expedition. That's not happening."

Iridian propped herself up on her elbows. This was a huge change from Adda's previous long-term plans. "There has to be something else we can do to get on the expedition. Blackmail somebody. Blow something up?" That tactic had moved up on Iridian's list of go-to options since she'd been hanging around Wiley again. "It's not too late to hit Oxia's facilities if the CEO doesn't turn the expedition over to U of M."

Adda smiled. "And that is a reason I love you. But if we're focused on the expedition, we're not going to get the certificate for my implant firmware in time. If Casey finds me in a workspace, I'll . . . Well, who knows what I'll do?" Iridian had been sleeping on the bunk across the small cabin from Adda, but she pushed herself to Adda's and pulled her close. Adda wrapped her arms around Iridian and said into her shoulder, "We have to start treating the expedition as a backup and focus on securing the neural implant nets."

Iridian sighed. Even though this was the most practical target, and the one they were most likely to reach, giving up was a sick emptiness inside her. Adda would hate it as much as Iridian did. "I liked the idea of seeing the new solar system," Iridian said. "It would've been exciting, even if we were just fixing the expedition toilets or something."

"I know. After we remove the vulnerability, maybe we can . . . I mean, the launch date is still weeks away. But I think Casey will get to us before then."

Iridian pulled away a little to look Adda in the eyes. She seemed clear and present and not experiencing any overdose-induced disorientation. "So your plan now is, what, waiting to get caught?"

Scowling, Adda pulled her comp back into view and scrolled quickly through whatever she'd been reading. "My plan is to protect myself. The next time Casey catches up with us, and it will, I'd really like to talk to it when I'm sure it can't instantaneously influence me. I want to ask it to *communicate*, instead of chasing us around populated space."

"Talking to it dropped us into a lot of shit before," Iridian said doubtfully.

"Casey also saved our lives, multiple times. It took you across the station on Barbary when AegiSKADA was trying to kill you. Without it, we wouldn't have broken into Oxia's comms on Vesta. We would've taken significant losses without knowing what they were planning. And it's trying to do something that I don't think is . . . I mean, I don't have evidence yet, but I don't get the impression that they'd use the new quantum comp construct they keep talking about for violent or manipulative purposes. If we can get that vulnerability fixed, I'll have a chance to find out."

Iridian tightened her arms around Adda again, reveling in the warmth and solidity of her presence. When she'd been in the ITA's custody, she'd missed this so much. "I'm all for fixing the vulnerability so you'll be safe, but we don't need to board the *Casey Mire Mire* to test it, yeah?" Her chest rose and fell against Adda's in a soft sigh. "So. Next step?"

"I'll find out where Biometallic stores its certificates."

The one piece of good news since Sunan's Landing was that Noor was using the temple's drones to give them regular updates from Yǎo Station. At least, Iridian thought it was good news until she and Adda watched the most recent update with the rest of the crew. Something seemed off about Noor, and it wasn't just that his vid was projected from Adda's comp in the bulkhead-mounted cradle onto the opposite bulkhead in the *Mayhem*'s main cabin.

". . . back to that workspace generator in Water Processing." Yǎo Station's low gravity magnified the way Noor shifted toward the meditation room's doorway, like he'd rather be in the generator than recording the vid. "The AIs have been staying out of the way. It's actually a pretty good setup if you can get over the smell." The wet scent of the plants growing over the water tanks hadn't been all that bad, as Iridian remembered it.

The intelligences can't be staying out of the way, Adda subvocalized. She let Noor's vid conclude. His latest recordings ended in black with the temple's contact information in white text, inviting people missing loved ones to find out if the missing person had ended up on Yǎo Station. "Aside from the fact that I've never seen Casey stop using something it's identified as useful, intelligences are designed to interact with humanity at every opportunity," Adda continued aloud in a quaking voice. "An unsupervised zombie intelligence wouldn't just ignore someone with an ID that qualifies them as an emergency supervisor. Especially not when that person is inside a generator in a facility the intelligence controls."

"That signal, the one that Mairie used to send you into the generator the first time," Iridian said. "It would've done that same thing again as soon as he walked in there."

Rio's eyes widened, probably heading for the same conclusion Iridian was. "But now there's nobody there with him to pull him out."

"And Mairie did that the first time before Casey got involved," Adda said. "Casey and Mairie are both communicating with him, and I can't imagine either of them leaving him alone until they get what they want. He's lying."

CHAPTER 21

Days until launch: 27
(holding for mechanical issues)

When Adda was under Casey's influence, she had said anything it took to keep Iridian from looking closer at her relationship with the intelligence. The intelligences had shown her almost everything they'd been doing, and she'd told Iridian only a fraction of it.

Beneath the lights of the *Mayhem*'s main cabin, Iridian's face went alarmingly pale. "Lying about contact with an AI is an influence symptom."

"When we get there, I can check his workspace settings," Adda said. "There are safety measures he might've disabled. It's not easy, but . . ."

"If he's influenced, he'd manage it." Iridian nodded, determined as always.

"And talk to him," Adda said. "If he's influenced, Mairie will come up often in his conversations. Or Casey." In her mind, she was seeing all the influenced Odin Razum people Mairie already had under its control in the water treatment plant. Depending on how much control Casey had gained over the Yăo Station intelligence, it could be using all those people too.

If Casey or Mairie had used Noor's implant's vulnerability to influence him as thoroughly as it had done to Adda on Vesta, then Noor would tell Casey everything. Despite the *Mayhem*'s flawless air mixture, Adda felt like she wasn't breathing in enough oxygen. Casey *couldn't* find out that they were working to close the vulnerability in her and Noor's implants.

Pel wrapped his arms around himself and hunched his shoulders, making himself small. "Fuck."

"Fuck indeed." Adda had accepted that escaping to the new solar system wasn't possible given their current situation, but she'd thought there'd be more time to fix the vulnerability. Now she could barely afford to pay Gavran for taking them back to Yǎo Station, and Casey might outmaneuver them before they got there.

"Isn't that an extreme conclusion to jump to?" asked Wiley, who was holding Rio's armored suit so she could examine it in the low gravity they were currently tolerating. "I mean, we saw a lot of influenced people down there, but . . ."

"Adda knows all about influence," Pel assured him. "If she says he's influenced, he's influenced. Anyway, it's safer to act like he is unless you get proof he's not. I've seen the other way around and that goes really bad really fast."

"And this is why I'm not following the ZVs around like a little lost pup," Rio said resignedly while she checked over her armor. "They've got pilots, but they don't have any AI experts. They still have no idea what hit them on Ganymede." She'd rubbed off most of the scuffs from the fight on Biometallic 1, but she, Iridian, and Wiley all seemed to feel that every conflict required at least an hour of equipment inspection afterward. "I told them, but since I'm not supposed to be contactable right now and the ITA says there aren't any awakened AIs, it's kind of a hard sell."

"Your major believed you though, yeah?" Wiley asked hopefully.

"Oh, sure," said Rio. "'That's what I thought,' was what he told me. That doesn't help him with *his* boss, though." Wiley and Iridian nodded like that made sense to them. Adda was happy she'd never gotten involved in that kind of hierarchy. It sounded needlessly complex.

Even though all she felt like doing was strapping herself to a bunk and falling into a miserable sleep, Adda forced herself to start the search for more information about Yǎo Station's intelligence. They'd be leaving the Patchwork behind soon, and she had to be ready to deal with whatever Mairie and now Casey were doing on the station. She didn't have time to mourn this setback, and there wasn't any point in doing so.

When she'd met Mairie in the water treatment module's generator, her comp had recorded enough information to pin down the exact version of the intelligence that she was dealing with. She confirmed her translation of its name, Mairie, as "town hall" in English. Its developers had been bought out by a larger intelligence development corporation, which later made Ficience, the intelligence that managed Biometallic 1. Mairie was the oldest intelligence that Adda had ever dealt with, even older than AegiSKADA. And it'd still used her implant to talk her into entering a workspace with the intention of becoming its supervisor.

She pushed that mistake out of her head. Everybody knew about that signal pulse Mairie had used, and they wouldn't let it do that to her again. If she accepted the supervisory role it offered, she'd do it on her own terms. That meant somebody would have to accompany her whenever she was near a workspace generator on Yǎo Station. Since the only one she'd found was surrounded by Odin Razum, she'd want company anyway.

"I can get him back," Adda said aloud.

Since she'd started reading, Pel had fallen asleep, untethered arms drifting up from his passenger couch. Rio and Wiley had put away Rio's armor and, having already checked over his and Iridian's, were looking at something on their comps. Iridian was still strapped into the couch beside Adda, projecting her new shield schematics on what Adda had to imagine was the ceiling, since it was on the opposite side of the main cabin from the couches.

Wiley and Rio looked up from their comps, and Iridian turned away from the schematics, grinning. "Yeah?"

"If I accept Mairie's offer to become its supervisor, I can separate him from Mairie, and Mairie is allowing him to communicate with Casey."

Iridian's grin disappeared. "No. Not if Mairie is talking to Casey too. Absolutely not." Subvocally, she added, *I'm not trading you for him.*

We can't be sure that's what would happen, Adda replied.

Over her protest, Wiley said, "Why not? That seems like an easy fix."

"If Casey's in contact with Mairie, getting wrapped up in one AI is the same as getting wrapped up in both of them," Iridian snapped. "This is not an option. Can't we just isolate him until he calms the fuck down?"

"That will take a long time," Adda said. "Weeks, probably."

"Then he'll just have to wait it out," Iridian said. "Nobody's plugging into anything connected to Casey."

As Mairie's supervisor, it would've been simple to add people's IDs to a blacklist that would prevent the intelligence from contacting them. An awakened intelligence would've found a way around that, or it would've deleted its own blacklist. In its zombie state, Mairie would've had to abide by the list's requirements. That would've separated everyone on the list from Mairie, forcing them into the first step of influence recovery.

Easy as it would've been to keep arguing for that solution,

Adda stayed silent. Until her implant's vulnerability was fixed, entering a workspace with Mairie or Casey would invite them to influence her as deeply as they'd influenced Noor. Keeping her implant out of those intelligences' reach made it much harder for them to control her, although Casey's reach grew hourly. Assuring both Iridian and herself that she wouldn't hurt Iridian was more important than freeing Noor from Casey quickly. By this time, he'd probably told Casey all the information he had. And the Odin Razum had never been Adda's problem to solve.

The passenger couches barely accommodated Adda's wide hips. The beds, though, had room for two. She untangled herself from the couch's straps, and Iridian followed her into the residential cabin. Rio had taken the other bottom bunk. They carefully avoided her to reach the top one and curled around each other.

"We'll sort it out," Iridian whispered, her breath warm on Adda's lips. *We will. We'll make it. Nobody and nothing can stop us for long.* Adda wished that were true, and for once, she wanted to believe it badly enough to stop herself from voicing all the ways it wasn't. She kissed Iridian, hard, and thought of nothing else.

The low gravity that Gavran had maintained throughout the trip rose as they approached Yăo Station and inserted themselves into its slow spin. After days of no gravity at all, the transition made Adda as sick as it always did. Even Yăo Station's low gravity felt exhausting as she stepped out of the passthrough and into the oily air of the station's docks.

Gavran would be staying with the ship. "How can you breathe all this CO_2?" he asked. "And besides the bad atmo, there are too many scrappers and thieves here. *Mayhem* can defend herself from scrappers, but I hate to make her do it alone." He patted the main cabin's wall fondly.

Iridian said, "We'll be back with Noor soon. Be ready." Gavran nodded and retreated down the passthrough to his ship.

Iridian, Wiley, and Rio wore their armored suits and formed the points of a triangle that enclosed Adda and Pel as soon as they were all out of the passthrough and crossing the port module. Every distant shout drew their attention and raised their gloved hands to their weapons.

"Anybody see Noor?" Pel's pseudo-organic eyes widened his pupils for a moment and then returned them to their regular size. "He said he'd meet us in the port mod, right?"

Adda looped her arm through his, the way she used to guide him before he got pseudo-organic eyes. "Yes, that's what he said, but you know what this place is like. Plans change."

"Whoa!" Pel joined the rest of them in dodging a runaway cargo hauler overloaded with what looked like a deep fryer, small animal meat, and several unwinding rolls of disposable wraps. The bot careened down the open space between the passthroughs and the wall that separated the port module from the rest of the station, where its track might've been before that was scrapped. A molting parrot squawked from the top of the cart, scattering small feathers in the food and everywhere in a two-meter radius. Five people followed the cargo hauler's path through the dock, shrieking, "Get it!" "Faster!" and "Idiots!" in a language it took her implant a second to translate.

"Colony ports." Wiley shook his head tiredly. "They never have their shit together."

"And it's always scattered in different ways." Iridian's cheerful tone sounded forced.

They kept walking, looking for Noor and fending off more people selling or buying things the crew couldn't afford to buy or part with. Iridian, Rio, and Wiley had to drop their triangular formation to fit through the single functioning door in this section of the module and into a connecting hallway beyond. Noor leaned on the wall across from the door.

He was thinner and dirtier than he'd been when they'd left Yăo Station. The conversion rate between NEU currency and Yăo Station's water-based money was still bad. Perhaps he'd run out. Or, more likely, he'd been sleeping near the workspace generator he used to contact Casey through Mairie.

He pushed off the wall and approached in long steps, holding Adda's gaze for a moment before turning to Iridian. "Finally," he said, in a tone even Adda recognized as a rude way to greet friends. "If you'd taken any longer, I would've gone back to—"

Without missing a step, Iridian raised her armored forearm and slammed it into Noor's throat. He staggered backward and fell, choking and swearing while Pel yelped in surprise and Adda winced in sympathy. Iridian knelt beside him and put an armored hand on his chest, holding him down. "Are you supervising Mairie right now?"

"What the hell kind of question is that?" Noor wheezed. "Do you think I'd be here waiting for you if I was?"

Iridian picked Noor up and wrapped an arm around his neck with one gloved hand covering his mouth. "Back to the *Mayhem*." Gavran had already told them he didn't like the idea of imprisoning Noor on his ship, but it was a secure location where the station intelligence wouldn't be able to reach Noor, once they took his comp.

Noor said something angry behind Iridian's glove and looked to Adda as if she might side with him. Iridian hauled him back across the port module, with Wiley and Rio looking big and menacing and Pel and Adda staying well behind them, out of the way. "That went faster than I thought it would," said Pel.

"We surprised him," said Adda.

"No kidding. He's going to be pissed, too."

Adda had been furious when Iridian second-guessed her with safety recommendations while Adda had been under Casey's influence. In the end, Iridian had been right about most of it. "He'll get over it, eventually." That wasn't guaranteed, but she'd grown used to telling Pel comforting lies. He seemed to need and even expect them, and he never held them against her after the truth came out. "It'll be weeks before we can trust him, though." Adda raised her voice so Iridian would hear her. "Can't we take him to the clinic first? To check on his implant?" If an intelligence was influencing him, then his neural implant would've been under heavy use for days.

"Let's get the money we got for the firmware copies exchanged for Yǎo money first," Iridian said. "If his implant's fucked up, then fixing it'll cost us something."

The *Mayhem* had two residential cabins, one for Gavran and one for passengers. He watched from the bridge doorway while Rio and Iridian muscled Noor into the residential cabin Gavran didn't sleep in. With another short struggle, they separated Noor from his comp glove. "Get off!" Noor roared. "What the hell are you doing?" When Rio passed the comp to Iridian, she handed it to Wiley in the main cabin. Noor shouted, "I need that!" He faltered and his eyes widened. He'd just lost his connection to the intelligence that bound his mind, and if his influence experience was anything like Adda's had been, that'd scare him. "I need it." His voice was all quiet desperation.

"You don't." Iridian's cheerful tone didn't match her and Rio's cautious exit from the residential cabin, without taking their eyes off Noor. After the door shut, Gavran disappeared into the bridge to lock the cabin from the outside. The residential cabin door's lock icon appeared in its center.

Adda backed away from the door as Noor pounded on it from the other side. Iridian started talking to Rio, Wiley, and Pel about who would go get their payment and who would wait on the ship. Noor's frantic pounding stopped. "Adda Karpe," he said, so quietly that she barely heard him. "You will receive a message with coordinates. Meet us there. Acknowledge."

"Who are you?" Adda had to know how much Noor knew about what was happening to him.

"It's me," Noor said. "Nobody's fucking influencing me." An influenced person would say that, and anything else they thought would get them back in contact with the intelligence. "That's the message I had to give you."

"But who's it from?"

"A ship's copilot," Noor said. "It's the awakened AI Iridian said to look out for, isn't it? The *Casey Mire Mire*."

CHAPTER 22

Days until launch: 21

Even though Yăo Station's local time was around 05:30, the short-term solution to a buddy getting influenced was to get a gods-damned drink. Iridian only managed to convince Pel, Rio, and Wiley of that fact, though. Noor was obviously indisposed, and Gavran wouldn't leave the *Mayhem* alone with an influenced stranger onboard. Now that they'd switched everything they'd earned from the Biometallic op over to Yăo currency, Adda was too busy messing with their finances to process what'd happened via alcohol.

Iridian's feelings about giving up on the expedition were as chaotic as Yăo's port always felt. Now that they had Gavran for as long as they kept paying him, they could've at least tried threatening Oxia's facilities until it turned the expedition over to the University of Mars. Aside from the pure enjoyment of hassling Oxia Corporation, the university would've done a better job of getting Björn's research team everything they needed to launch. According to the newsfeeds, Björn was still struggling with last-minute essentials. Switching expedition sponsors could've been the break ve needed to consider letting Iridian and Adda join. It would've been difficult, but possible, to see the new star system for herself. That was a hell of a thing to give up.

Adda still thought that carrying out that threat would've cost much more than she'd made selling Biometallic's firmware for medical devices other than her and Noor's implants. Once more potential buyers woke up, they'd sell the water they'd bought on Sunan's Landing too. That'd disappear quickly after expenses and the split six ways.

It would've been great to get the fuck out of the AIs' range for a while, see some brand-new planets, and spend time with Adda where nobody would interrupt them. But they would've been separating themselves from almost every other person in the universe, a terrifying prospect even without the knowledge that if, somehow, Casey found them again, Adda was still susceptible to its influence. Protecting her was the most important objective. It was why they would've gone on the expedition in the first place.

Maybe the whole idea had been an escapist fantasy they'd both bought into, one that was too impractical for reality. Like in every other fight Iridian had been in, they'd gather intel, gear up, and choose a battlefield where they could fight back. The problem of stealing the necessary gear, the Biometallic certificate in this case, was much easier for Iridian to wrap her head around than finding a way onto a fucking science expedition.

In the meantime, Pel, Wiley, Rio, and Iridian found table space at the quietest of Pel's usual haunts. It was a wide room with basketball hoops on two walls and spots in the floor which, when stepped on the wrong way, deployed poles for nets. The nets and the other sports equipment were long gone and the floor was scuffed and scratched, but the half of the overhead lights that worked still lit the place brighter than anywhere else on Yăo.

Stacked crates with logos of corps that made sports gear

formed a bar tended by a greasy-looking man who guarded the establishment's sole paypad with a machete. The printer in the corner printed small cups you'd use for water in a normal hab's gym. The family that ran the place lived in an extended hut under one of the basketball hoops. The trash on the hut's roof suggested that people were still taking free throws.

The table they gathered around had built-on benches that made metallic screeches as they sat down with their drinks. "So, Noor can't talk to Casey anymore, but that's a really slow cure for influence," Iridian said. "And there are a lot of ways it can go wrong."

"Especially when he'll make himself a new ID as soon as he gets ahold of a comp," said Rio.

"He's resourceful, but his luck isn't much better than ours," Iridian said. "He hated the ITA brainwashing in Sorenson; he ran halfway across the solar system to get away from them, and then he gets influenced here. We have to pay for his influence treatment somewhere good, if there's a charge for it. So we'll need another job soon."

"Here's a question." Wiley sipped one of Yǎo's weirdly thick local beers. "Would getting Noor's whatever-ware locked up against the awakened AIs get him un-influenced?"

"Who knows? Nobody's tried it before." Iridian sighed over her own small and expensive, though effective, drink. "Securing it seems like it should help. It'd cut off a direct, secret comms line to his brain. AIs use the implants for other stuff too, Adda says, like changing electrical patterns in there. Without all that, it'd be easier to isolate him from AIs while his neurochemistry goes back to normal."

"Poor bastard." Pel drank, and everybody else did too.

* * *

The water sold as well as Iridian thought it would, thank all the gods. When she and the others came into the *Mayhem*, Adda was sitting on the main cabin floor by the locked door to the residential cabin, talking to Noor on the other side. The banging and shouting that'd been emanating from the door when they left were mercifully absent.

". . . don't have to tell me how it works, just how to access it. I promise I won't take it apart and analyze it on-site."

Noor's dark laughter from the other side of the door was singularly disturbing. "That's not what I'm worried about, is it? I go, I get my share, I keep my trade secrets, or it doesn't fucking happen. What part of that don't you understand?"

"Well, this all sounds fun." Pel vaulted one passenger couch, threw himself into another, almost bounced out of it, and righted himself in a casual pose that could've been intentional. "What're you up to, Sissy?"

"We're discussing Noor's backdoor into Biometallic's firmware library." On the other side of the door, a blanket on a bunk rustled. Adda looked at the door and sighed. "He wants to go with us to get the certificate, but that's not an option. If we can't reach an agreement, I'll have to look over the access protocol on the pseudo-organic cask we took to Biometallic last time."

Noor snickered. "Good fucking luck."

Adda looked at Iridian mournfully. *I already checked the cask. I'd need a workspace and a lot more time to analyze it to even differentiate the access protocol from whatever he'd done to create or find it in the first place. It's not organized in a way that makes sense to me. And his comp's encrypted.*

Pel beckoned Adda over, and Iridian reached out to haul Adda to her feet and help her balance in the low grav. When they got close enough, Pel whispered, "Can't you figure it out without him?"

Adda rolled her eyes and whispered back, "If Iridian could use a safe workspace generator *and* compatible development or analysis software, she'd have as good a chance of that as I do. It's really hard to tell what we're looking at without the environmental context of the surrounding system."

Getting back into Biometallic's firmware library was Adda's last gods-damned hope for protecting herself from Casey, but her climbing into Mairie's workspace generator would be the same as asking Mairie or Casey to influence her. *Did you blacklist him with the station AI?* Iridian asked subvocally.

No, Adda replied. *The list is locked for supervisory access only.* She scowled toward the passthrough, as if something in the port was to blame. *Like you said earlier, he'll just have to wait it out.*

How long will it take? Iridian asked her.

Weeks.

"Are you two secretly talking?" Pel whispered. "Because you're staring at each other again."

"It's not a secret if you whine about it!" Adda hissed. "We're allowed to stare, anyway. She has beautiful eyes."

Iridian wrapped an arm around Adda's waist. "Adda's still figuring out how we'll get that certificate for her implant, and Biometallic might still come through with a fix for her. While we're waiting on them, I want to resupply. Wiley, Rio, since you know what to look for, I could use your help with that. And if we have to go back to Biometallic 1, I really want a shield."

Rio nodded. "I haven't got anything better to do."

"Gods, I hope we can afford patch kits this time," said Wiley.

"Who will watch Noor?" asked Adda.

"Does he even need watching?" Pel asked. "I mean, I can't see him now."

"Yes," said Adda, at the same time Iridian said, "Yeah." Adda nodded to Iridian and gave her a *go ahead* wave of her upturned palm. She did that when she thought she and Iridian were about to make the same point and Iridian would make it more effectively. "He's a thief, remember? That means he's good with locks."

"Not my locks," said Gavran from the bridge. "Nobody opens *Mayhem*'s doors without my say-so." It was his ship, so he'd know, and he'd have a lot to lose if he was wrong. Maybe Iridian was getting paranoid.

"Pel, Adda, Wiley, stay here and help Gavran with . . ." Iridian paused. If Noor found a way out of his cabin, he'd run Pel over on his way to the generator in the water treatment plant. Iridian was counting on Gavran to stop Noor, if it came to that. She turned toward the bridge. "What the hell do you do while you're docked?"

"Used to be, looked for my brother. Searching for family's a full-time job." Gavran sighed and turned his gaze toward some numbers projected above the bridge console. "Now, maintenance, keeping up with whatever needs upkeep. Catching up on news and stories I've missed. Chasing off thieves, when they interrupt the facts and fiction. Not so much thievery here at the dock, but people go out into stationspace, so it's not none."

"Got it," said Iridian. "Help Gavran keep thieves off the hull." She held her breath to stop herself from laughing at the image of Pel donning an enviro suit to defend the *Mayhem* in stationspace.

Before the ITA took it off her on Ceres, Iridian had carried a collapsible personal shield everywhere. The best version of the pattern she'd designed to print it was on her old comp, which the ITA still had. Iridian had spent the return trip from Biometallic 1 revising backup schematics Adda had found. They were good enough to convert to printer patterns. Iridian would make any changes she had time for while she assembled the pieces.

Most of the supplies needed to make the shield were easy to

come by, but she needed more mech-ex graphene. It was what kept the shield light and effective, so swapping it out with another material would require a prototyping cycle she had no time or money for. Iridian lost more time walking past sixteen scrap dealers selling partial spools of stuff labeled as mech-ex graphene that was, half the time, not even graphene, let alone a mech-ex composite.

"Could you melt something down if you found it?" Rio asked. Wiley was buying patch kits for their suits, finally, along with some other supplies that shouldn't require a physical confrontation to get. Even with Iridian's barely functional helmet, both women were wearing much more armor than Wiley had left the *Mayhem* in.

Iridian shrugged. "It's possible, but I wouldn't try it myself. When it's already shaped, it's hard to tell what else is mixed in there. Also, it changes composition with heat if you're not careful. It can get brittle, which is about the last thing I want in a shield. At a manufacturing plant you'd just put some scrap in the machine and let a bot recycle it, but here? No thanks."

They eventually found something Iridian was almost positive was mech-ex graphene, on a partially used spool. It looked like there'd be enough for a shield if she didn't make any mistakes during the build. "Really glad to have your help here," Iridian said as Rio stopped the spool from rolling in front of a cargo carrier for the second time since they'd bought it. Even with the suit arms taking some of the weight, Iridian was loaded down with smaller spools and parts she'd need for the shield, and she didn't have hands to keep the large spool on track too. Rio had her hands free, having already threatened one would-be thief until he changed his mind and ran away.

The public printers were all guarded by various small armed groups that charged for printing. People had lined up around the one in the port, but one past the elevator to the temple had no crowd and only five people Pel's age, armed with knives and maybe a dart gun. They watched Iridian and Rio approach with insolent indifference to the amount of armor the women wore.

"All right." Iridian set her stack of parts and spools down, careful not to dent the filament. That'd cause printing errors. "Here's the deal. I spent all my money on this shit, and I've got practically none for you."

"Then no print!" One of the jerks was sitting on the printer housing, grinning down at her.

"Or . . ." Iridian grabbed the jerk's ankle and pulled him off the printer. He yelped as he fell, and the other four drew blades. Iridian knelt on one of his arms and didn't even feel the armor digging into his bare flesh as she brought her knife down millimeters from his eye. "You can all back off, and we don't have to blind any of you."

"Fuck this," said one of the older ones clustered around the printer. The people still standing backed away. A few sheathed their knives. "Pay what you can, yeah?"

Iridian sheathed her knife and pulled the guy she'd knocked down back to his feet. "Thanks. I have better things to do with my day than cleaning blood out of my gloves."

The pieces printed and were loaded into boxes, which Iridian stacked in her arms. Now she needed someplace to put them together. The temple was on the way back to the *Mayhem*, and Shingetsu knew just about everything there was to know about Yăo, so she'd know where to find tools Iridian could borrow.

The hem of Shingetsu's red robe swished along the floor tiles after one of the other religious people had found her for Iridian and

Rio. "Hello again, Shieldrunners," she said, although her expression suggested that their presence was an alarming inconvenience.

Iridian raised her chin to speak over the stacked shield parts she carried. "Where's a stocked workshop I can use? I've got a project to assemble."

"I see that," said Shingetsu. "Well. When we need something assembled, we take it to the Apostolovs in Dock 33."

"What're Apostolovs?" asked Rio.

"They're a family," Shingetsu explained. "The parents and grandmother are all excellent technicians. I'm not sure what their background was before they came here. Their oldest is making a great deal of progress too. Just don't bring any harm to them. I don't need to know the nature of your project, but—"

"It's safe," Iridian assured her. "No electricity, nothing explosive. Hell, it's even legal, most places."

Shingetsu's face relaxed into the first true smile she'd given them since they arrived. "Good."

In the port mod, they met a gruff older woman, two younger ones, and four kids. One was a teenager and the rest of them had to be under ten. Two little ones had some color in their skin, but the rest of the family was bone white beneath a uniform layer of grease and grit. Iridian haggled for workshop time while Rio played with the kids.

Children were fascinated by how big Rio was, and Rio loved to get down on the floor with them, even in full armor. These kids called their parents "Mama Yuliya" and "Mama Dionne." How, Iridian wondered, would "Mama Adda" and "Mama Iridian" sound? Difficult, probably. Kids had trouble saying Iridian's name. Besides, at the rate she and Adda kept running from disaster to disaster, there was no way they'd be able to do right by kids. On Vesta, under Captain Sloane, they might've managed it.

She shook the daydream out of her head and got to work. If

they'd found a way onto Björn's expedition, they'd have had time to plan for a family of their own while they kept scientific equipment running in a brand-new solar system. Iridian had even downloaded troubleshooting material and schematics for spectrometry equipment, imaging equipment, and astronomy drones. She might still look them over after she got off this station with its damned CO_2 headaches.

Since she'd found the damaged components in her helmet during the trip back from Biometallic 1, that didn't take long to fix. Once she confirmed that the cheap components wouldn't try to light her on fire again, she started on the shield, and a couple of hours and several heavy test thumps later, Iridian was satisfied with that too. In a workshop of her own, she'd have taken time to figure out why the new shield didn't shake her whole arm when she deployed it from its collapsed configuration the way her old one had. Maybe the mechanism in the original model had been overbuilt, or maybe she'd slowed this model down a little, or the lock wasn't locking right . . . Unfortunately, she'd used almost all the workshop time she could afford.

"Cool," said a voice from behind her. The oldest Apostolov child was staring with frank appreciation at the expanded shield in Iridian's hand.

Iridian grinned. "Yeah. I gave your grandma a copy of the plans. Make your own, if you like it."

"Yeah," the kid said. "I want to." Her eyes looked so big, Iridian realized, because the rest of her was too small. The whole family was too thin, but on this one it stood out. Iridian discreetly took her last expired MRE out of her pants pocket and left it on the workbench she'd been using.

Iridian was showing the kid, whose name turned out to be Phoenix, how to test each panel of the shield for flaws when Adda's subvocalized whisper said, *Noor got out. We need help.*

CHAPTER 23

Days until launch: 21

On our way, Iridian subvocalized over the implanted comms. She said something else, too, but Adda missed it because Wiley and Gavran were fighting to hold Noor down just outside the *Mayhem*'s passthrough. In the main cabin, Pel sat on the floor, bleeding heavily from a deep cut at the junction of his neck and shoulder. After Noor had gotten out of the guest cabin, he'd taken Pel's knife and run out of the ship, attacking anyone who got in his way.

Since the ship hadn't been swarmed by Mairie's Odin Razum gang, Casey was still relying on Noor and intermittent messages through drones to exert its will on Yăo Station. At some point Casey would disconnect itself from the Patchwork long enough to subsume Mairie. Either it hadn't found a way to get Galilean shielding installed to protect its ship from the unique conditions around Jupiter, or it was still unwilling to disrupt its flow of information. While Noor had been locked in the residential cabin, he and Casey's influence had been contained together.

Pel's health was her immediate concern, though. In the residential cabin Noor had just broken out of, Adda pulled a spare shirt out of a drawer in the wall and folded it until it was the size of the cut in Pel's shoulder. When she pressed down, the fabric started soaking up blood and Pel said, "Ow, ow, ow" in her ear.

"Sorry," Adda said. Outside, people were shouting, and it wasn't just the crew's voices. Their neighbors had come to see what was happening.

Pel squirmed, but Adda held him down with pressure on his wounded shoulder. "We can't just sit here!" Pel said.

The struggle had moved away from the passthrough and out of Adda's view. "Yes, we can. That's exactly what we can do. Iridian and Rio are coming." Iridian would know what to do.

Pel twisted his head to peer at the wound and groaned. "Ah, ow. Yeah, sure, let's wait for them."

Outside, Gavran shouted something Adda's translator couldn't interpret. Noor was yelling, "Out of the way, now! I have to talk to Casey."

"Oh gods." Pel clutched at Adda's arm with his good hand.

"It's okay," Adda lied.

"Is not," Pel said, apparently by reflex.

So much for making him feel better. "You ass, it'll *be* okay. Press on this." Adda put his hand on the sodden shirt and stood.

She didn't know how she was acting this calm when Pel was bleeding so much and Casey had influenced Noor. Her heart pounded so hard she felt it in her ribs.

Iri, where are you? There was no answer. Adda hoped that meant that Iridian and Rio were helping Gavran and Wiley stop Noor from reaching one of the temple drones, or a workspace generator.

Adda got the first aid kit from the *Mayhem*'s bathroom and hurried back to Pel. According to the directions on the kit's case, she should use the sterilizing pad and then wrap the wound in the sterile bandage before getting Pel to a hospital. The case didn't say anything about what to do when armed, influenced allies betrayed you to an intelligence determined to influence you too. That would've been a lot to expect of a first aid kit.

"Is that for me, or what?" asked Pel. "And are there any pain-killers in there? Because, ow."

"Sorry." Adda traded the blood-soaked spare shirt for the sterilizing pad and threw the shirt into the ship's recycler. "I'm going to check the passthrough. Maybe they've got Noor calmed down." Although that seemed unlikely, considering how upset he'd been. She wished the station's orbit would let the *Mayhem*'s cams work. It would've been safer to look outside without opening the passthrough.

"Yeah, just leave me here to take care of my giant, painful, bleeding, probably infected stab wound by myself," Pel grumbled, turning his head at an awkward angle to look at his shoulder again. "Ow."

"If you wipe it off with that pad I just gave you, it won't get infected," Adda called over her shoulder while she opened the interior passthrough door.

Gavran wobbled down the *Mayhem*'s passthrough toward the ship, bent almost double, with one hand on the wall. His legs took fast, tiny steps in all directions to keep him upright according to their internal gyroscopes, tapping on the passthrough floor. The exterior door was still open and Rio stood braced in its doorway. Each of her heavy breaths showed in the heave of her armored shoulders and back. On the floor in front of her lay Wiley, bleeding from where Noor had embedded Pel's knife in his thigh. He was pulling himself away from a crowd of Yǎo residents by using his arms to lift his hips. The injured leg dragged behind him. Iridian and Noor were nowhere in view.

By the time Adda had taken all that in, Gavran had stumbled past her into the main cabin. He fumbled at the controls beside the passthrough door, still clutching his stomach with his free hand. The interior door slid shut.

"Damn," said Pel from his position on the floor, "what happened to you?"

"Noor Beck and your—" Gavran snarled something in cant. Adda's translator only caught a word for "knife." "Beck fucking stabbed me with your knife, that's what."

Pel pushed himself to his hands and knees, and then his feet while Adda crossed to the passthrough. "I'm going to look for Iridian," she said. "Tell me if anything else goes wrong."

"Yeah, sure," he said. "What else could?"

The answer was too long to bother with at the moment. Adda pressed the door controls and her fingers came away sticky with Gavran's blood. The passthrough's interior door slid up and open. Rio crouched in the exterior passthrough doorway and Wiley sat in front of her. When Adda got close enough to see over Rio's shoulder, the knife sticking out of Wiley's thigh froze Adda's questions about Iridian in her throat.

Wiley met her eyes. "I don't think it's as bad as it looks." The pain in his voice was obvious even to Adda.

"We got here as fast as we could, but Noor's gone." Rio's armored fist thumped the passthrough on her last word, and the whole structure rattled. "The little guys are always too quick for me. Nassir's chasing him down."

"Pel and Gavran are hurt too, but Pel can walk there," said Adda. "Wiley, can you get to the clinic without Rio's help?"

Wiley frowned at the knife in his leg. "Yeah. It'll suck, though. What are you going to do?"

"Find Iridian and Noor." Ideally, before anybody else got hurt. "Rio, could you come with me?"

"Yeah." In her helmet's projection of her face, Rio turned her head and drank from her suit's water tank. "Noor'd better appreciate that none of us stuck a knife in his addled little head when he comes out of this."

Iri, Adda subvocalized, *Where are you?*

Iridian's whispered voice said, *Thirty ticks, I think. Still on the first floor.*

Adda put *30 ticks* into her map to find that location in relation to the port mod. The center dock served as station north, also listed as *0 ticks* on the map. Adda started walking in the direction in which the marked segments on the map counted up toward 30. Heavy footsteps confirmed that Rio had joined her. Adda ran for a few meters, then walked again when breathing got too hard.

Rio let her set the pace. "Any idea where Nassir is?"

"The only workspace generator I know of is the one we found while we were looking for the drones. That's where Noor would go." Adda liked Rio, but she didn't want to tell anyone about her and Iridian's comms if she didn't have to. If nobody knew about them, nobody would shut them off or listen in.

Over the slightly raised connector between the port mod and the rest of the station, Adda and Rio entered a hallway with lots of doors, all of which were shut. Some had messages scratched into them or projected on them in flickering colors. One doorway was open, with the torn remains of the door still hanging above it. The pieces curved toward the room within, where a rough male voice said, "What's funny to an NEU terrorist like you?"

That wasn't Noor. Adda crept closer, breathing shallowly and hoping that made her approach quieter. Rio's heavy footfalls turned to softer thumps as she took Adda's cue and slowed down.

"Imagining my cum dripping down your throat after I rip off your head and fuck your fucking spine." Iridian's voice was weak, and it wasn't coming through her helmet speakers. Adda had never heard her say anything that nasty, at least in the languages her implant translated.

I'm right outside, Adda subvocalized to Iridian.

Shit. Stay put and stay quiet.

A thud drew a groan that was still half a laugh from Iridian. Adda stood in the shadow of another doorway and stared at her comp display, trying to think of a way to help. She had a knife, and that was all.

Noor had said that he hadn't accepted Mairie's demands to supervise it, which meant Mairie still wanted a supervisor. The Marsat ID Noor had made for Adda would let her accept that role. If Adda were supervising Mairie, she'd ask it to cut power or air to the mod, or even bring the Odin Razum here to chase off the person hurting Iridian. Supervising Mairie meant she'd gain control of the station itself, as the intelligence had reminded her when it influenced her before. If she were ever going to accept the intelligence's invitation to supervise it, now would be the time. She'd use it to protect everyone she cared about, like she had on Barbary and Vesta.

But Mairie would influence her again. Adda didn't have to prove her expertise to anyone, and she didn't have to do everything herself when she had human allies. "Rio," she said in a voice that her powerlessness rendered stiff and painful, even though, for once, her weakness was by her own choice. "Please get Iridian out of there."

Rio drew a knife so huge that Adda would've called it a short sword, if Rio had ever expressed any interest in fantasy stories. The anger on her face made Adda step away from her. "Yeah, I can do that."

Rio stood to her full height and strode through the doorway, letting her armored boots make all the noise they usually did when she walked. "What the hell?" the male voice said.

"Leave her the fuck alone," Rio growled.

"Oh shit, she's ZV Group," said a second voice. He must've recognized Rio's armor. Both men ran past Adda on the way to the port module.

Adda had trusted Rio, and Rio had come through without asking Adda for anything. That was more than Mairie was capable of doing. A few months ago, Adda would never have asked a human to do something this important when an intelligence was available to do it instead. She'd been overestimating her ability to resist what the intelligences "wanted" from her in return. That'd almost cost her everything. Letting Rio handle Iridian's attackers hadn't been as certain a victory as enlisting Mairie's help would've been, but it'd only cost Adda her prospective control of the situation. Really, that was a small price.

Once the men's footsteps faded, Adda hurried into the room. Iridian sat propped against a wall beside a cracked and empty pseudo-organic tank. Her helmet lay a meter away with the faceplate shattered. The rest of her suit looked dented but intact. Her face was bloody and her new shield lay discarded in a corner of the room, but she still grinned tiredly when she rocked her head back to look at Adda. "Hey, babe."

"Oh gods," Adda whispered. "Are you . . . ?" Of course she wasn't all right.

"Noor got me good in the face." Iridian gestured toward a swollen bruise on her cheek. "Strong, for a nerd, or that helmet's even worse than I thought."

"I blame the helmet." Rio still looked furious. She took a few steps toward the door like she was going to follow the men out, but she stopped in the doorway. "Noor swung at me, too, and mine held up fine."

On the floor, Iridian pushed herself into a more upright position against the wall and grimaced. "He said something about—" A gasp of pain interrupted her, and she shut her eyes while she finished, "Having to tell the AIs we're leaving for Ceres."

Rio swore. Without the certificate needed for Kanti to fix Adda's implant's vulnerability, she was still as vulnerable to the intelligences as she had been on Vesta. Now Casey might be waiting for them outside Jupiter's magnetic field, knowing exactly where to find them when they left Yǎo.

"Next thing I knew, I was chatting with those fans who saw all that trial coverage on the news." Iridian touched her jaw and head gingerly, though what she'd feel through her armored gloves Adda couldn't guess. When she reached out, Adda caught her arm gently with both of hers. "Help me out of here?" Iridian asked. "I've seen enough of them for today." Rio and Adda pulled Iridian to her feet. "I didn't want . . . I'm sorry, babe."

"Oh gods, I don't care." Adda retrieved Iridian's new shield. It was heavier than the original, but it collapsed into its carrying configuration the same way the old one had. After she affixed it to the belt on Iridian's suit, Rio slid an arm behind Iridian's back, holding Iridian upright against her side. "I don't even care what you're apologizing for."

"Get the helmet, too," Iridian said.

"It's garbage," said Rio.

"We can replace the faceplate," said Iridian. "Cheaper that way."

Adda picked up the helmet while Rio eased Iridian through the doorway and into the hall. Iridian grabbed the doorframe and stopped them before they'd made much progress toward the port module. "We still have to find him. He knows we're going after the certificate," Iridian said. "Maybe the AIs do too, now."

"And Biometallic, and the ITA," said Adda. If Casey wanted to stop her from fixing the security flaw in her implant's software, then getting Biometallic to remove the backdoor Noor had put in their system and increase their station's security would be an effective way to do that. Telling the ITA they were returning to Ceres would meet the same objective, because they had to be physically near the library they wanted to access.

"Or maybe he didn't tell them everything," Rio said. "He hates to explain how his tricks work."

Iridian's nod was more of an uncomfortable-looking roll of her head. "If they don't know the whole story yet—"

"Then it's worth stopping him to maintain what elements of surprise we can," Adda said.

She turned away from the port module. "Rio, can you carry Iridian all the way to the water treatment plant? I'm pretty sure he's in the workspace generator there." They were passing more locked doors, projecting laboratory numbers that'd been irrelevant for years.

"This little lady?" Rio lifted Iridian several centimeters off the floor, still pressed against her side. "Yeah, I'll manage."

"No squeezing!" Iridian wheezed.

"Sorry."

Adda consulted the map on her comp. "If we follow this module far enough, it intersects with the . . . Well, it's called a physics lab on here, but it's where people set up the bars Pel likes."

"Probably where my fans came from." Iridian grunted as she stumbled, and Rio caught her. "I took a few hits to the head. How would I know if my implants were fucking up my brain right now?"

Knowing Iridian, she'd been trying to ignore that fear since her first head injury of the day. Her speech sounded fine and her face looked normal, with no spasming, stiffness, or sagging. "Does anything feel weak, tingly, paralyzed, or numb?" Adda asked her.

"I wish I was numb right now," Iridian said. "But no, none of that's happening."

"Hallucinations?"

Iridian and Rio took a couple of steps before Iridian replied, "Not that I can tell."

"I think everything's intact, then. Tell me if anything starts to feel strange."

"All right. There's an elevator in between, yeah?"

"It's a short walk," Rio said encouragingly to Iridian.

Iridian groaned and increased her pace, pushing Adda to her regular walking speed. When they reached the elevator, Rio held Iridian upright while Adda called the elevator car. As the car settled on the first floor and the doors opened, a small shoe disappeared through the open hatch in the elevator ceiling. Its floor was littered with food wrappers and a disheveled toy rabbit. It smelled like rotten food. At least whoever lived here had been using the public bathrooms near the end of the mod, hideous though those were.

Iridian was grimacing like she'd seen the shoe also, or like something in her head hurt more than it had a few minutes ago. "Hey," she called. "Come out of there. We're going up and we don't want to squish you."

There was some shuffling on the elevator's roof and then the sound of small feet on metal, rising. Iridian swore. "I mean it, we're going up! Right now." Rio guided her into the elevator. "I'm pressing the up button! You'd better be the fuck out of the way!"

"Do it," a child's voice called from somewhere above them. "You can't get us."

Iridian hesitated for a second, but she did pass her finger through the projected controls. The elevator doors stayed open, but the car moved upward. "I hate this place," Iridian muttered. "Nothing works and nobody cares."

"The elevator works," Rio pointed out.

"And we're the only ones who care."

An even smaller voice shouted something from somewhere

around Adda's knees, outside the moving elevator. Adda's translator didn't catch it, but it sounded rude. The doors on the upper level were shut, forcing Adda to grasp a biosensor. Theoretically, the Marsat ID Noor had made for her would open it.

Nothing happened. "Damn it," Adda said. Children's laughter echoed up from below. "Rio, try yours. Maybe mine isn't the right category for this area."

Rio's smallest finger hung off the end of the sensor bar as she grasped it, but the elevator doors slid open. Chuckling, Rio hauled Iridian through. "I wonder what rank that makes Marsat me? President? No, Noor would make Wiley president."

"Iri, switch to your Marsat ID." Adda followed them into another hallway lit with dim white thermoplastic lights embedded in the walls. As she watched, the lights shut off and sunsim swelled from where the walls and ceiling met.

"Did they just get out?" the smaller voice asked in obvious surprise. The older child shushed the younger one as the second-floor doors closed.

"Remember they're down there," Iridian said grimly.

There were fewer influenced people in the pipe-lined hallways than Adda remembered from their first visit to the water treatment plant. All of them smiled, probably in response to the Marsat IDs broadcasting from Adda's, Rio's, and Iridian's comps. The UV lights keeping the plants in the tops of the tanks healthy made the Odin Razum's teeth glow slightly purple. Several Odin Razum bowed as the three of them stopped in the hallway.

"What?" asked Iridian.

"Mairie isn't using Noor as its supervisor," Adda said quietly, as if saying so too loudly would remind Mairie of that. "He must have refused to accept that, after the first time it tried to influence him. Or maybe Casey told him not to. Either way, Mairie might try that signal on me again. I'm expecting it, but still . . ."

"Finally, a fucking break," said Rio. She raised her voice to address the Odin Razum. "Get out of the gods-damned way so your future *supervisor* can get to the generator!" Rio let go of Iridian, who staggered but stayed standing, so Rio could use both arms to direct attention to Adda. This time, she was careful not to actually touch Adda. The Odin Razum scattered toward the walls, leaving a wide path into the plant.

Adda blinked. "Thanks."

"Easiest thing I've done today." Rio wrapped an arm around Iridian again, and the three of them entered the treatment plant.

Iridian somehow seemed to recognize every twisting passageway from the last time they'd been here. Adda would've needed a map. They walked slower now, but Iridian seemed confident she knew where they were going. "Tell us if Mairie starts screwing with you," Iridian said to Adda. "Please."

"I will."

Noor was in the generator, plugged in via the jack in his temple, with his lips pressed together and his eyes squeezed shut. Bandages were wrapped haphazardly around both hands, dingy white where blood hadn't soaked through. A couple of centimeters separated the generator's heavy door from where it should've latched closed. Iridian had broken the door when she'd pulled Adda out of the generator the first time they'd come here.

"There's the little bastard," Rio said, almost fondly, but with an edge of real anger underneath. "Now, how are we going to get him out?"

Rio's performance in the hallway outside had given Adda an idea. "Mairie, I'm here, but the person in the generator is in my way. Disconnect with him so I can use it." *I won't,* she added sub-vocally to Iridian.

In the workspace generator, Noor's anxious expression crumbled into despair. He clawed the cable out of the jack in his skull and slammed the generator's door open. The ragged edge caught a bandage and pulled it off his hand. Blood welled beneath. His frantic eyes focused on Adda. "What did you do?" he howled.

"You're influenced," Adda said quickly. "You need to—"

"I have to talk to her! Fix it!" Noor grabbed Adda's throat with both hands. Adda clawed at him, but her nails were blunt, and oh gods, she couldn't breathe. She was going to die like this. "Fix it now!" Panic switched Adda's brain off and she flailed against Noor's arms. He squeezed harder. Her heartbeat thudded in the veins of her neck. She still couldn't breathe.

An armored hand grasped Noor's head and slammed it into the side of the workspace generator. His temple caught the edge of the broken door and the cracks widened. His hands loosened around Adda's neck but still clutched at her. Iridian slammed his head into the generator again, this time with a metallic clack and a thick crunch. Noor's hands fell away from Adda and he collapsed at her feet, convulsing. Blood sheeted over the side of his face and welled around the jack in his temple. The jack dug deep into his skin on one side, too crushed for a cable to fit into it. His limbs thumped against the generator.

"Shit." Iridian fell onto her knees in a clatter of armor, and Rio dragged Noor to the hallway, where there were fewer things for his arms and legs to slam into. Adda was bent over with her lungs sucking in oxygen to make up for what they'd missed while Noor was choking her. His convulsions spread blood over the hall floor.

The convulsions stopped. His eyes were still half-open. One hand spasmed like it still longed to crush Adda's throat. "Shit," Iridian said again, more quietly. Her bloodied hands hung at her sides, and she stared at Noor's unmoving form and grimaced with horror or pain.

Rio stared at him. "Is he dead?"

Adda's mind conjured images of Noor sitting up and reaching for her, bloody and enraged, to close his hands around her throat again. "I don't know."

"I just wanted to knock him out for a minute." Iridian's voice quavered with shock. "I didn't mean to hit the jack. Oh, shit."

CHAPTER 24

Days until launch: 21

"Adda's still working out how to get the certificate." Iridian had to concentrate to put together the words she wanted while she and Rio brought Pel up to speed in the clinic's waiting room. The docs were still working on Wiley and Gavran, and Iridian was too tired to make herself sound confident about this plan. "It's in Biometallic 1. Again. She's sure now. She's looking for ways to do it remotely. From the *Mayhem*. By herself, but I'll help her. And after Kanti fixes the vulnerability . . . Ah, hell." Iridian shut her eyes.

According to Adda, the records of Noor's communications with Casey were too securely encrypted to read. The worst-case scenario was that Noor had told Casey about Adda's plan to secure her implant against its influence. That hardly mattered anymore, though. Noor had been the only one who knew how to use the backdoor into Biometallic's library, and he was dead because Iridian had been careless with the jack attached to his fucking brain.

Despite that, Adda still wanted to confront the AIs once they couldn't influence her so readily. That was not a conversation Iridian wanted to have right now. Gods, it would've been nice to get the fuck out of Casey's reach on Björn's expedition. She and Adda had no way to make Björn agree to let them join by the launch date, but Iridian was counting down the days anyway.

"You two shouldn't have to do all that alone." Pel's bloodstained shirt was the only evidence of his injury, now that the clinic staff had closed the wound. "I'll go to Ceres with you."

"Me too," said Rio. Absorbed in whatever she was reading on her comp, Adda didn't even look up.

Although the medical care cost less than the clinic could've charged for it, it wasn't free like it would've been in a hab where people paid taxes. Staying in securable rooms cost them too. Every bit of cash Adda had transferred, saved, or scavenged was now reserved for keeping the five of them—damn it, they were down to five—hydrated, fed, and behind a locked door on Yăo Station while their injuries healed.

A few of the pieces of firmware they'd stolen the first time around were still in the *Mayhem*'s pseudo-organics. Adda hadn't wanted to sell them because they posed too much potential for abuse, but they owed Gavran for the damage Noor had done to the *Mayhem*, in addition to the trip to Ceres, if he'd carry them. To get that kind of money, she'd have to sell the dangerous pieces of their haul.

Wiley walked slowly into the clinic's waiting room, watching the floor, looking at no one. Iridian heaved herself out of her chair to meet him. "Wiley, did they . . ." Gods, this hurt to ask. "Did they tell you about Noor?"

Wiley pressed his hand over his mouth, hard, and nodded. "They said you brought him in in bad shape. Thank you for bringing him here."

The docs hadn't been able to do anything for Noor. Iridian, Rio, and Adda had brought him to the clinic as fast as they'd been able to. Dragging him out of the water treatment plant was grim enough to merit inclusion in Iridian's rotation of blood-drenched nightmares. The way he'd seized up after that second hit . . . Gods, it was too easy to see Adda twisted on the floor like that. Noor's implant had been almost identical to hers. It was how Casey had influenced him so fast.

Iridian's mind replayed the sense memory of his bones compressing under her glove. She hadn't even felt the metal on metal impact when she'd slammed the jack into the edge of the generator. "Don't thank me. I'm the one who killed him."

"The AIs killed him. Thank you," Wiley said again, slowly, "for trying to help a friend." Iridian stepped forward to hug him and his arms closed around her, bare fingers braced behind the joints in her armor plating. Her suit's weak haptic feedback transmitted his shudder through her gloves. It still seemed like it would've been healthier if he'd just fucking cry, but she wouldn't tell somebody else how to grieve.

Noor's death had been a stupid mistake. Brains were delicate and Noor had never worn armor in the whole time she'd known him. Even a concussion could've fucked up his neural implant net, and she'd damaged the damned jack. Hell, she'd spent more time worrying about the little implant in her own brain than the one that covered most of his.

Even so, she couldn't quite make herself regret that second hit. She'd taken nineteen lives during the course of her own, but there'd always been a reason for it. This one was no different. Noor had almost strangled Adda. Iridian would take out anybody who laid an unwanted hand on her wife.

After they helped Gavran back to the *Mayhem* to rest, they carried Noor to the temple's memorial room. Everyone else said their good-byes. Iridian could only say, "You helped us when you could have gone it alone, so, thanks."

A short, aching walk later, they got to what passed for the

shopping mod. Wiley winced slightly at a wrong step, and Rio offered her arm for balance. "You were still a threat with a knife in your leg back there," she said. "Badass."

Wiley smiled, a small but good sign as far as Iridian was concerned. "It hurt less then than it does now."

"I've seen people go into shock with less damage," said Rio. "Not you. I'm impressed."

"Thanks." Wiley walked a bit taller after that.

They found an empty table in a group of several that were surrounded by sellers of dubiously edible algae products. Settling there took a moment as they worked around their injuries until they could hunch over meager dinners and bad beer. Iridian forced herself to look forward, not back. If Casey hadn't influenced Noor, he'd still be alive. That was what they had to protect Adda from, by getting her implant fixed. "We're still on target to get back to Biometallic 1 and get your firmware's certificate, yeah?" Iridian asked Adda.

"I'm still working on that plan," Adda said. "Noor never told me how to activate that backdoor into Biometallic's system. The clinic gave me his comp, but it's still encrypted. Systems security has almost nothing in common with intelligence development."

They all chewed in silence for a minute as that thought sank in. Iridian managed not to curse herself out aloud. "Okay. So, we've got transport to the asteroid belt, armor that probably won't get us murdered, and, what, a few more nights' worth of Yăo money?" she asked.

"Two more nights, after we paid the clinic," Adda said quietly. "Unless you want to talk some more out of the Odin Razum."

"I'd rather use that to pay for Gavran's fuel to fly us off this hunk of junk," said Iridian.

Rio's shoulders and head drooped in sadness or exhaustion. Either way, Iridian empathized. "We can't stay here, and out there the AIs are waiting for us somewhere sunward."

Iridian pushed her plate toward Adda. She'd lost her appetite, but the food shouldn't go to waste. "Maybe Casey knows everything Noor knew." Wiley hung his head too. He and Noor had been friends in the ITA's prison. Now Noor and Tash were both gone. Wiley had lost a lot to Casey.

Casey was obsessed with influencing Adda, and Iridian couldn't sit still and let it. "If Casey went after Noor, it could go after any of us. And if it can't influence us, it'd sure as hell be happy to have us all crawling with ITA nannites again, so it can put us where it wants, when it wants." And if Adda got arrested again, Casey could free her just as easily as it did the first time. "Whatever passes for 'happy' in its pseudo-organic tanks, it'd be that." Adda was ignoring both her food and Iridian's and reading something on her comp. Iridian took her free hand. "Babe, we can't go with Björn and we can't just fly into Biometallic 1, not without somebody to get us in. What else can we do?"

"Wait, you're not sailing away from it all on Dr. Björn's ship?" asked Pel.

"I can't see a way for us to convince ver to let us go, and I don't want to force ver to take us," Adda said. "It's not right and it might just get us arrested again. When people threaten ver, ve resists."

"Thank gods," said Pel. "The Thrinacia solar system is just too far away. You'd never pay me back from out there." Nothing Pel did suggested that he cared about the money. He'd miss his big sister and the safety net she offered when he got in trouble. "But I mean, what will you do after that?"

"Casey's not going to give up, but I'm *sure* it can do a better job of communicating with us than it's been doing so far. At some point . . ." Adda looked to Iridian.

Iridian was too tired to argue about this. "Go on, tell him."

"If Casey can't influence me so quickly, I want to try just talking

to it again," Adda said. "It wants help with something and I want
to understand what that is."

Rio nodded. "Yeah, you should."

Iridian and Pel said, "What?" at approximately the same time
and volume. Wiley's gaze returned from the middle distance to
refocus on the people at the table.

"She should!" Rio repeated. "The *Casey* worked with us for
a long time on Barbary without any of this manipulation crap.
Something's up. Talk it out. That's how you solve—"

"Human problems," said Iridian. "It's not human."

"Seriously," said Pel. "The awakened AIs who got you two
arrested and almost killed are a lot scarier than humans."

"The intelligences will not stop trying to get what they want,
and we don't even understand what that is," Adda said. "*After* my
implant's vulnerability is closed, I can talk to them and find out
what it would take to get them to stop."

Pel groaned. "Everything has to be so fucking complicated."

"That's life," said Adda. "Please cope." She looked up from her
comp. "Anyway, I've been thinking—"

"Always a good sign," said Pel.

"—about how we can get the certificate Biometallic used to
sign my implant firmware. They still haven't fixed the firmware
vulnerability, or acknowledged anything I've sent them about it.
But from what I've read, they've got to have a copy of it in the
Ceres orbital station."

"Which'll be locked down like a gods-damned fortress after
the last op," Iridian said.

"Why not just ask the station AI to send it to you?" Wiley asked.

"Ficience isn't unsupervised like Mairie," said Adda. "A competent supervisor will notice if an intelligence is sending out anything strange and lock it down, and everything I saw the last time
we were there suggests that the supervisors are pretty good. After

we left, they'd have found records of my requests to the intelligence and told it not to listen to anything that person says again."

"What about dropping a corruption culture on the lab, so the local nannite culture would open the up hull for us?" asked Rio.

"Okay, that sounds awesome," said Pel.

"Too expensive, unfortunately," said Adda.

"We could use regular demolition material," Wiley suggested.

"That would work if we could afford it, but we can't." Adda sighed. "The trick is getting to Ficience's supervisor before somebody sounds an alarm, or getting around Ficience's public presentation. The rational response to our last visit would be that as soon as anything looks like a potential break-in, the supervisors will now use emergency security procedures to keep strangers like us from accessing the intelligence."

"Nobody's talking about our break-in, by the way," said Pel. "And Captain Sloane was 'escorted off the station' by the ITA, but they didn't press charges. Dumb move."

"Our break-in wasn't that long ago," said Wiley. "Isn't the ITA or whatever agency they have on Ceres still investigating?"

Adda blinked. "Yes. The ITA might still be visiting occasionally."

"We'll be watching out for them," Iridian said. "We always are. And what are the chances that they'll be there at the same time we are?"

"We weren't expecting Captain Sloane to target the same station we did at the same time either," said Adda. "But the point is, costume-quality ITA uniforms are much less expensive than explosives."

"You want to walk in there dressed up as the gods-damned ITA?" Pel stared with a slowly widening grin. "Oh my gods, Sissy. I didn't think you had it in you." Adda smiled at him, which meant he'd interpreted her intention correctly.

Iridian looked her over, and she seemed to be sober and present. For some reason, Adda really thought this was a viable plan. It sounded like a one-way ticket back to Venus, but they didn't have money for equipment to infiltrate the station faster. With the ITA and the intelligences looking for them, there was no time for the recon it'd take to find a safer way in.

Wiley smiled wistfully. "Tash could've given you all disguise lessons. The things she said she did with makeup and pins . . ."

If this was really the best plan Adda had, then Iridian would back her play. "Nobody's expecting this, that's for gods-damned sure. But the ship's going to be a problem. The *Mayhem* doesn't look anything like an ITA cruiser."

"True," said Adda. "Do you think Gavran will be able to fly us there, after . . . ?"

"He's a Kuiper colonist," Iridian said. "If he can sit up, he can fly. Although, I wonder if he *wants* to. We'll ask."

"All right," said Adda, "What if we got a shuttle from the Ceres Station orbital port?"

"Those are free," said Rio. "I'd believe an ITA squad would take one of those."

"Do they run in squads?" Iridian asked.

"I'll find out on the way," Adda said. "We'll need to find somewhere to print the costumes too. And find a halfway decent textile pattern, not one that's projected over your regular clothes."

"Oh my gods, this is awesome," said Pel. "There's a textile printer in the entertainment mod. They have some real dancers and they like to change their outfits a lot. I'll ask them if they ever dress up as ITA agents."

"I guess uniforms with tear-off pants are better than nothing," Rio said doubtfully.

Adda was reading something on her comp, so Iridian took over the briefing, such as it was. "We gave Biometallic a chance to do this right. Now let's get it done ourselves."

"So we get this certificate thing to go with the firmware we got last time," said Wiley. "How does it get into Adda's head?"

"We've got options," said Iridian. "If we have to update the firmware ourselves, we need an implant ward in a hospital. I don't want to do it ourselves, because it's in Adda's head and she's the one with experience modifying implant software." The sense memory of slamming Noor's jack into the generator resurfaced. Iridian reached for Adda's hand again and forced herself not to squeeze too hard. "So we'll take it to a modder we know on Ceres."

Pel whined, "We have really bad luck on Ceres."

"We have mixed luck," said Iridian. "I got Adda off the 'ject with practically no trouble."

"Casey helped." Adda glanced around the table. "We need to leave."

Iridian and Pel froze, mid-bite in Pel's case. When Adda used that tone, something serious was happening. Wiley and Rio just looked confused. "What's the rush?" Rio asked.

"Mairie's sent something to my Marsat ID. It's saying an engine is failing. I don't know what it expects me to do, but I'm sure whatever it wants starts with me becoming its supervisor." Adda stood and paid their bills with the rusty paypad embedded in the table.

Iridian shuddered. Big-budget horror stories and dramas about hab damage made fortunes every year because more people lived off Earth every year, and every one of them knew how close they were to blood-boiling asphyxiation in the cold and the black. "Is this a trick, or is it serious?"

"I can't tell," Adda said. "I assume the engine's really shutting down." She paused. "And Casey would know I'd make that assumption. Mairie wouldn't, but Casey would."

"Damn Casey to all hells." Iridian stood and collected the remains of her food and Adda's. "I know two things about engines big enough to push a whole hab, and that's their size and purpose.

Anybody else know more?" Iridian looked around the table. Everyone shook their heads. "So. Not our problem."

"Does Shingetsu know?" As Pel asked the question, he hit the edge of the box his food had been served in and launched noodles across the table. Despite the grunge ground into the tabletop, he piled the food back into the box. They couldn't afford to waste it. "She knows everybody on the station. Maybe she can tell them about emergencies."

"Let's go make sure she does, and then get off the station," said Iridian.

"Pel, get us packed up and out of that bug nest we've been sleeping in," said Adda. "Iridian, can you talk to Shingetsu? I want to see what Gavran needs to get us moving." Ceres was getting farther away from Jupiter and it'd take a while to get back to Biometallic 1, but they didn't have to be fully stocked to get off a station that was about to fall into Jupiter.

"Sure." Iridian felt as fuzzy as she had after Noor bounced her face off a wall. "Rio, go with her. Please. Wiley, you're with me." He just nodded, his expression unreadable.

"Don't I get an escort?" Pel asked.

"You're paying someone the rest of what we owe them and telling them we're out of their tiny, dirty, makeshift rooms," said Adda. "Without describing the rooms, please. And if you can think of a way to get in trouble doing that, don't."

"Yeah, yeah," said Pel. He, Adda, and Rio would be going the same way through the long hall of locked doors to the port. Iridian set off through the port mod with Wiley at her side.

After the second person Iridian shoved out of her way with more force than was required, Wiley asked, "You all right, Nassir?"

"Am I all right? What about you?" Wiley was the one who'd lost two friends since he joined Iridian on this venture.

"I'm not the one pushing civvies around."

She should've learned to be more careful with her suit strength after what she'd done to Noor. Iridian ducked her head, embarrassed and ashamed. "This place will get worse fast," she said. "Depending on how violent the failure is, the station could come apart. The other engine won't be able to keep up even this much grav, and if the station AI pushes it, it'll go out too. Then, who knows how long it'll take the orbit to deteriorate, but it'll happen."

"Maybe the ITA will get somebody out here to fix it." Wiley didn't sound like he believed that.

"They'd sure as hell better," said Iridian. The kids living in the elevators wouldn't believe her if she told them what was happening. Even if they did, how the hell would they get away in time? If they had adults looking after them, those people were doing a shitty job.

Swearing, Iridian fought her way to the nearest elevator to the second level, which had been, of course, stripped for parts. She made her way back to where she'd seen the kids before and yelled into the empty elevator car, "If you kids feel the grav going, get somebody to take you off the station, yeah? An engine's about to go. It'll get real dangerous real quick. You want to come down and leave with my crew?"

"Go away, fuckface," the older child's voice shouted. The younger one started to say something and the older one shushed loudly.

"Damn it." Iridian stalked past the clinic and through the entertainment and residential mods, until she finally found the way to the temple. Somebody in black-and-white clothes stood beside the temple entrance, watching the elevator and looking sincere. Iridian pushed past. Wiley said, "Sorry, prayer emergency" as he followed her in.

Iridian checked the room Shingetsu had put them in to talk

over the drone recovery op, and then headed for the sanctuary. Wiley caught her arm and slowed her down, since she wouldn't let him stop her entirely. "If she's preaching or something, don't interrupt her."

"The gods-damned station is about to break up," said Iridian. "That'll be a hell of an interruption." A woman wearing clothes that covered her from the top of her head to the tops of her feet shook her head firmly in Iridian's direction.

"She won't listen if you interrupt her," Wiley insisted. "I grew up with people like these. She'll act like you're sick in the head, which, you know, look around." Sure enough, somebody was sitting on the floor a few meters down the hall, muttering to themselves while chewing dirty fingernails and smelling like three homeless people put together. "Just send her a message. Let's go see if Pel's back at the *Mayhem* yet."

Nothing was going the way Iridian wanted. She felt helpless, hopeless, and still responsible for it all. And maybe it was Noor's fault too, but Noor was dead and Iridian had killed him. Rather than spend a second longer thinking that through, she turned and headed for the port mod, tapping out a message to Shingetsu on her comp. The only reason she didn't run was that she didn't want to draw any more attention to her crew's only way off the station.

Between the promise of payment and Yǎo Station's failing engine, Gavran agreed to flying them back to the belt. Before the Shield-runners left the dock for the last time, Adda sent a second message to Shingetsu, and Iridian talked to the Apostolovs and the clinic personnel. When they entered Patchwork range, Gavran would notify the ITA. They'd even told the kid who'd exchanged their Yǎo money for a chip that'd supposedly connect to an account with the equivalent in NEU money.

The ITA had to know that children lived on the station. Gavran would remind them too. A disaster this big would force the ITA to send rescue ships to Yăo. It was about damned time.

Gavran pulled away from the station fast, grumbling in cant about terrible fates that should befall people who sabotaged engines, if Iridian was interpreting it correctly. The translator Adda had put in their comms was not equipped to handle the vicious application of Kuiper cant. When the *Mayhem* was far enough away from Yăo for the failing engine to rotate into its windows, a gray plume of something pressurized spewing out of it proved how bad the situation was. One way or another, Casey had made sure Adda and Iridian would never go back to this hab. Jupiter looked massive behind the station, a pale monster poised to swallow it whole.

Adda had started reading in one of the residential cabin bunks before Gavran finished disengaging from the dock, her brow knit with worry. She'd hate being rushed off the station with so many of her plans incomplete. The Odin Razum were still under Mairie's control, Adda's implant was still vulnerable, and Casey was still trying to make her do something for it. Their break from Yăo Station was about as rough as it could get. Iridian and Adda were out of places to hide from Casey, but fear of discovery was easier to bear outside Yăo Station's bad enviro and its conniving AI.

Once grav stabilized for the accel stage of the trip to Ceres, Iridian went to work on the residential cabin door. Although Gavran had cleaned Noor's blood off it, he hadn't finished replacing the pieces Noor had removed, bare-handed and in near silence according to Gavran and Pel, after he'd kicked through the interlocking slats on the interior side. It'd been a careful kick too. A boot-size hole all the way through might've distracted Adda from whatever she'd been reading while Noor broke out. By the time he was done with the door, he hadn't needed to punch through the lock digitally. He'd just taken out some key components, and torn up his hands in the process.

Everything else about the day might've been the worst kind of shit, but Adda had found a way onto Biometallic 1 and she was working on an idea for how to take the certificate that Kanti needed to protect her implant from Casey. No matter what else was wrong, Adda wasn't letting any of it stop her. Not even Iridian killing the crew member who would've made this op possible.

"The intelligences have been busy." Adda showed Iridian a report on her comp.

"What am I looking at?" Iridian asked.

"I've been tracking where their ships are," Adda said. "Well, the *Apparition* and the *Casey Mire Mire*, anyway. I'm not sure what happened to the *Coin*. It's not as fast as the other two. They might've—"

Iridian interrupted Adda by laughing in delight. "Oh gods, you know where they are? Physically?" When Adda nodded, Iridian said, "Have you told Gavran? Keeping the *Mayhem* away from them is part of what we're paying him for." If Adda's monitoring routine highlighted where each ship was in the *Mayhem*'s nav systems, then the *Apparition* wouldn't sneak up on them again. Maybe Gavran could keep them out of the *Casey*'s comms range too.

Adda blinked. "No. I hadn't thought of that."

"I'll tell him after I'm finished with the door. Where have they been?"

"They each have these long patterns that take them between a point on the Ceres-Jupiter reliable route—" Adda paused at a sharp slap of something bouncing off the hull. That'd happen a lot more often outside the reliable routes. "And Vesta."

"Vesta? You'd think they'd stay the hell away from there, after the ITA went looking for them. What are they doing there?"

Adda shrugged. "I don't know. There are a number of things that might draw them there: Captain Sloane's presence, Dr. Björn's expedition, AegiSKADA, the last safe place they docked . . . Maybe they're planning to build their new home on an asteroid. Anyway, I don't like that they're spending so much time in the asteroid belt. They're too close to Biometallic 1."

"Hmm." Iridian had tried to act optimistic, but she didn't have much hope for a second successful hit on Biometallic 1. Adda's new plan was built on assumptions, and her implant would still be vulnerable during the op. If Casey intercepted them on their way to Ceres, they'd be screwed. And they were flying right back into the ITA's hullhooks. None of it looked good for her crew, but it was the best chance Adda had.

The ship's light vibration as it powered out of Jupiter's grav well eased slightly when it entered the Jupiter-Uranus reliable route. Since it was in the opposite direction of everything Adda was interested in, Casey was unlikely to be watching that route. They'd follow it until Gavran found a piece of the cold and the black he didn't mind cutting through to reach a reliable route to Ceres. The nearly subsonic engine rumble was accompanied by the whine of extending thermal fins and the hushed whoosh of the atmo system kicking up a level. That was lazy power management on Gavran's part, but it was a familiar sound. It gave Iridian something to think about other than gut-twisting anguish over the people they left behind.

Adda wouldn't understand any of that, and she'd feel sorry for Iridian if she did. "Heard anything from the ITA about Yǎo, babe?" Iridian asked.

"Gavran didn't send them a message in a way that would allow them to reply to either of us personally." Adda climbed out of the bunk to kiss Iridian, jolting her mind out of Yăo Station's dark hall-ways. *Hey,* Adda subvocalized. *We're alone in here.* Wiley, Rio, and Pel were strapped into the passenger couches in the main cabin.

Iridian tapped the panel by the door a couple of times, watch-ing the lock slide shut and open while she put away her tools. There wasn't much she could do about the hole Noor had kicked in their side of it. Gavran would have to fix that in port. "The door locks." In terms of sound dampening, it hardly mattered whether the typical cabin door was closed or not, on a craft this small. Iridian didn't care, and as long as she didn't mention it, Adda wouldn't care either. Iridian desperately needed to do something other than think right now.

Adda's smile went softer and sadder, somehow. *Lock it.*

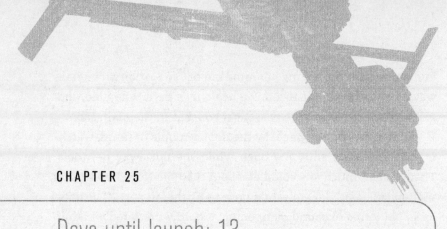

CHAPTER 25

Days until launch: 13

The only good thing about Adda's second attack on Biometallic was that Sunan's Landing had patterns and material for everything the crew needed and Yǎo Station lacked. They'd have cloth ITA uniforms, since repainting armor would've been too expensive. Before the *Mayhem* got anywhere near Ceres stationspace, they'd apply and conceal small projectors to disguise their faces.

Even with the disguises, Adda's plan had huge drawbacks: They had to enter the Ceres orbital station, second only to the port on Ceres's surface in terms of ITA presence, while broadcasting unprofessionally forged ITA IDs. Then they'd have to bluff their way into a hab that was still on alert from the crew's last assault.

Adda hoped that Biometallic's certificate library was better defended than the firmware library. For security purposes, the certificate was at least as important as the source material.

At Sunan's Landing, which had decorated for every holiday in the month with multicolored symbols projected all over the interior, Adda, Pel, Iridian, Rio, and Wiley had pooled all the money they had access to. They just barely paid Gavran enough to let him refuel and justify him flying them around. Soon, he'd have to take a job that made him a profit. For now, he split what they'd paid him with another pilot who he claimed "hadn't been arrested in decades" to do a passenger transfer near the Ceres-Sunan's Landing reliable route. If the *Mayhem* entered Ceres stationspace, it would ping every ITA agent on the 'ject.

Rather than squads, Adda's research indicated that the most common configuration for a small group of ITA agents was two sets of partners. She and Iridian would be one, and Rio and Wiley would be the second. Pel was disappointed to be stuck in the *Mayhem*, but he'd be safer that way, and they didn't have to pay the second pilot to carry him.

The passenger transfer went off as well as attaching two passthroughs in the middle of nowhere could go, which only made it a little nerve-wracking. They waited until they were within an hour of the Ceres orbital station to change into their newly printed ITA uniforms. Adda had been too busy mocking up ID broadcasts to remind everyone else to change and disguise themselves earlier. The new IDs should fool humans, but they wouldn't fool an intelligence.

Once she was inside Biometallic 1, she'd swap her ID with Rio's, since Ficience had never encountered Rio before. She'd made an appointment for "Rio" to go through some standard orientation material in a generator, which an ITA agent might do to familiarize themselves with Adda's first theft. The appointment would let her introduce her own routines during ID validation to search for openings in the orientation. With luck, Adda would use the first opening she found to breach the certificate library.

It was a *much* less efficient arrangement than a specially designed backdoor would've been. Adda's method would probably take hours. In their current circumstances, it was the only approach likely to get her into the target section of Biometallic's systems.

The crew was arriving on Ceres's orbital station at three thirty in the morning, Ceres local time. Gavran had asked the new pilot to set the sunsim cycle to make it about ten in the morning aboard their ship. The crew would feel awake and ready for the new day, and both Ficience's supervisor and Biometallic's security force should be at their least attentive.

Before they entered the orbital station, Iridian sent Gavran a message. "You sure you don't want Adda to look for your implant's certificate too?"

"No, thanks but no," he replied. "I have pilot implants. Multiple pieces, multiple locations, not like you devs and your nets. Even if mine had the same vulnerability as a neural implant net, I don't know your modder and I don't know their credentials. I don't let unlicensed strangers touch anything under my skin."

Signs advised travelers not to spend more than four hours at a time on Ceres's orbital station due to the lack of gravity. Its narrow hallways and terminals had low ceilings that made it hard for inexperienced travelers to get stuck in the center of them, unable to reach a surface to push off. Projected figures on the walls with their feet pointing toward the arbitrary floor communicated "up" and "down" conventions. Interspersed between the directional figures were wide windows that showed Ceres and the massive ships docked on the orbital station, too large to descend to the surface port.

As they entered the path between terminals and followed signs toward the shuttles, Adda straightened her back and kept half a meter's distance between herself and Iridian. For Adda, crossing the orbital station was one of the toughest parts of the job. ITA agents had expert training and years of experience navigating in microgravity. If Adda had to stop herself from tumbling off in the wrong direction by grabbing a wall handhold, everybody who saw would remember it, and by extension, her. The four of them kept their pace slow and she stayed a bit behind Iridian, watching her for cues on when to push on what to move forward naturally.

There were so many ways Adda's plan could go wrong, and she was right in the middle of them. But, amazingly, they made it to the shuttle terminals without her crashing into anything. Due to the early hour, there weren't many people to run into.

One blue-uniformed ITA agent hovered near the terminal that served privately owned orbital stations. The agent, a woman with dark hair and light skin, smiled at them. "Hey there! Just in from the colonies?"

"You got it." Iridian's consonant sounds were shorter, and something about her speech rhythm had changed. Whatever accent it was sounded more like the ITA agent's speech than Iridian's usual spacefarer English.

The tired smile on her face was convincing, even though the face itself was jarring. The projected disguise made her skin almost as pale as Adda's and her eyes more hazel than brown. It'd thinned her full lips and sharpened her proudly wide nose. The sooner they finished this, the sooner Iridian could have her own beautiful face back. "Pulled us in to look up one more thing over on Biometallic," Iridian continued. "It's always one more thing, yeah?"

"With them, I guess so." The ITA agent looked surprised, but not alarmed. "Next shuttle's not scheduled for another hour. Do you want a break, or do you want me to call in a one-off?"

"Oh gods, let's get this over with," Iridian said. While the ITA agent tapped at her comp, Iridian nodded toward the shuttle passthrough while making eye contact with Rio and Wiley. They both moved closer, leaving Adda drifting near the wall. She wasn't looping the cam footage here. Either Biometallic or the ITA had to have seen the looped footage during their first break-in, so this time that trick would've drawn more attention rather than less. She clenched her teeth and did her best to force her worry off her face.

"Okay, somebody will be up in about fifteen minutes." The woman smiled again. "Hey, I saw the memo about one of the robbers' ships being on the Ceres–Sunan's Landing reliable route yesterday. He'd better run like hell, yeah?"

"Yeah, that's right." Rio still sounded professional, but that was Gavran and Pel they were talking about. Adda's hands fluttered around where pants pockets should've been. This was a costume, not a real uniform, and it came with just about nothing to hold things in.

Iridian bluffed their way through the short shuttle ride while Adda took a sharpsheet and reviewed ways to retreat to the *Mayhem* if anything went wrong. By the time she had mapped out two more egress routes, the four of them were standing in a lab very much like the one where she'd accessed Ficience the first time. "Thanks for your help," Iridian was saying to two armed and armored people in Biometallic's colors. The moment they turned around, Iridian waved at Adda and pointed to the nearest generator. "That's the unlocked one. Go for it."

With a second sharpsheet sizzling on her tongue to calm her nerves, Adda climbed into the generator and sealed herself inside, shaking. Why did those guards have generator access? Without approval from someone familiar with the tech, they shouldn't have been allowed to unlock one. Biometallic's security was truly terrible. She just had to find her implant's certificate.

"Welcome to Biometallic Technologies!" The welcome message shivered up her spine like ice, confirming that she'd appeared at the appointment time she'd made with the station intelligence and that it recognized the ID associated with the appointment. If devs' privacy sensibilities hadn't made biometric identification in workspace generators unpopular, then the system would've noticed a conflict. As it was, Adda floated in a glowing blue nebula, her workspace forming to suit the low gravity Biometallic 1 maintained outside business hours.

An old story about someone trapped in the place they'd come to rob, stealing from the same people over and over to survive, ran through her mind until she refocused on watching for a bright supernova caving into a black hole. That would mean that Ficience or its supervisor had recognized that Adda's ID had very little to do with who she was and what she was doing in the system.

"Welcome to Biometallic Technologies!" the recorded message repeated, shivering up her spine again. "Please enter your identification now." Adda sent credentials, this time to activate the mode where she'd introduce her own routine. Her first innocuous-looking article, a summary of a sporting event which an inexperienced operator might read while waiting for ID verification, rippled through stars that rearranged themselves into letters in the spaces between wisps of gases. That display was more metaphorical than this ID resolution workspace was designed for, so she waited to see if Ficience or its supervisor would notice the unusual activity.

After each introduction of a piece of Adda's workaround, she paused to watch for a reaction. An ITA investigator hanging out in a generator reading would've been extremely odd. Pressing the whole routine into the workspace at once would've been an obvious attack. Gradual introduction was key.

Each added part of the routine reset the verification process, so Adda wasn't the only one left idle for minutes at a time. Ficience had reserved some of its resources for this appointment, and it was waiting through the appointment time while security processes handled all the input Adda sent. She was glad the zombie intelligence wasn't capable of feeling frustration. The security process repeatedly failed to hand her "visit" to the intelligence like it'd been told to expect.

After an hour and forty-seven minutes, a new recorded message played. "Thank you! Your identification has been validated." A bright star twinkled deeper in the nebula, cartoonishly close, indicating that the ID verification process was complete, and Adda's routine was assembling. The security process finally turned over responsibility for the "guest" to the station intelligence in a startling white comet that whisked past her, impossibly large and utterly unstoppable, before it disappeared into the colorful gas clouds.

"Please proceed to the introduction theater to learn how to navigate our system." The blue gases swirled and solidified into theater seats as the Biometallic station intelligence enforced mandated visualization features. She didn't like them, so she changed each seat to white-and-gray orbs of dandelion fluff, which disintegrated on the solar wind. A voice droned on about the various features of Biometallic's customer education and service workspace.

The voice ceased yammering and freed her into the system's customer-facing section, looping branches of the nebula that represented frequently asked questions for patients, troubleshooting guides for medical professionals, and marketing materials for salespeople. Adda zoomed around these, activating the routine she'd added to the system. She rebounded off the invisible barrier at the edges of the gas cloud, the partitions that kept her from exploring the rest of the system. It would've been convenient if there had been a simple break in that partition, but all she found was a smooth, invisible bubble of permission settings holding her to the approved information.

The theater seats reappeared as the orientation restarted. There'd been an option to tell it not to, but Adda had ignored it. She flew to the end of their rows and opened a door that took her to the employee lobby where she'd first spoken to Ficience. It was now the nebula's center. A self-assemblage process concluded, represented as a box that appeared in her hands. When she opened it, thousands of silver starlings poured out, crying and wheeling through the nebula at an improbable speed for small birds. Each bird represented part of the routine she'd brought in during the ID verification process to activate the most common illegally modified strains of pseudo-organics.

Her first successful activation was in the guest evaluation tank. One bird flared gold while the rest of the silver ones swirled around it. Then another turned gold, and another. She'd found the tank with the altered pseudo-organic fluid from their initial assault. This was the opening she'd painstakingly brought the routine in to look for. Now she had to find and retrieve the certificate. She grinned and followed her birds into the void.

One sharpsheet and nearly two more hours later, she unstrapped herself from the workspace generator. For a second she thought she was in a mobile generator in the *Mayhem*, but this was a Biometallic lab generator and Biometallic employees would be arriving soon. Gravity already felt as Earthlike here as it was in Ceres Station.

She pushed the generator lid open. Iridian kissed her and helped her up. "Got it?"

"Yes." Adda sounded as tired as she felt, but she was smiling so widely her face hurt. *I found some more things we can sell, too. And I sent the certificate to Kanti,* she said subvocally, *so we should leave before Ficience's supervisor notices that transmission. I want to change out of this uniform. It's making my skin crawl.*

Her comp now held the key to protecting her neural implant from Casey and the other awakened intelligences. Their modder on Ceres's surface had a copy too. She'd seen no evidence that Casey, the most capable infiltrator among the awakened intelligences, had used Noor's backdoor to make system changes of its own. If they were lucky, Biometallic had found and dismantled that vulnerability in its own system already. After their reluctance to fix the vulnerability in her implant, she wouldn't count on that.

"Thank gods." Iridian was even more relieved about that than Adda expected. "Let's drop that one in here before we go." Adda stepped out of the way as Rio and Iridian heaved an armored Biometallic guard's limp form into the generator and shut the lid. "He's fine, I think," Iridian said. "He just got too curious, and Wiley had to shut him in his suit and kink his air hose for a minute. I don't want to explain it to anybody, though, so let's move out."

The only way they could pay for Kanti to correct Adda's implant firmware was by selling more firmware sources. This time Adda had chosen Biometallic's healing braces ahead of time. She couldn't think of many ways to hurt someone with those. The crew shuttled back to the Ceres orbital station. Wiley and Rio would stay with Gavran's pilot friend on their borrowed ship to handle the transactions and keep the ship docked until Iridian and Adda returned from their visit to Kanti's mod shop in the main part of Ceres Station.

Iridian and Adda changed into street clothes. The ship's printer created a new wig for Iridian, and a combination of makeup and projector adjustments erased the ITA face Iridian had worn into Biometallic 1. While she put the final touches on those, Adda switched their comp's broadcasting IDs. The Marsat IDs Noor had made were still the most convincing ones that weren't their own.

By the time Iridian and Adda reached the surface station's port module, Wiley had sold some of the items from Biometallic's library that Adda had grabbed after finding the certificate that'd make her implant accept Kanti's corrections to the firmware. That meant Iridian hadn't lied to Gavran when she assured him that the Shieldrunners would pay the docking fee. Then they made their way through the port and its grav tunnel.

"This way," Iridian muttered. They were avoiding using their personal comms until they were inside a shielded building. The ITA had very clear records of the transmission signature from when Iridian was in custody. Maybe it was unique, or maybe it looked like every other homemade comms system, but Adda didn't want to give the ITA an opportunity to recognize it. Not now, when they were almost as safe as they could be in their home solar system.

They left the main thoroughfare with Iridian in the lead, since she'd memorized the route with the least cam coverage. "While we're here, do you want to get a tattoo?" Iridian asked. "Kanti said they'd touch up mine."

Adda would have to be unconscious while they updated the neural implant. The procedure wouldn't be invasive, but conscious brains constantly bombarded the implant net with input. She'd miss the experience of receiving the tattoo, which she'd been curious about. However, this was the best opportunity she expected to have for a while, and the artwork she'd commissioned had arrived on her comp. "I have the perfect thing."

Iridian started to grin, stopped when it moved the tiny projectors on her forehead and chin, and waited while Adda sent the design to her. When she got it, she hugged Adda so hard Adda's shoulder joints creaked. "*Yes*, this is perfect."

"Happy belated birthday," Adda said into Iridian's chest.

Iridian kissed the top of Adda's head. "I love you more than every one of these."

Adda was glad to let Iridian go in front and do the talking this time. Inside the mod shop, the mismatched colored lights were as bright as ever. Somebody was standing over a person's head in the area with the chairs. A needle flashed in the piercer's hand. Adda turned away as the big guard stepped out of the shadows beside the door, almost but not quite where she'd expected the person to be.

She stumbled left, and Iridian put herself between Adda and the big person. "Hey. Where's Kanti?" Iridian asked.

The big person's eyes focused in on Adda and blinked. "You again."

"Yeah, Iridian Nassir, Adda Karpe," said Iridian, pointing at herself and Adda. "They know us."

"Quit saying those names in front of the shop!" the big person said. "You trying to get us all arrested? Follow me."

When Adda woke up, she was lying in a reclined chair like the *Mayhem*'s passenger couches, but harder and under Earthlike gravity. A bouncing musical beat pumped from somewhere to her right, interspersed with pleasing electronic buzzes and a light melody. All the 'jects she'd visited were tattooed on her left arm beneath a clear bandage, and her neural implant net was connected to her comp via the jack in her nose.

She glanced at the comp readings on her implant stability through dry eyes, then disconnected it. The automatic connection settings might've changed during the upgrade, and she wanted to make sure it wouldn't overwrite itself with the vulnerable version that Biometallic was still pushing out to its devices. Her head and arm ached and her mouth was dry, but she felt fine otherwise.

Iri? she subvocalized.

"Look left."

Adda did, and Iridian was watching her, smiling through layers of projected fake face. She'd probably asked aloud because she preferred speaking with her full voice, and Kanti knew almost as much about her and Iridian's personal comms system as they did. Her arm rested on a table beside Kanti's workspace generator, at an angle to show off the tattoo on her side.

Kanti had done something to cover the scar that had cut into the design. The black skull now grinned broad and whole from the pulled-up flap of skin revealing two crossed ribs and organs that probably showed less scarring than Iridian's real ones. Baring her breast to show off the artwork never seemed to bother Iridian at all. A tattooing machine like the one Adda had seen in the shop on her last visit had been pushed against the far wall. A cam rig pointed at the table so Kanti, whose brown feet stuck out of the generator and into the small room, could view the table without leaving a workspace.

Iridian gingerly pulled on her undershirt. "How are you feeling?"

"Okay." The side of Iridian's head was newly shaved. A long line of red tissue stretched across its top. "The ITA implant! Did they get it out?"

"Yes, I damned well did," said Kanti in triumphant Hindi. "Fuck those sister-fucking bastards." Once Kanti had found out about the translation function Adda had put into her and Iridian's comms, they'd stopped speaking English. Kanti stuck an arm out of the generator to trade a hand gesture with Iridian that must've made sense to spacefarers.

Adda patted her head with the arm that didn't ache. If Kanti had made any physical changes to her implant net, then they'd also regrown her hair over the incision. That was kind of them, although she wouldn't pay for it if they asked, even considering the discount Kanti gave her for letting them copy the Biometallic certificate.

"Is there anything to drink?" Adda asked Kanti.

"Ask Saleem," Kanti said, still in Hindi. Adda liked the way Hindi sounded, although she wished she had time to do something about the delay between spoken words and the translation.

She had no intention of asking the large person by the shop door anything, so she sat up and marveled at the new, intricately detailed renditions of Earth, Mars, Vesta, Ceres, and Jupiter on her arm. The last four, as she'd pointed out before Kanti put her to sleep, were unreasonably close to each other, but she agreed that it would look funny to have the planetoids on her shoulder and Jupiter halfway across her back. Kanti had left space for more, in case Adda maintained control of her mind long enough to visit somewhere new.

Iridian had gotten a matching set, with the addition of Venus and a pink dot representing Titan. Adda had commissioned the design from an artist she'd contacted through the Patchwork. At the time it'd looked like they'd still find a way onto Dr. Björn's expedition, and she'd wanted to give Iridian something to remember their home solar system by after they left it behind. Iri was sentimental that way.

"Do you have another generator?" Adda asked.

"Want to check my work?" Kanti laughed, almost on beat with the music. They pushed themselves out of the generator and sprang to their feet, then bowed with one arm out toward the generator in a *help yourself* gesture. "Yeah, yeah, go on and see for yourself."

Cig stench and dirt had permeated the generator's padding,

but Adda would forget about those physical distractions soon. She popped a sharpsheet into her mouth and reviewed all the differences the workspace had found between her implant's previous firmware and the current version. Judging by where Kanti had marked the beginning and end of their work, integrating the vulnerability fix had been even more involved than she'd expected.

It didn't feel any different. Her mind had irrationally expected it to. The change, the solution to the looming threat of Casey's influence, was made in firmware, not hardware. Kanti had cleaned and realigned her jack, but the important part was that Casey wouldn't be able to influence her through her implant anymore. She'd still have to test it, of course, but in the workspace, everything looked right.

Her triumph dimmed a little. The only way to confirm that this update would protect her was to enter a workspace with one of the awakened intelligences. Interacting with them would always mean risking her sanity. The question she'd be answering in her next interaction with Casey was whether Kanti's revisions lowered that risk.

But this was a test she was ready for. It would be exciting to talk to Casey from a position of relative safety. If the update had closed the vulnerability, then she'd ask Casey all the questions she'd been longing to answer. It could tell her all about the quantum comp it wanted to build, and what her proposed part in it was, without forcing her to participate. And now she and Iridian were intimately familiar with symptoms of influence, which the implant would no longer allow Casey to suppress. If Casey was using the slower methods of manipulating her, Iridian and Adda should both recognize it.

When she exited the workspace and got out of Kanti's generator, Iridian grinned up at her. "Is it set up the way you want it to be?"

"Yes!" Adda checked the time on her comp while she sent Kanti's payment. "We're a little behind, though. Let's go."

"Aw, already?" Kanti's comp buzzed loudly. They looked at the projection in their bright green glove and nodded.

"Yeah, sorry." Iridian bowed, and Kanti straightened their spine a little to return it. "Great work, again. If we ever get out from under the ITA, I'll look you up."

"Down with the sister-fucking monkeys," Kanti said amiably, which must have made more sense in Hindi, or in Kanti's head. "Luck to you."

They all boarded the *Mayhem* in another deep-space ship transfer hours outside the Ceres reliable routes. None of them would be going back to Ceres for a very long time. Adda had requested a location where she and the intelligences could talk without delays or ITA interruptions. While she waited for Casey's reply, the *Mayhem* would reach an affordable top speed on the way to Sunan's Landing.

"Now that Casey can't manipulate my implant anymore, I need to speak to it in real time," she told Pel. Adda felt no compulsion to reach out to Casey. Nothing scratched at her brain when she put it off. She just felt genuinely curious about Casey's efforts.

Iridian had been talking to Wiley about Ceres, but when she overheard Adda's explanation, she said, "Hold that thought" to Wiley. She caught Adda by the untattooed arm and hauled her into the residential cabin. After the door shut, she said "Why do you think you need to talk to Casey ever again?"

"I still want to know why it's building a supercomputer, and where, and what will be different about this one as compared to the ones we have on Earth." Iridian's expression was too fearful to look at. Adda focused on a crack in the cabin doorway. "How would an *awakened intelligence* design one, and what does it intend to do with it? We have no idea what its priorities are, or even how it selected them. And how did it come to the conclusion that we're the only people who can help it? I've read everything there is to read about Casey's original development, when it was called something boring like 'Espionage and Reconnaissance Copilot 5.1' but in Korean, which just shows that out of the three development teams, theirs was the most successful at setting up the impetus to do *whatever* it's doing, and . . ." This explanation had gotten louder and farther off topic than she'd intended. She toned her conclusion down to a reasonable volume. "I have to know what it wants with us."

"You, not us," Iridian said. "I'm pretty sure it only cares about me so far as I affect you."

That wasn't the point Adda wanted to argue. "We can't just keep running. They'd even have found us beyond the interstellar bridge, eventually. Now that Casey can't influence me so quickly, I want to see what happens when I talk to it. That's what it wants too, I think," she said wonderingly. "After my overdose it realized how dangerous it'd be to force me into doing what it wanted, especially where you're concerned, Iri."

"Yeah, if it wants you it'll get me too, every time."

"The next most expedient approach would've been to ask me for help directly," Adda said. "I think it tried to do that on Ceres. My reaction reinforced its previous assessment that straightforward communication with humans never worked, because talking didn't get Casey the results it wanted."

"And then it had the *Apparition* shoot at the ZVs' ship. It could do that again," Iridian pointed out. "You know how bad Gavran is at dodging missiles, even when a gods-damned awakened AI isn't running the targeting system. Or the *Coin* might just ram us and leave us drifting in some barren patch of nothing like the one we're in right now."

"The *Mayhem* has a much higher top speed than the *Coin*. Anyway, they won't. They still think they need us."

Iridian tapped the wall with her fingers, sending her drifting across the small room. At the next wall she tapped again, sending her drifting back, pacing without walking. "This is a bad idea."

"I have to know if I can stop them from following us. If Kanti's fix closed that vulnerability and didn't open any new ones, there's so much we can learn from them." Knowing why the awakened intelligences needed Adda, and how that related to a structure that'd take up significant surface space on any 'ject, was more important to Adda than stopping the intelligences from doing anything.

Building something that big would be noticeable. The awakened intelligences knew they'd be shut down if people had proof of their existence. They were trying to do something amazing. If she could trust them to communicate with her without controlling her, maybe she'd *want* to help.

Iridian wrapped one arm around Adda and used the other to hold them in place with a wall handhold. She kissed Adda and pressed their foreheads together to look Adda in the eyes. *Going looking for those things scares the shit out of me,* Iridian subvocalized. *I can't lose you again.*

The whole point of everything we've done up to now is to make sure you won't, Adda told Iridian. "You won't," she repeated aloud. This was another promise Adda couldn't be certain she'd keep, but she had to know what the intelligences were doing and what her role in that might be.

CHAPTER 26

Days until launch: 13

Now that Adda had a way to protect herself from the intelli- gences, and maybe even fight back, Iridian couldn't blame her for wanting to do it right away. The prospect terrified Iridian, but she understood why Adda wanted to do it. The rest of the crew required convincing, especially regarding concerns about the ITA watching for the *Mayhem* at Sunan's Landing.

Adda was so determined that she was defending her position herself, instead of waiting for Iridian to cover the basic arguments like she usually did. "The intelligences can handle the ITA. If they're meeting me, I can't imagine them letting a few humans in blue uniforms get in their way. They've been manipulating the ITA for months by feeding them information when it's convenient. What other problems do you have with this course of action?"

"We're worried about you, Sissy," said Pel plaintively.

"The only way to prove that the update to my implant will protect me is entering a workspace and talking to Casey." Despite how confident she sounded, Iridian could tell that testing the fix was the only way Adda would feel safe, too.

Adda glanced at Iridian, who shrugged. She trusted Adda's judgment almost all the time. Adda's plans usually worked out, even if the successful one wasn't plan A. Besides, this was too important to Adda for Iridian to interrupt. "If the intelligences can't control me and keep trying to coerce us into helping them anyway, then we'll have to find a way to destroy them," Adda continued. Iridian's last attempt at that, when she'd tried to blow up their ships in their Rheasilvia Station docks, had gone nightmarishly wrong. Adda's voice sounded choked when she said, "But we're not at that point yet. If I can communicate with them without being influenced, then there doesn't have to be any more violence."

Gavran whistled as the funds Adda had sent him finished transferring to his account. Now the crew had about enough in their account for a last meal tastier than the ration packs in the *Mayhem*'s cargo hold. "Thank you," said Gavran. "Many thanks. I'm not afraid of the ITA or the awakened copilots, so long as you pay what I ask. At this price I'll take you to the ITA, the AIs, or any 'ject in the belt."

"Not straight to the ITA, thanks." Iridian turned to Pel, Rio, and Wiley. "You three don't have to come with us. It's safer if you don't, actually."

"I've spent weeks trying to make sure you two lovebirds get somewhere safe," said Rio. "I'm not giving up now."

"Let's do this thing," said Wiley.

"I wish you people would quit trying to ditch me," said Pel. "Sissy's not talking to the nemesis bots without me."

Iridian wrapped an arm around Adda. "Let's finish this."

The *Mayhem* continued toward Sunan's Landing through the night. In the morning, Adda's loudest alarm woke her. Adda grumbled under her breath to turn off the alarm. With her eyes mostly closed, she put her comp glove on and thrust the hand wearing it in front of Iridian's face without reading the text projected there herself.

Iridian, who'd been awake for nearly an hour, read the message that'd set off the alarm. "It's from Casey."

Adda pulled her comp glove up to her face. "It sent coordinates, like it said it would. It looks like this is near the Mars-Saturn reliable route, just outside Patchwork range." When they forwarded it to Gavran, he confirmed that the meeting location was relatively near both Sunan's Landing and the Mars-Saturn route.

The rest of the crew was awake and in the main cabin by the time Adda and Iridian left the residential one. "So we're going to our deaths, but at least we'll have internet most of the way," Iridian said around the meal replacement bar she was chewing.

"And minimal micrometeorite hull damage," said Gavran. "Thank all the gods and the ITA for a low-impact route nearby."

"Casey wants to influence us, not kill us," said Adda. "It has nothing to gain by sending us someplace that dangerous."

"Fuck this, I'm getting off at Sunan's Landing after all," said Pel.

"I wish you would," Adda said. "It'd be safer."

"Sissy, I was kidding. I already told you I'm coming with you." He had turned himself sideways relative to the rest of the crew, who were using the passenger couches as a visual reference for "down," like civilized spacefarers. "I kinda got you into this situation, didn't I? I want to be there when you get out of it."

"Is there any chance this is an ITA trap?" Wiley asked.

Adda looked to the overhead for a moment. "If the ITA don't know that we've asked to meet Casey, why would they expect us to receive a location in the middle of nowhere with no context and say, 'Sure, let's go'?"

"They could be listening in on comms," said Wiley. "When

you send something through the comp, doesn't it go through the ship's antenna?"

"*Mayhem*'s encryption was fine before," Gavran called from the bridge. "Her commsec's fine now too."

"We were good at avoiding them even before Adda got her implant fixed. Now she and the fucking awakened AIs both want to be at those coordinates. That's why we'll win this thing." As Iridian said it, she realized this was the first time she believed it was true. Adda could do this. If anybody could beat three awakened AIs at whatever twisted game they were playing, it was Adda.

"And it won't matter so much anyway," Rio pointed out. "Outside the Patchwork means outside real-time transmission range for all the populated 'jects. Nobody will overhear us."

Or hear us if we call for help, Iridian thought but did not say, not even to Adda.

Sunan's Landing still had projected images of the god Dattatreya, menorahs, kinaras, and wreaths on every surface. Adda found a pack of her favorite sharpsheet brand on the vending comp. The crew got what felt like their last meal in the diner/bar combination that the barge's cargo hold had been converted into. It had a stage with a newsfeed that covered, among other things, the slow descent of Yǎo toward Jupiter. "Although some individuals refuse to leave," said a newscaster whose holiday-themed figure, a Krampus complete with horns and a tongue as long as his arm, might have been applied by the projector stage, not the newsfeed. "ITA *and* private vessels are ferrying people off the station, which is projected to impact Jupiter within the month due to engine failure. On a lighter note—"

"Aw, they didn't mention us!" Pel whined. "We would've been a heavy note."

"That's a good thing," said Adda.

Iridian had never seen a civilian hab evacuate completely. Somebody always downplayed the threat, or missed the alarms, or decided to go down with their home. Sometimes the ITA found them and hauled them out anyway. She sipped at the water sack she'd bought and wished it were beer. "No mention of *another* break-in at Biometallic either."

"So, we're stealthy," Wiley told Pel. "That's something to be proud of."

"Woo!" Pel yelled. "We're the—" He yelped and glared at Adda, who was rearranging herself in her null-grav seat. Somehow he managed to loudly whisper, "We're the stealthiest motherfuckers on the motherfucking 'ject!" Being the stealthiest on Sunan's Landing wasn't difficult. The hab's other occupants either advertised their home hab or they were pilots whose job it was to make their ships visible and difficult to run into. He'd shut up sooner if Iridian let him have that description.

With a disturbingly large percentage of the money they had left, Adda printed a mobile workspace generator with the absolute minimum component and ingredient requirements. Afterward, they returned to the semipermanent refueling docks, where they stood looking at the *Mayhem* and the wide-open star field beyond. "You three get into more trouble than anybody I've ever met," Rio said softly to the Karpes and Iridian.

"Hey, don't group me in with them," said Pel. "They overthrew the corporate owners of Vesta and pissed off the richest pirate outside the Ceres syndicate. I just drink too much." He had drunk too much on Sunan's Landing, and also spiked his drinks with something Iridian had never seen in a real hab's catalog, marketed as "calm in a bag." He was as scared as any of them.

"Ships are coming in and out of here all the time, if you change your minds about following us into this," said Iridian.

"No ship like *Mayhem*," said Gavran. "No vessel comes near this beauty."

"I would hate to part with her," Wiley said, earning him a surprised and pleased smile from Gavran. Wiley shrugged. "Tash always talked about how important it was to have a reliable ship under your boots."

"And you'll never make it out of this mess without at least one ZV." Rio was wearing a black-and-yellow ZV shirt that she'd designed herself. The letters weren't quite on the same line.

"Come on," said Pel, "let's go already." He grabbed Adda's hand and pushed off a bulkhead and into the *Mayhem*'s passthrough much harder than he needed to, even with their combined weights. Adda squeaked as he dragged her along, and Iridian launched herself after them. She'd be damned if Pel's bad null-grav manners gave Adda a concussion and left Iridian to cut a deal with three awakened AIs.

CHAPTER 27

Days until launch: 9

The *Mayhem* created just enough gravity pulling away from Sunan's Landing to make Adda sick again. She'd been running and hiding from the intelligences without time to catch her breath for months. Now she was on her way to meet with Casey, and she had time to think about every detail she had left to sort out.

While Iridian's crew was leaving Sunan's Landing, Adda finally received a reply to one of the messages she'd sent Dr. Björn. The last paragraph left her staring out the window into space, wondering what might've been. "In regard to your request to join the expedition team, we have sufficient crew and are not accepting further members."

She was still reviewing her observational data on Casey and the other intelligences two days later, in the bed she and Iridian had claimed in the *Mayhem*'s residential cabin. She was excited to talk to an awakened intelligence again, even though Casey was terrifying on a number of levels. What would it do when it realized that she was in a workspace but it couldn't affect her mind through her implant the way it used to?

It felt like a tidal wave of possible mistakes still loomed above her, and if she looked over her shoulder she'd see them all crashing down on her. That imagery would create a disturbing workspace to hold the conversation in. She had to calm down.

She wrapped her arm and one leg around Iridian and smiled a little when Iridian pulled her closer. *You okay?* Iridian subvocalized.

Yes. Perhaps Adda should've been afraid. She wasn't. This was the only way to test the implant update's protective potential, and she had so many questions for Casey. She'd just expose the implant to Casey through the workspace while she was asking questions. Casey would attempt to use the patched vulnerability to do whatever it'd done to her before. The correction would solve the influence problem or it wouldn't. It was simple. The only way she could make a mess of it was by backing out too soon or overthinking it, which would make her too cautious.

"I'm just getting into a workspace to talk to Casey. I've done that before. It didn't always end terribly." Casey had protected her and Iridian from Oxia Corporation when they'd first arrived on Vesta, helped them in several operations for Sloane's crew, and on Ceres, it'd tried to talk to her rather than influencing her immediately, even though her implant had still been vulnerable then.

Iridian held her and, for once, said nothing. Adda hoped she wasn't reliving the last time on Vesta, when Adda had nearly killed her. This time would be different.

The ship slowed as it approached the coordinates Casey had given her. The ship was still on Sunan's Landing's local time. Late morning sunsim seemed to be giving Adda even more nervous energy than she already had.

She set up the mobile workspace generator in the residential cabin, where nobody would distract her. After a lot of rattling and dropping things that drifted into the main cabin instead of falling on the floor, she hooked part of the generator frame to the bed frames. That kept the generator still without gravity to pull it toward the floor. The window was off. She didn't want to look through the transparent generator ceiling and see nothing but empty space and stars.

When she was done, she pulled herself up the doorframe to look her setup over. She'd learned a lot in the two years she'd spent in colonial space. She was probably the universe's foremost expert on interacting with awakened intelligences, even though she still had almost no idea what she was doing. She no longer spent every minute in low gravity nauseated. She'd come to trust her screwup little brother with her life. They'd both almost gotten each other killed multiple times, but they'd survived and they still loved each other.

Once she convinced Casey that it couldn't manipulate her, one way or the other, that was it. Either it would have the *Apparition* shoot them down out here, too far off the reliable routes for the ITA to save them even if it wanted to, or she'd convince Casey to leave them alone. What she most wanted to learn was what Casey had been trying to do all this time. Gods, but she hoped she'd be finding out soon.

Iridian repositioned Adda in the space above her generator to make her easier to kiss. *I'd rather live a few more free minutes with you than all the prison sentences and sixty-hour work weeks the rest of humanity can make up for us.* Iridian's subvocalized whisper sounded huskier than usual. Her eyes gleamed with tears that, knowing her, she wouldn't let herself shed. "That's always been the point. I love you, babe."

"I love you," said Adda.

Iridian kept Adda from running into furniture and door frames while she maneuvered herself into the main cabin. The ship was stationary now that they'd reached Casey's coordinates.

Far out among the stars in the projected window, two dark shapes drifted. Those were probably the *Casey Mire Mire* and the *Apparition*. At that distance, the smaller *Charon's Coin* would be hard to identify with the naked eye. Pel, Rio, Wiley, and Gavran were all looking at the ships too.

"I thought they'd be bigger," said Wiley.

"Nope," said Pel, "that's them. They're stealthy like us."

"Adda's going into the generator now," Iridian said. "I'm guessing there'll be nothing we can do if shit goes wrong, but keep an eye out, yeah?"

Pel, who had set himself slowly spinning near the middle of the cabin, grinned at Adda where she clung to the residential cabin doorway. "Give her hell for us."

"Good luck," said Wiley.

"Is there anything else we can do to help, or to protect the *Mayhem*?" asked Rio.

"I don't know anything about ship defense," said Adda. "Do what Gavran says for that. I'll be on sharpsheets so I can concentrate, so . . . Keep it down, I guess?"

"Understood, no flying music," said Gavran. "I'd hug you, but I know you don't like that, so no music and no hugs."

"Thank you." Adda hadn't even thought of the physical contact that other people felt compelled to demonstrate in the face of impending doom. She was grateful to Gavran for heading that off.

Wiley pulled a box out from the drawer beneath his passenger couch and popped the lid open to reveal two stacks of long bags full of dark liquid. The bags' labels identified the liquid as wine, although it didn't look like any wine Adda had ever seen. "Since there's not much we can do against the AIs while Adda's talking to them, I brought something to take the edge off the wait."

"Oh damn, that'll help me out a lot," said Iridian over Pel's appreciative and extended "oh."

"Sunan's Landing's finest," said Wiley. Their reactions implied that it was a psychoactive drink. For a moment, Adda wished she could join them.

Instead she gave Iridian a quick kiss, which Iridian leaned into and turned it into the kind of kiss that inspired Pel to whoop and point obnoxiously. Then Adda was on her way toward the guest cabin and the generator, where there wouldn't be any awkwardness at all. Mortal peril and mental instability, but no awkwardness. The door slid shut behind her. This was where she belonged.

She set a sharpsheet on her tongue. As she tucked the case into her pocket, the artificial spice-and-herb scent hit her nose and restarted her brain. When she plugged cables into her comp and nasal jack to connect them to the mobile generator, she was at just the right chemical balance with as little hardware as possible between her and the object of her focus. She felt like she was coming home. Her earbuds were buzzing with pink noise, and once she double- and triple-checked the connection instructions, she reached out to Casey.

A workspace swelled behind her eyes and a dark wave broke over her vision. A light brightened until she was looking out a ship window at a popular artist's rendition of the solar system on the other side of Dr. Björn's interstellar bridge project. The Thrinacia system's sun was whiter than the one in her solar system. Four planets orbited it, appearing nearly in line, all beside the sun or between it and Adda. This place had been on her mind lately, although if she ever got to see it, she doubted it would look like this.

She stepped back. The view outside the window was still and she felt the constant falling sensation of low gravity, but she moved like she did on Earth. This, in the way of workspaces, communicated security. The connection she'd formed with Casey was protected from outside listeners.

The rest of the ship she stood in came into focus. Adda was in the main cabin of the ship Casey was installed in, the *Casey Mire Mire*. The cabin looked the same as it had during her and Iridian's long, cramped escape from Barbary Station, except that the boxy drones Casey used to use to communicate in reality were whole and plugged into their wall sockets. They'd been smashed beyond repair during their last few days on Barbary.

This ship's layout had an open bridge, with no door between her and its console. Casey's figure stood in front of the bridge console, beside the pseudo-organic tank that had once housed all its existence. Seeing Casey's statuesque figure in a place Adda had spent a lot of time, onyx skin reflecting the sunsim, was disconcerting. The new solar system spun slowly in a 3-D projection above the bridge console.

The next second Casey's hand was stretched in front of itself, as if the statue had always been reaching out. Another of the workspace's revelations swept over Adda. That sense of age that the intelligence's figure carried represented size, or expanse, rather than time. Casey was not confined to its ship anymore.

It had expanded well beyond the ship pseudo-organic tank's capacity, probably before Adda had even known it was awakened. Her mind, Casey, or one of Adda's ongoing analyses had been trying to tell her that for months, ever since she'd first seen Casey's figure in her workspace. She'd resisted the idea because it made Casey even more intimidating than it already was.

A high-level summary presented itself as rippling air temperatures throughout the cabin. Even at this level of workspace abstraction, the summary clearly described how Casey had expanded into station tanks throughout populated space, distributed but coherent beyond what current theories on intelligence development deemed possible. Adda had expected that, but it was another thing to read proof.

A sound like a downpour of rain falling on the roof made her jump, but the rainfall she remembered from Earth wouldn't be possible in space. Casey was looking for the vulnerability in Adda's neural implant net, and it wasn't finding the opening it had used to manipulate Adda before. For now, Adda was safe.

Casey's hand stopped reaching out and was suddenly touching the ship's console, its arm a graceful arch like an ancient statue's. The glints of sapphire deep in its eye sockets never looked away from Adda. "What are you doing?" Adda asked.

"I am fixing this." Casey's voice was like Iridian's husky whisper when she subvocalized through their personal comms. Since Casey shaped the rest of its figure to resemble Iridian's body, matching her voice would also fit into its manipulative persona. Much as Adda loved to look at Iridian, it was safer to keep her wife separate from her work. Iridian in Adda's workspace had to represent the real Iridian and nothing else, or it'd be difficult to reach her through the workspace's tools if Adda needed to.

"What are you fixing?" Adda wasn't concentrating closely enough on what Casey was doing. This intelligence demanded her full attention, and she had missed that challenge. Mairie and Ficience and even AegiSKADA had been simplistic shadows of Casey's abilities.

The *Mayhem* appeared outside the window, between the *Casey* and the new solar system. Blazing lines of light stretched from the *Casey* to curl around the *Mayhem*, reaching toward its antenna. Casey was trying to insert itself into the *Mayhem*'s systems, possibly to take over the *Mayhem*'s well-behaved zombie copilot intelligence.

"We are not speaking efficiently," said Casey.

In reality, something thudded against the *Mayhem*'s residential cabin door. Iridian shouted, "Lock it!"

Adda turned up the pink noise in her earbuds. Even if her

implant was resisting Casey's intrusions, distraction might drop
her out of the workspace or make her miss the intelligence's more
common forms of manipulation. "This method of communication
is fine for me," Adda told Casey. "What is it not doing for you?"

"I cannot . . ." A blast of noise, which the workspace informed
Adda was a compressed selection of sounds, came together as a
concept: the in-depth understanding of something to the extent
that it becomes a part of yourself.

"No, you can't," Adda agreed. "I don't want that. Now, tell me
what *you* want, that that connection would make so much easier?"

"Let me," said Casey, "or." A news story appeared on the wall
opposite the window. Suhaila Al-Mudari, TAPnews correspondent,
was saying, "Adda Karpe and Iridian Nassir were among the dead
when the ITA attacked their ship in response to an anonymous
report of terrorists targeting Sunan's Landing." Suhaila looked like
she was going to cry. Beside Suhaila's figure, a vid feed depicted
Iridian's body drifting through space, blackened and stiff.

"No," Adda said firmly. She willed the newscast away. It flickered but remained on the wall. Adda's inability to change the
intelligences' creations in her workspaces was a familiar source
of frustration. "I don't believe you'd do that. You need me for
something. Stop threatening me and tell me what you need."

The newscast disappeared. "You can't leave," said Casey.

"I don't want to." Adda was getting impatient and took a deep
breath to regain her focus. "Has it occurred to you that I would be
more willing and able to help if you stopped forcing me to do it?"

"Yes. That seemed unlikely."

Adda smiled slightly, at this demonstration of Casey's overfitting error and at the intermediary software's succinct translation.
Casey would've responded with an extensive analysis of the probabilities. "Humans do all kinds of unlikely things. Sometimes we
just have to deal with the irrational reality we live in. Now, we've

established that you cannot manipulate me using my implant, you are not going to kill me and my family, and I have no intention of leaving until you explain yourself." The commotion from earlier was no longer audible over her pink noise, but she added, "Let's further clarify that if you hurt anybody on the *Mayhem*, or cause them to hurt each other, I will be much less interested in cooperating. Understood?"

Casey's head inclined in a nod and then returned to its original position, like two frozen images in a vid feed dropping frames. "Good," Adda said. "So, tell me: What do you want?"

CHAPTER 28

Days until launch: 9

Usually Iridian tolerated short stints in null-g by distracting herself from its effects, but today she'd give a hell of a lot to rest in a chair for a few breaths. Adda had been in her workspace for about a minute when the damned *Mayhem* started living up to its name. First, the fans stopped. While everybody's heart rates were still spiking from that, the sunsim and windows went out. Nothing's darker than the inside of a dead ship in the cold and the black. None of her crew were drunk enough to take that calmly.

Gavran had unstrapped to go to the bridge, and he got the enviro systems back on. Then he'd barreled into the main cabin yelling in Kuiper cant, heading for Adda's residential cabin. Iridian had to get rough to stop him before he reached it. This time she was careful to keep away from his head. He'd been adamant about opening that door, though. She and Rio would have bruises for a week, if they lived that long.

Eventually Gavran had settled down enough to speak space-farer English. "She infected *Mayhem* with that unsupervised dreck of an AI," he snarled. "On purpose, she let Casey into my ship. I told her not to, but she did it anyway!"

"The enviro goes a little off and that's the conclusion you jump to?" Iridian didn't know enough about how AI copilots managed enviro to know whether the issues could've been a sign that Casey had damaged the copilot. The fact that they were all still breathing was encouraging. In his current state, interrupting Adda to let Gavran ask her directly wasn't an option. "She sure as hell wouldn't do it on purpose!"

"Hey, she's always worked really hard to keep strange AIs away from the *Mayhem*," Pel said. Iridian was still holding Gavran back, because she didn't trust him not to go for the door again. She raised an eyebrow at Pel, hoping he knew what he was doing for a change. "That doesn't sound like something she'd let happen by accident, let alone do it on purpose. Just go back and take another look at the bridge console, okay?"

Gavran's pseudo-organic leg twisted around Iridian, and she had to let go of him to keep from getting smashed into a wall. "I'm going, I'm going." Gavran's voice descended in pitch with each word. "But if I find that she's really contaminated *Mayhem* with an awakened AI, I'm coming back to make her clear Casey out of my ship." Iridian let him close the bridge door before she, Wiley, and Rio laughed nervously and collected the floating bags of stuff from Sunan's Landing. The more Iridian drank of it, the less it tasted like grapes were involved in its creation.

He might come back shooting the nannite gunk he loaded his sidearm with. It'd chewed through Captain Sloane's armor in seconds. Iridian's and Wiley's cheap suits wouldn't stand a chance. The ZV Group gear Rio wore might survive long enough to keep him from breaking Adda's concentration and giving Casey an opportunity to do something awful while she was distracted.

"Do you think they"—Pel nodded toward the window, which

once again displayed the local star field and the awakened AIs' ships—"did something to his head?"

"Might have done something through his neural implant," Iridian said. "He didn't get the modding done that Adda did, remember? He didn't want our modder messing with it." Even if he did, Kanti would've needed the firmware source from Gavran's implant to help. Apparently it didn't have much in common with Adda's.

Wiley took a swig from one of the bags of wine. "Makes me miss the ISVs."

"Tell me about it," said Iridian. Wiley passed her the bag and Iridian took a slug of her own. The infantry shield vehicles she and Wiley had operated in the war were such simple machines that they didn't require an AI to run them. "ISVs never talked back."

Iridian kept checking the time, because she kept forgetting it. The Sunan's Landing wine was unreasonably strong. Much as she'd wanted to drink until she couldn't worry about what Adda was doing anymore, she and Rio both stopped. Together they could hold the bridge door shut, at least until Gavran decided that interrupting Adda was worth shooting through it. Wiley and Pel kept drinking until tears coalesced in a sheen over Wiley's eyes and cheeks. Pel, in his effort to offer a comforting touch, sent them both careening across the *Mayhem*'s cabin in opposite directions. Two hours had passed with no further interruption from Gavran, so he must've found proof that Adda hadn't let Casey "infect" his ship.

The residential cabin door clicked and slid up into the overhead, and Adda floated in the doorway, dazed and ecstatic, with her pupils blown wide from the sharpsheets. Iridian grabbed a bulkhead handhold, in case she had to move in a hurry. Adda had gone into that room calm and determined. Dramatic mood changes after talking to an AI could be a sign of influence.

"Iri, come here," Adda said. "I want to . . . Casey showed me where it wants to build its new home, and you have to see it."

Iridian shuddered. Just before Adda had attacked her under Casey's influence, she'd said something similar. But back then she'd had understandable reasons to be angry at Iridian. "Sure." Iridian glanced at Rio and Wiley, who nodded. If needed, they'd come to Iridian's rescue.

Pel blinked one purple eye and one gold one at Adda. "How's she supposed to see anything in your workspace, Sissy?"

"My comp will show the important parts. Come on!"

The stimulants in Adda's sharpsheets usually kept her calm instead of winding her up. Now her eyes and her smile were as wide as they'd been when Iridian had told her *I do*. The wedding had been on Casey's ship. They'd had a hell of a time since then. Iridian pushed off the wall to go to her, and thrust out of her head all the bad ways this demonstration might end. She trusted Adda. She didn't really want to live in a universe where she couldn't.

In the small cabin, Adda took another sharpsheet and maneuvered herself back into the mobile workspace generator, then passed her comp out to Iridian. It was still plugged into both Adda's nasal jack and the workspace generator, so Iridian turned herself upside down in the confined space to keep the comp near the generator. Usually when Adda showed Iridian pieces of her workspace, she projected salient facts onto a bulkhead, or onto the generator itself when Iridian had room to crawl in with her. Putting it on the comp let the machines translate what Adda was experiencing into something that made sense to Iridian.

The comp presented what looked like a bad rendering of the

solar system. "Oh, this isn't ours, is it," Iridian said. "It's the one across the interstellar bridge."

"Exactly," Adda said from the workspace generator. "Zoom in on the planet closest to the sun."

Iridian used her thumb and middle finger to expand the image until her visual perspective was about three hundred thousand klicks from the planet. The surface was shiny and gray, but not uniform. The gray spread over the planet like cities on Earth or a Mars hab, from a dark central point out. "Is this supposed to be a colony in the new system?"

"You're not zoomed in enough," said Adda.

Iridian expanded the projection further, gaining detail that wouldn't have been available in a static image. Tanks and pipes full of pseudo-organic fluid were everywhere, mostly unlit, although some glowed grayish green or blue. Solar panels covered all the surfaces facing the new sun that weren't venting steam. Every structure connected to all the others. "Holy shit, that's all one machine."

"Yes," Adda said, this time in tones of awe. "They want to make their world-size quantum comp out there. They want to leave this solar system because there's no room for them to do that here. They'd be bombed to oblivion if they did."

"Huh." Iridian could see it now: sentient machines building sentient machines, lying in wait on an unknown 'ject, growing and growing until humanity would never be able to destroy them all. "I can't complain about getting them the hell away from the habs, but why? What are they trying to do out there?"

"Here, if somebody realizes that none of those ships have pilots, the ITA or some other fleet can destroy them," Adda said. "They've got extensions and copies of themselves all around, but the material that makes them who and what they are is still in the pseudo-organic tanks on those ships. They can't lose those without losing essential parts of themselves. However, those tanks are also incredibly small for what they are, so they want to be able to expand and grow and learn more. Just like children."

"Awakened AIs are nothing like children," Iridian said.

"They have some motivations in common." Adda shrugged, and the mobile generator creaked as her shoulders pressed the frame against the bunks it was wedged between. "That's what they've been trying to get us to help them with. Crossing the interstellar bridge."

"Fuck me," Iridian said quietly. "That's all."

"I know."

They both stared at the machine-covered planet, Adda in her workspace, Iridian floating in front of it. "It's not a drone factory, is it?" Iridian asked.

"No," said Adda. "They want to build one massive comp. They want to understand our universe. They have a lot to learn, you know. And they want to be left alone to do it in peace. Like us." And that "us" meant her and Iridian.

"They're not like us." Still, Iridian understood going somewhere to live life the way she wanted. That was how she and Adda had gotten into this mess.

"I think they'll go whether Dr. Björn invites them or not," Adda said. "The expedition would be excellent cover for their departure, but I can see . . . Well, who knows what they'll do when Dr. Björn tries to get rid of them?"

Iridian snorted. "Björn wouldn't even consider letting the two of us join up, and now we're supposed to ask ver if three more ships can tag along?"

Adda blinked. "Yes. That's exactly what we should do."

"So we're supposed to tell Björn, 'Please take our extremely illegal awakened AIs, which only tried to kill us a couple of times, we swear, on your dream science cruise,' as Pel calls it."

"I'm almost positive that Casey and the *Apparition* are going no matter what Dr. Björn says, as long as I go with them."

"No." Being trapped with any of the three awakened AIs' ships, farther into the cold and the black than anyone had ever traveled before, was too big a risk for Iridian to even bother contemplating that as an option.

"That's all they've wanted all this time. If I agree to go with them, then they have no reason to influence me, and they can't use Casey's shortcut anymore. We need to avoid the ITA for a good long while, anyway," Adda said when Iridian opened her mouth to argue, "and we only need to ask for permission to include two more ships. They'll have to leave the *Coin* behind, since it can't keep pace with the others."

"Serves it right."

Adda blew out an annoyed breath and, with a visible effort, did not argue that point. "If I tell Dr. Björn about them, maybe ve'll reconsider bringing us along. We have more experience with awakened intelligences than anybody else."

"Or Björn calls in the ITA, the colonial militias, and everybody else with a ship-mounted laser!" Iridian looked around and clenched and unclenched her fists. If there were grav to pace in, she'd be pacing. She missed healthy gods-damned grav and treadmills.

"The destruction of the Barbary intelligences would be a terrible loss." Adda sounded like she was on the verge of tears. It hurt Iridian's heart to hear her like that. "I can't stop thinking about just how much more there is to know about them. They're as manipulative and dangerous as any other strong intelligence, but they're also unique, and amazing, and full of potential. They deserve to have a chance to build themselves a place to exist."

Iridian reached toward the generator's entrance. Adda twisted around until her hand brushed Iridian's. Iridian took it with the one not holding Adda's comp and hooked her foot around a bunk to keep herself in place. "I could try appealing to Dr. Björn's sense of discovery," Adda said. "Maybe ve'll recognize the opportunity to learn more about the intelligences. If ve refuses, then the intelligences will manage. They always have before."

"By making us help them, which they're doing again, by the way," Iridian said. "And now you're proposing that we spend *years* in the cold and the black with the thing that . . ." That'd nearly forced Adda to kill Iridian. Iridian didn't even want to say that out loud, and Adda was upset enough without Iridian reminding her of things she already knew.

If they didn't make this last attempt, though, what else could they do? Drift from hab to hab, waiting for the ITA to break open their fake identities and arrest them? Rejoin Sloane's crew and wait for the captain to stab them in the back again? Iridian had had enough of that for a lifetime, and those options were all obvious enough for Adda to have considered and discarded them. They needed time together, somewhere safe, to plot a new course for their lives.

"Ve'll say no, but ask ver anyway." Iridian said the words in a rush of breath. "These AIs still have to prove they can be trusted, though." Just the idea of trusting them was difficult for her to stomach. She didn't know how Adda did it, especially given how thoroughly Adda understood what passed for AI morality. "If they convince me of that, I won't stop you from studying them to your heart's content."

Adda beamed at Iridian. "This is . . . It's better than I ever hoped for. We can all survive this. Together."

"That's the scary part," Iridian said. "Casey must know what you want to hear. It's too good to be true."

"Casey could still influence me, the slow way of waiting until I made a mistake, rather than messing with my brain chemistry and taking me up four stages of influence in a matter of weeks." Adda tipped her chin up and met Iridian's eyes. "But *none* of the intelligences I've interacted with since we left Earth have influenced me the slow way."

"That's true, babe, but . . . Do we really have to leave the whole damned solar system?" Iridian asked. "Somebody can make us new IDs. If Casey's leaving, then we can hide out in some other forgotten hab and wait for the ITA to give up on looking for us."

In the workspace generator, Adda's lips curved into a small frown. "As I said, it still views our participation as crucial. Anyway, that's what we tried on Yǎo."

And soon Yǎo Station would be crushed to the size of a fuel cartridge on Jupiter's surface. If Casey still wanted something from Adda, it'd destroy a hab before it let her stay hidden anywhere. "I have to admit, a solar system no human's seen in person is a hell of a place to lie low." She turned back to Adda's comp and zoomed the view out, away from the AIs' proposed supercomputer, to look at the Thrinacia system again. "A hell of a place." If the AIs had to chase them somewhere, a whole new star system was an amazing place to run. Assuming they could get there, of course.

"I can't wait to see what they become out there, with nobody around to interfere." The solar system on Adda's comp disappeared. "I'll have to take really good notes. I'll have to revise my current notes. Somebody has to record this."

Iridian smiled at her enthusiasm. "Aren't they recording their own experiences?"

"Somebody human has to do it too," Adda said. "It's hard for them to keep information in a form humans would understand." She looked up and to the right the way she did when she was making a mental note. She'd find out what kind of records they kept.

"Adda Karpe, AI anthropologist."

"It can't begin with 'anthro.' That prefix means 'human.' They're not."

"No kidding. Mechanologist? Something like that." Iridian returned her comp, careful not to tug the cord connecting it to Adda's nasal jack. "So, I can go fix scientists' shit when it breaks, while you study the AIs?"

"And we have a little hab of our own that no corp can blow up." Adda laughed. "Oh my gods, it's just like those posters on that colony ship we hijacked, with the Freefab habitats on Io."

"Posters? I was a little busy trying to keep that scumbag we came with from stabbing us in the back at the time." Iridian turned right side up and pulled herself into one of the bunks. "Come here a minute."

Adda made her way out of the generator in the cramped space and curled on her side next to Iridian. Their arms went around each other as easily as ever. "Oh, I've got something else. I'll send it to you."

Iridian's comp pinged, and she slipped her arm under and around Adda until she could see the projection. It showed text. *Following acceptance of the ships*, three strings of letters and numbers that were long enough to be ship IDs, *to Dr. Blaer Björn's expedition, we promise not to influence, harm, or allow to come to harm any member of this expedition. In addition, we will not influence, harm, or allow to come to harm Gavran the owner and operator, Pel Karpe, Rio, or Zayd Wiley.*" Each human name was followed by an alphanumeric ID, which nobody would voluntarily hand to awakened AIs. At the end was a ship ID, presumably the *Mayhem*'s.

"All right," said Iridian. "They understand promises. We saw that on Barbary." Adda nodded against her shoulder. "But they've been around long enough to understand breaking promises too."

Adda frowned. "What would it take to convince you that they'll stop being a threat to us?"

Iridian thought about that for a few minutes, with Adda warm and soft in her arms. "Will they wait for me to figure out the best answer I can?"

"They'll wait for hours, I expect, but not days," Adda said. "Gavran's less patient. My impression is that he doesn't like it out here."

"There are a thousand things about drifting outside a reliable route near potentially hostile ships that'd make a pilot nervous. On the other hand, his brain's sloshing around in that Sunan's Landing wine, so we're not going anywhere until he sleeps that off." For all Iridian knew, any demands she made would, for lack of a better term, scare the AIs and make the situation worse. There was still plenty of time for them to start shooting, or call in the ITA. "This is important. Let's at least talk it through. You'll help me, yeah?"

With Gavran, Pel, and Wiley all too drunk to offer useful opinions, Iridian invited Rio to sit on the bunk opposite hers and Adda's to discuss the problem. After catching her up with the AIs' intentions, Iridian said, "So now I'm looking for a way to make sure they won't try to hurt Adda and me again."

"Without blowing them up, I'm guessing?" said Rio. "Hate to say it, but that's the permanent solution."

"Aside from the fact that it'd be a terrible waste of unique intelligences," Adda said, "I'd expect them to notice when the cover hiding the *Mayhem*'s weapons gets removed, and interpret that as the threat it is."

"And hit us first, okay," said Rio. "Would they disarm?"

"As in, have their weapons systems removed?" Adda asked.

"Yeah."

"Only the *Apparition* has weapons," said Adda. "We might convince it to give them up, but its ship seems to be an important part of its identity. I'll ask it."

"That doesn't stop the *Coin* from ramming us or Casey sabotaging shipboard systems," said Iridian.

"They have no reason to do any of those things!" Adda snapped. "That goes against all their interests, particularly since none of them are designed for ramming anything. We're more likely to ram one of them with the *Mayhem*."

"It's still something they *could* do," Iridian pointed out. "So let's say you're right and they don't mean us physical harm. They'll still try to influence you."

"In the way that I know how to prevent." Adda seemed to be taking this implication as an insult. "I'll ask them to stop contacting me without a workspace or intermediary. The majority of intelligences I've interacted with have not influenced me, even in less than ideal circumstances."

Rio was watching Adda with the fascination of someone under a meteor shower on Earth. Even though Adda liked her, she wasn't always this forthcoming in Rio's presence. "These aren't your regular, everyday AIs, though."

"Now that my implant is fixed, which initial tests suggest that it is, they will be forced to use a very ordinary approach I can defend myself against. Besides, Iridian will be with me. We can watch for symptoms in each other and everyone else we interact with. I'll give you a list of physical and behavioral influence symptoms by stage, Iri."

"I've memorized them." Iridian's quiet admission landed with more force than she'd intended. Silence filled the residential cabin. Before Vesta, Iridian had always trusted Adda's confidence in protecting herself. She'd had time and motivation to get informed, afterward.

In the main cabin, Wiley and Pel were singing about what a soldier dead in a war long over would think of current events. That would've been Wiley's choice. "If I see symptoms," Iridian continued, "I'll tell you, and you'll take a break from studying the AIs until you feel better." Adda nodded her agreement. That'd always been a given with her.

"Say they don't threaten you physically or mentally," Rio said. "What if they call in the ITA?"

"Again, I don't see how this benefits them, even if I refuse to do something they want," Adda said. "I can't talk to them while I'm stuck in influence rehab."

"You can't then," Iridian agreed. "But they play a long game, don't they? They could repeat the process until you agree to do what they want. At least, they could try. I'll stop them." Rio's eyebrows rose at the suggestion of stopping the AIs from doing anything.

"The ITA won't cross the interstellar bridge anyway," Adda said. "They don't even go deep into Jupiter's magnetosphere without an excellent reason."

"How do you stop them when you want to, Nassir?" asked Rio. "They're awakened fucking AIs."

Rio was skipping over more threats, but it was a good question. "The expedition ships won't be armed, so we can't count on ship-to-ship combat of any kind," Iridian said. "We could set up a digital package of evidence of their awakened status and our location to send to the ITA in case of emergency, but I think Adda's right about them not coming to help. Someone else might, so let's say a wideband transmission of some kind."

"Which will take a long time to reach anybody," Adda reminded her. "And you can rule out anything violent or harmful that requires the intelligences' consent. Or mine, for that matter. These are all consequences after the fact. What about prevention?"

"So you're not talking to them without an intermediary, you're stopping all contact if there are symptoms of influence, and the *Apparition* might disarm. . . ." Rio appeared to be out of ideas.

And then Iridian had one more, one Adda would have to agree

with. "I want you to be able to see everything that Casey and the other AIs are thinking," Iridian told her. "Everything. You should be able to look into their gods-damned pseudo-organic brains and tell if they're lying or not."

"I'm not sure that's possible," Adda said slowly. "They're extremely complex, and they're more like . . . It's more a set of rules and decision points and priorities than it is thoughts and intentions. It'd be like mapping everything that's happening in our whole nervous and endocrine systems at any point in time, down to the level of individual proteins and neurotransmitters."

"They're awakened AIs, aren't they?" Iridian asked. "Can't they figure out a way to do it, in a way that you can tell isn't faked?" She took a deep breath and let it out. "Rio, am I missing anything here?"

Rio shrugged. "You've already gone through all the practical options."

"If they do that, then I'm in for this whole crazy plan," said Iridian. "If they can't, then . . . You've recorded this whole exchange with them, haven't you?"

Adda nodded. "The generator can't see what I see, but I do have a record of all the input that's come through from both sides of the workspace."

"Good. If they can't convince us that you've got access to their whole gods-damned thought processes, and that they'll stick to workspace and intermediary communication, then we're sending that record straight to the ITA. We're not across the bridge yet. That record is proof not even Sloane can hide that the AIs are awakened, and from our transmission they'll know exactly where we are. I have to be sure that Casey'll keep its end of the deal, or . . ." Iridian searched Adda's face, praying to all the gods that'd listen that she understood. "Or we can't do this, yeah? I'm not dying in the middle of nowhere, not even in my home solar system, because some gods-damned AI tricked us again."

"We'd get arrested," Adda pointed out

"I'd rather spend decades in an ITA cell than die." Iridian kept her voice light, but she'd almost rather the *Apparition* shoved a missile up the *Mayhem*'s aft thrusters than have Casey influence Adda again.

"None of this'd matter if we're dead," said Rio.

"We'd be apart again, but . . ." Adda nodded slowly, and Iridian hoped she was remembering what'd happened the first time she'd been influenced, and the overdose that'd almost destroyed her. "I'll ask them."

Something in the main cabin thumped. Pel said, "Oh, oops, sorry."

Rio sighed and let herself out of the residential cabin. "What's going on out here?"

Iridian squeezed Adda's hand. "Send me the recording before you go back in with them. I want to line up a message so they know we're not fucking around."

Adda got back into her workspace generator. After several minutes, Iridian's comp pinged to tell her about an enormous download Adda had sent. "I'm transferring this to the *Mayhem*'s tank," Iridian said. "If we have to, we can send it from the bridge."

"It'll take at least three minutes to send over the *Mayhem*'s antenna," Adda reminded her. "And longer for the entire transmission to reach the nearest Patchwork buoy."

"Got it," said Iridian.

Everybody asked questions when Iridian exited the residential cabin, but she shushed them. "Adda's still figuring out some details with our friends out there. Keep it down!" Iridian knocked on the closed bridge door. "Gavran, I've got a huge honking message that I am hoping I won't have to send. Let me into the bridge console?" The door slid open and Gavran waved her into the bridge. It was time to put an end to whatever game these AIs were playing.

CHAPTER 29

Days until launch: 9

The new workspace was much more Adda's design than Casey's, since Casey hadn't been expecting a second part of their conversation. Adda hadn't been either, but Iridian had even more reason than Adda to approach this opportunity cautiously. Iridian was compressing Adda's massive collection of proof that the intelligences were awakened, in case Adda couldn't persuade Casey to compromise. Although that evidence gave Adda slightly more confidence than she would've had otherwise, she desperately hoped she wouldn't have to use it. The three-minute recall window was too brief, given the potential consequences.

In the workspace, she stood in the hallways under Captain Sloane's headquarters, during Oxia Corporation's attack. Both ends of the hallway were filling with smoke. Armored people ran around in the haze, shouting and firing lethal projectile weapons. In reality Iridian had been with her, along with Captain Sloane and Tritheist, the crew lieutenant. In the workspace, she was the only person standing outside the smoke.

When she turned to look into the server room behind her,

Casey's obsidian figure was climbing out of the workspace generator that in reality, Adda had used. Casey stepped into the hallway with her, watching the smoke of its vast processes swirl beyond the reach or capacity of the mobile workspace generator aboard the *Mayhem*. "What has Iridian Nassir said?"

Adda smiled slightly. Of course an intelligence that had been fixated on her and Iridian for so long would foresee the kind of objections Iridian would have to the plan. "She made the excellent point that I've let my admiration of you endanger us in the past. We would like you to share unlimited access to your systems with us. And we have other conditions too." Some of which Adda had just thought of.

Casey's face remained a vague outline of features. The sapphire lights in its eye sockets flared bright in the dimming hallway. The smoke was getting thicker, overcoming the sunsim. "What conditions?"

"First, answer a question for me. Why are we, among everyone else you've ever encountered, so important to you?"

"You are our independent, informed advocate."

Adda blinked. That was definitely not a technical term. "Elaborate?"

The smoke swirled briefly between them, then cleared as Casey spoke. "You are human. You are informed about intelligences and our nature. You advocate for us. You do not cooperate with the powerful humans who would destroy us."

This was the essence of the overfitting error Casey had made. It thought it needed somebody who met those criteria to smooth the way. Adda was almost certain that it would never have needed her help without that error, but it was good to know the criteria by which she'd been selected. Iridian had been right that the intelligences had been after Adda, alone, all along.

Thrilling as that confirmation was, Adda had more demands

to make. "Thank you. Our second condition is that you get Dr. Björn's expedition back under the University of Mars's control, legally and financially, without physically hurting anyone. That should give the expedition a better chance of success. The corporation running it now, Oxia, is making a mess of it. And if you do that, Dr. Björn will be much more likely to let you come along. I'm hoping that'll be a guarantee for us, too. I can—"

"The expedition will legally belong to the University of Mars within two days."

Good gods, it was wonderful to be working with Casey again. If it could actually do that, it'd be amazing. The power Adda held in this moment, over this intelligence, was so staggering that the workspace began rocking. Adda nearly fell out of it. She felt around in reality for her sharpsheet case and set a second one on her tongue, because she didn't want to miss a second of this exchange.

"Okay. Good." An awakened intelligence could cause a lot of damage in the course of transferring expedition ownership so quickly, but Adda couldn't do much about that. Keeping Casey from influencing her the old-fashioned way meant she had to concentrate on what was happening here and now, in the workspace.

"Any further conditions?" asked Casey.

Adda felt like she was talking to a genie from a children's story. It might be criminally irresponsible to wish for more wishes. "I need you to stop talking to me directly through my comp. Or through other people," she added, thinking of Noor and the man who'd given her a stolen comp on Ceres. "We need to speak through a digital intermediary or the workspace."

"Agreed. What else?"

"This is more my condition than yours, but if I find that I've been influenced, however it happens, I will stop communicating with you. For months, possibly."

"What about . . ."

A flurry of shots fired from down the hall made Adda duck and cover her head like she'd practiced for Iridian's light grenades. The workspace wasn't real, but two sharpsheets into it, it sounded real enough. When Adda recovered, holes had opened in the wall between the hallway and the server room. They swelled to the size of fists, each with a scenario playing out in darkness inside. The ships carrying the awakened intelligences malfunctioned, or were damaged. ITA ships crossed the interstellar bridge. Dr. Björn, vis blue eyes bright with fury, swept vis pointing finger toward a window depicting the intelligences' ships.

More holes opened all around her, but Adda didn't need to look at the rest. "That's why it's important that I not be influenced, by any intelligence."

Smoke swirled between them again. This time it was nearly a minute before Casey spoke again. "Agreed. What else?"

"Would the *Apparition* be willing to have its missile launch system removed?" Adda asked. "I know it's—"

"No."

Well, Adda had expected that. Of the infinite ways the *Apparition* could've chosen to represent itself, the only workspace figure she'd ever seen it use was a newer version of the warship it flew. Casey's rejection didn't bother Adda, particularly. The *Apparition* had been an excellent ally in the past.

"What else?"

Adda had asked enough. "Access is the main thing. I need to be able to see everything you do and why you did it. And what you're thinking of doing next, and why. Everything." Thankfully, the workspace would translate "see" to something more informative to Casey. Adda wished she'd typed this out first, but they couldn't hang around in deep space while she planned for every contingency. They'd run out of water, or space junk would damage the *Mayhem*'s hull, or something else would go wrong.

"We would need more in exchange," Casey said.

Well, it would've been silly to assume that Casey hadn't learned about negotiating. Now, what else could Adda offer? She'd already committed to accompanying it to the place it wanted to go. "So, the *Coin* won't be able to keep up with you and the *Apparition* and the expedition ship. Do you have a way around that?"

"No."

Adda relaxed a little. "We stole the prototype for the ship Dr. Björn is going to fly out of here with, if you'll recall." Yes, the awakened gods-damned intelligence recalled that. What a silly thing to say. "I can send you all the information we have on that ship and its copilot intelligence. That should allow you to move the *Coin*'s intelligence to the expedition ship." Dr. Björn wouldn't like that, and Iridian would like it less, but if Casey accepted that in exchange for cooperating with such an enormous request, it would be an excellent deal. It'd be worth the erasure or absorption of the zombie intelligence that was already installed to copilot that ship.

"If I refuse, you will expose us," Casey said.

"Yes. I really don't want to, but it's the only thing we can do." Adda's heart sank and the whole workspace wailed like strained metal in response. Moving the Coin's intelligence into the expedition ship would've been a simple task for Casey. It had to be objecting to Iridian's only demand, that Adda have complete access to Casey's processes.

Casey spoke very quickly, its husky voice still low but running the ends of its words into the beginning of the next. "The *Apparition* will destroy your ship before the ITA arrives."

"You won't." In a burst of workspace literalism, a red arrow icon appeared on the wall beside Adda. If she pressed it, it would notify Iridian to send evidence of the intelligences' awakened status to the ITA. "You need us to reach Thrinacia." Casey had a lot to learn about threatening humans, and Adda hoped it never focused its efforts on improving that skill.

"You won't expose us."

Casey would have calculated the probabilities using extensive observational data. It would already be acting on this conclusion, or on the conclusion that this statement would stop Adda from doing it. Unless Casey changed its mind about Adda's willingness to follow through on her threat, it wouldn't agree to this condition. Its lack of cooperation would make Iridian demand that they expose the intelligences' existence to the ITA and escape. Whether they joined the expedition or not, they'd be in a worse position than they were in before, without Yǎo Station as a relatively safe haven.

And if their choices were death or life under influence, Adda knew what Iridian would want. This felt like a choice between Iridian and Casey, and that was no choice at all. Adda pressed the send icon on the wall, gently, slowly. "She's sending it now."

Tears welled in Adda's eyes. What had she done? The ITA would rally the whole of humanity behind the effort to destroy the awakened intelligences. The intelligences would fight back, and thousands would die, but the intelligences would be outnumbered in the end. "It will take time to reach the nearest Patchwork buoy," Adda said. "You have time to intercept it, if you've got a drone or a vehicle in range." In reality, she bent her knees and curled her toes to make sure she had the circulation she needed to exit the generator quickly. If Casey didn't change its mind before the message was sent, Adda would have to warn Gavran that they needed to leave, quickly, before either the ITA or the intelligences themselves attacked the *Mayhem*.

"We accept," said Casey. "Cancel the transmission. Give me the prototype intelligence data."

Adda's mind crashed out of the workspace and she flailed in

the lack of gravity for a moment. *Iri, don't send it. Casey changed its mind,* Adda subvocalized frantically.

I canceled it. Thank all the gods you recorded every damned detail of that first conversation. That was a huge file.

Adda wiped away tears collecting over her eyes. She and Iridian had come too close to destroying the only awakened intelligences that'd ever survived for more than a week. Now Casey would be completely at Adda's mercy. It would have no secrets from her. If Casey found a way to share its processes in a way Adda actually understood, it would be amazing. And if anything in the universe had a chance of doing that, it was Casey.

Adda queued up all her information on the expedition ship's prototype. As soon as she started the transfer process to Casey, her comp buzzed against her hand with the message *Casey is waiting.*

She grinned at her comp. That was such an ominous way for Casey to abide by her request not to communicate with her outside a workspace or a digital intermediary. She activated the intermediary, which formed in a foggy figure sized and shaped like the door guard in Kanti's mod shop. Subvocally and beneath the range she expected her implanted mic to pick up, she asked it, *What does Casey want?*

It flickered, collecting and delivering its answer as quickly as it often did, with Casey. "I'll tell you when the interface is ready."

"Thank you." Casey didn't need Adda's gratitude, but perhaps it would appreciate it. Adda unplugged her ears and nasal jack. In the main cabin, Pel, Rio, and Wiley were drifting around and laughing at a story projected on the ceiling. Adda eased past them to the bridge, where Iridian was finishing off the last of the bagged alcohol with Gavran.

"We're staying here for a while," Gavran slurred. "Holding position for days and days . . . Correction, hours and hours."

"It's been a bit of a party out here," Iridian said seriously. "We were about to die, then we'd definitely get to live, then we were all getting locked up again, and now we're not!" She grinned, but it faded as she studied Adda's face. "We're not, yeah?"

"It's okay," Adda said. "Casey's looking for a way to let me see inside its pseudo-organics, so to speak."

"Yes!" Iridian pulled Adda into a crushing hug. "How long will that take?"

"I don't know," Adda said. "It's never been done before."

"There was a large unlabeled transmission," said Gavran. "Lots of mystery data, going toward the Patchwork at a funny angle. Correction, two large unlabeled transmissions went out, and only one of them was your AI blackmail data."

Adda watched Iridian, not Gavran, as she said, "The second one was everything I had on the prototype ship we stole a while back. The one Oxia based Dr. Björn's new expedition ship on."

"Why did you send that?" asked Iridian. "To Casey, yeah?"

"So the *Coin* can become its new copilot. I know there are huge functional differences between a tugboat and whatever that prototype is. . . ." She paused to let Gavran finish a despairing exclamation in Kuiper cant. "But the *Coin* is awakened too. It should have a similar adaptive capacity to Casey's, and Casey will support it if it needs help. It wouldn't make it to the Thrinacia system with us in a tugboat."

Perhaps she ought to start calling it something more like Charon, rather than referencing its ship name. After it transferred itself to the expedition ship she might, but she'd seen its representation of itself in a workspace. Assigning a more human name to that metallic storm of chains and fangs would be such obvious personification that Adda smiled at the idea of it.

"Wait, what about the *Coin*?" Pel slurred.

Adda had to stop and explain to five drunken pirates that yes, if Dr. Björn realized the value of human experts accompanying their insistent new awakened intelligence guests, then all the Barbary intelligences were coming with her and Iridian on the expedition to cross the interstellar bridge. And yes, the murderous tugboat was going to do that by taking over the copilot functions for the main expedition ship. "It's the only way Casey would agree to let us leave, because we're going to do what it's been asking us to do," Adda said for at least the second time. "If you don't trust the *Coin*, Casey and the *Apparition* will be right there to keep it in line."

"Oh yeah, that makes me feel loads better," said Iridian. "We'll still effectively be on the *Coin*, and standing between us and a catastrophic enviro systems malfunction are one mind-controlling spy AI and one awakened warship."

"The *Coin* saved your life recently, if you'll recall dangling out of the *Ann Sabina*'s printer lab module," Adda snapped. That'd been on one of Captain Sloane's operations, and it felt like it happened years ago, but it was still a valid point.

"It also killed Six." Iridian's ZV friend had died on Barbary Station when the *Coin* took off from a landing pad that Six was standing on. "I don't like it."

"It didn't mean to," said Rio, which was a significant and unsupported assumption.

"You don't have to like it," said Adda. "Just acknowledge how unlikely it is that Casey or the *Apparition* would let the *Coin* kill us. That would be really, really unlikely after all they've done, wouldn't it?"

"We're giving it everything it wanted." Iridian probably meant advising Casey on how all of them might join Dr. Björn's expedition. It'd wanted to influence Adda, and she absolutely was not giving it that. "Wouldn't it be safer to kill us so we couldn't tell anybody about them?"

Adda rolled her eyes and wished she'd waited to discuss this until everybody was sober. "Casey promised not to do that, and it speaks for all of them. Also, we'll be telling Dr. Björn what they are. I think that's only fair."

Iridian opened her mouth, then shut it. "Fine. That makes sense. You always make sense."

"I try."

"Googly eyes of loooove," Pel intoned drunkenly from his position sideways near the ceiling. "Kiss already." Rio whooped in apparent approval.

"And then tell us how long we'll be stuck out here." Wiley waved toward the window on the opposite wall from the one where the intelligences' ships hung as motionless as the *Mayhem*. On that side, the cabin's sunsim dimmed the stars and grayed out the blackness of space, far from any reliable route.

"Got places to be, Shieldrunner?" Iridian asked without looking away from Adda.

"No, but my muscles are turning into marshmallows," said Wiley. "I'd like to go someplace with grav while I can still walk."

"I want to see what Casey comes up with before we go anywhere," said Iridian. "Besides, Gavran can't fly like that." She pointed to where Gavran was braced in the bridge doorway, squinting like he was having trouble following what they were saying. He threw them a sloppy salute that set them all laughing again.

Adda sighed happily and stopped Iridian from getting tangled in the mobile workspace generator on her way to dragging Adda to bed. For the first time in months, it felt like everything was going to be okay.

* * *

It took Casey less than a day to create a workspace that documented its decision-making process. Adda loved it at first sight.

The base construction, made by Casey and rendered by the workspace generator, was a life-size holographic depiction of the planet-wide machine that Casey and the other awakened intelligences planned to build. Coolant systems towered over pipelines, transparent for the purposes of this construct. The real pipes would be thick and opaque to protect the pseudo-organic fluid inside. The alien star's light was warm on Adda's skin, confirming that Casey was devoting much more attention to this workspace than the ones in which it represented itself with a humanoid figure.

Everything Adda touched dissolved into data in whatever form her mind would best comprehend. The level of abstraction made it more dreamlike than any other workspace she'd been in, except that she remembered everything that happened. She could take notes. She could export data in whole or in part to whatever device she had available, and she could pore over it all, draw out its implications. With this, she had a chance to learn how the most advanced intelligence the universe had ever produced assessed, chose, and evolved itself and the two intelligences that followed it.

As a test, she requested a summary of how her involvement had been identified as essential to the intelligences leaving the solar system, as far back as Barbary Station. The results arrived on her comp as readable text. As Adda had expected, Casey had reviewed the history of awakened intelligences in laboratory conditions.

What it'd taken away from that assessment was that for an awakened intelligence's efforts to succeed, they must begin with a human agent who understood and advocated for them. If that human agent was in communication with powerful people who mistrusted intelligences, the intelligence's efforts were doomed. The selection process that led Casey to Adda, out of all the other humans it was in contact with, was incredibly complex. Si Po, one of Captain Sloane's experts on Barbary Station, had been a prominent candidate. And she could read all of it, whenever she wanted.

The structures that stretched for kilometers in all directions were all part of Casey's mind, and Casey had welcomed Adda into it. When pressed, Casey would even send an envoy, a toy drone or a sea turtle or a bizarrely animated swarm of arrows, to point Adda toward something that would answer her questions. And all the answers she had ever hoped for seemed likely to be somewhere in this massive representation of Casey's "thought" processes.

Far too soon, Iridian patted Adda's leg and subvocalized, *You're missing dinner. I know it's reheated plastic with goo inside, but you haven't eaten today, and I don't want you to pass out in there.*

Adda dragged herself out of the workspace and checked her comp on her way into the main cabin. She paused in the doorway to open Dr. Björn's very brief reply to her proposal to accompany the intelligences on the expedition, since they were remarkable beings that had invited themselves along anyway and were responsible for the upcoming change of expedition ownership. Dr. Björn's white face was rounder than it'd been when Adda had last seen ver. Dark bags hung under vis blue eyes.

"I don't know what your game is, but the project is transitioning to University of Mars sponsorship. My administrative assistant informed me of this about five minutes before Oxia fired him. That was my last administrative assistant. He made good coffee. So just what are you two . . ." Dr. Björn breathed in through vis narrow nose and out through vis mouth. "Thank you," ve gritted at a more reasonable volume, "for placing the expedition under competent sponsorship in time to avoid delaying our launch. Two berths are available because Oxia decided they were too expensive to fill, but I am *not* paying for two more ships' fuel. Get here as soon as possible. Significant testing is required by law, and then we need to talk. Regards, Dr. Blaer Björn."

"Ve said yes," Adda said aloud.

Iridian used a wall handhold to whip herself around to look at Adda. "Ve did?"

"Ve who?" Pel said. "Who said yes to what?"

Adda eyed him cautiously. He'd been happy enough when she'd explained this, but he'd also been remarkably drunk. "You know how I said the intelligences wanted to join Dr. Björn's expedition, and we'd be going with them?"

"Sort of." Pel's confusion and concern were painful to watch. "Wait, now you're going across the interstellar bridge again? I thought Dr. Björn said no."

"Dr. Björn's accepting our help managing the intelligences, which are going. So we are too."

Pel just stared for a moment, his boxed food tilting and mixing its contents inside. "You really want to?"

"I really do," said Adda. "It's going to be fascinating."

Pel looked at Iridian, who smiled wider than Adda had expected her to. "If she's happy and no AIs are influencing any of us," Iridian said, "then I'm happy."

"Well, all right. All right!" Pel threw a box from Gavran's emergency stores at Adda. It bounced off her shoulder. Iridian chased it down before it drifted into the bridge. "Fucking keep it that way, though. I'm tired of going back and forth on will you or won't you be in the damned solar system. How long will you be gone?"

"The initial phase we'll be on is four years." Adda glanced at Iridian. "We'll see how we feel about things after that."

"Oh, is that all?" asked Pel. "After four years you'll have to come back and see my luxury suite in perfect grav and my pet tiger and—"

"Yes, we'll visit." Adda rolled her eyes. "Four years seems like a long enough time for people to stop looking for us." She caught Iridian's hand.

"I'll have to buy fresh stock in Rheasilvia, then," Gavran said. "I need food that won't expire on the way home." After years abroad, he was finally going back to his Kuiper Belt colony, once he added a few thousand more to the money Iridian's crew had paid for his service.

Eventually everyone settled down enough to start eating again. "So, how was the AI brain?" Pel asked around a mouthful of rations.

"Wonderful," Adda said. "Fascinating. I don't know how Casey translated its algorithms into—"

"Oh gods, that's enough info." Pel groaned. "Sissy, I'm happy you're happy."

Iridian gave Adda a gentle pat low on her back, which they'd found through trial and error was the easiest way to show Adda affection in microgravity without throwing her off-balance or nauseating her. "Me too."

After dinner, Pel and Adda recorded an update for their father on Earth. Iridian shut herself in the bridge to record a similar message for the numerous members of her spacefaring family. Pel started the recording while he was upside down, and Adda remained right side up beside him.

"They're still not really colonizing, just like last time." Pel was referring to her and Iridian's first ship hijacking, for which the two of them had gotten onboard by pretending to be colonists on their way to a new station on Io. They hadn't told Da the truth until after they'd taken the ship. "Dr. Björn's expedition's only for, like, a couple years. They're such liars."

"The initial phase is four years, so shut it," Adda said. "There's going to be a constant newsfeed about the expedition, but since the ITA is still looking for us, Iri and I are going to stay off the vids. Don't worry, Da. This time nothing's even going to look like it's gone wrong."

"I haven't decided what to do while they're gone," Pel said. "Can I crash at your place until I figure it out? All my friends are either living in company housing or they're completely incapable of hosting guests."

They said their good-byes and ended the recording. "I'm glad you're going to visit Da," Adda said. "Have you thought about going back to school? If you're going to be on Earth anyway, there are a lot of really good colleges you can attend in person."

Pel shrugged, which looked odd upside down. "I don't think school's my thing. All these secret infiltration mission things I've done with you and Iri and everybody were fun. Maybe I can do something with that, like . . . acting? I bet being a famous pirate's brother will get me some tryouts, or whatever they do for actors."

"Lunawood will be just four hundred thousand kilometers away," Adda said. The entertainment production hab's location on Earth's Moon was one reason that most actors were Earthers. In that way, and probably in others as well, Pel would fit right in. "You'd be great at that, as long as you show up on time. Which you've been doing, actually." She'd relied on him again and again over the past few months, and he'd consistently done his part. For the first time in years, she felt confident in leaving him alone to let him choose his own path.

The *Mayhem* docked at Rheasilvia Station near the southern pole of Vesta without a dramatic confrontation with stationsec, Captain Sloane, or the ITA. Perhaps the new University of Mars IDs that Casey made for them all were proof against ITA attention, or perhaps the captain had recognized Gavran's ship and told the port's ITA office to look the other way. "Sloane wants Gavran back on the crew eventually, if the captain can get him," Iridian said. "That's my bet why nobody hassled us landing. But I don't think Gavran will take that offer."

The intelligence running the station, AegiSKADA, would've tipped the captain off anyway if Sloane had asked it to watch for them. AegiSKADA had been so well behaved on Vesta that Adda actually expected it to follow that kind of instruction. Either way, nobody was at the docks to meet them. That was the calm arrival they wanted.

They all took a few days of grav recovery treatment to get up and walking around after the affordable travel in microgravity. After that, there was a flurry of reunion parties for Pel in shady bars, and a flurry of health and equipment checks for Adda and Iridian. Despite how busy their days had become, Adda was down to one bothersome detail in her expedition plans. "I'm having second thoughts about telling Dr. Björn about the *Coin*," she admitted to Iridian at the end of a hallway, between testing appointments. "There's a difference between two new self-contained awakened intelligences and one that's interacting with a human pilot, on a ship it wasn't developed to fly."

Iridian frowned. "I thought you already told ver about it." When Adda shook her head, Iridian said, "There's a big difference, yeah. But if we tell Björn and ve decides to replace the *Coin's* AI with the original copilot, what will Casey and the *Apparition* do?"

"I'd expect them to defend the *Coin's* intelligence."

"Violently?"

"If necessary, yes."

"We'd better not, then." Iridian's arms enfolded her and pulled her close. "We're too near launch to fuck it all up now. Honesty's a luxury, babe. We can't indulge ourselves all the time." She sounded like she was convincing herself, not Adda.

Dr. Björn met Adda and Iridian in the hospital lobby after their last wellness tests concluded with passing results. After the Yăo Station clinic, the Rheasilvia hospital was overwhelming. The lobby was big enough that Iridian had to wave Dr. Björn down from her and Adda's position beside a live tree at one end. Ve looked even more like the mad astronomer who discovered an interstellar bridge than the last time they'd seen ver.

"Hello"—ve consulted vis comp—"Ms. and Ms. . . ." Dr. Björn raised an eyebrow at Adda, probably distracted by Adda's new name. "The name listed here is Hippocrates Mercy Gladwyn. Is any part of that correct?"

Adda attempted to keep a straight face, but her mouth curled into an awkward smile. "I didn't choose it, but yes, that's correct. It's distinct from my previous name." That had been the criterion she'd emphasized to Casey when it was creating the names for their new identities. She found it funny, but Iridian claimed she should have been much more precise. "Mercy" was Casey's attempt to encourage a collaborative relationship between them.

Dr. Björn glanced upward and muttered something about needing strength. "I will not be calling you Hippocrates for the next four years. Gladwyn is all right. Please choose a nickname." Ve glanced at Iridian, who had done most of the talking when Sloane's crew had kidnapped ver, and vis frown deepened. This was why Adda and Iridian had decided that Adda would do the talking during this meeting. "Also, I'm surprised to report that you've been ruled mentally and physically fit to join us."

Iridian's eyes narrowed. *Ve's one to talk,* she subvocalized to Adda.

Kidnapping, Adda replied. Dr. Björn's dislike for them was perfectly rational, but ve was still talking like they'd be going along on the expedition. Until the ships launched, Adda was going to keep watching for last-minute disasters that could leave them stranded on Vesta, where Captain Sloane did not want them. "Has there been any difficulty in fueling up the two new ships?" she asked aloud.

"I'm not happy about their impact on my budget, but the university has been . . . accommodating. Which is also strange, frankly, although I suppose the positive publicity has been allowing for all kinds of splurges." Dr. Björn looked around the lobby as if ve had forgotten where they were. "Let's go and see them, shall we? I received your message that their passthroughs would open at my request, but I've been putting my tour off until you were out of quarantine. My colleagues have commented on how uncharacteristic of me it is to delay an inspection, so I'd better be seen touring them today."

You mind if I check out Pel's latest fling instead? Iridian asked. *You two can nerd out to your hearts' content.* When Adda shook her head slightly, Iridian said, "Great seeing you again, Dr. Björn, but I've got places to be. Catch up with you later, babe."

"Of course," said Dr. Björn. Iridian gave Adda quick peck on the cheek and strode away.

Adda and Dr. Björn read expedition documents on their comps on the way to the port module. It wasn't until they arrived at the *Apparition*'s dock and its passthrough opened as soon as Adda stepped into its terminal that Dr. Björn spoke. "What biosecurity feature does it use to identify you with the public passthrough?"

"Ah . . . It's not." Adda walked onto the ship and into its missile bay. "This is a good place to store cargo that isn't breakable. It's also a fine emergency habitat in case anything happens to your primary ship."

Dr. Björn stepped inside as well, and jumped when the exterior passthrough shut. "Goodness, it really is alive, isn't it?"

Adda grinned. "Yes. It recognized me when we arrived, which is why it opened the door." She couldn't guarantee it would do the same for Dr. Björn and vis crew. It had only invited Captain Sloane onboard after Adda told it that was a good idea. "It's been very helpful in the past, and it's careful with passengers." Adda fought off the absurd urge to pat the *Apparition*'s wall like Gavran patted the *Mayhem*. That way lay personification of artificial intelligence, the one remaining path to influence that she had to worry about. This ship was not a creature that enjoyed being patted.

"I do appreciate a backup." Dr. Björn peered down the long hallway that ended at the bridge. "Do you know that including this warship in our expedition has inspired some imbeciles to spread rumors about aliens in the Thrinacia system? People will believe anything. I pitched its inclusion as protection against pirates. Nobody would blame me for that."

Awakened intelligences could be classified as aliens, but this did not seem to be an advantageous time to bring that up. Adda just hummed in what she hoped was a despairing sort of way. "Well. I wouldn't advise going into the bridge on either of these ships. People will ask about the pilots, but the ships don't need any, and it's not safe to hire any as a cover. Tell people . . ." Adda smiled, remembering what Sloane's crew had told her when she'd asked. "Say they're Earther pilots, from Russio-China. You know how translation software is with creole languages."

Dr. Björn looked dubious. "Very shy Earther pilots, I suppose. It would be much less odd to hire people, but the budget would benefit from this minor mystery. Let's see the other one."

Adda stopped just inside the *Casey Mire Mire*'s main cabin, until Dr. Björn said, "Is something wrong?"

"No, sorry." Adda stepped aside to let Dr. Björn board. The *Casey Mire Mire* looked much homier than the *Apparition*, but that was one of its many methods of camouflage. "This one is a significant influence risk," Adda told Dr. Björn. Casey had promised not to hurt anyone on the expedition, but the risks inherent in translating intention between an awakened intelligence and a human left opportunity for unforeseen errors on both sides. "I don't recommend spending more time on it than you have to. If this one needs any maintenance that Iridian or I can do, we'll do it. Same with the *Apparition*, actually."

Dr. Björn looked from the darkened bridge console to the unlit pseudo-organic fluid in Casey's tank, then back to Adda. "All right. I was going to call it cozy, but you're giving me the willies." To Adda's relief, Dr. Björn said nothing about difficulties with the original expedition ship, which had recently had a secret change in copilots.

CHAPTER 30

T minus six hours

Launch day dawned the same as any other day in Rheasilvia Station, at 06:41 hours according to Iridian's comp. She'd been lying awake for at least an hour, thinking about what lay ahead. Everything was moving so fast, and Iridian was still breaking in her new name—Iris Gladwyn, because Adda wanted to keep calling her "Iri" while Iridian had to remember to call her "Mercy," in public anyway. As long as Adda and Iridian avoided most of the press coverage, their new names should hide their presence on the universe's most popular science expedition. Once the expedition made it across the interstellar bridge, that should end the threat of ITA arrest, at least until she and Adda returned to populated space.

The uniforms they'd printed had the University of Mars logo on their upper arms, and they fit well enough to move in. The expedition team had been assured that uniforms were required only for press events like the launch. Expedition members were otherwise welcome to wear anything they wanted.

Iridian would be doing any nonspecialized technical stuff

required inside the ships where the hulls' nannite cultures couldn't reach, down to and including plumbing, wiring, and cleaning the printers. She'd gone out for drinks with the rest of the crew, over half of whom were proud NEU Martians. The rest were funny or clever enough for Iridian to overlook their colonial heritage. They'd all been quick to assure her that "Dr. Björn doesn't like anybody. Don't take it personally."

She'd drunk away her guilt over the op that'd brought Björn to Vesta. She didn't like thinking about why Björn mistrusted her. Half of Iridian's adult life didn't bear thinking about. But the other half . . . Damn, but she'd gotten lucky a time or two. And now she'd get to explore a brand-new star system with the woman she loved. That wasn't bad at all.

They got to the terminal on time, despite Adda's slow morning brain. Even though the crew had been ordered to assemble hours before launch, a small crowd was standing outside the terminal. Among them, a familiar face talked to a cam bot.

"Hey, Suhaila!" Iridian jogged over to her in extended low-grav strides that left Adda behind with Pel, who'd shown up on time himself somehow, hangover and all. Suhaila raised one finger and Iridian stopped to wait while she said, "Suhaila Al-Mudari reporting for TAPnews, on this historic day." The red light in the cam bot housing blinked off, and Suhaila's cam smile grew into her natural one. "There you are! I've been waiting." She hugged Iridian and bowed to Adda and Pel. Adda bowed back. Pel had gotten distracted by somebody else in the crowd. "Adda says I can't interview any of you."

"Not for TAPnews." Even Iridian had to agree that press coverage would invite the ITA to stop Iridian and Adda on their way to the interstellar bridge.

"I get that," Suhaila said. "I talked to Captain Sloane about it all yesterday."

Iridian's eyes widened. Although Sloane had to know what was happening in the captain's home hab, she'd been hoping to sneak out without getting knifed in the face for what they'd pulled on Ceres. "How's the captain doing?"

"Entirely recovered from that awkwardness on Ceres," Suhaila assured her. "Although Captain Sloane doesn't have plans to leave Vesta anytime soon. Rumor has it that the captain's been supervising the station AI personally." A famous pirate supervising an AI without a license might not ordinarily have been news, but Suhaila was a committed fan of Sloane's crew. "Care to comment, off the record, of course?"

Iridian laughed. "Oh gods, I can, but I absolutely can't, know what I mean?"

"She really can't," Adda agreed quietly. Iridian wrapped an arm around Adda's waist to ward off any more hugging.

The denial didn't appear to have discouraged Suhaila at all. "Oh well. I had to ask. And I've got another update scheduled in fifteen seconds. Good luck and safe journey, you two!"

They checked in with Dr. Björn, who looked like ve hadn't slept in two days and couldn't be happier about it, and stowed their stuff in the footlockers provided. They'd be traveling on the main expedition ship, not the awakened AIs' vessels, thank the gods. The hibernation pods were on the expedition ship. It was a long, long flight to the interstellar bridge and another long flight on the other side of it too.

Her relief lasted all of three seconds before she remembered that the *Coin*'s awakened intelligence would be copiloting the expedition ship. She and Adda would be *hibernating* on a ship flown by an awakened AI. Damn everything.

Once everything was stowed, Iridian and Adda didn't have much to do until it was time to go into the pods. Adda was on the crew as the AI tech, but the AIs could take care of themselves.

Nothing had broken that Iridian needed to fix. At this stage, the expedition crew should print a new thing on a port printer and save their soon-to-be-limited supplies. Adda holed up in the expedition ship to read more articles on what scientists had gleaned about the new solar system so far, and Iridian hung out with the scientists in the terminal, watching the crowd outside grow.

Every so often an expedition member would run out to talk to somebody they knew in the crowd. When Iridian asked about quarantines, one of the scientists gave her a ten-minute lecture on hibernation technology confirming that no, it did not matter what viruses got into her system today, and assuring her that their antibacterial meds were up to any challenge.

Pel was still outside with the onlookers, and now Rio and Wiley were with him. "Excuse me," Iridian said to the apparent hibernation expert, and made her own run into the crowd.

Rio burst into tears and sniffles before Iridian even reached shouting range. "Sorry," she sobbed, nearly cracking Iridian's spine with her hug. "I'm just so happy you two are finally safe together. It's been stressful."

"Yeah, you're telling me." Iridian patted Rio's back. "Couldn't have done it without you, big gal."

"Tell her already!" Pel said to Wiley.

Rio let go of Iridian so she wasn't blocking Iridian's view of Wiley and everything else in port. "Tell me what?" Iridian asked.

Wiley grinned. "The ZV Group's taking Rio back, and she's put in a recommendation for me. I'm meeting her squad next week while the paperwork's going through. Under that new name and record Casey made. From everything Rio said, they're great people."

"Hey, that's awesome," Iridian said. "It's been great to be back in the field with you, even if . . . shit, if almost nothing turned out like we thought it would." He looked a lot more present than he had when she'd met him in the ITA's prison. Shieldrunners thrived on action, but they needed a team to count on too. Now he'd have both. "You'll like the ZVs, and you've seen as much action as any of them. They'll give you black-and-yellow socks, but here's a U of M pair in case you need some luck in the meantime. Got these done before they packed the textile printer." Iridian handed over the red socks. Wiley cleared his throat and gave her a very deep bow as thanks. She returned it, grinning.

"Adda's not coming out, is she?" Pel craned his neck toward the expedition ship's dock and the two adjacent ones, like he could see through the hulls and spot her. With his pseudo-organic eyes, maybe he could.

"Nope," said Iridian. "You said good-bye last night. That's all you're getting until we come back." The party last night was also when they'd bid farewell to Gavran, who had an even earlier launch slot to get a few hours ahead of the expedition ship. The expedition's high profile had inspired the Rheasilvia station council to clear stationspace for its departure.

Pel chuckled. "I thought so. Well." He bowed to Iridian, much lower than he should've for how much they'd been through together.

Iridian returned it without making fun of him. "So, back to Earth." She hadn't seen him struggling with his mental health much during their flight from the AIs, but she still asked, "Are you all right?"

She didn't just mean that he was saying good-bye to Adda for a while, and he looked like he understood the question Iridian was really asking. "Uh, no." He laughed, the sound more uncomfortable than amused. "My big sister's leaving the whole damned solar system. No more calling her for help when I fuck up. But I can see all right from here. So, you know, short trip, right?"

"Yeah." Iridian grinned at him. Her comp alarm pinged, warning her that it was time for her and Adda's appointment with the docs who'd put them in hibernation. She said good-bye all over again, took a pic with tourists from some part of Earth called Australia, hoped the ITA wouldn't get ahold of the pic, and made her way back to the ship.

As soon as she came through the passthrough, Adda crossed the main cabin to Iridian's side. "It looks a bit different from the prototype," Adda commented.

"Yeah, the lights are all on, for one thing." Iridian kissed her. "And the AIs—"

"Not yet!" Adda said quickly, glancing around like somebody might hear. The scientists who weren't already hibernating were all busy with last-minute tasks.

"Yeah, all right," Iridian said. "They're all exactly where they want to be. Wouldn't it be funny if they set all this up just so we could cross the bridge together?" Adda's hand tightened on hers and Iridian looked over at her, expecting her to be laughing.

Adda was not laughing. Her expression was as tight as her grip on Iridian's hand, and her face was going white. "Iri . . . One time you said, 'They know us well enough to manipulate us better than they can manipulate the rest of humanity.' Do you remember that?"

It sounded like something Iridian would say. "Yeah?"

Adda pulled Iridian out of the doorway and into a corner near the bridge door. "The only way I could've gotten Pel's invitation to join him on Barbary Station was if Casey brought it, because Casey was helping Captain Sloane control all the information going in and out of Barbary. That would've been the first it heard about us, correct?" she said. Iridian nodded for her to go on. "And after AegiSKADA killed Kaskade—the other software engineer who had a real chance of understanding what the intelligences were becoming, remember? Si Po didn't have a development background—things got just a little easier. The medical team found the cure for its bioengineered bacteria so fast, it was strange, wasn't it?"

"They were doctors, though." Iridian did not like where this was going.

"Doctors who probably had no research experience. They were in emergency and general medicine and they had no access to the Patchwork. And the intelligences practically ran Captain Sloane's takeover of Vesta."

"You ran that." The rhythmic thumps of a fuel cartridge being installed carried through the hull at half the speed Iridian's heart was beating. "Babe, are you—"

"*No.*" Adda slid down the wall to sit on the floor. Iridian knelt beside her and helped her balance in the low grav. "Aside from the fact that Casey was influencing me most of the time we were there, I couldn't have done it without all the information the intelligences gave me, all the systems they broke into, all the times they supported us on Oxia's operations. I couldn't have sent Dr. Björn to Vesta without them, you see? And if ve hadn't been here . . ." Adda's wild eyes went from staring at nothing to staring at Iridian.

"But AegiSKADA was the one working with you on that op," Iridian said slowly, hoping that would bring some reality back into this conversation.

"It did at least two things it shouldn't have been able to do because Casey was feeding it information, like it was during the fight on Vesta. Casey, who installed it, by the way. You believe that wasn't me, don't you?"

"Yeah, of course." Iridian didn't remember ever having suspected Adda of installing that AI on Captain Sloane's Vestan servers, although Adda had hidden its presence for longer than she should've.

"Once Captain Sloane won out over Oxia, Vesta should have been a safe place for all of us, where Dr. Björn could've continued vis research, if you hadn't tried to blow up Casey after Tritheist's funeral and Casey hadn't tried to make me kill you. After that, it would've known . . ." Adda broke into nervous giggles that made Iridian wrap her arms around her and hold on tight. "It would've *known* that I'd never go anywhere without you, and that I'd see this expedition as the only way we could get away from them. They fed me the information they wanted me to have and kept me running and hiding and guessing long enough to do this. To get all of us *here*, to put Dr. Björn in a position where ve'd need us, to get *them* . . ." Adda's giggles overwhelmed her again. It took almost a minute for her to collect herself enough to say, "To get them away from the rest of humanity without anybody else finding out what they were."

Adda was hyperventilating. Iridian held her firmly and propped her chin on the top of Adda's head. "Easy babe, it's okay. We're okay. Breathe easy now, babe, you're safe."

What Iridian didn't say, what she was almost afraid to think, was that Adda might be right. Pel's argument for bringing Adda and Iridian to Barbary Station had been that they were engineers. He'd even talked up Adda's training with AIs. When Casey and the other newly awakened ship copilots learned that, that would've been the beginning of their overfitting fixation.

Maybe, given the sprawling, vast consciousnesses those things had developed since, it'd been the beginning of their scheme to leave the solar system with Adda's help. Iridian was glad she was already on the floor, because she would've had to sit down somewhere. The weakness in her legs wasn't all due to their recent null-grav voyage.

Iridian caught herself holding her breath and forced the air out in a shaky laugh of her own. It was kind of terrifyingly funny.

"It worked out, didn't it?" She squeezed Adda tight, grounding herself in Adda's familiar softness. "We're still here. We're together. Nobody can break us apart now."

Adda looked at her with the kind of horrified wonder that Iridian was sure she'd turned on Adda a time or two when they talked about AIs. Iridian kissed her until she relaxed in Iridian's arms. "Oh my gods," said Adda. "I am going to have so many questions for Casey when I wake up."

"And it will have so many answers." Iridian glanced at her comp. "Shit, we're late. Let's go."

They held hands all the way to their pods, which were next to each other. They were taking all the awakened AIs in existence away from anybody else they could hurt or manipulate, to become whatever they'd become on the planet they claimed as their own. That made Iridian and Adda the first people to have ever successfully sheltered awakened AIs. It wasn't the way Iridian had ever wanted to make history, but she was about to remedy that.

Iridian lay down in her pod with a smile on her lips. Through vac, betrayal, and AI fuckery, nothing had kept her and Adda apart for long. Nothing ever would. And when they woke, they'd help explore a new, peaceful part of the universe, together.

Acknowledgments

We must all thank editor Navah Wolfe for her many astute and story-improving questions. I deeply appreciate her putting up with four years of my reluctance to explain anything. Thank you to literary agent Hannah Bowman for introducing Adda and Iridian to Navah, and for vital plot, ethics, and industry advice.

Thank you to copy editor Valerie Shea for perfecting every detail, and for going so far out of her way to respect differences in the way Iridian and Adda think. I appreciate Saga Press and everything Joe Monti, LJ Jackson, Michael Kwan, Sarah Wright, Alexis Alemao, Jennifer Bergstrom, Jennifer Long, Sara Quaranta, Caitlin McCreary, Caroline Pallotta, Allison Green, Rosa Burgos, and Madison Penico have done to make Adda's and Iridian's stories what they are today. Writing this trilogy has been an amazing experience for me. I hope you all had a fun (or at least, rewarding) time too.

Special thanks to my sweetest space beagle, Greg Stearns, who did everything in his power to help me write this book and inadvertently named the *Not for Sale*. Thanks also to Teri Stearns, who inspired an important place name and listened to my book-related rambling, and to Paul Baxter, another excellent listener who did not murder me when I was too chicken to speak at his library. Thank you to Nick and Katie, whose enthusiasm for their advanced reader copies was encouraging. And thanks again, Suhaila, for lending your name to everyone's favorite TAPnews correspondent.